THE TIME OF
CHERRIES

MICHAEL S
HOLLINGTON

The Book Guild Ltd

First published in Great Britain in 2023 by
The Book Guild Ltd
Unit E2 Airfield Business Park,
Harrison Road, Market Harborough,
Leicestershire. LE16 7UL
Tel: 0116 2792299
www.bookguild.co.uk
Email: info@bookguild.co.uk
Twitter: @bookguild

Typeset in 11pt Minion Pro

Printed and bound by CPI Group (UK) Ltd, Croydon, CR0 4YY

ISBN 978 1915603 999

British Library Cataloguing in Publication Data.
A catalogue record for this book is available from the British Library.

MIX
Paper | Supporting
responsible forestry
FSC
www.fsc.org FSC® C013604

For Sarah

AUTHOR'S NOTE

The Paris Commune, the largest civil insurrection of the nineteenth century, ended in the last week of May 1871. Many called it *la semaine sanglante* – the bloody week – where over twenty thousand Communards were massacred by the government army taking back control. Others named it after a song: 'le temps de cerises' – the time of cherries.

MSH
May 2023

The square of light had disappeared up the wall. I turned over to block out the cell, drew my nails across the sheet, the scratch loud in my head as if I were picking at the strings of some strange instrument. I must have fallen asleep.

I awoke. The light was now high on the opposite wall – morning outside. I rose and checked the grate at the bottom of the door. No food... what did I expect?

Nothing I could do but lie down and consider my predicament again. No sound but the whump-whump of my heart. The gloom held the reek of decay. I exhaled. The walls. I wondered whose breath had mouldered the stone, an aristocrat or two in the time of the guillotine?

What day was it? They had slammed the door shut yesterday, or had it been the day before?

Waves of anger, starvation, prayer, anger again. Fear. Would Oreste's plan work? Could I trust him? I reached for the tin, took a sip – no more than a day's water left.

I saw Lucien in my mind's eye. The park. Framed the only word he had ever said to me: P-O-G-O, my lips moving, my tongue fat in my throat.

I couldn't sleep. My life came back to me as if it was yesterday. The boy in the church...

ONE

1861, ten years earlier

MEURSAULT, A SMALL community in Burgundy, was planted with vines by Cistercians monks in medieval times. Some say the Romans were the first to turn the earth there. Others will tell you of tribes of flaxen-haired Gauls, the Mandubii or some such. All would have been drawn to the south-eastern aspect of the hills, the marl and limestone composition of the soil, components for the production of full and flavoursome wines.

My family, the Vellays, have worked this land for generations as labourers. Everyone who lives in the town is in their own way dependent on the grape – from the priest who blesses the wine in church to the butcher and baker who provide us with sustenance.

The crop is king. Men, women and children divine the sky at sunset and sunrise, gauge the drift of the wind, observe the rise and fall of the barometer, kneel in prayer on Sundays, all in fealty to the grape. A late frost, hailstones, tempest and snow can bring disaster – there, sent by God to test man in his quest for a decent drop to drink.

The land, the *domaines*, are owned by a handful of proprietors – men who control our lives, pay a man a miserable two and a half francs a day to sweat and toil on God's own ground. To become a proprietor, you have to be born to it, or marry into it, or be of sufficient fortune to obtain it. *Or by whatever means are deemed as necessary.*

One such proprietor was staring at my back. I was convinced of it. I dared not turn around to look at Junius Gerard lest the congregation saw me and shook their collective head. Only last week, he had turned in his saddle and smiled at me with his large brown eyes. Now, those eyes were on me again, on my back. His family were the owners of Domaine de l'Oubliette, an estate on the edge of the town. I had seen him over the years, high up on his horse and as ignorant of me as a cat is of God.

Until now.

Father Alberic stood and blessed the wine. I shifted down the pew with the rest of my family, convinced that everybody was looking at me. I knelt, felt myself tense when he placed the wafer on my tongue. The blood of Christ tasted acidic – in Meursault? I looked across at my sister Aliette and wondered again how different we were: she with her fair hair and blue eyes; me with my dark hair, brown eyes and olive skin.

I followed Maman's bulk as she clattered back to her pew. She was large, the child within her a surprise, as Alie was supposed to be the last of our generation of Vellays. Papa plonked himself next to me. He was large as well, *and* flushed. Hair gathered at his Adam's apple; his collar tight against the flesh of his neck. I could see he was chafing to be away… for his Sunday drink. My brothers sat the other side; the male Vellays tended to stick together.

My given name is Christine, after the saint whose feast day, the twenty-fourth of July, was the same day as my birthday. As an infant Alie had struggled with my name. 'Kikine, Kikine,' she would say. The family had settled on Kiki.

Soon it was over, except the ignominy of walking up the aisle, of avoiding his stare. At last, I was outside in the warm spring air. I chanced a look behind me. Junius was there. Smiling, he waggled his fingers at me without raising his hand.

'Come on, Kiki,' said Alie, taking my arm. Walking to our house on rue du Moulin Judas I might have been walking on air with an idiotic smile on my face. My mood was short-lived. Maman had prepared mutton stew. Alie and I diced vegetables. The men, as per their custom, were drinking in the square by the church.

I dreaded Sunday lunches, but that particular day was especially awful. They had lurched into the parlour, slamming the door behind them. Slurring his words, Papa splashed himself a glass of wine. My brothers Dagobert and Salvat ate noisily, their elbows stuck out, with not a word of thanks to Maman. I was of a mind to say something but held my tongue. They scrapped over the last drop of wine. Papa brushed them aside, swigging the dregs from the bottle then dashing it against a wall.

Everyone was shouting. Alie burst into tears. Father apologised to her. 'There, there, my pretty,' he repeated, slurring his words. Then, sticking his nose in my face: 'It's all your fault, *salope!*' My brothers were fighting, knocking over chairs, plates crashing to the ground. Maman was sprawled on the floor, her face covered in slop. I worried she might lose her child; it had happened before. Strange, but I felt calm when I smashed two saucepans together, shouting for them to, '*Stop!*'

Silence.

Then Salva apologised and everybody slunk away, except Alie and me, so we could clear up the mess.

School was on Tuesdays and Thursdays in Beaune, seven kilometres away. Alie and I had to walk there and back. I didn't mind except when it rained. Father wanted me to work, while insisting that Alie had an education. Maman had put her foot down: 'Someone has to take her to school.' Walking always heightened my mood; anyway, it was a relief to be away from the house. The country was wide and open with few trees, the leaves lush on the vines at that time of year. When the sun shone it lit the *côtes* in a light so clear and intense it made me wonder about nature and God and His mysterious ways.

For Alie the walk was not so pleasant. Sometimes she dragged on my arm.

May in Bourgogne is cherry season. Monsieur Blanc was generous, doling out handfuls of the fruit when we passed by his orchard in Pommard.

The school was housed in a building on place Saint-Étienne. Lessons started at nine thirty. Lunch was at one o'clock. Madame Thierry, our headmistress, often spoiled us with cheese or *saucisson* wrapped in paper so none of the other pupils would notice. She was small and dark and, like me, had a lilt to her nose. I often imagined her as my mother, me as her only child. She made me feel special – winked when I gave her a correct answer.

She taught us French and geography. And history. In those days we French were ruled by Emperor Napoleon III, nephew of *the* Napoleon, the one Papa talked about. The one my grandpa lost an arm for at a battle in a place called Leipzig.

And religion. What we were supposed to think about at Saint-Nicolas' every Sunday. I often thought of Jesus Christ – *dying on the cross for all our sins.*

There were eighteen of us in my class, including one boy. We were fourteen- and fifteen-year-olds, except Simone who was sixteen. Some of us had to work, in my case at Madame Lonjons' four times a week. Others had an easier life, such as Simone who was from a well-to-do family.

A week later Arlette was born. The Vellay men were at work in Monsieur Monnier's fields and Alie was out. With no time to fetch Dr Barolet, it was up to me.

I boiled some rags and wiped Maman's body. She trembled, her thighs twitched, her legs spread. She screamed the house down. The baby eventually emerged, a blue membrane wrapped around its neck. I instinctively knew what to do, gently pulling then cutting the cord. Blood and secretion ensued. After tapping it on the backside, it bawled. *It* was a she. I tied a knot and checked her body. Nothing missing. Crossing my chest, I gave thanks to God.

Soon after Arlette was born, Alie and I were slogging our way to school, the wind in our faces. I thought about my family. There *was* an atmosphere in the house. The men appeared to have something on their minds – held discussions behind closed doors. Maman had let slip that Dago was intent on buying land so we could grow our own grapes. I had overheard Father shouting at him: 'You're a *gros con*, Dago. Where do you think we'll get the money from?'

Maman was in a better mood, even smiling from time to time. Arlette took after Alie, with wisps of blonde hair, blue eyes and bow lips. We fussed over her. I carved her a dog from a piece of wood, which she promptly stuck in her mouth.

Alie tightened her grip on my hand. Clouds scudded across the sky. The light was intermittent. The wind freshened, the vines rippling in great crescent waves across the hillsides. Workers hoed the ground, their hats drawn down.

Monsieur Blanc was at his gate. 'Take as many as you want,' he said, smiling, handing me a bag of cherries, his eyes narrowing as he looked over my shoulder. A carriage had pulled up, drawn by a chestnut mare. Monsieur Monnier, my family's employer, leaned out of the window and asked us if we wanted a lift into Beaune.

'No, but thank you all the same,' I replied.

'It's a long way… Looks like it will rain.'

I looked up at the sky. Clouds masked the sun. The wind gusted again. Alie looked at me in that wheedling way of hers. 'All right,' I said. 'Thank you, monsieur.'

Monsieur Monnier opened the door and we squeezed in. Alie wore a foolish grin – her first time in a carriage. Mine as well. The inside of the coach was clad in wood, the seats in leather. I thought it could do with a cushion or two, make it less austere. The ride was smooth with the occasional bump. I wrinkled my nose, the smell not entirely alien to me: eau de cologne, something Papa wore on special occasions.

Monsieur Monnier sat straight-backed in his morning coat. His stare unsettled me. He fingered his moustache with its pointy ends and smoothed his beard. I offered him a cherry.

'The time of cherries,' he said, picking one out between two bony fingers. Sticking it in his mouth, he sucked on the fruit, his mouth slack. My stomach turned when he spat out the stone.

'Dagobert wants to buy some of my land,' he announced.

'Men's business, monsieur.'

'Oh?'

'Where, may I ask, monsieur?' I heard myself saying.

'On the edge of my *domaine*, half a hectare, not the best piece by any means.'

'How much will you sell it for?'

'You're an inquisitive little thing, aren't you?'

I smiled sweetly.

'Three thousand francs.'

'Sounds a lot,' I said, knowing that vine workers earned two and a half francs a day. *Where would we find such an amount?*

'Your brother fails to understand that Meursault prices are rising, that Paris has an unquenchable thirst for the stuff.'

'Are you going to sell him the land, monsieur?'

'That depends.'

'On what?'

'Never you mind' – squinting at me. Then: 'Kiki, how old are you?'

'Fourteen, monsieur, fifteen in July.'

'Hmm, that would be the twenty-fourth, Sainte-Christine's Day.'

'How do you know that?'

Turning a shade of pink: 'Dagobert told me.'

Silence the rest of the way. I felt Monsieur Monnier wanted to impart something to me but could not bring himself to do so.

Why had Dago been discussing me with him?

We arrived in Beaune. Thanking Monsieur Monnier, I followed Alie out of the berlin and heaved a sigh of relief.

At school Madame Thierry made an announcement. The class was to walk through Beaune. Taking me aside she handed me a black shift with a blue pinafore. 'They belonged to a friend of mine, Kiki. Try them on.'

Behind a door I dressed in my 'new' clothes, securing the pinafore by tying its laces in a bow around my waist. I pirouetted then curtsied in front of her.

'Perfect,' she said. 'Suits your dark looks.'

I thanked her in the knowledge that charity was unacceptable to the Vellays, especially Papa who would confiscate the clothes and throw them away. I would have to swear Alie to secrecy.

We emerged onto rue du Pain, a pretty group, all eighteen of us, two by two, Madame Thierry at our head like a proud mother hen. Pierre, the only boy, made sure he was paired with me, and clasped my hand.

Beaune was alive with activity. Barrels on the streets, dray horses with their tufted fetlocks pulling carts full of wine, men hauling on ropes lifting goods via a pulley to a *grenier*, nuns walking, huddled as if for protection from the outside world. We walked the road that circled the town. Old forts with battlements, trees, their lofty canopies providing us with shade from the midday sun. Madame Thierry explained the history of the town – wine, wine and wine – that Beaune was the capital of wine, producer of the finest wines in all of France and therefore the world.

Back in the centre we arrived at a vast building where a nun greeted us. After a few words with Madame Thierry, she led us through an archway to a courtyard and another large building. Pierre squeezed my hand. The red, black and green tiled roof was intertwined in elaborate geometrical patterns, dormer windows with pinnacles above, rows of wooden columns, timbered galleries.

The Hôtel-Dieu.

'The hospices are a charity with a wine auction every November,' explained Madame Thierry. 'They support people less fortunate than ourselves.' We filed inside the salle de Nicolas. I was reminded of a church – it *is* the hotel of God – with its arched ceiling and altar with candles below a painting of the Virgin Mary.

Beds under red canopies lined the walls on either side. The place reeked of medicine and bodies. A nun attended a man whose leg was swathed in bandages. Another patient groaned in his sleep.

I turned away and looked at the floor; a glass strip ran across the middle. I looked closer; water flowed below. 'La Bouzaize runs under the hospices,' the nun explained.

Outside the Hôtel-Dieu I saw it: Junius Girard's black horse tethered to a rail. I loitered in the hope of seeing him but Madame Thierry hurried us away.

We returned to school for lunch and afternoon lessons; then it was time to walk home. I was on a tear to be away and told Alie we were going via the Hôtel-Dieu. She whined. I made an excuse and we walked there as fast as our legs could carry us, but the horse was no longer there.

Madame Lonjons' house on rue de Cîteaux resembled the Vellay's: single-storey, stone, a kitchen scullery at the back, a parlour facing the street with two rooms either side. She lived alone and used one of the rooms as her atelier. Maman often told me how fortunate I was to be working for such a respected seamstress. Inside was neat and tidy. Sparse furnishings made the place feel bigger than ours. The smell of wax pervaded.

Madame Lonjons reflected her surroundings – her shift, black and severe, her grey hair secured in a tight net at the back of her head. She rarely smiled. I had no idea what I was paid as she settled with Maman directly. I dropped hints, hoping she would give me some of her failures – garments that hadn't turned out appropriately – but they never came my way. Sometimes she gave me titbits from the kitchen, a biscuit or a glass of milk, as though I was a cat.

We worked in silence, save for the tick of the grandfather clock. Time passed slowly. Madame Lonjons communicated mostly in sign language – a chop of the hand meant stop, a rhythmic sewing motion with her fingers meant sew. She took her customers' measurements in the parlour. Sometimes she asked me to jot down their dimensions, dictating in a crisp, high-pitched voice. I once made a mistake and she told me off. 'Your mistake has cost me and will be deducted from your pay, Kiki.'

She drew lines of white chalk on the particular cloth and then cut the material with a large pair of scissors. She would always start the sewing, handing me the item to finish. Sometimes I had to embroider flowers or patterns on a garment, which I found less boring. She often dispatched me on errands, delivering finished items to her customers.

One afternoon I was embroidering a rose onto a blouson when she summoned me. A lady was sampling one of Madame's materials. She was of similar height and build to me and not much older, and pretty despite her short hair. Her face was round and vaguely familiar. A dress was lying on a table. I remembered sewing the lapels and thinking it would suit me.

Madame Lonjons said, 'Mademoiselle feels the hem is not straight – difficult to tell when wearing the dress oneself. Since you are of a similar build, Kiki, I thought you should put it on, afford Mademoiselle a different perspective.'

I changed in the atelier, arranged myself as best I could and brushed my hair. I looked in the mirror. The dress *did* suit me – maroon and complementing my complexion.

Determined to present myself to advantage I entered the parlour with my shoulders back, my head held high. Madame Lonjons shot me sharp looks while Mademoiselle inspected the hem.

'You see, I was right,' said Mademoiselle. 'On the left, near the back, it sags as though a couple of stitches are missing.'

Madame Lonjons glared at me. 'Kiki, this is your responsibility. I see I will have to give you more menial tasks as you cannot be trusted.'

I was about to protest, but Mademoiselle spoke first. 'Madame Lonjons, I am partial to the dress. Please redo the stiches and ask Kiki here to deliver it to Domaine de l'Oubliette. I have to wear it tonight.'

Domaine de l'Oubliette: where Junius Girard lived. I could barely contain myself. *Mademoiselle… she must be his sister.*

Mademoiselle left. And, with a snarly look at me, Madame Lonjons retreated to her atelier.

A short while later she emerged. 'Here,' she said, handing me a parcel. 'Oubliette is on the edge of town at the end of rue des Plantes. Now go' – shooing me away dismissively.

Every step filled me with trepidation – would Junius be there? Madame Lonjons' instructions were unnecessary: I knew where Domaine de l'Oubliette was, close to Domaine le Merle where Monsieur Monnier lived.

Stone columns supported a pair of iron gates, one with 'Domaine de l'Oubliette' carved into its top. The cobbled courtyard was orderly, green and stippled with colour, with roses and flowers in tubs. I felt dowdy in my shift. Swept back my hair. While my hand was on the knocker the front door opened. Mademoiselle was dressed in riding attire: britches, black boots, tweed jacket.

'Thank you, Kiki,' she said, taking the parcel and handing me a one-franc coin.

I made a show of being tired, panting and wiping my brow

with the back of my hand.

'Oh, all right,' she said. 'Come in. It is warm.'

She led me through the hallway to the kitchen at the back of the house. The walls were decked with pictures of the harvest: peasants treading grapes, portraits of ancestors – some holding bunches of the fruit, others nose down in wineglasses. One depicted a sailor in uniform brandishing a sword, a three-masted ship in the background, cannon firing, plumes of smoke.

The kitchen was large, everything in its place. Mademoiselle summoned a maid, and a glass was handed to me.

'Grape juice,' said Mademoiselle.

I took a sip.

'My name is Eloise' – resting a hand on my arm. 'You looked lovely in my dress, lovelier than me.'

'I doubt it, mademoiselle' – feeling myself blush.

'You should keep me company when the family is away.'

'Away, mademoiselle?'

'Please call me Eloise.'

I nodded.

'My father and Clément often go to Paris to look after our wine interests. We have a house there.'

'A house in Paris?'

'Yes, for Clément's convenience.'

I smiled politely. *Why is she confiding in me?* Her hand lingered. 'I better be going,' I said unconvincingly. 'Madame Lonjons will be wondering where I am.'

'If you must,' she said, removing her hand.

I felt disappointed. *Where was Junius?* I tried to eke out the time, pretending to study the painting of the sailor. 'Who is this?' I said without looking up.

'My grandfather,' replied a low voice.

I turned around.

'During some battle, showing off.'

Junius.

I tried to hide my confusion, avoid blushing.

'You're the girl in the church.'

'I worship there every Sunday with my family' – avoiding his gaze, watching Eloise instead, with her folded arms and stern look. 'Your sister looks upset,' I continued.

'Sister? Eloise is not my sister,' he whispered. 'She is my wife.'

I tried to hide my confusion. 'Madame Lonjons introduced her as Mademoiselle.'

'An old trick of hers' – rolling his eyes. 'She likes to pretend, flirt. Thinks "mademoiselle" is more exciting, more evocative.'

I stood there. *What could I say?*

'Forgive me for being so forward, but I need to see you again, to explain.'

'You are married.'

'Please' – his brown eyes urging me.

'I can't,' I mouthed.

'You should leave,' said Eloise, indicating the door.

Head down, I hurried through the hallway.

Words were being exchanged – harsh, loud words. Hauling open the front door I flew across the cobbles and through the gate.

TWO

S UNDAY. JUNIUS WAS sitting in the mid-pews alone. I turned around subtly. He was staring at me then winked. I prayed no one was watching.

The service took an hour. I was bored, visualising patterns in the flagstones, configuring the shape of a cross. Taking Communion, I imagined that everyone was looking into my very soul.

Outside Saint-Nicolas', Junius slipped a fold of paper into my hand, walking by without breaking step.

I found a quiet spot to the side of the church.

23 June

Dear Kiki,

Forgive me for what happened at Oubliette.

Please agree to meet me. There are things I need to explain to you. I suggest the cabotte to the right of the road, just before Volnay, at six this evening. If you can't be there, please leave a note on the inside of the chimney with a time that would suit you.

I can't stop thinking of you,
Junius

As usual the men arrived home the worse for drink. Papa went to bed without eating. Dago and Salva shot me dark looks. Alie was sweet, but her excuses on behalf of Papa annoyed me. Maman seemed beyond caring, Arlette guzzling at her breast. With lunch over I nipped outside to reread Junius's note. *I can't stop thinking of you.* I read the sentence over and over again. I might have run my finger over it.

I made myself scarce for the remainder of the afternoon, slipping quietly outside when the time came. With every step closer to Volnay the more nervous I became. Fear and guilt pulled at me, and something else: excitement, a delicious expectation. Turning off the road, I walked through the vines. The *cabotte* was of stone and looked new; the windows were vaulted. A statue of Jesus occupied an arch above the door. I made the sign of the cross and went inside; the place was basic but clean with a small fireplace. Outside, the vines shifted in the summer breeze. Sparrows skittered in the ivy of a tumbledown wall.

Junius arrived, not on his horse but on foot and dressed as a peasant: black britches, grey shirt, a kerchief round his neck, a worker's cap. He smiled, doffing the cap, but remained silent. Unexpectedly he wrapped his arms around me and kissed me – his tongue probing. I found myself responding in kind. I had never kissed a man before. I used my tongue as well. Soon I was losing control. My stomach felt weak as though I had butterflies fluttering inside of me.

My head was awash with the tales I had heard, the things men did to women, the times I had been warned. At the very moment Junius touched my breast I saw the statue of Jesus above the door, so I pushed him away. He laughed and I slapped him hard.

'You're married,' I said, panting.

'After a fashion.'

'What does that mean?'

'Eloise is not like normal women. You saw the way she dressed.'

'She wore britches.'

'Did she touch you?'

'I don't understand.'

Wrinkling his lips: 'She doesn't favour, how should I say... men. She finds intimacy uncomfortable, if you know what I mean.'

It dawned on me. Simone had told me of women like this. 'So why did you marry her?'

'Her family owned the *domaine* next to ours. Eloise is an only child. Her father is an old but practical man and approached my brother Clément with a view to merging the estates. In the end I had to marry her.' He pulled a face. 'The land was the price I had to pay.'

'So you don't...'

'We do, but it's a farce and rather unpleasant. This is what I wanted to tell you, Kiki.'

'Why? What do you want, Junius? A mistress? Someone you can use... at your beck and call, an amusement. I am only fourteen years old.'

'Thirteen is the age of consent.'

'So you admit it?'

'I can't help myself... when I see you in church.'

I sighed. He looked so beautiful that I couldn't help but wrap my arms around him. We kissed again.

'There's something you should know,' he said.

I looked up at him, wide-eyed in my innocence.

'Clément runs the estate, a family tradition—'

'Then why didn't Clément marry Eloise?'

'He was already married.'

'Oh.'

'I am destined for a naval career and leave for Brest next week.'

'Brest?'

'The Naval Academy in Brittany.'

I remembered the painting of the sailor at Oubliette. 'The picture on the wall, your grandfather...'

'Yes, he was also a second son and fought for Napoleon... knew the great man personally. He lost an arm at Trafalgar. That's enough of me; tell me about your family.'

I explained that my father was a drunk and that my brothers were loathsome. 'My mother is indifferent to me. Anyway, she's preoccupied with her new baby. It's as though they are trying to rid themselves of me.'

He squeezed me to his chest. 'How could they? You're adorable. If only...'

I sighed. 'I don't know what you expect of me, Junius. You're married and about to go away. Anyway, your family is of a different caste to mine.'

He smiled. 'You're in a class of your own.' Taking my hand: 'Let me show you something.' Entering the *cabotte* he jiggled some masonry to the side of the fireplace. 'Our letterbox' – indicating a small nook. 'Find a small container to put your messages in. If you want to stay in touch, that is.'

'I want to, Junius. It's so sudden. I feel overwhelmed.'

He squeezed me again. 'I will never forget you for as long as I live, Kiki.'

After a prolonged kiss we said our goodbyes. I departed first and walked down the path. I tried to resist but turned to wave at him. He waved back, his cap in his hand. My head was so full of dreams as I walked back to Meursault.

If only Eloise did not exist.

Monday afternoon. I was about to leave for Madame Lonjons'. Maman shook her head. 'She doesn't want you to work for her anymore.'

I was half-relieved but felt irked as well. Tears pricked my eyes. 'Did you ask her why?'

'Don't ask silly questions. You've lost the job and that's that. I will have to speak to your father… your schooling.'

'I don't understand.'

Pursing her lips: 'The pay from Madame Lonjons will no longer be available for your education. It's tight moneywise with a new baby to feed. Putting food on the table is not as easy as you imagine.'

The next day I was dressed and ready to go to school. Strangely, the men had not left for work. Dago appeared and said, 'Papa and I want a word with you.'

'I am off to school. Waiting for Alie.'

He frowned. 'You're not going to school today, or any other day for that matter. Come, Papa is waiting.'

I felt my legs sag. Dago grabbed my arm, closing the kitchen door behind me.

Papa was pacing and looked stern, avoiding my gaze.

We sat at the table, me on one side, Papa and Dago the other. Papa's eyes were bloodshot; he belched into his fist.

Dago cleared his throat; his normally ruddy complexion was pale. I choked down the bile in my throat. My eyes stung.

'Madame Lonjons has let you go,' he said.

I fidgeted with my hands.

'Christine, you have to face the truth – we can no longer support you.'

My head was whirling. 'But we are family.'

'No, you don't understand.' Papa turned away.

'I'm your daughter,' I said.

He ignored me.

Dago continued, 'The money from Madame Lonjons almost covered your school fees.'

'I will find another job.'

'Space is very tight here. We share a bedroom. And where will Arlette sleep?'

'Arlette is only six weeks old and can stay in Maman's room for at least a year.'

He closed his eyes. 'There's something else… we have been talking with Monsieur Monnier. He has agreed to give us the land.'

'Why would he do that?'

'Because you will become his wife.'

I shook my head. I couldn't take it in. I gripped the table for support.

'It's the best solution. He is wealthy. You will have all you desire, clothes and books *and* money. You will be the mistress of Domaine le Merle, fifteen hectares of prime Chardonnay grape. This is a huge advancement for you, for our family.'

'You are selling me for a half-hectare of land?'

'Half a hectare, how do you know?'

'Monsieur Monnier told me himself on the way to school. He gave us a lift into Beaune.'

'So you've met… that's good. He's a real gent—'

'Papa, tell me you haven't agreed to this.'

'Where else can I find three thousand francs? Touching fifty is hard enough.'

'Then stop your drinking. God knows what you spend.'

Levering himself to his feet, he shook his finger at me. 'How dare you!'

'How dare *you*. He is three times my age *and* disgusting. No, I won't do it. You forget I am only fourteen years old.'

'The age of cons—'

'—is thirteen. Do you think I don't know *that*?'

'The kings and queens of France have been doing this for centuries, *la marriage politique*,' said Dago. 'If they can do it, you can do it. You *will* do it.'

I thought of Junius, forced to marry Eloise for much the same reason.

'You'll do what I tell you and that's final,' said Papa.

I jumped to my feet. 'No, I won't! You are a couple of unloving *conards*, bâtards! I hate you! I wish I'd never been born. You're a drunk, Father, a filthy, nasty drunk. Lay a hand on my mother ever again and I will kill you. Understand?' The rage had me by then. I don't know what possessed me but I stood and upended the table with all its contents. Dago was splayed across the floor and so I kicked him as hard as I could, again and again.

I stormed out of the room, slamming the door behind me. Pencil and paper somehow found their way into my hands as well as a tin on the dresser, 'Pastilles de Vichy' inscribed on its lid. Papa and Dago barged in. There was blood on Dago's face.

Alie ran in, screamed and grabbed my arm. I shoved her aside. After slamming the front door my feet took me to Saint-Nicolas' as though I was being led there. A while later, having begged God for His guidance, I wrote out a message.

25 June

Dear Junius,

Please help me!
My family is forcing me to marry Augustave Monnier. I have no one to turn to. What can I do?
I hope this message finds you.
I'm desperate!

Your friend,
Kiki

Dear and *Your friend* sounded appropriate. I considered rewriting it – *Dearest* and *I love you* – but dismissed the idea.

After a hate-fuelled walk to the *cabotte* I removed the stone and placed my note inside the nook. The tin was thin, the stone flush to the wall when I replaced it. Outside, I knelt in front of the statue and prayed to Our Lord that Junius would rescue me.

I dreaded going home – the recriminations. Any remorse I might have felt at kicking Dago died almost as soon as it entered my head. He had conceived the marriage-for-land idea. Not Papa who did not have the imagination. The effrontery: their rotten piece of land for my future, and that rubbish about the kings of France and their *marriages politiques*. At that moment I realised I had changed. I had been kissed for the first time, experienced impulses in my body I had never felt before. I knew I loved Junius. My family had rejected me. My life could never be the same. The days of innocence were gone. I was no longer the child who would do as she was told.

THREE

SATURDAY, 27 JULY was the day I became Madame Augustave Monnier, just three days after my fifteenth birthday. Alie and Maman helped me dress at our house on rue du Moulin Judas.

'Stop pouting,' said Maman. 'You look ridiculous and spoilt, on the most important day of your life.'

'The worst day... Do I really have to go through with this?'

'You'll get used to it. I married your father, didn't I?'

'At least he wasn't a hundred years older than you.'

'Stay still,' said Alie, buttoning my dress at the back. It was white, décolleté, the waist nipped in, though for all I cared I might as well have been wearing a sack. My hair was worn down and crowned with a 'ring of thorns' to secure the train. Crown of thorns more like – Jesus would not have approved. He said that marriage was God-made. Not mine. Mine, because of a piece of rock-strewn land.

Maman held the mirror in front of me. I pulled a face. At least Madame Lonjons had not had the satisfaction of making the dress. Serves her right. Alie slipped the strand of pearls round my neck.

'I can't believe that Monsieur Monnier paid for all of this,' said Maman.

'Say that one more time and I will scream.'

Alie sighed.

The barouche arrived – open-topped and drawn by Monsieur Monnier's chestnut mares. I kept it waiting for as long as I could. Maman almost manhandled me into it. Papa and I were seated in the back, Alie and Maman facing us. Saint-Nicolas' was a short drive away. People gawped as we passed them by. Someone hurrahed. Papa tried to make conversation but I ignored him. Muttering, he swigged from a silver flask which I took from him, tossing it over the side onto the street.

'*Salope!*' he said.

Maman said, 'Kiki, try to be sweet to your father on this joyous day.'

I replied by sticking out my tongue.

We arrived at Saint-Nicolas'. Two bridesmaids I had never met carefully gathered my train when I stepped out of the barouche. Maman and Alie entered the church. After a short wait and clutching the posy Alie had put in my hands, I walked down the aisle on Papa's arm. The organ groaned out a dirge. Only the pews at the front were occupied. The people were meaningless to me. Most were old and grey with absurd hats. I had not been privy to the guest list. Why would I, a simple *paysanne*? Everyone turned to gape at me, let out an intake of collective breath when I tossed my hair. 'My goodness,' someone said. 'She's exquisite,' said someone else.

Augustave was clad in a long black frock coat, double-breasted, his top hat on the ground beside him. I was tempted to stamp on it. He looked fit for a funeral and turned to show me his yellowing teeth. I looked away and took my place by his side.

The Bishop of Dijon, no less, stood in front of us, a block of flesh, vast in his raiment, mitre in his hand. His chin was greasy as though he had just enjoyed a plate of roast pork. *And* he was looking down the top of my dress and licking his lips.

How could someone like this represent Our Lord?

Placing his mitre to one side, he opened a prayer book and started prosing in Latin. I understood the gist of what he was saying. The liturgy ground on; even my husband-to-be yawned.

When he came to 'If any man can show any just cause let him now speak or else hereafter forever hold his peace...' I held my breath and prayed that Junius would materialise and whisk me away.

Nothing. No Junius. Silence instead.

When he said, 'Wilt thou have this man Augustave Olivier Baptiste Monnier to thy wedded husband, wilt thou obey him, and serve him, love, honour and keep him so long as ye both shall live?' I let myself down.

'If I have to,' I said.

The church went quiet – not a mouse heard to yawn – as though the world had stopped.

The bishop's jowls slapped against his neck, his piggy eyes peering at me. '"I do" would suffice,' he intoned.

'I do,' I said, at length.

Then we were out of the church, Augustave clutching my hand. Rose petals were dumped over us. He grinned, and I stood there like a turnip.

Then something strange: a man with a contraption covered his head with a black cloth. 'Smile. Still as you can for two minutes,' he said.

Monsieur said, 'Stop wriggling, Kiki, it's a photograph. One for the archives.'

Archives, *mon dieu*! I didn't want to be in an archive that had anything to do with Augustave Monnier.

Then we were off in the barouche down the cobbled streets to Domaine le Merle. People were cheering, some waved at me, more rose petals. The Blackbird Estate... *bah*.

A tent had been erected in the courtyard at the back of the house. I entered on my husband's arm. A momentary lull: then

23

everyone was talking at the same time. Hats everywhere, flowing gowns, a couple speaking English, men in uniform, staff serving wine from bottles stashed in bowls full of ice, flowers, and tables laden with food.

I savoured a moment to myself, gazed at the hill beyond the stream. Somewhere up there was *the* half-hectare of land.

A waiter handed me a glass of champagne, breaking my reverie. *Steady*, I thought, *I'm not used to this.*

There must have been a hundred or so people, some from as far as Lyon, landowners or something to do with wine. Some came up to me, congratulating me. The women were polite; most of the men had that look in their eyes. I found I was enjoying myself despite what lay ahead. My education allowed me to make conversation; anyway, most of the talk was of wine, the upcoming *vendange*. I was introduced to Monsieur Guiod, the Mayor of Beaune, who invited me to the Hôtel de Ville. 'You may be able to serve the community, the hospices, perhaps,' he said.

Despite my ease, I could see the Vellays were out of their depth. My brothers hung around the back of the tent. I even felt embarrassed for the *conards*.

Eloise sidled up to me. 'You caught the old crow,' she said.

'We are neighbours now. As the crow flies, not that far apart.'

'Close enough to lure my husband.'

Her comment deflated me, reminding me of my 'duties' that night. I was tempted to ask her about Junius but thought better of it.

She laid her hand on my arm. 'Junius will be away for two years, so forget him. You can always visit me if you like.'

I was of a mind to tell her I was not of her persuasion.

She clung to me. For once Monsieur came to my rescue, introducing me to a man of similar height and looks. 'Kiki, I am pleased to introduce you to my twin brother Oreste.'

I studied Oreste: he was the very image of Augustave, minus

the hirsute superfluities, although his eyes were different – more severe, less vacuous – as though they held secrets known only to the man himself.

He bowed. 'I missed the service. My apologies. I have been working on a case. And the train from Paris was delayed.'

'Oreste is a policeman in Paris,' said Monsieur.

I nearly said, *Why did you not tell me you had a brother, a twin at that?* Instead: 'An interesting case, I trust, monsieur.'

Judging from his expression he was working out why a fifteen-year-old girl would be interested in policework. He attempted a smile. 'We discovered a plot to assassinate the emperor and arrested the suspects last week. I was delayed… tying up loose ends.'

'Oreste is known to the emperor himself,' said Monsieur.

'Although we are twins, Augustave was born first. I wasn't interested in viniculture. I was always drawn to the police. A vocation, you might say.'

'How long have we the pleasure of your company?'

'Three days and then it's back to Paris, I'm afraid.'

'A pity,' I said, aware of sounding sarcastic.

Oreste stared at me, his eyes inscrutable. A waiter saved me by topping up our glasses, affording Oreste the excuse to move away.

'You didn't tell me you have a brother, a *twin*, Augustave?'

Monsieur mumbled an excuse along the lines of him not wanting to distract my pretty little head.

'Well, that's not good enough,' I said, walking away.

While helping myself to a radish, a man introduced himself. 'Sir Reginald Markham,' he said, bowing extravagantly.

I tried to smile but he was almost too much – too male and very tall with black whiskers and fierce dark eyes.

'So you snared the old coot,' he said.

'What's it to you, monsieur?'

Puffing his cigar: 'I always admire a girl on the make, trying to better herself. Admirable, some would say.' Sidestepping a couple of paces, he rubbed his chin. 'Yes, you seem the right type to me, pretty in the sort of way that would appeal to the older man.'

I was tempted to grind his foot with my heel. Instead: 'Quite the reverse, Sir Whatever-your-name is.'

'Huh, you're common. I can see that. I'm told your family work in the fields for Augustave.'

'Hardly fields. Now, if you don't mind' – turning my back on him.

'But, madam.'

I readied myself, thinking he would grab me, and walked swiftly away. I had learnt a lesson: never lose your temper under fire. Fight fire with ice. I seethed nevertheless – the nerve of the man, rude to me at *my* wedding. I would have to be wary of Sir Reginald Markham.

The Vellays really were out of their depth. Papa was drinking with a group of artisans who had inveigled their way into the tent. Dago and Salva were on their own and looking forlorn. Maman was engaged with some flowery women, expounding, no doubt, on the virtues of breastfeeding.

I spotted Simone from school. She looked very grown-up. 'How did you manage to worm your way in here?' I asked her.

'My father is a *négociant* and has known your husband for years.'

'A négociant?'

She sighed. 'You need to grow up, Kiki. You're married to a wine producer.'

'Well?'

'Father assembles wine from *viticulteurs* and sells their produce under his own name, as does Sir Reginald over there.'

'Why would a grower do that?'

Rolling her eyes: 'Economies of scale and Father knows the buyers. If he does his job properly the grower will sell his entire crop.'

I nodded. 'Lovely dress, Simone.'

'You don't look bad yourself… for a peasant.'

I laughed. Simone was never one to hold back.

She laughed as well. 'A beautiful peasant, though.'

'Simone, you seem to know what you are doing. You are obviously comfortable in this world. I may need your help.'

Later, a violin accompanied by an accordion played a ditty to dance to. Dago made a fool of himself, asking Simone to the floor. She laughed and turned her back on him. I asked someone the time, worried at the prospect of performing *my duties* in Monsieur's enormous bed. I had taken the precaution of visiting 'le Merle' a week before to check my future abode. Apart from staff, Monsieur lived alone. His parents were dead. His only relative appeared to be Oreste.

On leaving the party I found the housekeeper in the kitchen. Madame Gaillard favoured black clothes. Like Madame Lonjons she wore her hair in a tight grey bun. A look of crossness never seemed to leave her face. The folds of her dress did nothing to conceal her bulk, though her dark eyes and prominent features suggested a certain kind of beauty, albeit faded.

I asked her to remind me where I was sleeping. After a black-eyed stare she led me up a galleried staircase to Monsieur's bedchamber. Three large round wooden beams supporting the ceiling dominated the room. The prospect of looking up at them made my stomach turn. The bed was large, four-posted with candelabra on either side. The windows were closed and curtained with brocade. *At the height of summer!* And an odour – ripe and clawing – of stale eau de cologne.

Living and sleeping here was so repugnant to me that I blurted it out: that I wanted my own room. 'A small bed will do, if it's not too much trouble, madam.'

'No, no, that would not suit Monsieur Monnier at all.'

I reminded her I was now mistress of le Merle, that she would do my bidding. After glaring at each other she led me down a corridor, muttering to herself. The room was modestly proportioned. An unmade bed faced a single window. I asked her to make it up. *Please.*

I returned to the celebrations. Music filled the tent. A group of older men including Monsieur and Sir Reginald stood in a circle, cognac and cigars on the go. The younger guests were dancing a jig, whooping, their legs kicking high. Tempted to join in, I resisted: I had to be in my room pretending to be asleep before Monsieur came up. Alie was dancing. Grabbing her by the arm I bid her goodnight.

'So soon?' she said.

'I can't explain, but I have to go.'

She pulled a face. 'I hope all goes well' – putting her arms around me.

Bed linen and a bolster had been dumped on the mattress, so I made the bed, mouthing curses at Madame Gaillard. After struggling out of my wedding dress I closed the curtains and slid between the sheets.

The following morning I awoke to find Monsieur perched on the end of my bed in his dressing gown. 'Kiki, you were not in my bed when I came up last night.'

'Not now,' I said.

'Kiki' – clearing his throat – 'I am aware of the difference in our ages. Nevertheless, I am now your husband and will provide for you; you will live as a gentlewoman at le Merle with all your attendant needs.'

I was tempted to tell him that the one need I had was not available to me.

'I propose an arrangement. This room will be yours... not ideal, but something I can live with.' Clearing his throat again: 'But I have my needs as a man, so to speak. What I am trying to say, Kiki, is that we should have congress, limited to, say, twice a week.'

'Congress?'

'Umm, sexual intercourse, my dear.'

I remembered what Madame Thierry had told me: *Never rush an important decision until you have thought it through.*

I cocked my head. 'Let me think about it.' Then: 'Which nights do you have in mind?'

He leered. 'We'll talk over dinner.'

After breakfast I decided to inspect the estate. Roughly half was planted with vines on a hill facing Meursault. I trudged up the incline, crossed a track and walked to the side of a coppice to arrive at 'my bride price': the half-hectare my family had traded me for. Weeds grew everywhere, brambles and wild roses, a sea of dandelions. And rocks. Trees as well, some quite large. The land sloped towards the south-east. My brothers had got something right: a south-east-facing aspect ideal for the ripening of grape.

I wondered how they would cope. They would be after money – *my money*, rather my access to it. I would have to be on my guard.

It was magnificent up there alone with Meursault spread below me. I was reluctant to leave. On my way back down, a team of workers were taking their lunch. Two sticks of bread, a raw onion and a wicker-covered flagon set on a strip of cloth. I thanked God that Papa was not amongst them. One young man, about my age, jumped up and removed his cap. 'You're the new mistress, ma'am. Old Albert's girl?'

'You're right there,' I said, aware I had changed my accent. 'Who are you, may I ask?'

'Roget, ma'am.'

'Happy to make your acquaintance, Roget.' I failed to tell him he was the first person to ever have addressed me as 'ma'am'.

'What are you doing?' I asked.

'Ensuring there are no weeds 'tween the vines, ma'am.'

'Oh… why is there a rose bush at the end of each row?' I asked, full well knowing the answer.

'Distracts the flies, ma'am. Aphids. Not sure I believe it, though.

Old wives' tale, if you ask me.' He fidgeted with his cap. 'I 'eard Dagobert bought some land.'

'Yes, up there beyond the thicket.' I paused. 'What do you think of it, Roget? The land.'

Scratching his chin: 'Facin' sou'-east, that's good, ma'am. Rough piece, mind, needs a lot of work. Won't be producin' for many a year.'

He indicated the flagon. I politely declined, leaving him to his lunch.

Monsieur had made an effort, the large dining table strewn with flowers and a candelabrum – ten candles, all lit. A bottle in a silver bowl with ice, its label facing upwards: 'Domaine le Merle' inscribed above the etching of a blackbird. Madame Gaillard served roast pheasant with haricots and carrots, going about her duties without once looking at me.

Monsieur poured the wine. 'To us,' he said.

I touched my glass.

'Well, have you considered our "arrangement"?'

'I have and I accept. But I need answers and I have conditions.'

He leered, imagining, perhaps, what awaited him.

Without warning four dogs bounded into the room – dark and sleek with a bob for a tail, thick in the shoulder, powerfully muscled. They whined in the hope of a scrap. I loved dogs, but these were overwhelming. One was snuffling at my legs.

'Castor and Pollux, Scylla and Charybdis,' Monsieur announced. 'The loves of my life… apart from you, of course, my dear.'

I stroked the brute at my leg.

'Careful,' said Monsieur. 'They are remarkably strong.'

Up on hind legs, the dog pawed me. I could feel his weight, his strength. I braced my legs. He licked my hand with his huge, wet tongue. His eye teeth were long and pointed.

'Down, Scylla!' snapped Monsieur. 'Down!'

The beast sloped away and lay under the table.

'Well?' he said.

'Two nights. Wednesdays and Saturdays would suit me.'

He wrinkled his lips, which I took as a 'yes'.

'When we finish our, um, "congress", as you call it, I will be entitled to return to my room.'

'Acceptable,' he said.

'I also require freedom of movement.'

'Acceptable as well, but I don't want you going to Paris every other week. Were that the case, you would be unable to fulfil your part of the bargain.'

'I'm not interested in Paris,' I lied. 'To move about the district, Beaune, for example.'

'All right…'

'I will require my own horse, monsieur.'

'We have the berlin.'

'I *want* my own horse.'

'Acceptable. Yes. Not a problem.'

'I will also require an allowance. I have never been one for fripperies; the basics will do. And I don't want you buying me anything, clothes, that is.'

'We will drive to Beaune, meet a banker friend of mine and open an account in your name. Three hundred francs will be transferred to you on the twenty-eighth day of each month.'

Three hundred… I could barely imagine such an amount. 'Thank you, August,' I gushed. Then: 'Lastly, and this is not a condition, but I would much prefer if you were clean-shaven, like your brother Oreste.'

He touched his beard.

'I don't want to nuzzle up to, well… to some sort of furry animal. Oreste looked more handsome than you.' I smiled prettily.

We ate in silence. To make conversation I suggested I could

involve myself in the wine business. 'My family, it's all we know,' I concluded.

'As labourers.'

'So what? It's in our blood. We Vellays are rooted in the soil.'

Silence.

'I spoke to the Mayor of Beaune at our wedding. He mentioned the hospices… charity work.'

Monsieur made a face. 'Oh, him.'

'You have a problem with *him*?'

More silence. I tried again, but Monsieur appeared uninterested in what someone like me had to say.

Having finished our dessert of caramelised pears, Monsieur indicated it was time for bed.

'Today is Sunday, if I'm not mistaken. Three nights to go,' I said, feeling like a cow.

On Tuesday I took the berlin to Beaune for the first time. Monsieur had supplied me with money to buy clothes. I sent Alie a note telling her I would arrive at rue du Moulin Judas at eight o'clock. *Outside*: avoid having to answer all sorts of tiresome questions from my family.

Alie was on the corner. 'You look very fine,' she said, taking her seat. 'You seem so grown-up, Kiki,' she said after a while.

'I've had to grow up very quickly. Too quickly.'

'How do you mean?'

'Alie, I have been sold by my family to a man who is twenty-eight years my senior. I had to make up my mind what I was going to be… a wilting rose – sweet, shy and accepting – or someone who would stand up for herself.'

She bit her lip. 'You're so much more mature than me.'

'Be patient. Don't rush. One day the family might let *you* down. Talking of let-downs, how are my "delightful" brothers?'

'Dago's assumed control. Even Papa does his bidding. He

imagines he will become a big grower now he has his piece of land.'

'He's fooling himself. A lot of sweat will be required, and money, with no grapes to speak of for at least five years.'

The carriage trundled on. I couldn't help myself, looking out of the window as we passed the *cabotte*.

We arrived at place Saint-Étienne. I hadn't planned on going inside the school but was tempted to see my old classmates, show off my new-found status. I did bump into Simone who shot me a sly look. We agreed to meet at one o'clock.

Madame Thierry spotted me. 'Ah, Madame Monnier,' she said with a wink. 'How is married life?'

I shrugged.

'Kiki, I've been thinking, you should complete your education.'

Strange. I had been thinking the same. 'That won't be possible given my present situation. My husband would never agree to it.'

'I am sure you're right. A reminder he is married to a schoolgirl. His friends would never let him forget it.'

Stroking my chin: 'We could have private sessions. I want to learn all there is to know.'

'Hold on,' she said. Entering a classroom, she soon re-emerged, handing me a book: *Madame Bovary* by Gustave Flaubert. 'Come in next week and we'll work something out. And try to finish the book by then.'

I leafed through the pages. 'What's it about?'

'A young woman who marries the wrong man and leads herself astray.'

'Astray… how do you mean?'

'She takes various lovers and is let down. She burdens herself with debt. Society catches up with her. The plot is a comment on bourgeois folly. Read it. I don't want to spoil it for you.'

I left the school clutching the book, having changed into the clothes Madame Thierry had given me. I told Blanchet, Monsieur's driver, that we were to leave at four o'clock. I wondered at my situation – a girl with some francs in her purse at liberty to do as she pleased. A freedom of sorts, one for which I would have to pay the price the following night. I tried to banish the thought, relegate it to another place.

Beaune in late July is always hot. People went about their business – carts laden with barrels, one man unloading rounds of cheese from a handcart. A wagon drew up, the driver jumping down in front of me. I asked him, 'The barrels and cheeses, monsieur, to where are they bound?'

He was young and looked me up and down, displayed his teeth. 'Paris, especially the wine, thirsty lot, they are, up there.'

'Yes, but how are the barrels shipped there?'

'Most via the Canal de Bourgogne, on barges, mademoiselle.'

'The others?'

'By train.'

I thanked him and turned away, not wanting to encourage him.

Crossing place Saint-Pierre I entered Jeannine on rue de l'Hôtel-Dieu. The place reeked of leather.

At first, I was ignored – my mode of dress, perhaps. Eventually, a man asked me if he could be of assistance.

'I require a saddle, monsieur.'

He looked at me from under his brows. I pulled the fold of francs from my purse.

'My apologies, mademoiselle.'

I sat on a model of a horse where he took my measurements. He looked somewhat put out when I told him I rode 'English'-style.

I emerged onto the street with a pair of britches, a hat and a crop. The saddle would take a month to make.

With time on my hands, I visited the dressmakers on rue du Faubourg Madeleine. Once again, I was changing out of my shift and being measured, this time by Madame Hermann who, unlike Madame Lonjons, was young and full of interesting advice.

I purchased all sorts of intimate things: underwear, chemises and camisoles; two peignoirs (yellow and blue); and three pairs of stockings.

Madame Hermann was *au courant* with the 'latest' in Paris. I settled on two dresses of similar style: tight bodices, high necks, buttoned fronts, white lace, low sloping shoulders flaring into wide full sleeves. The skirts were also full, ankle-length and bell-shaped. 'Ready in a couple of weeks,' she assured me.

A young woman entered the shop, her hair worn in low ringlets with a centre parting and tied in low chignons at the nape of her neck. I admired what I saw and decided to copy her.

I had almost forgotten Simone and hurried across place Saint-Pierre to a patisserie for brioche, and cheese and ham from an épicerie nearby.

I stashed my purchases in a locker at the school, then waited outside. Simone turned up wearing her know-it-all grin. 'You look like the dog that ate the bone,' she said.

I must have been smiling – dreaming of the things I had bought.

We walked and talked, and settled on a bench in place Monge. After arranging our lunch on a cloth, I broke the brioche in two.

'Your wedding night?' said Simone. Typical Simone – no subtlety.

I felt my cheeks turn red. 'Well, er, nothing happened.'

'Nothing happened…? Is Monsieur Monnier a sheep or a goat?'

I told her what *happened* – me sleeping in another room. After further interrogation I confessed to 'the arrangement'.

'So tomorrow night is when it happens?'

'Yes' – shrinking inside.

'You'll be pregnant in no time.'

'Pregnant? I don't want children, at least not with Monsieur Monnier.'

'You're not thinking properly. A child will provide the Monniers with an heir and you with a life of security.'

'Are you deaf? I do *not* want his children.'

'Preventing a pregnancy is not as easy as you may think.'

'Simone, have you ever... well, have—'

'Have I done it, you mean?'

I pulled a face.

'I am fifteen months older than you. That makes a difference at our age.'

'Who, may I ask?'

'Huh, do you really think I'm going to tell you *that*?'

I paused for a moment. 'Well... aren't you scared, the risk you are taking?'

Shooting me a look she pulled her nose. Digging into her reticule she extracted a black drawstring pouch. After looking around she took out a strange-looking object.

'What's that?' I said.

'God, you're naive, Kiki. A pessary. What did you think it was? Here, have a look.'

The thing was black, about six centimetres long, made of metal with a coin-sized buffer at one end and twisted wire in the middle flaring into two wishbone-like ends. I turned it over. 'How...?'

Rolling her eyes: 'You pinch the ends together and insert it into your you-know-what, the shield end nearest the entrance – prevents your husband's seed from entering your uterus.'

I gasped at the thought of putting the thing inside me.

'It's painful at first but you'll get used to it.'

'Can I borrow it?'

She rolled her eyes again. 'Very well, I have a spare... I'll treat you to one from my supplier. A wedding present, so to speak.'

I grimaced. 'Thank you, Simone.'

'Just a thought... Augustave will be expecting you to, well, bleed the first time.'

'What are you trying to tell me?'

'Tomorrow night, don't use it. Dispel any suspicions he might have. Men are very sensitive to this sort of thing. They expect their brides to bleed. A risk, though.'

I nodded blithely.

'Once he's done the deed, stand up and let his seed seep away. Clean yourself, if you know what I mean.'

I left Simone, the contraption in my reticule. Deep in thought, I entered Scordel-Pécot where I purchased two pairs of shoes. The assistant measured me for riding boots.

At four, I met Alie outside the school. We boarded the berlin and drove out of Beaune, the clip-clop of the horse's hooves lulling me to sleep. Alie woke me outside Volnay. I had an idea. 'I need to wake myself up. I'll walk the rest of the way,' I told her.

Inside the *cabotte* I removed the stone from the wall. The tin was still in its nook. I unfolded the paper inside and hung my head – my 25 June note had remained unanswered.

Junius had been away five weeks.

FOUR

W EDNESDAY, 31 JULY 1861. The day had arrived, the day I had tried to put off. At dinner, I picked at my food while Monsieur darted looks at me. I tried to wear my cheerful face, making light of my feelings and drinking more wine than I ought.

I had agreed to visit his bedroom at ten o'clock.

At nine, I took my leave.

'Ten o'clock,' said Monsieur, as though I needed reminding.

I climbed the stairs – gallows, more like. In my room I undressed and inspected myself in the mirror. I sniffed an armpit: it smelt fresh. It should – I *had* washed before dinner. The tufts of hair – some women, I'd heard, shaved there to please their man.

Was I to wear an undergarment beneath the peignoir? With Junius I wouldn't have bothered.

I stepped into the blue peignoir and looked in the mirror again – there in all my bridal pulchritude with a sour look on my face. I did look beautiful, if beauty could be associated with a cornered doe with large and frightened eyes. I tossed my head – my hair hung in dark curls down my back.

Madame Bovary lay on the bedside table. I was at the part where Emma was secretly meeting Rodolphe Boulanger. During the day the book remained concealed behind the wardrobe. I didn't want

Madame Gaillard snooping, to know what I was reading.

The clock on the mantelpiece told me it was five to ten. With a deep breath I opened the door and crept down the corridor.

Monsieur was sitting on a chaise longue in his dressing gown. He rose to greet me. 'You look beautiful, my dear.'

'It's a pity you couldn't have shaved.'

'Kiki, if I did everything you required, where would that leave me?'

The curtains were closed. The air was laden and humid. The room reeked of eau de cologne.

I have tried to forget what took place in my husband's bed that night: his breath, his beard, him on me grunting like a pig. The shock when he penetrated me. The pain. As soon as he had 'finished' I hurried to my room. Remembering what Simone had told me, I stood over my bowl and rubbed myself clean. The serviette was smeared with blood and other fluids.

I was no longer a virgin. I had imagined my first time as something magnificent – two beings locked as one, a continuum of seeds being sown in the glorious propagation of humankind.

I cried myself to sleep.

Next morning, on waking up, I pulled the bolster over my head, the night before alive in my head. All the clothes, the house, the food, the allowance and the horse-to-be were not worth this. I had visions of stealing out in the dead of night on my new horse, with clothes in the panniers and francs in a belt. I had francs, but where would I go? A woman didn't travel alone. I thought about the alternatives: Paris to the north or the Mediterranean to the south, with its cities of Nice and Marseilles.

My family was out of the question, as were Simone and Madame Thierry. Beaune was too close – Monsieur would simply take back his possession. A wife belonged to her husband, to do with as he pleased. To escape I would have to go far away – London, perhaps. America even. I did speak a little English.

No. My one true chance lay with Junius Girard.

I washed in the bathroom, scrubbed myself from head to toe, expunging Monsieur from every pore. I looked in the mirror and cleaned my teeth *again*. I felt better. I had to calm down and work out a plan. One thing was certain: nothing would happen quickly – slowly and surely was the only way.

Downstairs, Monsieur was nowhere to be seen. Madame Gaillard was in the kitchen and shot me a salty look. I imagined her look of disgust when it came to washing Monsieur's sheets.

I poured water from the hob onto tea leaves. The pantry was large and cool. I helped myself to some fruit. Cherries lay rotting in a bowl, reminding me of Monsieur Blanc – of bygone, happier days.

Madame Gaillard went about her business, never saying a word or acknowledging me.

Feeling uncomfortable, I rushed my breakfast and returned to my room and *Madame Bovary*. After a while I put the book down. I was bored. I didn't have the bulk of my purchases to amuse me. I had riding britches but no boots. The idea of wearing a dress in the middle of summer was unappealing. My wardrobe needed to be more practical, suited to spending time outdoors in the sun.

I decided on the britches, a long-sleeved shirt and a pair of new shoes. I looked in the mirror; my hair was long and unruly. In keeping with the britches, I tied it up in a ponytail. The shoes looked ridiculous.

Out of the house, I felt better. I had learnt the lesson of being positive when one was up against life, far better than moping in indecision. Outside in the fresh air was the best place to be.

I checked on the mares. One was in her stall. The berlin was not in its usual place. I stroked the chestnut, her mouth soft against my hand. Something struck me: Castor and Pollux and the other dogs – where would they be?

A lad entered, pail in hand. He couldn't be much older than me, and was tall and raw-boned. He pulled up short when he saw me. Turning red, he proceeded to gawp at the outline of my breasts beneath my shirt.

'I'm Madame Monnier,' I said. 'I'm new here. Who are you?'

Doffing his cap: 'Florian, ma'am.'

'You work here, Florian?'

'I am the stable hand. I look after Flo and Floss. This one here is Floss. Flo is with Monsieur Monnier in the berlin.'

It struck me how well spoken he was for a stable lad. He looked vaguely familiar. 'How come you're working here, if you don't mind me asking?'

'My mother works at the house.'

'Madame Gaillard?'

He tipped his head. I could see the likeness.

'And your father?'

'He died eight years ago.'

I encouraged him with my eyes.

'He was hit by a carriage crossing a road in Lyon.'

'Oh, I am sorry. Poor you.'

He shrugged.

'By the way, where are Monsieur's dogs kennelled?'

He brightened. 'I'll take you there if you like.'

I followed him as he loped across the courtyard. I imagined him as a backwoodsman in the Americas, tracking Iroquois, a *longue carabine* in his hand. He turned around and smiled. I felt he didn't want to lose sight of me. My heart squeezed for him.

He opened a gate to a walled enclosure with a caged-off area. 'The dogs are kennelled here,' he said. 'They are out exercising with Monsieur Monnier.'

'My husband tells me they are mastiffs.'

'From England – he was given them when they were pups. They are three years old and unbelievably strong. Huh, I wouldn't want to get in their way.'

'How do you mean?'

41

Twisting: 'Oh, nothing.'

I felt he was concealing something. I threw him a lifeline: 'I look forward to seeing you soon, Florian.'

I wandered over to the largest of the outbuildings. Inside were barrels stacked in rows. Some were branded with a date, others with chalk marks. And two large vats, there, I imagined, for the maturation of grape juice. Equipment littered the place: presses, bottles, ironwork and crates. The place was cool, a relief from the summer sun, and had a musty, oaky, earthy smell.

A man with a pipe in his mouth was tapping a barrel. He looked me up and down as if to say, *What is a woman doing in my winery?*

'I am Madame Monnier,' I said.

He shrugged.

I gave him my best smile. 'How long have you worked here, monsieur?'

He took out his pipe. 'Thirty-two years, and before you ask, my name is Benoît.'

'Well, Benoît, what do you do here?'

Knocking his pipe against a wall: 'I'm the winemaker, ma'am. You are Albert's girl, if I'm not mistaken, sister of Dagobert and Salvat.' He looked down his nose as if to say I was married above my caste, so why waste time on the likes of me?

I ignored his rudeness. 'The grape is Chardonnay?' I knew this, of course.

'For the white…'

'Oh, yes.'

'We make a red as well, Pinot Noir.'

'I didn't know that.' In fact, I did.

He nodded.

'What happens in these vats?'

'Maturation, ma'am.'

'I would have guessed that, Benoît, but I'm new to this. Could you please elaborate?'

He filled his pipe, shooting me a look as though he had just noticed me. 'We ferment the Chardonnay twice.'

'Twice?' I knew this as well.

Sighing: 'After the *vendange* we add yeast, convert the sugar in the grape to alcohol.'

'How long does this process take, Benoît?'

'Six to eight weeks. In the spring, we initiate malolactic fermentation, convert the malic acid to the softer-tasting lactic acid. Also takes six to eight weeks. The wine gains its buttery taste by stirring the sediments, the lees, giving the wine a rounder, fuller feel.'

'And the red?'

Striking a match, he lit his pipe and sucked. 'Pinot Noir is the grape. Although we add Pinot Blanc and Pinot Gris as accessory grapes.'

'How many bottles does a hectare produce?'

He looked at me as though I was from the moon. 'Depends on the *terroir*.'

I understood *terroir*. 'An average *terroir*… le Merle in a reasonable year.'

''Bout fifty hectolitres per hectare, provided the grapes are fully mature and the weather has behaved.'

I did the arithmetic. A hectolitre was a hundred litres. Dago's land would eventually produce about two and a half thousand litres – some three thousand bottles – *in five years' time.*

'One more question, Benoît, if you please. At what price does Monsieur Monnier sell a bottle?'

He blew smoke, scratched his chin. I could see he was reluctant to answer me.

'Oh, come on, Benoît. It won't hurt.'

''Bout three francs a bottle, ma'am.'

Three francs: my family would pull in about nine thousand francs a year if they were lucky. Didn't sound much to me, with the costs of production.

I was about to leave Benoît to his barrels when a youth in a leather apron appeared. 'Papa,' he said, brandishing what looked like a poker, 'I've just done the fifty-sevens.'

He was florid, his face pitted with acne scars. He was overweight and his fringe was drenched with sweat.

An awkward silence fell as he stared at me, licking his lips.

'My son Guillaume,' said Benoît.

I forced a smile and indicated the poker. 'What's that for?'

Guillaume scratched his head. 'We brand the barrels with Monsieur Monnier's initials, so they don't fall into the wrong hands.'

'Curious.'

'Common practice 'round these parts,' Guillaume said, waving the thing in my face.

'Steady, lad,' said Benoît.

I mock-played with Guillaume, dodging away from the iron, laughing. 'Please let me have a look.'

He looked dumbfounded when I took it from him. Ignoring the fact it was hot, I inspected the branding end – the initials **AM** thereon.

He tried to snatch it back. 'That's mine,' he said.

Handing it back, I made my excuses to leave. *The wine business.* I shook my head. The idea of working with Benoît and his son did not fill me with joy.

Outside, I tracked the stream that ran along the back of the courtyard to a wrought-iron gate set in a wall. The catch was rusted and, after my pushing and pulling, the gate scraped open. The area was small and bounded by the stream and the wall. The layout told me that this little corner of le Merle had once been a garden. Now weeds grew everywhere, as well as thickets of brambles. Sinewy vines with their yellowing leaves wound along the ground and up the walls. Fruit trees leant forward off their walls towards the weed-infested beds below. Flowers in clumps: blue agapanthus in bloom;

sunflowers, their heads bunched; rose bushes, their branches straggly; other plants, blighted and deformed. And vegetables and herbs: onions, their stalks pale and wilted; strands of mint; a large clump of sage. Grass spouted in ugly tufts between daisies, dandelions and clover. A broken trellis, its slats entwined with rambling rose. A rusting roller in a corner, its wooden handle split. Near the stream an upturned watering can that hadn't watered anything in years.

Butterflies fluttered and settled on clusters of purple buddleias. And bees, their low, continuous humming as they lifted from flower to flower, their legs laden with gold dust.

It could be beautiful, this place within these walls.

I knew about gardens. I had maintained the patch at the back of rue du Moulin Judas. I had enjoyed the freedom, away from my family.

This would be my garden, my project, something to occupy my time. Moreover, it would provide me with an excuse to be out of the house. The feeling that life wasn't so bad after all.

FIVE

THREE WEEKS LATER my horse arrived – a five-year-old bay mare with a black tail and mane that matched my hair. I had found her in a farm near Arnay-le-Duc and named her Lapin because of her large ears. I presented her with a carrot and stroked her nose. Her nostrils flared.

I smiled at Monsieur. Life was a little easier between us, though Wednesdays and Saturdays *were* a detestable chore. I realised I might be a whore. Apart from dreams of escape, what alternative did I have? My allowance came through at the end of the month; I was both surprised and thrilled. I intended to hoard it, spend as little of it as possible. I continued to wear the pessary Simone had given me. Monsieur had complained that it felt strange down there. I soon discovered the more 'active' I was, the faster he sated himself – enabling me to return to my own bed.

I had finished *Madame Bovary*. My situation was similar to Emma's, except she was silly and I was not. And I had no intention of falling into debt.

All my new clothes were now in my room. My hair – I had decided against the central parting with the bits and bobs. Anyway, it would belie my age, make me look older.

Not much to do in the garden, the sun-baked earth too hard

for fork and spade – a little weeding and tying the fruit trees back to their walls. I looked forward to planting in the autumn.

I visited the *cabotte* whenever I made a trip to Beaune – checked the tin two days previously on 3 September. Nothing. Junius had been away nearly ten weeks. Perhaps our kiss was a figment of my imagination, a flight of fancy, self-deception, if you will – an aid to cope with my predicament.

Florian taught me the rudiments of riding; he said I had a 'good seat'. I was a fast learner. It wasn't long before I could gallop with confidence. I purchased two extra pairs of britches, a waistcoat and more white shirts with billowing sleeves.

Monsieur was busy with the *vendange*. One day over lunch he announced he was going to Paris for three weeks 'to make sure they keep drinking my wine'. Any annoyance I felt was soon dispelled by thoughts of what I could do while he was away.

I will never forget the day I first rode to Beaune on Lapin. I set off mid-morning. The autumn sun was warm on my back. The vines were various shades of yellow, gold and russet. A breeze caressed my face. I don't know why but I surged with optimism, in a world of my own until another rider came into view. As we neared, I could see it was a woman, one who rode English-style – none other than Eloise. The sight of her brought my thoughts back to Junius.

Her horse was taller than Lapin and she looked down at me. 'You've learnt to ride, Kiki.'

I was desperate to ask her about Junius. Instead, I made pleasant conversation: the *vendange*… would it be a good year… things wine.

'We should spend a morning together,' she said.

'I would love to, Eloise,' I lied. 'At your convenience.'

'Oh, not for a least a week. I am, well, indisposed.'

'Indisposed'. *Had Junius returned?* I was tempted to ask her. My

47

face felt hot and I dabbed it with a kerchief. We agreed to take coffee at le Merle in a couple of weeks' time. We said our goodbyes, smiling at each other, me somewhat flirtatiously.

With Junius in mind I headed for the *cabotte*. Removing the stone, I opened the tin; my note was still there. I noticed that it was folded in two, not in four as I had left it. I felt a frisson of excitement as I read.

7 October

Dearest Kiki,

I have returned to Oubliette.

I have a lot to tell you, should you wish to meet. I will be at the cabotte at ten o'clock every morning. I'll wait for twenty minutes, then leave.

I depart for Brest on 14 October.

Your note – that you are now married to M Monnier – shocked me.

In hope.

I think about you all the time,
Junius

My mind raced: *Dearest, In hope, I think about you…*

The note was dated 7 October – he would be here six more days. I reread the note several times, every word a jab to my heart, every dot and comma.

I had come without a pencil and swore to myself.

I do not remember mounting Lapin. I screamed at myself – part bliss, part trying to gain control of my senses. Lapin sensed my excitement, snorting out steam and trotting triumphantly. I stroked her neck, trying to calm us both down. Nevertheless, my mind was full of the possibilities, of escape.

My first stop in Beaune was the school where I sought out Madame Thierry.

'You look hot and flushed, Kiki. You feeling all right?' she said.

'My *règles*,' I lied, handing her the copy of *Madame Bovary*. 'Monsieur Monnier will make a prolonged visit to Paris. A chance for me to have those private lessons with you.'

She kneaded her chin. 'Mondays and Fridays would suit me. Why don't you come to my house on Monday?' – jotting down her address.

'Mind if I borrow your pencil?'

She handed me a book and the pencil. 'Read this,' she said. I scanned the title: *Pride and Prejudice* by Jane Austen.

'It's English?'

She nodded. 'You appear distracted, Kiki.'

I mumbled an excuse… my first trip to Beaune on a horse. 'I've had a rather eventful journey, madam.'

'Quite.' Madame Thierry was not easily fooled.

I walked to Banque Villiard. My first time alone in a bank and they kept me waiting. The clerk was sniffy when I asked for my balance, looking down his nose at my riding garb.

I left the bank secure in the knowledge that the balance of my account was 474 francs and twenty-eight centimes. I smiled. This time next month I would have over six hundred francs, enough to support me for a year were I to escape.

Next stop was the Hôtel de Ville. I gave my name and asked to see Monsieur Albert Guiod. The clerk behind the counter wrinkled his lips. 'No, I do not have an appointment,' I said, glaring at him.

'Very well, wait a minute,' adding 'please' as an afterthought. He returned five minutes later. 'Monsieur Guiod will see you at three o'clock.'

I was making progress. Meeting the mayor would help fill my afternoon.

Lunch with Simone was in place Monge on 'our' park bench. 'Well?' she said, slicing cheese onto a knob of bread.

'I now have a horse—'

'I'm not here to discuss Dobbin.'

'Oh, you want to talk about the weather.'

'You are naughty, Kiki.'

'You go first, Simone. Are you still seeing "Monsieur Duval"?'

She eyed me in her Simone way. 'He is not a monsieur, more a *maître*. And no, I am not seeing him anymore, not that it's any of your business.'

I grinned.

'Oh, come on, Kiki, stop playing games. How is your arrangement with Monsieur Monnier?'

'If you are talking about the sex, which of course you are, then it's bad.'

'Bad, you say.'

'It does nothing for me.'

She looked at my riding attire. 'You're not a…'

'No, I am not.'

Simone blushed.

'I don't feel anything. I just want to get it over with and return to my room.'

'Your room?'

'We have separate sleeping arrangements.'

'*Mon dieu*,' she exclaimed, rolling her eyes. 'How's the "thing" working?'

'It hurts a bit… sometimes Monsieur complains.'

'Ah,' she said, rummaging in her reticule, 'a little present for you… the latest from Paris. Much the same but lighter, thinner, easier to insert.'

We chatted pleasantly. She stood to leave. 'I must get back. Be careful, Kiki.'

'How do you mean?'

'Men can be manipulated for a time. They will even accept they are being fooled in matters of sex. But eventually their pride gets in the way. Get the wrong man and he will erupt. They erupt in a number of ways.'

'Such as?'

'Some will just cast you aside. Some will exact revenge. Others will inflict physical damage. The worst will resort to murder.'

'Ha! What makes you such an expert?'

'You would be surprised. Take the *maître*, for example. A typical young man, vain to the rooftops, thinks he is Adonis. Sex was good at first and then he started to, well, you know, do his thing too quickly. He couldn't stand himself... blamed *his* problem on *me*. It was as though he had a gift, then lost it. Composed a sonata one day, next day whoosh: nothing, no semiquavers, very frustrating for him.'

'What did he do to you?'

'Well, he didn't murder me, did he? No, he threw the mattress out of the window and me nearly with it. He was in floods of tears, Adonis brought to earth. I escaped down the stairs.'

'Oh. You still see him?'

'I can't avoid him. When he sees me, he crosses the road, hides his face.'

'Stupid little boy.'

'Boy is the word, Kiki. But your husband is a man in his middle age. As a wife you have no rights. *He owns you.* You are his to do with as he pleases. What are your choices were he to rid himself of you?'

'I'd return to my family.'

'Don't be stupid, you'd be miserable. Remember what I said last time... produce an heir for Monsieur. For God's sake, use your head, Kiki' – wagging a finger. 'Now I really must go.'

Before my meeting with the mayor I visited Dumilly-Girard on rue Saint-Pierre, where I purchased embroidery materials: needles, linen, silk and wool. Although not very skilled, I had learnt the basics of needlework from Madame Lonjons. Sewing would help pass the winter nights.

What Simone had said bothered me. She was right: my situation with Monsieur could not last. He would snap, and I had to be prepared. I entered the Hôtel de Ville just before three. The clerk led me through to a large ornate room.

Monsieur Guiod swept in. 'My apologies for not seeing you this morning, Madame Monnier,' he said. He wore a grey frock coat – the lapels short but wide, à la mode – a white shirt, a black cravat. A small wooden cross was pinned to one of the lapels. Apart from my wedding I had seen him at church in Meursault.

Bowing, he waved me to a chair. He appeared uninterested in my mode of dress or how I looked, not fixated on the swell of my breasts as most men were. I took the initiative: 'Monsieur, you are very kind to see me at such short notice.'

'The pleasure is mine, Madame Monnier. I trust the *vendange* at le Merle was plentiful, despite the storm we had at the end of August.'

'Monsieur, I cannot attest to the storm, the effect it had on the grapes at le Merle.'

'The storm was not so bad in Meursault. In Nuits-Saint-Georges some growers lost half their crop.'

'I am sorry for that.' I coughed. 'Monsieur, at my wedding we discussed charity work, the hospices. Forgive me for being so direct, monsieur.'

'Ah, my apologies. A delicate matter, madam, if I may confide.'

I leant forward.

He avoided my eyes. 'Humph! Forgive me, but your husband has not paid his taxes for the last two years. Embarrassing for us and for him, I'm sure.'

'Oh, I am sorry, but what do you expect me to do?'

'Administering the district has been especially expensive –

street lighting, the new station, building works. I'd be obliged if you had a word with him.'

'Le Merle seems to me to be prosperous. In fact, my husband is visiting Paris this month to promote our wines.'

'That's good,' he said. 'Very good.'

I sensed he was trying to lead me somewhere. 'Do you like animals?' he continued.

'Yes, of course.' I explained that I had just been given a horse, which I was very fond of.

'That's good,' he said again. 'Um, if you see anything untoward would you let me know? We are all good Christians here.'

I asked the mayor if he could clarify what he was trying to tell me but he waved his hands. He stood and, with a curt bow, concluded the meeting.

Walking back to the centre of town I wondered what Monsieur Guiod was on about. I felt the non-payment of taxes was a side issue; there was something else. *Do you like animals?* What did he mean by that?

I collected Lapin from the stables and fed her a carrot from a pannier. She stamped her hooves, anxious to be away.

Next stop was the *cabotte*, and after removing the tin I took out the pencil and composed a reply.

8 October

Dearest Junius,

I read your note and am excited you are back at Oubliette.
I will meet you tomorrow at ten o'clock.

I miss you,
Kiki

At dinner I decided not to mention my meeting with Monsieur Guiod. Monsieur *le Maire*, with his strait-backed-religious-zeal act, could do his own dirty work, man on man. Monsieur wore pince-nez for the first time. 'My eyesight is failing me, my dear,' he said, peering at me. 'I will travel to Dijon tomorrow on my way to Paris.'

I managed to keep my face blank.

'I would be obliged if you would accompany me there. We leave at six in the morning. You could pack some knick-knacks. We'll stay the night in a comfortable hotel and you'll return here the following day. A pleasant excursion for you, my dear.'

I coughed down my panic, pretending to choke on the apple I was eating. I hid my face behind a napkin. 'W-why don't you take the train from Beaune, August, dear?'

'They're dirty. Anyway, I prefer to travel by coach, drive between the vines. I know a lovely place for lunch in Nuits.'

'I would be delighted, August' – groaning internally.

'That's good.' Clearing his throat: 'Kiki, the *vendange* this year has been rather disappointing, the storm at the end of August...'

'I heard that the growers around Nuits-Saint-Georges were worse affected than us.'

Dabbing his mouth: 'We are experiencing a small hole in our finances.'

I didn't know where this was going, but I was mindful of my meeting with the mayor. For once he had said 'we', not 'I'.

'Your allowance, Kiki, three hundred a month, I recall. We'll have to cut it to 150, I'm afraid. You have all you need, your clothes, equipment for the horse.'

I nearly said, *Cut my allowance in half and we cut 'congress' down to once a week.* Instead: 'But what of our arrangement?'

'I won't be at le Merle for three weeks. The arrangement is therefore suspended. Should all go well in Paris, I will restore your allowance to the full amount.' He took my hand. 'We start at six in the morning.'

Settling back in his chair, he struck a match and lit a cigar.

I worried about Junius. After my night in Dijon only three days would be available to us. If he really wanted to see me, though, he would go to the *cabotte* every day, as promised in his note. The allowance. I was thinking like a whore: half the allowance, half the congress. It almost seemed like a bargain. The night in Dijon was a Wednesday. I would have to perform but for the last time in three weeks. Then I would be free.

How could Monsieur be experiencing a small hole in our finances? His family had owned le Merle for three generations, so presumably no mortgages burdened the estate, but what did I know of such things?

I had worked it out: Dago's land would turnover nine thousand francs a year when fully productive. Monsieur's land, on the other hand, was thirty times the size of Dago's, which meant le Merle was earning nearly three hundred thousand francs – a fortune, even with expenses. I shook my head. Something was wrong, or was Augustave an old skinflint trying to cut the cost of his biweekly rut? Surely, he could afford to pay his taxes to the Hôtel de Ville? My skinflint theory did not hold water.

The mayor had mentioned animals? There were Flo and Floss, the mares. And the mastiffs. *Was I missing something?*

SIX

WE SET OFF for Dijon at six in the morning. Madame Gaillard handed me a wicker basket, her sour look firmly in place. Floss was on duty, with Flo hitched to the back of the berlin.

The journey was pleasant enough. I was wearing one of my full-length dresses with the billowing sleeves. A proper lady, I'm sure, but useful when it came to helping old Blanchet change the horses. Monsieur enthused about wine, especially when we passed the villages of Aloxe-Corton and Comblanchien.

We arrived in Nuits-Saint-Georges at just past eleven. Nothing remained of Madame Gaillard's measly offerings, and we stopped at La Côte d'Or for a glass of wine and a plate of chicken salad. Blanchet watered Flo and Floss. I fed them a carrot before we set off again.

Monsieur was wrapped in his thoughts, uncommunicative until we drove through Vosne-Romanée. 'The finest red wine in the world, without a doubt,' he said, punching his palm. I had never seen him so worked up.

Late afternoon we arrived in Dijon. Blanchet dropped us off at Hôtel La Cloche. A bellboy took our bags while the manager welcomed us. Plenty of hand-wringing: 'Yes, Monsieur Monnier, of course, Monsieur Monnier,' before he escorted us to our room via a wide, carpeted staircase.

The room was large. A four-poster bed stood there ominously, plumped with cushions, the curtain drawn back. I was of a mind to remind Monsieur of the 'hole' in our finances but kept quiet. Once the manager had bowed his way out of the room I started unpacking. I soon felt trapped. 'I'll check the horses,' I said to Monsieur.

'Don't get lost, my dear.'

Downstairs I asked the doorman for directions. I had seen a train before from a distance. I felt excited, not sure what to expect. A short walk later I arrived at the station. Inside, I checked the arrivals' board: a train was due in from Paris on Platform Two in twenty minutes' time.

I took in the sights and sounds. The glass and iron roof had me wondering how they'd constructed it. Posters dotted the walls, one promoting tooth powder, another a circus.

There were four platforms in all. I looked down onto the tracks – two parallel lines of iron. Time passed quickly; soon I heard a distant thumping sound. I craned my neck. The train hove into view, black and surrounded by steam – the noise was irresistible. People on the platform leant forward. Men in a variety of hats, women dressed like me – all heads turned towards the panting beast. A young girl holding a doll grabbed her father's hand and proceeded to jump up and down. Perhaps she was meeting her mother and was thrilled at the prospect of the presents that surely awaited her. My insides literally shook as the sound buffeted within the confines of the roof. Clouds of steam billowed from ironclad flanks as it slowed. I almost jumped out of my skin when a whistle screeched. Great wheels churned, rods of burnished steel pumping in and out. Cheers came from a group of young men when the contraption finally ground to a halt.

I was caught up in it all: doors opening, men in uniforms, one with a flag, people pouring out onto the platform.

Walking out of the station I was almost envious of Monsieur. Paris. I wished I were going. On the other hand…

I walked into a park, the *jardin botanique*, exotic plants everywhere – palms, surprisingly. I knew roughly where I was headed. After crossing some roads I arrived at a bridge – a stretch of water on either side, the Canal de Bourgogne. I remembered what someone had said: that most of the wine in the area was shipped to Paris via canal. A barge approached. A man shouted instructions as a lad detached the tow rope from a large horse. I called down to him: 'What are you carrying, monsieur?'

'Coal,' he replied.

'Bound for Paris?'

'All the way to the Seine.'

The river Seine. Paris. My head was full of images and dreams. I lingered, not wanting to break the spell, aware that I had to return to my husband and our stuffy room.

Monsieur was lying on the bed and gave me a quizzical look. I sighed and told him of my adventures. He looked disinterested in what I had to say and patted the sheets. 'Come to bed, my sweet.'

'The journey has tired me, August.'

'Don't be a sourpuss. I'll be gone for three long weeks.'

'Later. I need to bathe.' Changing the subject: 'Who will be looking after the mastiffs while you're away?'

Another quizzical look. 'Guillaume. Why?'

Dinner passed agreeably enough. Monsieur ordered two bottles of Domaine de la Romanée-Conti. 'We passed by Vosne-Romanée this morning,' he said, as if I needed reminding.

He was spending money like a duchess. I couldn't help but think of the unpaid taxes.

'Try some, my dear,' he said, swirling the wine round a glass.

The waiter poured, looked down his nose. Perhaps he was wondering why he was serving a mere girl this fabulous wine: one incapable of fathoming its structure, texture, flavour and finish.

Swirling the glass, I inhaled the bouquet. 'Autumnal woods. Truffles. Orange,' I said. I sipped the wine – a velvety texture that lingered in my mouth. 'Deep fruit. Ripe plum,' I continued. 'Pepper and red berries. Cherries. Grains of coffee. The palate is rich and deep. The tannins have flattened out. Delicious.'

The waiter looked at me as if for the first time. 'Madam has a discerning palate.'

Monsieur rolled his eyes.

I smiled modestly.

Somewhat flushed, Monsieur waxed lyrical about his trip to Paris – drinking six glasses to my two. Again, I resisted mentioning my conversation with Monsieur Guiod. I did, however, venture onto the subject of his beloved mastiffs. 'Why four of the brutes and why all male?'

Slurring his words: 'All male, eh? I would have thought that was obvious.' Then: 'I will breed them, my dear.'

Dessert arrived, a confection of raspberries, meringue and cream. Monsieur ordered cognac and a cigar. I declined the cognac. He blew smoke at me. His breath stank. The thought of bed made me squirm.

A man approached the table and pumped Monsieur's hand, wittering on about the *vendange* while stealing looks at me – particularly my cleavage. He showed me his teeth. Eventually Monsieur waved him away.

Time for bed. Monsieur made it up the stairs with my help, although I felt like leaving him there to stew. Taking my time in the bathroom, I emerged to find Monsieur slumped, fully clothed on an armchair, snoring. I crept into bed and prayed he stayed that way.

Next morning I awoke to find Monsieur asleep next to me. I had got away with it. I smiled in the mirror as I brushed my teeth – no congress for at least three weeks. Dressing quickly to be on the safe side I went downstairs and ordered breakfast – poached eggs, *tartine* and coffee. A magazine on my table: *The Illustrated London News*. Indulging myself, I thumbed through the pages.

Photographs of Paris and the emperor with Eugénie roused me, as did those of the 'beau monde' enjoying the season: aristocrats as well as artists and writers and musicians who had made Paris their home. 'A Golden Age of Creativity', one caption proclaimed. 'War a Thing of the Past', another.

The return journey to Meursault was a delight in the autumnal sunshine. Vines carpeted the *côtes* in hues of red and gold as far as the eye could see. *And* I didn't have to put up with Monsieur. Junius, however, occupied my thoughts. I had let him down. I prayed he would be at the *cabotte*.

We made good progress and stopped at La Côte d'Or for a salad and a glass of wine. I chatted to Blanchet, edged the conversation to the subject of the mastiffs. That look again and, mumbling under his breath, he took his leave. We arrived at le Merle late in the afternoon. I changed into my britches and wandered outside. Florian was mucking out Flo and Floss. I presented Lapin with a turnip. Her soft mouth tickled my hand.

Florian looked surprised then went red when I told him he was doing a good job. He tried to say something but stammered, turning his eyes away from me.

I entered the garden. Raking leaves was all I could do, the earth still hard and dry with no rain for a least a month. I drew water from the stream and splashed it over the beds. The mastiffs entered my head, and I found myself walking to their enclosure. All four were cooped up in their cages. A new contraption in their patch: a pole suspended between two wooden posts, a rope dangling down with a bone at the end. Some sort of exercising device, I imagined.

After breakfast the next day I set out on Lapin. My stomach felt like blancmange. I tried to visualise Junius, his round face and brown hair, his brown eyes, the gap between his front teeth.

I arrived at the *cabotte* feeling as though I was going to be sick. Junius was not there. I dismounted and pulled the stone from the wall. The tin – my note was still there, undisturbed.

I was early and tried to compose myself. What if he did not come, and if he did how would I react?

I paced, turning and thinking. The next thing I knew he was walking down the path. I waved. He doffed his hat in return. Junius repeated his performance – taking me in his arms and kissing me without saying a word. I responded in kind, our tongues intermingling. I found I was undoing his belt as he undid the buttons on my britches.

'*Chérie*, are you sure?' he said.

'As anything in my life.'

'Over here,' he said. 'Avoid prying eyes.'

He guided me to a place beside the *cabotte*, between the vines and out of sight from the road. It crossed my mind that he may have taken other girls there.

A spark of mental anguish: I had forgotten the pessary.

I pushed him away. Grimacing, he spread his hands as if to say, *What did I do wrong*?

'I forgot to bring my contraceptive' – shaking my head.

He took me in his arms again, kissed my ears. 'Kiki,' he whispered, 'I will wait for you… on your own terms.'

'But you only have two days left in Oubliette.'

He stared at me, took his time. 'What will be will be.'

I went cold all of a sudden. This was not how I'd imagined it would be.

He was beautiful standing there, but I no longer felt the urge, the rush in my stomach gone. 'Tomorrow,' I said.

He stroked my hair. 'Don't go, Kiki. Not yet.'

'You leave on Monday, Juno.'

'Yes, but I'll see you tomorrow?'

'There's nothing to prevent me. Ten o'clock. Oh, Juno.'

He drew me into him. I wanted to stay. But I couldn't and so I pushed him away.

I left first, feeling a complete fool – a silly little schoolgirl. The heat was on me again; I was desperate to turn around, submit to him, to my desires. Instead I ploughed on, cursing myself, trying to rationalise what I had done – at least I had not risked having a baby. I longed for tomorrow. He was there in the vines and available. All I had to do was turn around.

Next morning I could hardly keep still, such was my want of Junius. I informed Madame Gaillard I would be out riding… no need for her to prepare lunch. The clock in the hallway said nine twenty-five and, crop in hand, I opened the front door. I stood there fixated as Alie rounded the gate, running full pelt towards me red and perspiring.

'Kiki,' she gasped, grabbing my hands. 'Papa has taken ill. He fell over in the kitchen. You must come now. Maman can't cope. Now!'

My heart literally shrunk inside my chest – Junius would have to wait. Although I despised my father, it was about him, *not me*. 'Where are Dago and Salva?' I demanded.

'Working at le Merle. We need to find them immediately.'

'Wait here. I'll speak to Florian.'

Florian was in the stables. 'Find Dago and Salvat. Tell them they are to return home at once,' I told him. 'Then saddle Lapin and bring her to rue du Moulin Judas.'

His eyes flared. 'I hope everything is all right. Anything else you want me to do?'

'A family problem. Now, please, do as I ask.'

Alie and I hurried home. Papa was lying on the kitchen floor covered with a blanket, a bolster under his head. The left side of his face resembled a punctured balloon. His eyes were closed.

Maman waddled in, Arlette clamped to her side. 'Kiki, thank the saints you're here. It happened an hour ago. Praise the Lord he was sitting down when he collapsed.'

I felt his pulse. 'Have you called Dr Barolet?'

'Of course not. No one was here except Alie, with the boys at work and you in your big house.'

Arlette started crying. I kept quiet – now was not the time for recriminations.

'Where have you been the last two months?' she continued.

I ignored her. 'I'll fetch Dr Barolet.'

She pulled a face.

I turned to Alie. 'Papa needs another blanket. He must stay warm and you should move him onto his side. I'm going.'

'You can't go now!' screamed Alie.

'There is nothing I can do except stand here and fret. He needs a doctor. And you need to calm down and use your head.'

Alie slumped and started weeping, setting Arlette off again.

Soon I was outside on the street. My impatience was killing me but eventually Florian arrived, riding Lapin. A fly of a thought: that I should go to the *cabotte*. Shaking my head, I mounted Lapin. 'Have my brothers been told, Florian?'

'I told Guillaume to fetch them, madam.'

I beamed him a smile. 'Well done, Florian.'

Three minutes later I arrived at rue de la Goutte d'Or and thumped on Dr Barolet's door. A youth appeared, only to inform me his father was away in Dijon.

Scratching my head: 'Dr Leclerc in Chagny is on rue de l'Artichaut, if I'm not mistaken.'

'I believe so.'

I mounted Lapin – felt I was on a mission. In fact, I was enjoying myself – the action, the drama, the race to Chagny and Dr Leclerc. I squeezed my heels, and Lapin responded. Junius didn't enter my thoughts until I was halfway there. I cursed out loud at my family. Was this God's way of keeping me faithful to my ghastly husband?

At rue de l'Artichaut Madame Leclerc answered the door. I recognised her from my wedding; she had a kindly, careworn face.

'Papa has collapsed and is lying on the floor unconscious. We need your husband to come immediately,' I said.

She fidgeted with her hands. 'Christine, oh my dear, he's out on a ca—'

'Where?'

'I don't know.'

For ten excruciating minutes I paced up and down, thwacking the crop against my leg.

'Where is he?' I repeated several times.

Madam shrugged, looking uncomfortable.

Then, at last, Dr Leclerc arrived in his pony and trap.

Half an hour later I rode into rue du Moulin Judas, Dr Leclerc behind me. After a brief examination he announced that Papa had had a stroke.

Then it was Maman's turn to collapse.

Dr Leclerc took out a phial, placing it under her nose.

'What are we to do?' said Alie, wringing her hands.

'She needs bedrest for forty-eight hours,' said Dr Leclerc.

Alie stared at me. 'Kiki, you'll have to move in with us.'

I scowled at her.

'Who will look after the family? The men have to be fed. Papa needs care, and what about Arlette?'

'I could employ a housekeeper,' I said, rather unconvincingly.

'What's wrong with you, Kiki? A housekeeper? What can you be thinking? For God's sake, be responsible. *We* need you.'

I cringed. She was right, of course. At times I hated my family. Junius Girard would just have to wait.

SEVEN

T HE NEXT THREE days I was occupied with the family, only returning to le Merle to collect clothes and whatnot, including Madame Thierry's copy of *Pride and Prejudice*. I had reached the part where Lydia Bennet was about to elope with Mr Wickham. Madame Thierry was definitely trying to deliver me a message: young women involved with the wrong men.

I was cook, nursemaid and washerwoman. Alie helped a bit, ran errands, but she got in the way and had the habit of making fatuous comments. At least she attended to Papa – administering to his personal needs.

Two days after Papa's stroke I was tempted to visit the *cabotte*, aware it was Junius's last day, but I was too occupied at home.

Dago and Salvat were their usual obdurate selves, never thanking me for meals and for washing their filthy clothes. Instead, they afforded me shifty looks. Sometimes I caught what they were saying – always the same – how hard it was clearing their land while at the same time working for Monsieur. Their faces were thin and streaked with dirt when they came home at night. Dago complained they couldn't make ends meet with Papa no longer able to work.

Life, however, started to return to normal. Maman was up and about, and I felt I could return to le Merle. I had read *Pride and* alidadᅳ

Prejudice in dribs and drabs. I identified with Elizabeth Bennet, although I was sure she would not have aspired to the likes of Junius Girard.

I returned to le Merle and ten days of relative freedom.

On Monday I rode to Beaune for a lesson with Madame Thierry, stopping at the *cabotte* in the hope Junius was there. He was not. Instead, a note, undated.

Dearest Kiki,

I came here the last two days of my stay and alas you were not here.

I understand that your father has had a stroke. I pray for his swift recovery.

I don't know when I will return from Brest. I will leave a message as soon as I am back.

I hope my unbecoming behaviour has not put you off me.

I miss you,
Junius

Madame Thierry plied me with work: history, arithmetic, English, geography as well. I especially enjoyed studying maps of various parts of the globe, the seas and rivers, the capital cities. I dreamt of the larger world out there.

One evening I rode Lapin up the hill to my family's half-hectare plot. The land had been partially cleared. Most of the trees had been removed. Stumps, branches and tangles of thorn and rose were clumped in piles to the side. A strip of soil had been turned. Bending down, I rubbed some between my fingers. Reddish-brown and crumbly, it was flecked with limestone. Stones were good for ripening the grapes, as they retained heat from the sun. But what really mattered was the *terroir*, the schist – conditions below the surface – whence the wine derived its special character and flavour.

Dago and Salva still had a lot of work to do.

The time approached for Monsieur's return. Madame Gaillard informed me he would be back on Friday, 1 November. The nights were lengthening. The prospect of winter in le Merle filled me with dread. At least I would have my diversions: reading, sewing and my garden. Although Monsieur was returning on a Friday, he would expect me to 'perform'. Seemed reasonable, except I found the prospect loathsome. My mood darkened as the date approached. I tried to justify my existence – at least I was not stuck with my family. And I lived in luxury, with my own bedroom. I was cooked for, had adequate clothing and an allowance – reduced as it was. I reminded myself that it was equivalent to the pittance my brothers earned in three months. *And* I had Lapin and the use of the berlin.

In truth I was a whore paid for sex with a man I physically abhorred.

Monsieur arrived in the early afternoon. I had decided to go to his bed that night, put him in a good mood, get it over and done with.

At dinner I told him about Papa.

'I heard,' he replied.

'You *heard* from Madame Gaillard?'

He nodded.

I looked him in the eye. 'What happens when an employee of yours is ill… such as my papa?'

'It's up to me. I would of course pay what I owed, plus an extra month were I feeling generous.'

'And when one of your workers dies?'

'Again, my decision… I might give his widow a couple of months' wages.'

'After that I suppose her family would starve.'

He shrugged.

I asked him about Paris.

'Not very profitable, I'm afraid. This year's yield was disappointing, the quality average. And there's always the competition.'

'Did you manage to sell last year's wine?'

'I did, all of it,' he sighed. 'Not at a good price, and what with the shipping costs…'

'You ship the wine by canal?'

'Of course.'

'Have you considered using the train? A day's journey to Paris.'

'No. Good point, though, Kiki. I will check with the train company.'

At ten I stole into Monsieur's bedroom to find him reading in bed.

'What an agreeable surprise,' he said.

Taking off my peignoir, I crawled in next to him. Silence. The occasional glance. After a while he indicated he wanted to try something different. No snuffing out of the candles as was his usual practice.

I cringed.

Struggling out of his nightshirt, he kicked back the sheets and lay on his back. His manhood was stiff, although rather miniscule. According to Simone some men had erections upwards of twenty centimetres. Monsieur's was a little more than ten. A relief, in a way: less chance of him detecting the 'device'.

He wanted me to mount him, so I climbed on top. Not an edifying sight, having to look at the wretch. Aware I was dry, I tried to show some enthusiasm by dangling my breasts in his face. I wiggled my backside – the quicker done the better – and Monsieur soon obliged with a groan. Closing my eyes, I kissed his forehead. 'That was pleasant,' I lied.

Back in my bed it struck me what a perfect little slut I'd become.

And Monsieur on his back? Perhaps in Paris he'd availed himself of a prostitute, several, maybe, who had 'educated' him. The more I thought of it the more certain I was. If so, *my* allowance had been spent on *them*. Another thought: disease. I'd heard stories. I would have to be careful, so much so that I returned to the bathroom and purged myself of any affliction he may have acquired.

Two weeks later we had settled into a routine – congress on Wednesdays and Saturdays. Monsieur was in the habit of taking off in the berlin early on Saturday mornings. Needless to say he didn't have the grace to tell me where he was going or what he was doing. A reprieve, though, not having to engage in forced pleasantries. Next day, Sunday, having worked in the garden, I decided to check the mastiffs.

Only three were in the enclosure. Charybdis was missing. Pollux was looking sorry for himself, his faced bloated, his stub of a tail down, his neck smudged with blood. I edged to where he was lying. The abrasion was just below his jawline. Salve had been applied to staunch the wound. His baleful eyes watched me. Meanwhile, Castor and Scylla were pacing and growling.

Unpleasant thoughts circled my head. To the side of the enclosure was an object covered by a tarpaulin, underneath a large cage with space for two dogs and supported on two small wheels. A shaft of wood angled out from the front so, presumably, the cage could be hitched to a carriage. A blood-flecked carpet covered the floor, reeking of dog, blood and sweat.

It had been raining; fresh trails were discernible in the mud – the tracks, four large and two small wheels. I traced them back to the main gate.

My immediate reaction was to confront Monsieur. He had to be using the dogs as fighters. *Conard.* I was mindful of what the mayor had been trying to tell me.

The following Saturday I resolved to confirm my suspicions.

Monsieur always departed at seven thirty in the morning. At dinner I told him I felt out of sorts, that I would not be down for breakfast.

Early the following morning I dressed by lamplight. After an apple and a glass of milk I headed for the stables. Being cold and dark with no hint of dawn, I was tempted to change my mind for the warmth of my bed. Battles, however, are not won by the timid. I was heartened when I found an old cloak in the tack room.

Florian walked in, a smile lighting his face. Flo and Floss were head down in their pails of oats.

'Monsieur is going out this morning, Florian?' I said.

'Yes, his usual outing on Saturday—'

'With the dogs?'

'That's right' – avoiding my stare.

'He usually leaves at seven thirty?'

'The berlin will be ready at a quarter past.'

'Where does he pick it up?'

'In the yard.'

'Florian,' I said, my hand on his shoulder, 'I am taking Lapin for a hack. Monsieur Monnier must not know. A surprise. You won't say anything, will you?'

'Not a word, ma'am.'

Leaning forward I kissed him on the forehead – a kiss to ensure his loyalty. He turned a shade of pink.

Following Monsieur was a risky endeavour. Wanting to be ahead of him, I walked Lapin down a strip of grass bordering the yard. The hint of dawn on the hills, the outline of roofs etched in mauve. An owl hooted in one of the outbuildings. The moon was wreathed in cloud. Rather than risking the sound of Lapin's hooves I led her under an arch and round to a side entrance. Unhitching the gate, I then mounted her. I had to make a decision: turn right to the centre of Meursault or left towards Auxey-Duresses. I decided on Meursault. Fear and doubt gnawed at me, *and* I felt ridiculous. *What on earth did I think I was doing?*

On the road to Puligny-Montrachet, I found what I was looking for: a wall higher than a horse's head. Manoeuvring Lapin behind the wall, I wrapped the cloak round me and held her fast with the reins. From time to time I stamped my feet and stroked her flank.

The wait seemed interminable. Freezing and about to give up, I heard the faintest clip-clop of hooves. Lapin trembled – time to feed her the turnip I had saved her.

The berlin rolled into view, Monsieur at the reins. A passenger on board – I couldn't make him or her out. It trundled past, the dogbox in tow. Once the sound of the hooves had faded, I mounted Lapin, held her in a trot, slowing to a walk when I detected the clip-clop again. The light had improved; I could see the berlin as it passed the graveyard at the entrance to Puligny. Clicking my tongue, I squeezed my thighs.

Soon we were through Puligny, in open countryside. The berlin was two hundred metres ahead. I felt exposed and hung to the side of the road. We passed through Corpeau, a village on the outskirts of Chagny.

I arrived at a junction with no sight of the berlin. *What would Monsieur do? Indeed, what would I do? Would he drive straight ahead in the direction of Montceau-les-Mines or left into Chagny?* I chose Chagny and dismounted at the entrance to the town. My breath roiled the cold autumn air. Vapid light strained through leafless trees. No sign of the berlin and eerily quiet, except the echo of Lapin's hooves. And no signs of life save the curl of smoke from several chimneys. Out in the open I felt nervous. After remounting Lapin we trotted up a small incline and into the countryside again. The road was straight. The light had improved to the extent that I could see a fair way – but not the berlin. I had to face it: I had lost Monsieur, and so I turned around.

Back at le Merle I unsaddled Lapin, brushed her down and settled her in her stall. I felt compelled to check the mastiffs' enclosure. Only Pollux was there in his corner, lying down, his jaw on his paws. He growled at my approach. The tarpaulin was stashed against a wall.

I crept in through the front door. The hall clock told me it was nine fifty. I climbed the backstairs to avoid Madame Gaillard. After undressing I slipped between the sheets, playing out that I was poorly. Anyway, I was exhausted and, after wondering what had happened to Monsieur, I fell asleep.

At supper Monsieur appeared to be in a good mood, slurring his words. Evidently, he'd had a good day with plenty to drink. It was Saturday night – and when I stole down the corridor into his room, he was fast asleep. I tiptoed back out.

Next morning I inspected the mastiffs. The three of them were there, although Castor seemed too exhausted to move. On closer inspection I could see that his face was bloated and that one of his ears was torn and bloody.

EIGHT

ORESTE ARRIVED A few weeks later. Trips to Beaune, Volnay and Pommard were planned. Dinner was a bore. I would take my leave as soon as I dared. My ears pricked up, however, when the Emperor Napoleon was mentioned – Oreste had uncovered a spy network, something to do with the Italians.

'Why would they want to spy on him?' I enquired.

'All governments spy on each other, my dear. Part of the diplomatic process.' He turned away – the end of the conversation as far as he was concerned.

The one advantage of Oreste in the house was Monsieur's consumption of alcohol. On Wednesday after dinner Monsieur lay slumped in his chair. I would avoid congress again.

I was alone with Oreste and took the initiative. 'Tell me about your work, monsieur.'

Oreste took out a case and offered me a cigar. I declined but was flattered nonetheless.

'I am a senior *sergent-de-ville* reporting directly to the *préfet* of Paris.'

'A big responsibility. Why you, Oreste?'

Indicating his sleeping twin: 'Luckily, I was born after him. I'm sure I would have enjoyed producing wine, but policing is far more interesting. As a twenty-year-old I arrived in Paris and trained in policework. I did well. Although I say it myself, I am tenacious and once on the trail of a criminal I never let go. I don't like giving up. The press call me le Blaireau, "the Badger".' Smiling, he lit his cigar.

'Tell me about one of your cases.'

He reached for his glass of Armagnac. 'Two prostitutes were murdered in 1849. I was a junior *sergent-de-ville*. One was discovered in a laundry basket in a hotel off boulevard Saint-Germain, a good-quality hotel, I might add. The second was found in Cour du Commerce, in the street, also in Saint-Germain. Both were in their early twenties, blonde and pretty, and both had been strangled. I studied the imprints on their necks and determined the perpetrator was one and the same.'

I leant forward. Oreste topped up my glass.

'I checked the hotel register, only thirty rooms, but it was April, the hotel fully occupied. We narrowed the suspect down to six men. I interviewed them; they all had an alibi. One said he stayed there because of the restaurants nearby. He came to Paris to eat.

'I visited Cour du Commerce and inspected the immediate locale. There is a famous restaurant nearby, Le Procope, duck their speciality.'

'Aha, a restaurant.'

'Indeed. Remembering what the gourmand had told me, I checked the reservations list, the night the second body was found, comparing it to the list of hotel guests. Guess what?'

'Two of them matched?'

Oreste heaved smoke. 'No match, I'm afraid.' He continued, 'An artist friend did sketches of the victims' faces.'

'What happened to their bodies?'

'Usually we try to find a victim's relatives, hand back the bodies for burial. If we fail, they are buried in a common grave.'

'Oh dear.'

'Luckily, we found the father of one of the young ladies, the other, alas…'

'The common grave.'

He nodded, heaved more smoke. 'I showed the maître d' the sketch of the "Cour" victim. A man of his position achieves his status for his ability to recognise people, remember their names. Sure enough he recognised the girl – a huge advance in our investigations as we could now link the second murder with Le Procope.

'"With whom was she dining?" I asked him. "A man," he replied. Then he hesitated: "Well, this man *was* strange – thin, small-framed, with slicked-back hair, a birthmark to the side of his mouth. Husky voice. Small hands." Small hands! I failed to tell you that the imprints on the victims' necks indicated the perpetrator had small hands.'

'Your perpetrator was a woman dressed as a man?'

'Correct. From then on it was simply a matter of boots on the ground. We hauled in twenty-two delinquents known to masquerade as men. The maître d' recognised one of them. We took measurements, the span of her fingers and thumbs. Guess what? They matched the ones on the victims. Seemed the woman had a thing against prostitutes and wanted revenge. In the end she confessed.'

'And *Sergent-de-ville* Monnier is a hero. The Blaireau strikes.'

He smiled. 'One has to be careful about being a hero.'

'So now you work for the emperor?'

'The *préfet* has assigned me to the emperor in matters of security.'

'Assassination attempts?'

'That sort of thing.'

Silence, save Monsieur's snoring.

'Kiki,' said Oreste from under his brows, 'a delicate matter… you strike me as intelligent. My brother, your marriage, it must be difficult for you, the difference in your ages… I'm not married myself – married to the police, you might say. Augustave always thought he would never find a wife until you arrived.'

Arrived? Surely Oreste was aware of the land-marriage arrangement? I had to tread carefully. 'Our marriage is not ideal,' I replied. 'But I have a life that would otherwise not be available to me – clothes, a horse, good food and wine, and an allowance.'

He frowned. 'There is only Augustave and myself, you see. Barring a miracle, I will not produce a child. Le Merle is in need of an heir, someone to manage it after we pass away. Been in our family three generations.'

'We *are* trying.'

'You are a beautiful woman, Kiki. I wouldn't want you going astray.'

'Astray, monsieur?'

'Well, you know, take a lover, another man. As I said, you are attractive. Some men can be very persuasive.'

Two days later we waved goodbye to Oreste as the berlin rumbled across the courtyard. I was almost sorry to see him leave. Dinners were always livelier with his anecdotes on *la vie parisienne*: the artists and writers, their proclivities. Café life. The new street plan and buildings implemented by Baron Haussmann under the aegis of the emperor himself. And his meetings with the emperor, his description of the man and Empress Eugénie. I allowed myself to be transported to the place – a place where I longed to go.

Dinner that night was a dull affair. I casually asked Monsieur if he was taking his usual Saturday-morning trip. He angled an eyebrow as though it was none of my business. I shivered, dreading the following morning.

I rose at six thirty and opened the curtains – no clouds, the moon was almost full. I brightened a little. I had found a suitable cloak, freshly laundered and folded on a chair in my room.

The procedure was much the same. Florian was feeding Flo and Floss, and beamed when I entered the stables. 'Seems to be a habit of yours,' he said.

'I couldn't sleep. Is my husband taking the berlin this morning?'

'I wouldn't be up and about if he wasn't.'

Once again, I led Lapin down the strip of grass. Mounting her outside the side entrance I headed towards the centre of Meursault and Puligny-Montrachet. Moonlight helped. This time I hid between two buildings in Corpeau and bided my time. I was stamping my feet when a fox slid round one of the buildings and stood stock-still, its body hunched down flat in front of me. I didn't know who was the more startled – the fox or me. It was young, a vixen, its red fur thick and lustrous, its russet eyes appraising me, unblinking. Lapin flared her nostrils. I stroked her flank. The fox eventually turned and slunk away.

My spine tingled. A peculiar sense of detachment imbued me. I tried to hold onto it, but the feeling ebbed away, and then I was back in the world and waiting for Monsieur. Not long, though, before the berlin passed by with the dogbox in tow. Monsieur's profile was pinched, his chin thrust forward. Again, the carriage carried a passenger, one I recognised: Guillaume, the youth with the branding iron.

After a short wait I edged Lapin onto the road. We arrived at the junction outside Chagny. This time I took the road to Montceau-les-Mines. All was quiet, not a soul about. Trees lined the road. Oily black water slid by to my right – the Canal du Charollais, tranquil in the silence of dawn.

Now it was a matter of self-control, utmost carefulness: in touch with the berlin but not too close, but close enough to hear the clip-clop of Floss's hooves. It struck me I was somehow suited for this. Made for it – native caution tempered by an urge to take a risk. Too much caution, I lose my quarry. Too much risk, I lose everything. And so I erred on the side of caution. I felt my body thrill. Lapin was like a well-tuned instrument beneath me – aware of every shift, every nuance of my thighs, my hands and my heels, my brain even. We were as one.

Despite the light I could make out the back of the berlin. To stay out of sight I kept to the side of the path. I passed Remigny where the path veered to the right, causing me to lose sight of it. Touching my heels to Lapin's flanks I soon arrived at the bend where I tugged the reins, not wanting to run into the back of Monsieur. Dismounting, I inched forward. The path was now fairly straight. The berlin was a good one hundred metres away.

Passing Santenay I began to feel uncomfortable; I was a long way from home. Anything could happen. But no, being Kiki, I forced myself onwards down the path.

Ten minutes later another bend; the berlin again out of sight. I upped Lapin's pace but slowed her to a walk as I rounded the curve.

No berlin.

It must have turned off, but where? I decided to risk it and urged Lapin to a trot. In the distance a bridge. Then a sign: Cheilly-lès-Maranges. With no choice, I turned right and crossed the bridge towards Cheilly. Water flowed in rivulets towards the canal. Pasture, woods, a pigsty to my right. Farm buildings ahead. Two possibilities: an unkempt drive with overgrown trees either side and, further on, a property behind a wrought-iron gate, the word 'ORTOLANO' carved into a plinth.

Backtracking to the first entrance I dismounted and crept down the side of the drive, under the trees, my heart in my mouth. After fifty metres or so, a tumbledown farmhouse appeared. I held my breath then edged forward for a better view. No vehicles were outside. No berlin. An ivy-infested wall bordered the ruin. *Is the berlin parked at the back?* I shook my head.

Remounting Lapin I rode back to Ortolano. 'This is it,' I said to myself. A wall protected the front of the property. The gate was new, the black paint still fresh. The owners were likely not poor.

At the sound of hooves, I dismounted Lapin and led her behind a tree. A carriage drew up, a dogbox in tow. The driver jumped down and proceeded to scramble over the wall. The dogs started whining.

A man alighted from the carriage. The top hat he wore made him look taller and darker, his black whiskers and moustache, his dark eyes, adding to his aura of indestructability. 'Shut up, you bastards,' he said in English, slashing the cage with his whip.

I had seen him at my wedding, remembered him telling me I was common, that I had 'snared the old coot'. Sir Reginald Something or Other. An Englishman. Pacing back and forth he cursed to himself. When the gate opened, he climbed back on board. The carriage trundled down the drive, the gate closing behind it.

I breathed down deep and pumped myself up. I couldn't help it – the risk was compulsive yet terrifying. After a moment's hesitation I ran and shimmied over the wall. Ducking down, I crept forward, my heart thudding in my chest.

The setting was typical Bourgogne: a main house with outbuildings clustered round a courtyard. I half-expected someone to shout, *Whoa there, who are you and what are you doing on my land?*

There were no carriages. So where had the Englishman gone?

A man emerged from under an arch to the right of the house. I flattened myself against the perimeter wall and held my breath, letting it out when he entered the house. I picked my way along the wall to opposite the arch. Looking to my left I dashed towards it. The door to the house opened, a girl emerged carrying a jug, her head turned away as I nipped beneath the arch. The sound of blood pulsing in my head. To my right open fields. Straight ahead more fields that led up a hill. On my left the return wall of the house. Chickens clucked as they pecked at the dirt.

Then I heard it – the sound of men cheering, of dogs barking. Any sensible person would have turned and bolted, but no, not Kiki: the stubborn streak in me – a curse, a morbid curiosity, if you will – so I edged my way along the side of the house. Reaching the corner I chanced a peek. To my right was a stone barn with carriages outside, including the berlin.

The cheers grew louder. The barking was unlike anything I'd ever heard – insistent, manic, blood-curdling. Fear clenched at me. I was sweating despite the autumn chill.

My bastard of a husband was a dog fighter.

Balling my fists, I breathed down deep.

A barrel abutted the barn. I dashed across the cobbles and hunched down behind it. The clamour intensified: barking, men cheering, some screaming. Judging by the noise, the fight was taking place at the front of the building. I was at the back, *and* there was a door. I tried the handle; the door creaked open. The space was full of tools and gardening paraphernalia.

I could smell the dogs – the sweat, the odour, the fear. A ladder propped against a wall, a loft above. I mounted the rungs as though I was treading on glass, popped my head up when it came level with the floor – more clutter with a wooden rail at the end. Cataclysmic noise, screeching dogs; I wanted to run. Instead, some insane version of myself impelled me upwards. I hid behind an old door. Recovering my breath, I chanced a look. Two mastiffs in a ring of straw bales – one howling, its paws scrabbling pitifully, the other's jaws clamped round its opponent's throat. Men surrounded the ring, cheering wildly. Some clutched wads of francs. One man was sitting on a bale, his head in his hands. I spotted Monsieur who was not cheering, his face drawn down. In the ring crouched two rough types – 'handlers', I assumed – shouting, urging the dogs on.

Ruffians, farm labourers and what I took to be servants were on their feet, shrieking as though they were in a madhouse. I thanked God that neither of the dogs was ours. Two of the men shook hands, one nodding to the handlers who then entered the ring to separate the dogs – no easy task as the 'victor' refused to let go of his victim's neck – one slashing down at the beast with his crop. The dogs were prised apart. Money changed hands. 'Your winnings, Reggie' – Monsieur handing a wad to Sir Reginald, the Englishman snatching it, laughing all the while.

One of the types poured sawdust onto the ring; another raked it smooth.

Two handlers emerged, each with a dog on a leash. One was Scylla, his fur slick with water. His handler was Guillaume, with his pitted face and sweaty fringe. Men whistled and jeered; some called out numbers as money changed hands. Whining, their leashes taut, the dogs were led into the ring.

A man with a top hat stepped in, kerchief in hand which he dropped somewhat theatrically. Guillaume released Scylla, the other ruffian his dog, both bellowing at their 'charges'.

The noise. The crowd was a mob, a crazed, baying animal. The dogs circled each other, the handlers shouting and swearing.

'Go on, you *bastards*!' screamed one man, a florid fellow in a bulging waistcoat, a flask in one hand.

The dogs continued to circle each other, sparring, up on their hind legs intermittently. Scylla was the smaller dog, quicker, I would imagine, than his opponent, a brindle mastiff with a huge head and black facial markings. Then, quite by surprise, Scylla darted in and nipped at the brindle's ears. Monsieur was on his feet and cheering loudly.

Without warning the brindle rushed Scylla, intending to knock him over, but Scylla darted to one side. Now behind the mastiff, he leapt onto its back, sinking his teeth into the brute's neck. The noise was deafening. Monsieur jumping up and down like a madman. The brindle charged into the bales, knocking Scylla off his back. I choked down a scream. Before Scylla could regain his feet, the brindle charged again. Then Scylla was on his back, the brindle on top of him, its jaws fastened round his neck. Scylla squealed. I blocked my ears. Unable to bear it anymore I crept back towards the ladder. Unbeknownst to me, my cloak had snagged a nail attached to a plank of wood which came crashing down – the arena below at once silent, save the yowling of poor Scylla.

'Somebody's up there,' someone shouted.

'Get up there,' another.

The scrambling of feet, chairs knocked over. Letting my cloak fall to the ground I almost slid down the ladder. Bolting through the door I ran and ran.

'There he is,' someone yelled.

I looked behind me – they were only twenty metres behind. Soon they caught up, dashing me to the ground. I felt my bladder go, the wet warmth between my legs.

'Take him to the barn,' a voice said.

I was wearing a riding hat, my hair tucked in. They carried me back and dumped me in the ring. I cast about – Monsieur was not there.

Sir Reginald stood over me. Bending down he ripped off my hat. 'What have we here?' he said in French.

'A girl,' someone said.

I stood and snatched my hat back.

'A spirited little wench.' Sir Reginald scanned the crowd, gestured with his hands – an actor milking his lines. He had failed to recognise me, *yet*.

'She's wet herself,' someone yelled.

'So she has,' said Sir Reginald.

'Change her clothes!' shouted the florid man in the waistcoat.

'Good idea.'

The crowd howled, whistled.

'Change them here and now,' the man urged.

'If you insist,' said Sir Reginald.

As I lashed out with my feet, he fell. The crowd screamed. Soon I was on top of him – scratching, biting and punching him. He nonchalantly pushed me away, and then *he* was on top of *me*.

The crowd was now quiet, sensing, perhaps, that it was all over for me. Then a voice…

'I'd be obliged if you detached yourself from my wife, Reggie.'

Sir Reginald stood and brushed himself down. 'Your *wife*, Augustave?'

Monsieur looked at me. 'Madam, your carriage…'

I tipped my head at Monsieur, kicked Sir Reginald for the sake of it, then stuck out my tongue at the crowd. They whistled and jeered. 'Reggie' leered and winked at me, bowed extravagantly. Nose in the air, I offered my hand to Monsieur who proceeded to walk me out of the barn.

On board the berlin I arranged myself as best I could. Monsieur sat prim and proper while Guillaume was up in the driver's seat. Lapin was hitched to the back of the carriage, as was the dogcart.

The berlin rolled away from Ortolano and soon we were on the towpath. Monsieur remained silent as far as Santenay. Then he started: 'I gave you your freedom, Kiki, and you abuse it. What were you doing there anyway?'

'I wanted to see how you lose our money, Augustave.'

'Our money? You mean my money.'

'*My* money when it comes out of *my* allowance.'

'Bah, your allowance. You don't know the half of it.'

'I know you can't afford to pay your taxes to the municipality.'

'How do you know that?'

'The mayor. By the way, how is Scylla?'

'He will live to fight another day.'

'There won't *be* another day. This has to stop forthwith.'

'Madam, you will not presume to tell me what to do. You seem to forget that you are living in *my* house in the lap of luxury.'

'In return for congress and a reduced allowance' – glaring at him.

'Oh, that. Huh. You know that most men would not tolerate such a situation. Twice a week, bah. Things will have to change.'

Not wanting to demean myself I changed the subject. 'What was Sir Reginald doing there?'

'Reggie… he sold me the dogs. Why?'

'He is immoral. He would have raped me had you not intervened.'

'If you were married to Markham, you would be raped on a regular basis *and* knocked about. Consider yourself fortunate, madam.'

We sat staring at each other. I was surprised that Monsieur hadn't blown his temper. Instead, he was cool and matter-of-fact.

Once home, I attended to Lapin then retired to my room. Sometime later Madame Gaillard entered without knocking, removing the key from the lock. 'You are to take your meals in this room from now on. Should you wish to avail yourself of the closet, you will have to use the chamber pot which I will empty twice a day. For washing you will have to constrain yourself to the use of the ewer and basin provided.'

I tried to snatch back the key. With surprising strength she twisted my arm up behind my back. I did not give the witch the satisfaction of me yelping with pain.

'What about Lapin's daily exercises?' I said, panting.

'The mare will no longer be available to you. She will be sold.'

I refused to crumple in a heap, although I was sure I had gone white with shock. 'How long am I to be confined?'

'As Monsieur Monnier sees fit.'

'What about my books, my writing materials, my sewing equipment?'

'You will be allowed to keep them.'

'And new books?'

'Supplied to you upon request.'

'Why are you doing this to me?'

'I'm not doing anything...'

I sneered.

'Though if you want my opinion I would—'

'I am not interested in your opinion.'

'I would say that you have acted like a child and are being treated accordingly.'

'Get out!'

Madame Gaillard grimaced and, waving the key in my face, closed the door behind her. The sound of the roundels turning in the lock had a finality to it.

I was a prisoner of Domaine le Merle on that last day of November 1861.

NINE

CONGRESS OCCURRED WHEN it took Monsieur's fancy. Possessing a key, he came to my room and clambered on top of me. He hardly ever said a word, grunting when he had sated himself.

I always asked him when my 'confinement' would end. 'Sometime in the New Year' was his standard reply.

After a couple of weeks, I noticed I had gained weight. It occurred to me I could be pregnant: impossible, given my *règles* had finished just five days ago.

Horse riding, I am told, is good for the figure – for the legs, backside and torso. Hooking my feet under the end of the bed, I levered myself up from the floor, not giving up until I had completed a hundred 'lifts'. It was cold. My room had a fireplace but often I would run out of wood. Exercising helped me stay warm.

I read several books, including *Jane Eyre* by Currer Bell. I became absorbed in Jane's world: her miserable childhood, her unhappy schooldays, her Christian values and her off-and-on relationship with Mr Rochester, and how all ended well.

I perceived less of Jane in myself than I did Emma Bovary. I was less pious and not as plain as Jane. And certainly not as mindless as Emma nor as flighty and self-important as Lydia Bennet in *Pride and Prejudice*.

I recognised that indecision was corrosive and decided I would escape le Merle, come what may.

Time dragged, though sewing helped pass the hours. The cumbersome clothes men forced women to wear were ridiculous. Cumbersome was 'covering up', a man's way of screening his wife – his chattel, his possession – from the rest of the world.

I started work on a dress I had in my mind's eye: the bodice suspended by thin straps from the shoulders so the neck and cleavage were exposed as well as the arms, hugging the torso down to a nipped-in waist, gently flaring over the buttocks and thighs to its full length, and secured by buttons down the back as far as the waist so it could be slipped over the head. No billowing, no bustles, no layers; it would have a simple shape, less material and would hang naturally. Woman in all her glory would be on display, not swathed in reams of cloth. The more I cut and sewed, the more excited I became. I had something to live for. Madame Gaillard was a creature of habit; knowing when she would bring in food and empty the chamber pot, I hid the dress under the bed when she did so.

Despite my self-control and diversions, I was given to outbursts of temper. At times I felt like smashing something, including my head against the bedroom wall. My pragmatic nature saved me. I swore revenge on Monsieur and the witch Gaillard, devising all sorts of gruesome ends for them. I imagined pushing Madame Gaillard over the wall of the dog enclosure, her being torn to pieces. For Monsieur, I envisioned myself, cleaver in hand, grabbing his manhood – hacking it off with several not-so-well-aimed blows.

Christmas was approaching; the nights were long. Opening the curtains one morning I was pleasantly surprised: a light dusting of snow covered the ground outside. I would have loved to be out with Lapin and prayed Monsieur had not got round to selling her. I looked at my diary: Sunday, 22 December. I hadn't attended church in over a month.

Strange I should have been thinking this when Madame Gaillard brought in my breakfast. 'There,' she said, setting down the tray. 'On Tuesday you will be permitted to attend Mass. Make sure you are ready. We leave at eleven. And no tricks.'

I doubled my exercise regime. Recovering my breath from the afternoon session, I looked in the mirror: not a pretty sight – my skin was pasty, my hair lank. No great surprise; I had not been outside in three weeks. When the witch brought in tea, I asked her to provide me with make-up. A hint of a snarl but half an hour later she handed me a stick of rouge and a tub of powder. The first time I had worn face paint since my night in Dijon with Monsieur. I applied the minimum I could get away with. At least I now had a semblance of colour, albeit false.

At eleven o'clock I was primped and ready for church. Monsieur entered my room. I was of a mind to tell him he was a coward, using Madame Gaillard to do his dirty work. Instead: 'I am looking forward to Saint-Nicolas.'

'We're not attending church in Meursault. No, we're worshipping in Monthelie.'

'Why Monthelie?'

He shot me a look: a do-I-have-to-explain-myself look.

I crossed my arms.

'All right, I do not wish to worship at Saint-Nicolas' anymore,' he said.

'Why?'– standing my ground.

'I-I do not wish to meet certain people there, have to talk to them afterwards.'

'People like my family?'

'I don't want them asking me about money, and will I do this or that for them.'

Monsieur was as transparent as a pane of glass: me telling my family I was a prisoner in his house would make life awkward for him.

He turned to leave. 'By the way, Oreste will be spending Christmas at le Merle.'

After a short drive up the hill into Monthelie we entered Saint-Germain's just before midnight. The church was full. Candles lined both sides of the aisle. A sprig of ivy was pinned to the end of each row of pews. I imagined all eyes were on me. Being late, we had to stand at the back. I scanned the worshippers – was there anyone there I knew? No one, except Madame Gaillard and Florian who were sitting together.

Halfway through 'Silent Night' the door opened and in walked Junius and Eloise Girard. I managed to stifle my surprise. He looked different: the whiskers were gone; he sported a goatee; his hair was swept back. It suited him. Eloise looked no different, with her short hair and full-length dress. After failing to find a seat they stood close to us. Monsieur was to my left, so when I caught Junius's eye he was none the wiser.

Junius mouthed, 'Where have you been?'

I shook my head. He was too blatant. Eloise was sure to notice.

We hadn't been in touch since Papa's stroke. Many weeks since I last visited the *cabotte*. With his comings and goings I had seen no point in pursuing him. But now he was here my hopes for escape were revived. No one else could help me.

I remembered Junius's ploy at Saint-Nicolas'. My purse was bereft of writing materials. Of course, we could not be seen together after Mass. People would notice, especially Eloise and Madame Gaillard. On impulse I feigned to swoon, clutching Monsieur's arm, rolling my eyes.

'You all right, Kiki?' said Monsieur.

'Yes, August, I just need some air. I won't be a minute.'

At the back of the church I searched for something to write with. A visitors' book with a pencil attached to a string. Looking around I tore out one of the back pages and wrote.

Dear Junius,

I am a prisoner in le Merle, locked in my room. This is my first outing in a month.

   I have to escape.

   Try to arrange a social event with M Monnier so we can meet.

   Sorry to burden you but my life is intolerable.

   I have not been able to visit the cabotte in over a month.

   I will explain all.

Yours,
Kiki

Pocketing the message, I returned to my place.

I enjoyed the Mass – the coming together – and the hymns which I sang with gusto. Monsieur looked down his nose. Not having the best of voices, I sang even louder. I took the opportunity of looking at Junius as much as I dared. Him the same – darting me looks when he thought no one was looking.

Outside, I managed to avoid the Girards until Eloise flounced over to me. 'You look rather strange, Kiki,' she said, touching my arm. 'A little flushed. Oh, you're wearing make-up. I can see that.'

'Long nights mean confinement with little fresh air. It doesn't take much to lose one's summer bloom. But you know this, Eloise.'

'We should ride together once Junius returns to Brest.'

I was desperate to ask her when that would be. Instead: 'That would be nice.'

Junius walked over and stood between us. 'You two having a good natter?'

'Not particularly,' I said.

Someone approached Eloise and, when she turned, I slipped the note to Junius.

Eloise managed to extricate herself. 'You and Augustave should come to Oubliette for supper in the New Year.'

'That would be good' – touching her arm. It was as though she had read my note. I concealed a smile.

I looked up and noticed that Florian was gawping at me. Leaving the Girards to themselves, I walked over to him. My presence caused him to blush, more so when I told him he looked smart in his white shirt. Stammering a 'thank you', he asked where I had been the last four weeks.

'Indisposed,' I said, omitting to tell him that his darling mother was my jailer. 'Tell me, Florian, how is Lapin?'

'Healthy. I exercise her twice daily. May I ask where you have been?'

I was tempted to tell him the truth. Instead: 'I haven't been feeling well.'

After Mass, Oreste arrived at le Merle. I worked out he was the reason behind my 'release' – sparing Monsieur the embarrassment of explaining my whereabouts to him.

Dinner would have been a bore except I was enjoying my freedom. The twins talked of wine and Paris and of Oreste's latest case – something to do with the emperor and the Italian ambassador. Supper was first-rate – roast pork and chicken washed down with three bottles from Domaine de la Romanée-Conti.

Oreste said something about the emperor's latest team of horses: greys – Holsteiners – from northern Germany. My opportunity to talk of horses, leading me specifically to Lapin – *Has she been sold?* – full well knowing the answer. I acted surprised when Monsieur informed me it was not a good time of year to sell a horse.

'So I can ride her in the morning?' I said brightly.

'Why wouldn't you?' said Oreste.

So, Monsieur had *not* told his brother of my confinement. He shot me an indignant look then hesitated. 'Well, of course you can, my dear. I wouldn't want you leaving the estate, though.'

'I thought I would visit my family, wish them *joyeux Noël*. I haven't seen them in a long time.'

Another angry look from Monsieur. 'Go if you must.'

Oreste gave us each a quizzical look.

I had got what I wanted – exuded charm. Madame Gaillard cleared the plates away. Time for smokes and Armagnac. Oreste played his usual trick by offering me a cigar. I declined, making my excuses to retire for the night.

I would ride as soon as it was light and wedged the door so the witch couldn't lock me in without waking me. She tried half an hour later when I managed to snatch the key out of her hand. I remember jamming her up against a wall. 'Madame Gaillard,' I said, 'why do you hate me so?'

'Let me go,' she said, panting.

Releasing my grip: 'Well?'

Straightening her shift, she looked me in the eye. 'You think you are the bee's knees, don't you? Cleverer than anyone else. You came here expecting everyone to do your bidding... the run of the estate... do anything you want... go where you please. If you want my opin—'

'I've had enough of your opinions.'

'Monsieur Monnier has been far too lax with you. And... and why aren't you pregnant?'

'Pregnant? That's none of your business, madam.'

'My business is Monsieur Monnier's happiness.' She hesitated. 'You're not wearing anything, are you?'

'Wearing what?'

'You know, a device.'

'A device?'

'You know perfectly well what I mean.' Opening her palm: 'Now, give me the key.'

'No. Not that it's any of your business but Augustave said I could ride in the morning. I will do so as soon as it is light. After that you can have your silly key back.'

She huffed and puffed and, giving me the evil eye, she left, slamming the door behind her.

I kept the door wedged in case she had a spare.

Snuggling between the sheets I realised that Madame hated me because I was what she perceived me to be: a spoilt little bitch, twenty years her junior. She was jealous. Or was there something more?

TEN

CHRISTMAS DAY, 1861. I rose from my bed in the dark. By the time I had washed and dressed, grey light daubed the cobbles outside.

After breakfast, and when Madame Gaillard had left the kitchen, I searched for something to give my family. Two partridges hung from a hook. 'That'll do,' I said to myself, putting them in a muslin bag together with two bottles of Pinot Noir.

Florian was absent from the stables. Lapin stood in her stall. Her ears were pricked and, swishing her tail, she took the carrot from my palm in her soft mouth. I threw my arms around her neck. Tears pricked the back of my eyes.

Soon I had her saddled. It felt strange to be astride a horse again. The snow glistened in the early-morning sun. Lapin's hooves crunched down into ice-crusted puddles as I walked her across the courtyard.

My spirits soared; everything was good in the world that was not of man. All was quiet save Lapin's footfalls. Her breath roiled the air, steamy snorts in the frozen dawn. As we turned out of the drive a hare bounded down the road in front of us. The trees were naked. Rooks lifted out of a distant copse. I felt strong and squeezed my heels to Lapin's flanks.

Rue du Moulin Judas was a short ride away, but I turned Lapin around. The field opposite le Merle beckoned me. Once more I squeezed my heels, this time harder. Lapin started to canter, and harder, and soon she was galloping with abandon. I found myself whooping wildly, uncontrollably. The cold air seared my lungs, but I didn't care.

A while later I arrived at the Vellay family home. Knocked on the door several times – hoping I wasn't too early. Alie eventually opened up, threw her arms around me. Then she hushed me, indicating we remain outside. She wrapped a shawl round her shoulders and we walked a short distance down the road.

She turned to me. 'Where have you been, Kiki?' Irritation marred her face.

'I've been locked up in le Merle. Today is the first time I've been allowed out in a month.'

Clutching my hand: 'Locked up? Why?'

I related the dog-fight saga to her, my suspicions and subsequent discovery of Monsieur's activities. My confinement. I swore her to secrecy. 'No one, and I mean no one, can know about this. Promise me.'

She promised.

'How is the family?'

Her face clouded. 'A lot worse, not helped with you being away.'

I spread my arms.

'Papa is bed-bound but still manages to find a bottle of something.'

Rolling my eyes: 'And those brothers of ours…?'

'They are struggling. Salva's pathetic, follows Dago like a puppy. They work all God's hours. Stubborn as mules. Typical Vellays. They are planning to plant next spring.'

'And Maman?'

'Working hard as always. The prospect of producing our own wine keeps us all going.'

'It'll take five years.'

Alie grimaced.

'Are you still going to school?'

Shaking her head: 'We can't afford the fees. Anyway, it's too far to walk and I have to help Maman with the chores and Arlette.'

'I'm dying to see Arlette. You should keep up your education. It's your way out of here.'

'All right for you to say, all high and mighty.'

'I will pay the fees.'

'Huh, you think I want your charity? As I said, I have to help Maman.'

I nodded. Alie had matured. I noticed how pretty she was – the hint of a bosom beneath her shift.

We continued to talk of my confinement, what I did to pass the time – sewing, my ideas for a dress, my exercise regime, the books I had read. She appeared vaguely interested, paying lip service to my enthusiasm.

'You should read,' I said, 'broaden your horizons.'

'My horizons are in that house, with my family. I will leave *horizons* to you, Kiki.'

I folded my arm in hers, feeling chastened. We walked back to the house on rue du Moulin Judas.

The family was up and about. Maman wrapped her arms around me. 'Where have you been?' she wailed.

I looked at Alie. 'A long story, Maman, but I have not been away on purpose.'

I entered Papa's bedroom. The smell was rancid – old man's clothes and urine. He was asleep, an unhealthy glow to him; his jowls hung in layers down his neck. I made an attempt to touch his hand but drew back.

Deep in thought I entered the kitchen. Dago stood there and crossed his arms, stared at me from under his brows. 'Back then, are you?'

Handing him the muslin bag: 'And a merry Christmas to you,

Dagobert. Something for your lunch.'

He looked inside the bag. 'Bah, thanks, but we don't need your charity here.'

'It's my Christmas present to you all.'

Dago tried to hand back the bag. 'As I said…'

I kept my hands to myself, and he eventually put it down.

Maman plonked Arlette in my arms, an Alie lookalike – it seemed to me – blue eyes, a bonnie nose and ringlets of honey-coloured hair. I tickled her belly. She twisted and turned – wouldn't look at me. And when she burst into tears Alie took her away.

I loitered for a while. Tried to involve myself with the chores – brought in wood for the fire. It dawned on me that I didn't fit in with their routine. I felt I was in the way. I finally seduced Arlette, though, taking her outside to stroke Lapin's nose, lifting her onto the saddle and repeating my name to her.

Salvat emerged, scratching his arse. He said hello, looking to Dago for reassurance.

I felt I had to leave. Promising Alie I would stay in touch, I mounted Lapin and trotted back down the road towards le Merle. I thought of turning around and visiting the *cabotte* but thought better of it.

At le Merle I retreated to my room. Taking my part-sewn dress from its hiding place I began work on the hem. Unable to concentrate I put it down, telling myself to be more productive. I had an idea and replaced the dress under the bed.

I still had the key and walked through the house to the outside. I was determined to do some gardening – a waste of time, it turned out, as the ground was icy hard. After stacking some pots, I decided to visit the half-hectare of Vellay land. No one would be there on Christmas Day.

I arrived near the top of the hill out of breath. Meursault was spread below me, crystal-clear in the midwinter light. Significant progress had been made: mounds of rock and stone to the side, tree stumps and branches in piles, turned earth rather than weeds. My brothers were *conards* but I had to admire their resolve.

Back down the hill I checked the enclosure – only two of the mastiffs were there. The dogbox was under the tarpaulin.

I felt a presence behind me: Guillaume. I covered my surprise with a smile.

'What are you doing?' he said.

'I live here, Guillaume. And a merry Christmas to you too.'

He grumbled under his breath.

'I see that Charybdis and Pollux are missing. Huh, you must be very proud of yourself.'

Guillaume advanced, a lopsided grin on his face, his arms extended. Pretending to play his game I smiled again. And when he was about to lay a hand on me, I kicked him as hard as I could between his legs. Gasping, he then squealed like a pig, covering his crotch with his hands and stumbling away.

I stormed back to the house. Monsieur was in the hallway. I couldn't look him in the eye. I wanted to rant and shout at him but kept quiet.

'You've seen your family?' – looking down his nose.

'Yes, monsieur.'

'By the way, the Girards have invited us for tomorrow night.'

I feigned indifference. 'So?'

'So I will make an exception. I will allow you to attend.'

I pretended to think about it. 'That's very gracious of you, August.'

Next day, *le lendemain de Noël*, I took the precaution of putting a pencil and paper in my reticule. I had to be careful, treat Junius as though he was just a neighbour – keep Monsieur in the dark. Eloise was another matter; I would flirt with her a little.

From what few clothes I possessed I decided on one of the dresses made for me in Beaune after my wedding. I decided to pin up my hair, not have it flowing down like a raven-haired, neophyte witch.

Oreste was impressed. 'You look lovely, my dear,' he said as we prepared to leave.

Monsieur grunted.

We squeezed into the berlin, me in the middle – a rose 'twixt two thorns.

I determined the role I would play for Monsieur – meek and mild, speak only when spoken to – composed my features accordingly. Monsieur smiled. Perhaps this version, this little mouse of a wife, is what he craved. A wife he would, hopefully, no longer confine to her room.

Oubliette was at its best: candles everywhere, a toasty hearth in the hall and the main room, Christmas decorations, a pine tree with baubles hanging down, an angel at the top, sprigs of holly here and there.

I was handed a glass of champagne.

Two other couples were there. I smiled politely when introduced. The husbands were growers. I wondered if they were dog fighters – dismissing the thought as fanciful until Sir Reginald Markham entered the room.

Markham looked ferocious, his black whiskers stark in the whiteness of his face. Rapier-thin, his height was accentuated by the black tails he wore. After talking to Monsieur and one of the growers he made his way over to me. He took my hand and kissed it. 'Sir Reginald Markham, ma'am.'

'The last time we met you were not so polite.'

If he felt embarrassment, he didn't show it. Quite the opposite, affording me a toothy leer. 'Do you mind?' he said, cutting the end off a cigar. Trapping me with his eyes, he struck a match and lit the thing, blowing smoke at me. 'You're quite a girl… in many ways, Christine,' he said, his gaze lingering on the swell of my breasts beneath my dress.

'My friends call me Kiki, so you can continue to address me as Christine. By the way, is there a Madame Markham?'

'There is no *Madame*' – with the slightest of bows.

'I'd pity the poor wretch if there were.'

He smirked.

'How do you know the Girards?'

'I am a *négociant*, I act for—'

'I know what a *négociant* is, monsieur.'

Ignoring me, he talked of his business: purchasing wine from a coterie of growers for sale under his label in Paris and London. 'It enables them to sell their entire crop,' he concluded.

'The name of your label?'

'Markham père et fils. Your husband's wine, Markham père et fils, Meursault.'

'*Père?*'

'My father… he's dead. "*Père*" on the label is an embellishment, so to speak. Imbues my clients with confidence.'

'Is Meursault popular in London?'

'Very. Goes well with seafood – fine-textured fish, lobster – and poultry. Dishes with crisp textures that match with the lively mineral acidity of the wine.'

I yawned theatrically.

He grinned, exhaled smoke.

Junius interrupted us. 'Time for us to eat,' he said, frowning at Markham.

Junius arranged the seating, placing himself to my right with one of the growers to my left. Opposite me was one of the growers' wives. Eloise and Markham were seated at the end of the table.

The grower was Monsieur Prouhin, the owner of a *domaine* in Aloxe-Corton, famous, he explained, for their Pinot Noir. I asked him how many hectolitres per hectare he could produce.

'Depends on the year. About forty-five,' he replied. 'That's roughly six thousand bottles per hectare in an average year.'

I did the calculation: the Vellays' plot might produce three thousand bottles of wine a year – a year in the distant future when their vines had matured.

I turned the conversation to the question of prices.

Monsieur Prouhin gave me that look: why is a woman asking questions like this?

I smiled sweetly.

Sighing: 'Forty to fifty francs a case. Oh, but if I allocate a quota to Sir Reginald over there, slightly less.'

'Why would you do that?' I said, knowing the answer.

'To ensure the sale of my entire production.'

There was talk of war at the Markham end of the table. Markham wagging a finger: 'The French army's expedition to Mexico is complete folly. The emperor is trying to emulate his uncle, seeking glory whilst the Americans have their backs turned, fighting their futile war. Establish an empire in Mexico? Bah. He'll have trouble with his supply lines. It'll come to no good, of that you can be sure.'

Just when I was thinking I should discuss the war with Madame Thierry, a hand touched my thigh. Junius. Feeling for his hand I took the piece of paper, stroking his leg to let him know how I felt.

The main course arrived – jugged hare with *purée de pommes de terre*, an assortment of vegetables and a *jus*. Not up to Maman's standards – not bad, though. The wine was Monsieur Prouhin's Pinot Noir 1855.

I toasted Monsieur Prouhin: 'A touch light on the nose, but has adequate length, monsieur.'

That look again.

I steered the conversation to Sir Reginald Markham.

'Reggie? He's the second son of the Earl of Bradford. The family own coal mines in the English Midlands,' said Monsieur Prouhin. 'The eldest son, Harold, operates the mine. Reggie, never one to play second fiddle, established his wine business in London and Paris.'

'Coal mines – I've read the conditions are atrocious.'

Monsieur Prouhin pursed his lips.

'The miners in England indulge in all kinds of sports particular to themselves, monsieur: pigeon fancying, greyhound coursing and dogfighting amongst others. The breed English Pitbull derives its name from "pit", as in coal pit.'

'They're a bloodthirsty lot when it comes to their pastimes – fox hunting, for example.'

Studying his face carefully I concluded that Monsieur Prouhin was not a dog fighter. Standing up I made my excuses to visit the *toilette*, where I unfolded Junius's note.

Le lendemain de Noël 1861

Dearest Kiki,

I read your note with concern. How could he?

I am here in Oubliette until 13 January.

I have a plan centred on my return to the academy at Brest. First you escape from le Merle. We meet at the cabotte, ride to Dijon, from there we take the train to Paris. Stay a couple of nights with friends of mine, then on to Rennes by train, where I also have friends.

Rennes is not too far from Brest. We will see each other every weekend.

I will provide you with accommodation there and, through my connections, you will be able to take a position somewhere.

I have to tell you that I intend to leave Eloise. Life with her is intolerable.

The key to the plan lies at the beginning: escaping from le Merle. Place a candle outside your window so I know where your room is, then drop a message to the ground, which I will retrieve.

Kiki, I feel a deep affection for you. I dream about you

all the time.
     Courage is required. Consider my plan.

I adore you,
Junius

Panic, as though I was suffocating. I felt overwhelmed. I thought of Madame Thierry and took a deep breath. I was in no right mind to make a decision. I needed to think it through very carefully. I wrote on the back of the note.

Dearest Juno,

Your plan makes me both excited and fearful at the same time. I need to consider what you propose very carefully.
     I will place two candles (avoid confusion) inside my bedroom window on the first floor overlooking the courtyard. I will lower a message in a box below the window at six every evening when it's dark.
     Are you sure you want to risk all you have… uproot your life?
     Is Rennes a comfortable place in which to live?
     I am sorry to hear things are intolerable with Eloise.

Affectionately yours,
Kiki

I took my seat at the table, slipped Junius the note. Dinner was a struggle. Eloise insisted we moved places for dessert and sat next to me. She chattered incessantly, told me I looked distracted. I flirted with her – touched her arm, giggled girlishly, made light of my marriage to Augustave – all the while thinking of Junius's plan.
     Markham wanted to talk as well. He had moved opposite me

and was polite save the way he stared at me. The idea of Markham made my skin crawl – not the way Monsieur did – by virtue of his overly masculine, ape-like demeanour.

The journey home was oppressive, stuck, as I was, between the twins, who reeked of Armagnac and cigars. Oreste's presence prevented me from discussing my confinement with Monsieur.

Home and in the kitchen, I opened a drawer and took out a ball of twine. I then searched for a container, settling for a small walnut box with a hinged lid.

I prayed Monsieur was in no fit state to 'visit' me. I washed, put on my nightdress and wriggled between the sheets. Try as I might, I couldn't sleep – Junius's message in my head. He assumed my leaving le Merle was not a problem. I visualised taking my usual morning hack on Lapin, meeting Junius at the *cabotte*, riding to Dijon. Easy. But if I was locked in my room escape would be nigh on impossible.

The train and the Paris part of the plan were agreeable, exciting even. I had doubts about Rennes. I would be a kept woman in a provincial town – Junius's little bird in her gilded cage. Was this what I wanted? Equally, was it what he wanted? We might grow tired of each other. And one day he would join the navy, follow his career… then what? Sailors tended to sail away. *And* he was still married.

My account in Beaune – I resolved to withdraw my francs as soon as possible.

But did I want to do this? Really do this? I knew I was spoilt, used to a life of comfort. But since the dog fight my life had changed. I detested Monsieur, would do anything to avoid his 'demands'. Would another opportunity come my way? Yes, there were always opportunities. But I knew I was dreaming. Wives had no rights. And I was isolated – on the edge of a small town. I needed help from the outside. There was no alternative other than Junius.

Next morning, I was resolved. I still had the key and went downstairs for breakfast. Madame Gaillard was sitting at the kitchen table, her usual po-faced self. 'Help yourself,' she said. I busied myself in the pantry, selected some leftovers and a lump of bread. I was about to eat when Oreste put his head round the door. Madame Gaillard stood, smiled sweetly, offering to cook him a mess of eggs and ham.

'That would be perfect, Marie.' Then: 'Kiki, what are you doing here? Come, join me in the dining room.'

We sat. He stared at me. 'Kiki, forgive me, but I can tell all's not well between you and Augustave.'

'We're all right,' I said, forcing a smile.

'Oh, come now, Kiki, I can see what's in front of my eyes.'

I shook my head, but he wheedled at me.

'All right. Before you arrived here, I *was* confined to my room.'

'For how long?'

'Over three weeks.'

'Three weeks! Why?'

'I don't want to say.'

He pierced me with his policeman's eyes. 'Last time I was here you said your marriage was not ideal. Remember? And I said something about le Merle being in need of an heir.'

The mess arrived, Madame Gaillard providing me with temporary respite as she fussed over Oreste.

'Marie,' said Oreste, 'I hope you are looking after Kiki, here.'

I cringed as Madame Gaillard shot me a hate-filled look. She recovered quickly. 'Of course I do, monsieur. Don't I, Kiki?'

'You do, madam.'

Nodding at Oreste she left the room, closing the door quietly behind her.

'There,' I said.

'Yes. Right, Kiki. Humph. I don't believe her. Or you, for that matter.'

'That is up to you, monsieur. Oh, and how long do we have the pleasure of your company?'

'The second of January' – from under his brows.

We continued in silence. My freedom was guaranteed for six more days.

Upstairs I checked the dates: Monday, 30 and Tuesday, 31 December were the only days available to visit the bank. Tuesday was New Year's Eve and might be a half day. I had no choice but to go to Beaune on Monday.

I checked my purse: eighty-five francs.

I drafted a note to Junius, telling him to meet me at the main square at ten on Monday morning. At five thirty I lit two candles, placing them by the window. After putting the note in the walnut box, I secured it to the twine and lowered it out of the window. It was dark; I had no chance of being seen. At six o'clock I peered out of the window – no Junius. At six thirty I raised the box – no reply.

What did I expect?

I chewed my knuckles, fought back the tears. I rationalised that Junius must have been disrupted somehow, Eloise making demands on his time at the *wrong* time.

Next morning, Saturday, I took Lapin for a hack, not only for the exercise but to familiarise the household with me being free. I contemplated riding to Oubliette, waiting outside the gates for Junius, but dismissed the idea.

The afternoon was spent in the library – another 'habituation' exercise. Monsieur came in twice, snorted then left. I prayed he was growing accustomed to me being around the house. Oreste came and told me it was good to see me up and about, as though I was recovering from some awful disease.

Just before six I lit the candles and lowered the box again, raising it half an hour later – again nothing.

I tried to read, then sew, to no avail – my concentration was just not there. I was perched on the chamber pot when I heard a tinkle against my window, like hail. I shook my head and it happened again. I stood, adjusted my shift and opened the window. Despite the dark I could just make out Junius below.

'Psst, Kiki,' he said. Shushing him, I dangled the box out of the window.

K,

Sorry, E had me running errands.
Will see you in Beaune as per your note.
Courage.

I adore you,
J x

I heaved a sigh of relief. Whispered, 'Goodnight.' I nearly said, *I love you*, but held back.

With four days left I became the model wife. Sunday night, Monsieur visited my bed. I undressed him, groaned at the right times, pretended to swoon when he did his thing. I told him *it* was wonderful. Pulling on his nightshirt he gave me a roguish grin. I imagined he thought he was Don Juan. As soon as he was gone, I crept down the corridor to the bathroom. And having thoroughly scoured myself I stuck two fingers down my throat.

ELEVEN

I LAY IN bed worrying about the day ahead. The fire was out, the room freezing cold. Grey light eventually filled the gap between the curtains; I forced my way out of bed. Having washed and dressed I crept into the corridor, treading gingerly down the back staircase. Opening the kitchen door, I made my way to the stables. Lapin was on her feet, sensing my arrival, perhaps.

Soon we were on the road. Not a soul about. And cold. I felt my waistcoat pocket – the note inside, the items to discuss with Junius.

I double-wrapped the shawl round my neck. Lapin snorted, vapour rolling in clouds from her nostrils.

I arrived in Beaune with time to spare. With no sign of Junius I made my way to the stables, leaving Lapin in their care. Banque Villiard was a short walk away on rue Armand Gouffé. The sign in the window said the bank opened at ten and closed at twelve thirty. I felt relieved – at least the bank would be open. But my rendezvous with Junius was at ten.

The bank could wait. I treated myself to a slice of brioche from Mignet on place Saint-Pierre. An idea entered my head on passing Dumilly's.

Crossing the main square, I spotted Junius who indicated I should follow him. Despite the cold I felt myself flush, heat flooding my stomach, my spine tingling – fear and expectation, of feeling entirely alive.

Past the market he turned right into rue Paradis. Halfway up the street he took out a key and waggled two fingers at me.

After waiting a couple of minutes, I climbed a narrow flight of stairs. I could hear my heart thump – felt breathless and confused. A door was ajar and, despite my turmoil, I crossed the threshold.

Junius gently pulled me towards him and kissed me. I responded in kind and found myself clawing his back. Gazing into my eyes he picked me up and edged open a door with his foot. The sheet on the bed had been drawn back. Again, the feeling he had been here with other girls. Beyond caring, I struggled out of my clothes. We were both naked. Sun streamed through the window, and I lay on my back with my legs apart. Then he was in me. A moment of bliss until I realised I was not wearing my device, my resistance momentary when he started his slow, rhythmic undulations while kissing my breasts. 'I love you,' he repeated. Then he was deep inside me, deepest deep, deeper than Monsieur could ever have been. It seemed to last forever. My stomach turned to liquid. I closed my eyes, iridescent points of light in my head. Then my insides seemed to collapse as though I was turning inside out. I heard myself groan. Junius was not finished, and went on and on, me groaning again and again.

Eventually he let go – a flood of molten heat. My body convulsed, every nerve vibrating, every sinew tingling – twitching.

He withdrew slowly, deliciously. We lay there gasping for breath, drenched in sweat. I buried my head in his chest and wept. A while later I managed to gather my senses and told him I simply *had* to go to the bank.

He whispered endearments, kissing me. 'Well, of course you must, *chérie*. I will find us something to eat.' Rising from the bed unashamedly, I washed from a bowl and dressed. After kissing him

I descended the stairs and walked onto rue Paradis. Paradis. I *was* in Paradise.

At the bank I gave my name and requested the manager. I sat and dreamt of Junius. Monsieur Tausend emerged. 'The balance of your account, Madame Monnier' – handing me a folded note.

I unfolded the paper and read, reread what I thought I had read, then swooned, gasping for air.

'Can I fetch you a glass of water, madam?'

I closed my eyes, tried to will away the pain – the balance was fifty francs. *Fifty francs!* 'This is impossible, Monsieur Tausend. I had nearly five hundred francs when I was here five weeks ago. Since that time I've spent very little. Oh, and I would have received 150 at the end of November. There should be over six hundred francs in my account.'

'There, there' – handing me a glass.

I gulped the water. 'Surely there is a mistake, monsieur?'

He peered at me over his spectacles. 'No, no mistake, madam. You are correct, 150 francs were credited to your account on the twenty-eighth of November. However, Monsieur Monnier withdrew 592 francs on Friday, the thirteenth of December.'

I felt I was going to be sick. 'B-but it is my account.'

Monsieur Tausend avoided my stare. 'Husbands are permitted access to their wives' accounts, Madame Monnier.'

'This can't be?' I said. But I knew there was nothing I could do about it.

Back in the suite of rooms I found Junius at the table with food – a *tarte* and a flask of soup.

'You look as though you've seen a ghost,' he said.

I told him about the account.

He tried to calm me, telling me he thought the treatment of women was scandalous. 'Things have to change,' he said. 'They will change.'

I took a slice of the *tarte*. He asked me about my husband.

Between mouthfuls, I told him of the arrangement with Monsieur, and the events leading to the dog fight at Cheilly-lès-Maranges. 'Your friend Markham was there.'

'I am no particular friend of Markham. We sell a portion of our production to him every year. We could probably do without him, but Clément has dealt with him for years.'

I told him of life at le Merle, Madame Gaillard and Oreste.

'I knew Augustave and Oreste when I was a child, of course. I never got on with them. As twins they kept to themselves. Oreste went to Paris as a young man, became a policeman. Done well by all accounts.'

Nodding, I experienced a squeeze of guilt – not letting him know about the device, or rather, the lack of it. 'Juno, we need to discuss our plans. Our escape,' I said, flattening the piece of paper on the table.

He eyed me expectantly.

'Item one… the date.'

'I've given it thought – Thursday, the ninth of January. I have to be in Brest on the nineteenth. We'll ride to Dijon and stay in a hotel, take the train the following day, spend Friday night in Paris and travel to Rennes by train on the fifteenth – time to install you with my friends.'

'Who are these friends? How long have you known them?'

He told me of his friendship with Pierre Lamarck and his sister Anne, who lived in Rennes. 'They are the salt of the earth,' he concluded.

'I wouldn't want to inconvenience Anne for too long.'

'Finding accommodation will take no more than a day.'

Making notes: 'I would seek a position as soon as I arrived there. How much could I expect from employment?'

'With your talents, Kiki, about thirty francs a month, forty, perhaps.' Leaning across the table he brushed my lips with his.

'The cost of accommodation?'

'About thirty francs a month.'

'So, I'll be running at a loss. Monthly expenses about sixty francs including rent.' The scene at the bank would not go away. I must have been close to tears. My plans had been predicated on the francs I had saved. Junius must have sensed my indecision.

'I will cover the difference,' he said. 'We will open an account in your name. I'll put in seventy a month. As soon as you have a job, we'll review the situation.'

I wrote it down.

'That's good, Juno, and thank you. But I would hate to be a drain on you and would gain employment as soon as I am able.'

'You'll never be a drain on me, Kiki.'

'But seventy francs is a lot of money. How will you be able to afford it?'

'Oubliette produces eight thousand cases of wine every year…'

'All right, let's talk about Thursday, the ninth.'

'Simple, we meet at the *cabotte* at nine in the morning.'

'And if I'm confined to my room?'

'I will wait until ten should you be delayed.'

'And if I can't get away?'

'I've considered the possibility. Your room is on the first floor, the window ledge about four metres above the ground. I will arrive at five in the evening, when it's getting dark, on some pretence – a neighbourly visit, a case of wine as a New Year's gift. You would have made a rope from your sheets. On my signal, when I'm in place, you throw down your belongings before you descend.'

'Hmm, let's assume your plan works and we are outside the gates and on the road.'

'I've also thought of that. You will have no time to saddle Lapin.'

I sighed. I had worried how she would find her way back to le Merle.

'I will have a spare, a mare, a four-year-old with the heart of a lioness.'

'We'll be travelling in the dark.'

'Horses can see in the dark.'

'Then what?'

'Meursault to Dijon is sixty kilometres, about ten hours, including rest and water for the horses. We would arrive at about four in the morning. The Paris train leaves at ten o'clock on a Friday.'

I made a note.

I reached out and squeezed his hand. He had thought it through. 'It's risky, but I can't think of a better alternative. A lot can go wrong,' I said.

'It won't.'

'Suppose it does… I've thought of something: we use my sister as a postbox. Write to me but use her name. We are close and she is loyal,' I said, writing down Alie's name and address and handing it to him.

After glimpsing at the note, he told me to stick out my right arm and to close my eyes. I obliged. Something cold and metal slid over the top of my hand. 'You can open them now,' he said.

A thin gold bracelet encircled my wrist. I rotated it admiringly. 'It's beautiful, Juno, you shouldn't have.'

'Well, I did,' he said, caressing my cheek with his lips.

We kissed goodbye at one o'clock, having made love one more time. My body had been set free, albeit being a little sore. He was still in my mind's eye looking at me, telling me how much he loved me, how beautiful I was. Despite my efforts to clean myself I could still smell him on me.

I collected Lapin from the stables. As we trotted across the main square, I spotted Eloise on her horse. I pretended not to see her but she beckoned me. I steered Lapin in her direction and spoke first: 'Eloise, had I known you were coming to town we could have ridden in together.'

'That would have been pleasant, Kiki.'

Conversing with someone whose husband was making love to you a short while ago was difficult, but I forced myself to look her in the eye. 'Thank you for the other night, by the way.'

'Lovely seeing you, Kiki.'

'You know, Eloise, when I first saw you riding English-style I thought it very practical so I copied you.'

'More comfortable, don't you think?'

'And one can ride faster.'

We continued our small talk, me flattering her at every turn. Eventually, she made her excuse to leave. 'I'm meeting Junius for lunch.'

With Eloise gone I heaved a sigh of relief.

After hitching Lapin to a rail, I walked up rue Saint-Pierre and entered Dumilly's where I purchased two metres of serge at a cost of eighteen francs – a substantial amount considering my circumstances.

Would I tell Monsieur of my discovery at the bank? No, definitely not. Ensuring my freedom for the next few days and continuing to play the perfect little wife was paramount. I had a strange feeling on riding out of Beaune, as though I had forgotten something. I couldn't put my finger on it. I shook my head but, no, it just wouldn't come.

At le Merle I went straight to my room. Had I seen Monsieur I might have throttled him. I took the dress from under the bed. 'A good project,' I told myself. But I had to concentrate on the serge. Tape in hand I measured the inside of my leg, my thigh, my waist, my hips. With only one length of the material, I could not afford a mistake and drew out the design on letter paper. 'Measure twice, cut once,' Madame Lonjons had told me. Scissors in hand, I started to cut.

Next day was New Year's Eve, yet another formal meal with the Monniers – just the three of us. No guests, except Castor and Scylla, who growled and prowled round the table. Oreste looked down his nose. I girded myself for the long haul of too much food and wine.

We talked of the emperor, his plan for Paris. Baron Haussmann. 'The place will be a gigantic mess for a long time,' said Oreste. Mexico was discussed – the emperor, the war there. Monsieur supported the emperor. 'France needs a presence in the Americas to protect our Atlantic trade.'

Oreste thought otherwise. 'We can get away with it while the so-called "United States" are fighting each other, but when it's over they will not tolerate a foreign power on their border.'

I repeated what Sir Reginald Markham had said at the Girards: 'Surely conducting a war so far away will be difficult… supplying the army… all that equipment.'

They both stared at me like Cerberus with identical dog-like eyes.

'You may have a point, Kiki,' said Oreste.

New Year's Day. I breakfasted downstairs (my door remained unlocked). Madame Gaillard was her uncommunicative self and gave me a look as though she was sucking on lemons. I smiled, wished her a happy New Year and cut slices from a loaf of bread.

I decided to play a game, give her the impression I was here to stay at le Merle. 'Marie, it is 1862 and I have been married to Monsieur for five months. We should try to be friends… patch up our differences… better for the two of us.'

Wiping her hands: 'We can never be friends, Christine, unless you change.'

'Change? How do you mean?'

'You know… being honest with the people you live with, less calculating. It doesn't suit a woman to be manipulative. Doesn't pay either,' she said, walking away.

The night before my 'escape' Monsieur *visited* me, catching me unawares – I had not inserted the device. After trotting out an excuse I visited the bathroom, but the pessary was not behind the mirror where I had hidden it. *Where could it be?* Back in my bed I put on a performance. It was for the last time, after all. When I returned to the bathroom to purge myself, I searched again. Nothing. I prayed Monsieur hadn't impregnated me.

Monsieur was gone by the time I returned to my room. Again, I searched for the device – opening and closing drawers, looking under clothes, repeating my actions until I convinced myself it really was lost.

Or had Madame Gaillard found it?

I finally fell asleep, having forgotten to put the wedge under the door.

I woke early, such was my preoccupation with the day ahead. I thought of packing – I would only be able to take one of my dresses. I tried the door; it was locked. I cried out, such was my shock, and rattled it again just to make sure. I breathed in deeply and fought the tears away. Soon I was incoherent with rage, swearing I would tear Madame Gaillard apart, devising tortures for her – imagining her chained in a dungeon where I was pulling out her fingernails one by one with red-hot pincers.

I was tempted to make the rope out of sheets, climb down and make my way to the stables and Lapin but discounted the idea immediately – it was daylight.

I sat on my bed. I would have to wait until five when Junius was due to arrive. I knew I had to stay calm, were I to escape le Merle.

Madame Gaillard entered my room with food on a tray. 'No use complaining,' she said before I could speak. 'Monsieur Monnier's instructions.'

'Why? I have done nothing wrong.'

'As per his instructions.'

'Until when?'

'Until he decides.'

At four o'clock I was stuffing as much as I could into my bag – a nudge here, a tuck there. The dress did not fit. Oh well, I would just have to leave it behind. Then it came to me – what had been bothering me – the notes I made during my tryst with Junius. How could I have been so careless? Lovemaking with Junius had been a distraction. I had left the notes on the table. *Had Eloise gone there after I met her in the square?* Of course, she had.

At just before five I tied three sheets together, tested the knots and paced out the length on the floor. The 'rope' measured about five metres. Just after five I heard hooves on the cobbles below. Despite the light I could make out Junius. He faded into the shadows. The sound of voices and of doors closing. And the sound of my heart as it thumped against my ribs. With the rope tied to the end of the bed I dangled it out of the window. I felt a tug. Junius was below. 'Psst, now,' he said. I dropped my bag out. I was dressed in my riding outfit so it was easy climbing down. We kissed. 'Let's go,' he said, taking my hand.

'You're not going anywhere,' a voice said.

My blood froze. A door slammed. I was aware of a fracas – swearing and scuffling. Junius was on the ground, Guillaume on top of him, his knees on his shoulders. Darting behind Guillaume, I placed my arms around his neck and heaved for all I was worth. Then light, torches – Benoît and Madame Gaillard, Castor and Scylla straining on their leashes, barking. Junius was now on top of Guillaume and raining down blows.

'Come on!' I shouted, just as Madame Gaillard seized me from behind. Bracing, I stamped on her foot. She howled and let go of me. Junius stood and grabbed my hand, and we ran pell-mell towards the gate. We were both screaming. The barking was intense, staccato. Then something heavy thumped into me and I must have blacked out.

The pain woke me – my shoulder. I thought I'd been stabbed. Someone shouted, 'She's awake.' They looked down at me: my *conard* of a husband, Madame Gaillard, Benoît and Guillaume with his blood-spattered face. Not to mention the mastiffs, the brutes keening and whining, drool flecked white on their muzzles.

I was on the floor of the winery and cast about, strewn as it was with barrels, bottles, vats and piles of corks. A cart lay rotting in a corner. Light from the lanterns made the beams in the roof appear to move and shift.

'Thought you could get away with it, did you?' said Madame Gaillard.

I turned to Monsieur. 'Where's Junius?'

'Never you mind.'

He held up a piece of paper as though he was addressing a judge. 'Notes found by Junius's wife in rooms on rue Paradis in Beaune. "The train," he read, "10am, Friday, the tenth". It's your writing. I could go on.'

Grim-faced, he held up another piece of paper. 'A note also found by Eloise: "Aliette Vellay, number 6 rue du Moulin Judas". I require an explanation, Kiki.'

'Not until you tell me where he is.'

'You are in no position to make demands. For what it's worth, he's in the stables.'

'Is he all right?'

'I wouldn't say that. No, Scylla made good work of him.'

'You bastard.'

'Your explanation, please, Kiki.'

I stuck out my chin. 'Our plan was simple – after making our way to Marseilles we planned to sail to Bombay.'

'India,' snorted Monsieur.

'I don't believe a word of it,' said Benoît.

'Or further… Australia. In other words, as far away from you as geographically possible.'

Monsieur glanced at Guillaume who sidled away. 'So she

admits to an elopement. Where they were bound is a detail,' said Monsieur, as if I wasn't there.

'Unless there are accomplices,' said Benoît.

Madame Gaillard made a business of searching her bag and brought out, in the pinch of her fingers, the pessary, holding it as though it was infected with syphilis. It did look gruesome, with its coil and wishbone. 'I found this in her bathroom two days ago,' she announced.

'A contraceptive,' said Monsieur. 'Ah, now I understand…'

'I would rather conceive of Satan,' I said.

'Your clever words mean nothing to me. That you misled me does. Guillaume!' he shouted, nodding to Madame Gaillard.

My wrists were bound – nothing I could do as the witch stripped me of my clothing, even my underwear. I struggled, to no avail.

Benoît gawped.

Then Guillaume lumbered in with a branding iron in one hand, a pail of water in the other – licking his lips when he saw me.

His presence had the effect of unsettling the dogs – low growls in the back of their throats.

After a nod from Monsieur, Guillaume dropped down and straddled me.

'Is this really necessary, Monsieur Monnier?' said Benoît.

Forcing my legs apart with his knees, Guillaume then blew on the end of the iron – the letters **AM** at the tip, red-hot. He looked at Monsieur.

Monsieur nodded once. I kicked and struggled then my world exploded, the shock so sudden and so extreme that I screamed and screamed and screamed until I could scream no more. Guillaume stood and threw the water over my lower parts.

Through my tears Florian swam into view. I could see that he was brandishing a sword. Madame Gaillard was shouting: 'What are you doing here? Go! Now! Do you hear? Get out!'

Stepping behind me Florian sawed at the rope round my wrists. Guillaume lunged at him with the iron. Florian parried the blow, and they stood there glaring at each other. Guillaume ran at Florian, his arm outstretched. Florian appeared to shift his weight and almost nonchalantly back-slashed at Guillaume's outstretched arm. Then surprise, horror, the severed hand flopping onto the floor. Guillaume looked at where his hand used to be and started to scream, a sound I will never forget. Benoît was shouting. Blood pumped from Guillaume's wrist. The dogs were snarling, up on hind legs, their leashes taut. Monsieur looked fit to burst. Madame Gaillard had gone white, standing transfixed. I wrenched at my wrists with all my strength and my hands came free. Then the dogs were on top of Guillaume, ripping and tearing him – Castor, his jaws round the youth's neck. Loud sobs from Benoît as he beat Castor with a broom.

Despite the unimaginable pain, I knew I had to do something and dressed as fast as I could. Monsieur was flailing at the dogs with a whip. Without warning Scylla turned, leaping on Monsieur, followed by Castor, Monsieur falling to the ground, screaming and kicking, his hands fending them away.

Florian dropped the sword and stood in front of his mother, taking her by the shoulders. 'Get out of here, Maman, now move, please,' he said calmly.

Madame Gaillard stared at me then turned to leave. I will never forget her eyes: red-rimmed pools of hate. The dogs were all over Monsieur, grunting and ripping, grinding and slobbering. I was unable to tear my eyes away until Florian grabbed my arm and dragged me outside.

'Where's Junius?' I said.

'In there' – inclining his head.

Junius lay in the straw. His eyes were closed, his face a mess of scratches and bites. One leg was perforated by what must have been a row of teeth. His britches and shirt were suffused with blood. I knelt and tried to shake him awake. Groaning, he turned away.

I stared at Florian. 'For God's sake, help him.'

'Nothing we can do.'

I hesitated. I felt pulled – stretched – in many directions. The pain in my lower parts was unendurable.

'You have to go *now* if you want to leave this place.'

'What about Junius?'

'He will survive, rest assured.'

Shouting from the direction of the winery.

Florian's eyes flickered to my midsection. 'Are you fit to ride, Kiki?'

I winced.

'Well?'

My mind was a battlefield. One thing I knew for certain, though, was that my life with Monsieur was finished, irreparably destroyed. I had no choice but to leave le Merle.

'I'll go,' I said, hobbling towards Lapin. Taking hold of her halter I gritted my teeth.

'Wait. I have this for you. For you to remember me by,' Florian said, handing me a necklace with a cross attached, its silver chain coiled, ever so delicate and fine. 'It belonged to my grandmother.'

I kneaded the cross with my fingers. 'It's beautiful, Florian, I will never forget. Never.' He stood there, bold and beautiful, so I kissed him on the mouth. I couldn't help myself.

After a moment's hesitation, he lifted me up and placed me in the saddle. 'I'll open the gate,' he said.

I yelled. The pain was white-hot. Then I remembered my bag. Steering Lapin to below the window I dismounted and felt along the bottom of the wall until I found it lying there.

Florian stood at the gate – more a man, less a boy. 'Go,' he said.

'What are you going to do, Florian? You can't stay here.'

'I'll look after myself. Now go!'

TWELVE

EVERY PART OF me stung as I rode towards Beaune. The pain near my vagina forced me to stand in the stirrups.

It started to rain.

I had packed the cloak. Reaching into my bag, I draped it round my shoulders. Soon we were climbing the hill into Monthelie.

I was barely out of the village when it started to pour. Lapin was down to a walk, and I wrapped my face in the cloak. I was drenched and gasped when my backside bumped against the saddle. My right shoulder felt as though someone was punching nails into it.

The rain was relentless. Although on the outskirts of Beaune, I knew I had to find shelter. I had no idea of the time. My clothes were sopping wet. Lapin's ears were back. I prayed Madame Thierry was at home.

A while later I knocked on her door. Prayed again. She opened up, lamp in hand. 'It's me,' I said. 'Kiki.'

'Oh my goodness, come in, child.' She stared at me. 'Take off your clothes. In there' – opening a door.

I undressed – very careful when removing my britches. In that moment I resolved never to let anyone know of my branding, not even Madame Thierry. The shame it entailed. I went through my bag and took out my clothes, water dripping onto the floor. I opened the door and asked Madame Thierry if she had something for me to wear. A hand full of clothes appeared round the door.

Soon I was warming my hands by Madame Thierry's oven and sipping from a large mug of soup.

'My horse Lapin, where I can put her?' I said.

'There's a covered area at the back.'

Later, having settled Lapin, I dried myself in the parlour. Madame Thierry stared at me, her brows furrowed.

I told her everything: the marriage/land transaction, the state of my marriage, the arrangement, the device, Junius, Madame Gaillard's strange behaviour, the dog fight, my escape, Florian. Everything: except the brand. She appeared shocked when I described my botched escape and the fight in the winery, gasped when I told her of Guillaume's severed hand and the dogs.

'The state of your marriage is of no surprise to me. Dogfighting… the man's a monster.'

I nodded.

Kneading her chin: 'There's only one thing for it, report to the police in the morning. I'll come with you. Ah, and I know a good lawyer.'

'Police? Lawyer? No. What are you saying?'

'It's the only way, Kiki.'

'I have committed no crime. Quite the reverse.'

'The longer you leave it, the more it will *appear* as a crime.'

'Please, madam. No.'

'All right, we'll leave it a couple of days.'

I slumped in my chair.

She continued, 'Madame Gaillard's behaviour is illogical to me.'

'She hated me the day I arrived.'

'This Florian who rescued you – her son – where is his father?'

'He was killed crossing a road in Lyon eight years ago.'

A shooting pain in my shoulder, my hand going there as I pulled a face.

'Your shoulder, Kiki, let me have a look.'

She pulled down the top of the smock. Sniffed the wound. 'You silly girl, why didn't you tell me?'

I shrugged.

After scolding me more, she rummaged in a cupboard. 'Bite marks – the injury could be infected.'

She gently bathed the wound. 'Courage,' she said while applying a liquid. I winced through gritted teeth.

'Vinegar,' she said. 'Brave girl.' She opened a jar of salve and I winced again. Stripping off a length of bandage she wrapped it round my shoulder. 'There. Now off you go to bed. We'll talk in the morning. I have to go to the hospices and leave at eight o'clock.'

On waking, I wanted to blot out the world; pain and recollections bombarded me. I forced myself to my feet and dressed. Outside was bright, the night's storm a memory. Lapin's ears were back; she scraped a hoof. She must have been starving. I found some turnips in the kitchen. She needed straw. I would have to visit the stables in the centre of town.

I washed in Madame Thierry's tiny bathroom and inspected the brand. It was blistered and weeping and livid, the imprint **AM** barely discernible. The pain was a continuous sting. The bottle of white-wine vinegar and the jar of salve were by the basin. Closing my eyes, I dabbed on the vinegar.

After downing a large glass of milk, I busied myself with Madame Thierry's books. *Stielers Handatlas* was on a shelf. I thumbed to the map of India and found Bombay, tracing the route there round the southern tip of Africa. I imagined the heat and myself on an elephant, enjoying the smells, the spices and the exotica of it all with Junius by my side, handsome in his naval uniform.

I read some old newspapers and was just about to bite into an apple when Madame Thierry came in.

She looked me up and down. 'You seem recovered, Kiki.'

She busied herself in the kitchen, stoked the fire, filled the kettle. Disappearing into her bedroom she reappeared in her day shift. Having made coffee, she joined me at the table. 'Your thoughts, Kiki?' she said.

'Will the authorities be aware of what happened last night?'

'Hmm, I would think so... maybe not. But if a fatality occurred...'

'A fatality... Guillaume *did* lose a hand.'

'They'll pass it off as a farming accident, caught in some infernal machine. Happens all the time.'

'Let's hope you're right.'

'You mentioned dogfighting.'

'I actually witnessed a fight.'

'Well, it's illegal in France so they won't want anyone poking their noses in.' Wrinkling her lips: 'You should report to the police.'

'Why? As you said, they will pass off Guillaume's hand as an accident.'

Shaking her head: 'There's no telling you, is there, Kiki? By the way, how much money do you have?'

'One hundred and seven francs.'

'Enough to last you a couple of months.'

I told Madame Thierry of Monsieur's thievery. 'No doubt to cover his gambling debts.'

'Gambling debts?'

'His dogs.'

Pulling a face: 'Kiki, where are you going to go?'

'I know where I cannot go – Meursault with my family or back with my husband. Impossible.'

Madame Thierry pursed her lips.

'Junius has friends in Rennes, close to Brest where he's a cadet. He said he would see me every weekend.'

'Nonsense. "Close to Brest"... Rennes is two hundred kilometres from Brest, Kiki? Use your brain.' She sighed. 'Have you met these so-called friends of his? Do they have names?'

'Pierre and Anne Lamarck.'

'Their address?'

'No address, I'm afraid.'

She shook her head. 'Rennes is a fair-sized town. A city, more like.'

'If I could get a note to Junius.'

'He will be confined to his bed. In disgrace. And watched very closely by his wife.'

'I could try.'

'You're not thinking, Kiki. This Eloise will intercept the note and go straight to your husband. They will question whoever delivered it and track you down.'

'Who are they?'

She rolled her eyes. 'The police.'

'Oh.'

'Kiki…'

'Do you think they really want to find me?'

'Oh God, yes.'

I grimaced. 'Junius does have a brother in Paris – Clément.'

'Again, have you met him and do you have his address?'

I shook my head.

She pulled her nose. 'You'll have to stay here a few days. We'll await news. Meanwhile I'll see what I can glean. I have a friend who lives in Chagny, a busybody who knows everything and everyone. I'll get word to her.'

'Seems like a good idea, madam.'

'You can't go out – too risky until we know what we are dealing with.'

'And Lapin?'

'Kiki, I may be a dowdy old schoolmistress but I once had a horse of my own.'

On Sunday, three days after my 'escape', Madame Thierry attended church while I prayed to Our Lord in the parlour. My hand went to my neck. I looped the chain over my head. The cross was of silver and small. I turned it over. Minute initials: AG – 'G' for Gaillard. Florian had said it was his grandmother's.

Tuesday afternoon. Madame Thierry returned home from school, looking severe in her black dress and tight grey bun of hair.

She placed a newspaper in front of me, *Le Figaro*, Sunday edition. 'Not good news, I'm afraid.'

GRISLY DEATHS AT MEURSAULT DOMAINE

Beaune's coroner has ordered an investigation into the cause of death on 9 January of M Augustave Monnier, owner of Domaine le Merle, and M Guillaume Ligerot, an employee. Our correspondent understands that dogs attacked the two victims – mastiffs owned by M Monnier.

Long-time housekeeper Mme Marie Gaillard is under sedation and will be making a statement to the police in due course.

Benoît Ligerot, le Merle's winemaker and father of Guillaume, has made a statement.

M Monnier's young wife, Christine, was at the scene but has disappeared. A source said she had fled the domaine and was travelling to Marseilles.

I bowed my head and fought back the tears. Reread the article. Madame Thierry said, 'Now you will *have* to go to the police.'

'Madam, can't you see? Benoît has made a statement. He would have blamed it on me.'

'You don't know that.'

'Of course, he did. He and his son hate me.'

'Hmm, perhaps you are right. This changes everything.'

I burst into tears.

'You will have to leave this house, Kiki. The authorities will come here and ask questions.'

'Where will I go?'

'We'll think of something. Stop crying, dear, it won't help. They may not blame it on you. Someone, Madame Gaillard or this Benoît character, may tell the truth.'

I snuffled and dried my eyes. 'Florian will tell the truth.'

'Strange, no mention of Florian in *Le Figaro*.'

'And no mention of Junius…'

'No point in speculation. Let's see what my friend comes up with.'

'I suppose.'

'Kiki, we have to rid ourselves of Lapin. Find her and they find you.'

My face dropped.

'I know someone in Savigny, very discreet. And you need the money.'

I shook my head. I had to clear my mind, look to the future.

Madame Thierry glanced at the mantelpiece. 'Half past eleven. No time like the present.'

Outside, I nuzzled Lapin for the last time. Tears streamed down my face. I felt as though I had betrayed her, that I was about to lose a part of me, something sacred. Lapin swished her tail as Madame Thierry mounted her side-saddle. She looked at me, her eyes molten and brown. I couldn't bear it and went inside.

When sufficiently recovered, I placed the kettle on the stove and recalled Madame Thierry's words: *You will have to leave this house, Kiki. The authorities will come here and ask questions…*

I decided to conduct a thorough search of the house – take my mind off Lapin. The ground floor consisted of a parlour, kitchen and storeroom. I climbed the stairs. The upper floor contained two bedrooms and a bathroom. An attic was accessible via a ladder on the upper-floor landing. I climbed the rungs, pushed the hatch open and levered myself upwards. It was uncluttered but full of cobwebs. An oblong wooden box lay on the floor. My inquisitiveness got the better of me: I opened the lid. Inside were mallets and balls made of wood, and iron hoops. Downstairs, I found a small door leading to a cupboard under the stairs – all was neat and tidy, coats and cloaks and kitchen appliances. I lit a lantern. At the back, a piece of old carpet, a wringer on top. I moved the wringer and flapped back the carpet to reveal a trapdoor which looked as though it hadn't been opened in years. I heaved and the door creaked open. The space was about four by two metres and less than two metres in height, with rungs down one side. It was full of cobwebs and reeked of damp.

Madame Thierry returned home and handed me an envelope. 'Sorry about Lapin – it's not as though you won't ride again.'

I led her to the cupboard under the stairs. The trapdoor was open. 'My hidey-hole in the event of visitors,' I declared.

'All right, Kiki, we'll run a test. When I give the word, I want you to climb down into it. Shout when you are about to close the trapdoor; thump on it when you can't stand it anymore.'

'Let me clean it first.' And, climbing down, I brushed the dirt away, cobwebs and all.

'Sit at the kitchen table and move when I clap my hands. Ready?'

I sat. Madame Thierry clapped her hands and when I leapt from the chair she started counting: 'One, two…'

I climbed down the rungs. 'I'm down,' I shouted.

'Twelve, thirteen…' I closed the trapdoor shut over my head; it was pitch black. I tried not to move – expend energy, consume oxygen. I breathed evenly to blot out the claustrophobia. A dragging noise overhead – Madame Thierry replacing the wringer. No sound. I wondered how long I could last with almost no air. I started counting. Three minutes later I was bursting. After giving it a few seconds more I thumped on the underside of the trapdoor.

The dragging noise again, then light, Madame Thierry peering down at me. 'Two hundred and twenty-two,' she said.

I was doubled up and gasping. Felt dizzy. I struggled up the rungs.

'You all right, Kiki?'

'Never better,' I said, panting.

She handed me a glass of water. 'Took me twenty-eight seconds from when I clapped my hands to replacing the carpet and wringer. You were without air for all of three minutes.'

'How long will it take to search the house?'

'Ten minutes at the very least.'

I grimaced. 'I have an idea. We drill a small hole in the trapdoor and ensure the carpet does not cover the hole.'

Soon Madame Thierry was wielding a drill.

'Here, let me,' I said, taking it from her.

In the corner of the trapdoor nearest the rungs I drilled a hole about two centimetres wide. Brushing away the shavings I said, 'Let's repeat the game.'

'This is no game, let me assure you.'

This time it took only twenty-six seconds for her to replace the carpet and wringer. I stood on the bottom rung, my mouth close to the hole. Ten or so minutes later I thumped on the trapdoor.

Madame Thierry chuckled as she handed me a glass of water. 'We'll make a spy out of you yet, Kiki.'

'A spy?'

'You have all the attributes, education, physical and mental toughness, beauty, *and* you are highly resourceful.'

I put my arms around her. 'We've earned ourselves a glass of wine.'

We enjoyed a bottle of Pommard. Madame Thierry talked of her husband Marcel, how they met, their life in the West Indies. She sighed, looked serious. 'All right, Kiki, this is what we'll do. It's mid-January. A girl on her own, even as capable as you, will find it difficult to survive in the middle of winter. We will wait until the fifteenth of March and then you must leave. The Ides of March, Kiki.'

'Julius Caesar's assassination.'

'Year?'

'Forty-four BC.'

She smiled. 'Life will be tedious without you. If our cellar plan is to work you will have to tidy your room constantly, create the illusion no one is sleeping there. To pass the time I will set you a programme of education… make school seem like a kindergarten.'

'I have an idea, madam. I will move into the storeroom downstairs, next to the cupboard under the stairs.'

'Good idea.'

Back in my room I opened the envelope – one hundred francs. Tears pricked the back of my eyes.

One hundred: the amount Junius had promised to give me. I rotated the bracelet and whispered a prayer. Lapin. The tears flowed.

THIRTEEN

WE SETTLED INTO a routine. Every morning I cleared my room to look as though no one lived there. Madame Thierry was a slave driver: English, German and arithmetic with tests every night. And newspapers – 'I want you *au courant* with European politics, Kiki.' My skin had a sallow look and I was putting on weight, stuck inside as I was. So I resumed my routine of exercises.

The nights were long. Madame Thierry allowed me to walk outside at dusk. 'Not too long, Kiki,' she always insisted. I looked forward to it: the cold air on my skin and time to think.

Two weeks into my stay Madame Thierry handed me an edition of *Le Figaro* dated earlier in the week.

MEURSAULT KILLINGS:
HOUSEKEEPER BLAMES MONNIER'S WIFE

On 10 January M Benoît Ligerot, winemaker, reported the deaths of his son, Guillaume, and M Augustave Monnier, his employer.

The deaths occurred on the evening of 9 January at Domaine le Merle, M Monnier's wine estate in Meursault.

This paper reported that long-time housekeeper Mme Marie Gaillard was under sedation at the time and was unable to make a statement to the police.

The police announced yesterday that Mme Gaillard has since made a statement corroborating that made by M Ligerot.

Both statements allege that M Monnier's dogs – mastiffs – attacked and killed the deceased under the control of Mme Christine Monnier.

Mme Monnier, aged fifteen, has disappeared and is sought by police for questioning.

This paper has learned that Mme Gaillard's son, Florian, aged fifteen as well, was at the scene and has also disappeared.

Speculation has it that Mme Monnier and Florian Gaillard are lovers and have fled to Marseilles and possibly India.

'God, that woman must hate me.'

'Kiki, now we have to be especially careful.'

'Huh, to think Florian and I are lovers.'

'Sells newspapers. And why Marseilles and India?' Madame Thierry looked faintly amused.

'I made it up on the spot.'

She shook her head, which I took as a compliment. 'Seems to have worked, *so far*,' she said.

'Still no mention of Junius.'

'Strange.'

'As you said, he'll be at Oubliette and in disgrace.'

'He should come forward, report to the police. Give his version of events.'

I clasped Madame Thierry's hand. 'I'm on the run, aren't I? And you are harbouring a fugitive.'

'A fact not lost on me, Kiki. Now, make sure your room is spotless.'

A day later it happened: the knock on the door.

I was in the parlour and Madame Thierry shot me a look. Twenty-five seconds later the sound of the wringer being dragged overhead. I counted off the seconds in my head. After about eight minutes I heard muffled voices, the wringer scraping across the floor. The trapdoor opened; I breathed down deep and held my breath.

'Ugh,' said Madame Thierry. 'A rat.' Then: 'Ah, my husband's croquet set; I wondered where it had got to. Marcel must have put it here when I complained it cluttered the house.'

A familiar voice – 'Madam, my men can lift it out for you?' – one I couldn't quite put a name to.

'Certainly not,' said Madame Thierry. 'There's enough mess in my house as it is. Now I know where it is, I may take up croquet myself. Marcel loved to play, you know. Do you play, Sergeant?'

The voice again: 'I once tried it in the Tuileries. A game for the ruthless, I'm told.'

'Quite so, Sergeant.'

'Shall I close the trapdoor, madam?'

'No, leave it. I need to clean down there anyway. And get rid of that rat. Ugh.'

The voices drifted away. I breathed out. And once I was satisfied they had left, I lifted the lid and clambered out. Despite the time of the year, I was drenched in sweat.

Lantern in hand, Madame Thierry grinned at me. 'Kiki, you didn't tell me about the croquet box.'

'Croquet, what's that?'

'A game. Marcel took it up the year before he died.'

'Oh, I wanted you to act with genuine surprise when they opened the trapdoor.'

'You can say that. I was scared witless. Thought the game was up... for both of us. And the rat, how did it stay on the lid after you climbed in?'

'I pinned it there, from inside its body. A decoy...'

'My, you are devious. Now, up you come. Give me your hand.'

When I was sufficiently recovered and drinking my second

glass of water, I questioned Madame Thierry. 'The "sergeant", his voice was familiar. Did he give his name?'

'He did. Let me see… it was a common name, that's right, it was Monnier. *Monnier*… oh my goodness' – slapping her forehead – 'I thought he looked familiar. Dear, dear, silly me.'

'Madam, Sergeant Oreste Monnier is Augustave's twin. What exactly did he say?'

'He wanted to question you about the le Merle killings. As your ex-schoolteacher had I seen or heard from you? I told him I had read of the killings and found it difficult to believe that you could have been involved in such a thing. I said you had had private lessons with me, the last at the end of November. He asked about your character… your disposition, the state of your marriage? I said you were one of my best students. As to your disposition I told him you were pleasant yet self-assured. I lied a little… you *are* my best student and although your disposition *is* pleasant you are tough and extremely cunning.' She looked at me from under her brows. 'The rat on the croquet box was ingenious.'

'And you are an accomplished liar, madam.'

She pulled a face.

'Was my marriage discussed?'

'I told the sergeant that I imagined life must have been a little wearisome for you, being married to an older man, that I was sad you had failed to complete your schooling.'

'So you didn't tell him how unhappy I was. That I knew about his gambling, his dogfighting activities?'

'Think, Kiki. How could I possibly know such things about an ex-pupil who had left my school six months ago?'

'Ah, you're right.'

'He asked if I would mind him searching the house. "Help yourself," I said. He checked the attic himself. Luckily, he did not associate the loose mallets and balls with the box.'

'I threw the equipment away, madam. Sorry.'

'Humph, I won't be taking up croquet then, will I? Oh, I forgot to tell the sergeant how ruthless you are. My God…'

The following day, after school, Madame Thierry returned home later than usual. 'I have some news,' she said. 'My busybody friend from Chagny visited me this afternoon. It seems that when Madame Gaillard's husband died, she transferred her affections to your husband. She has lived at le Merle since 1853.'

'Huh, those two, they'd make a fine pair… Why didn't he marry her?'

'He didn't have to. They were living under the same roof as master and housekeeper, concealed from polite society.'

'So why did he need me?'

'Kiki, sometimes you are blindingly intelligent but occasionally thick-headed. Why do you think?'

I wore my thoughtful face. 'Ah, he wanted me as his broodmare.'

'*Voilà*' – rolling her eyes.

'So no wonder she hates me… She gave birth to Florian, though.'

'Perhaps Monsieur is, how do you say… impotent.'

I nearly said *I hope so*, but kept quiet.

Later, while brushing my teeth it made sense: Madame Gaillard was jealous to the extent she was prepared to blame me for the death of her former lover.

The 'brand' tickled, so I angled a hand mirror to inspect the inside of my thigh just behind my vagina. The scar was pink and worm-like. I could make out the mark of shame – **AM** – and imagined what it was like being a convict, or Milady de Winter in *The Three Musketeers*, the fleur-de-lis seared on her shoulder.

I tried to read but my mind was elsewhere. January 1862 had almost run its course. I prayed for Madame Thierry. God bless her. I knew that staying with her could not continue – one day they would find me, and her life would be ruined. I couldn't let that happen, I really couldn't.

I extended my walks and planned my route of escape. One night I was out for an hour. Madame Thierry gave me one of her strict headmistress-like looks. 'Half an hour is all you need, Kiki.'

Making an excuse I retired to my room and tried on my disguise: the serge trousers, as yet not worn, my shirt with the billowy sleeves and my waistcoat. *And* the old beret I had found in the street. I put it on, tucking up my hair inside. I checked myself in the mirror – additions and adjustments would need to be made.

Madame Thierry was in the parlour. I made an entrance and bowed. 'What do you think, madam?' I said, my voice low.

She arched an eyebrow. 'What are you planning, Kiki?'

'The next stage of my life. I can't stay here forever.'

'Hmm, you will have to cut your hair, of course. That shirt is a woman's. I have several of Marcel's upstairs.' She circled me. 'The trousers are far too clean and you need a jerkin, rough and stained with wine and other effluvia. And you continue to converse with me in your low voice.'

I growled, 'Right, chef.'

'And your mannerisms. Think male. Think of a dog walking down the street and in need of a bitch to fuck and something to drink. Lengthen your stride, swagger, look people in the eye. You're a man, you're a man, *Chris*.'

I laughed, was shocked nonetheless – Madame Thierry using the F-word. 'Where did you learn such language, madam?'

'You forget I'm from Martinique. My father was an overseer at a sugar plantation. Anything goes with colonial life. Swearing was the least of our sins, Father especially. It is you who will have to learn foul language, *monsieur*.'

'Madam, I have a father and two brothers.'

'So you do.'

'And I suggest you don't call me Chris, madam. Christine, the association, is the same as Chris. I will think of a name. And I will need some papers.'

'*Un passeport intérieur.*'

A week later, Madame Thierry returned home looking grim. 'Someone is watching the house, Kiki. A man was lurking outside yesterday… he was here again today, hidden in the shadows, or so he thinks. I acted as though he wasn't there.'

'We will be searched again?'

'A certainty, Kiki.'

'What does this do to my plans?'

'No more evening walks for a start.'

'You really think Rennes is the right place?'

She sighed. 'We've been through this. Rennes is closer to Brest than Paris and those friends of Junius live there.'

'Are you sure you know of no one in Paris?'

'Kiki, I've already said that I do, but not well enough to ask them such a favour. I'm from the West Indies, not Île-de-France.'

'It's just that I feel drawn to Paris.'

'I can see *that*. Beware. Paris will swallow you up, Kiki, and is very expensive compared with Rennes.'

My plan was to take the early-morning post to Dijon, catch the midday train to Gare de Lyon in Paris, thence by cab to a *pension* near the station at Montparnasse, onwards to Rennes the following day.

Madame Thierry had given me one hundred francs. I had over three hundred francs – enough to last me six months. We decided that Friday, 14 February was *the* day.

Next day, 6 February, there were loud thumps on the door after supper. I was dressed as a youth, except for my hair. Madame Thierry gave me a look I will never forget – a fraction of time, a message conveyed – love certainly, for I certainly loved her. I nodded in reply and blinked away a tear. I tucked my hair into the beret, picked up my bag and looked at Madame Thierry one last time before walking out of the kitchen door and into the night.

Madame Thierry's house was close by a stream, la Bouzaize. In an oft-rehearsed move I climbed over a wall to its narrow bank below. As my eyes adjusted to the dark, I could make out its oily churn as it flowed towards the centre of town. I wore a neckerchief and shawl, a woollen vest, a shirt (Marcel's), a waistcoat, a jerkin, my old cloak, and the serge trousers (daubed in mud and washed several times). My feet were clad in my riding boots, the tops covered by my trousers. Double-wrapping the shawl round my neck I probed my way along the bank.

Madame Thierry thought she could string them out for at least ten minutes.

For once she was wrong.

I was aware of men scrambling over the wall. Then shouts: '*Stop. Police.*' A whistle trilled. After a moment's hesitation I stepped into the stream. Soon I was up to my thighs in water, my feet instantly drenched and instantly freezing, the breath knocked out of me – the shock of the cold as it smacked into me.

Two men were looking for me – the light of their lanterns reflecting off the ripples as they closed in. I felt like giving up but sank lower down, holding my bag above my head, my body pressed against the bank.

One said, 'Did she climb the wall?'

The other: 'She won't have got far.'

A stick jabbed down, missing me by millimetres. I closed my eyes and prayed.

'Not here,' said one.

'She must have gone the other way,' the other.

The voices drifted away.

I remained stock-still for a while and then waded through the stream towards the centre of Beaune. I was numb from the waist down. The flow took me to the mouth of a tunnel black as Hades. I remembered the school trip to the Hôtel-Dieu, the stream that ran underneath. No one would look for me here – little comfort, as I would soon freeze to death. Mercifully, my bag was dry. The stars were out, a vast array of diamantine points, the moon a slice of lemon light slung low in the blackness of space.

I heaved myself up onto the bank. First thing to do was change my clothes as far as I was able. With no spare pair of trousers, I took them off and wrung out the water as hard as I could. My teeth were chattering. My body was shaking. One thing, though – I had brought a spare pair of shoes and several pairs of socks.

I took off my riding boots and socks, and stashed them in the bag. After putting on dry underwear, I trod back into the trousers, the serge damp on my skin. I dried my feet and toes as best I could, pulled on a pair of fresh socks, and buckled my everyday shoes.

Beaune was like a morgue, with no one on the streets. I imagined the police were watching the railway station and staging post. The canal was the only alternative – apart from freezing to death I had no choice. Soon I was walking down rue du Faubourg Bretonnière. Hugging the side of the road I was soon in the countryside. A dog barked, lonesome and forlorn. At last I felt safe from Oreste Monnier and his policemen.

A while later I stopped to rest. After feeling for my purse, I checked my bag to reassure myself. Its contents were male: socks, underwear, two shirts, a toothbrush, a tin of tooth powder, a razor and a comb. And food – a stick of bread, cheese – together with a box of matches, two candles and a knife. Junius's bracelet and Florian's cross, and my hair, were my only female superfluities.

I set off again, the moon my companion. I was on the route de Bouze, headed for Bligny-sur-Ouche – a road I had once travelled with Lapin.

A sign: 'Bligny 8 kms'. The time must have been close to midnight. My feet were sore. An owl hooted from a nearby tree. The road wound through an endless corridor of trees. I summoned the spirit of a fox, its hearing, its instincts.

A while later I stopped and took off my shoes, massaged my feet, then dug in my bag for a fresh pair of socks.

I felt parched, having brought no water, but convinced myself that the river was only an hour away. I concentrated on planting one foot in front of the other. Walking to school twice a week helped. When I eventually stumbled into Lusigny-sur-Ouche, I cupped my hands in the Ouche and drank until I was bursting. I delved into my bag again, cut bread and a chunk from the cheese. Wolfed it down. All was quiet save the sound of water gently flowing.

With a groan I started to walk again, treading evenly to preserve my feet and working out how I could scrounge a lift on a barge. My youthful imagination had it that some kind old river skipper would put me to work and pay me a wage till we reached Paris. Madame Thierry had not had time to provide me with a *passeport intérieur*. I had already settled on the name I would give myself: Gaston Artagne, after D'Artagnan in *The Three Musketeers*, who had travelled from Gascony to Paris as a youth.

I arrived a Le Pont d'Ouche; it was still dark. Ate the last of the bread and cheese. Nothing to do except keep warm and wait for dawn. I huddled in the nook of a wall and dreamt of Paris.

FOURTEEN

O N AWAKING I tried to work out my bearings. Shapes materialised in the early dawn. A bridge spanned the canal. The village was nothing more than a handful of dwellings. The canal was wide, lazy spirals of vapour floating from its surface. The place was desolate, utterly silent. A barge was tied to the jetty. I could just make out its name: *La Fleur de l'Yonne*. The bow faced upstream in the direction of Paris.

Gritting my teeth, I started to cut my hair – my beautiful long dark hair – the strands drifting down.

Junius's bracelet and Florian's necklace prompted memories as I took them off, concealing them in a fold at the bottom of my bag.

A man clambered off *La Fleur* onto the quay. He reminded me of a gypsy – the kerchief round his neck, his black raggedy beard.

It was now or never, so I walked down the bank to the quay. A barn door was open. The sound of hooves as the man emerged, leading a large black horse with white fetlocks.

'Fine-looking animal,' I growled, my legs apart, my arms akimbo.

'Says who?'

'Says Gaston, who knows about horses.'

'What do you want, lad?'

'Passage to Paris, monsieur.'

'How old are you?'

'Seventeen.'

'Run away, have you?'

I swaggered. 'I'm on my way to Paris and a job.'

'A job, as what?'

'As a chef… at Le Procope in Saint-Germain. We Gascons know a thing or two about duck.'

'Come, take hold of Descartes here.'

I took Descartes' reins, rubbed his nose and whispered in his ear. Snorting, he fanned his tail.

'Well, you know about horses.'

'*And* duck.'

'What do you *really* want, Gaston?'

'Passage to wherever you are going. Whatever task you choose, Gaston will perform.'

He held out a hand. 'Your papers, lad.'

I gave him my broadest of Kiki smiles. 'I have no papers, monsieur.'

He scratched his beard then his crotch. 'No papers. You in trouble, lad?'

'Me…? No.'

Giving me a weary look: 'I won't pay you a sou, Gaston. But you cook, wash clothes, scrub the deck and lead Descartes here down the towpath. Understood?'

I smiled. 'Your name, please, monsieur.'

Puffing out his chest he stood tall. 'Achille de Bonnetain, skipper of *La Fleur de l'Yonne.*'

'Monsieur, to where you are bound?'

'Paris.'

On board *La Fleur* I descended into a small cabin to find a woman in a chair, a damp cloth draped over her forehead. 'Madame de Bonnetain,' announced her husband.

I stood over her. 'Is there anything I can do for you, madam?'

She looked at me through rheumy eyes. 'Who are you?' she rasped.

'Gaston, ma'am. Would you like me to make you a dish of tea?'

'That would be nice.'

Filling the kettle, I placed it on the stove.

'Be careful, lad, that thing catches fire and there'll be hell to pay,' said Monsieur de Bonnetain.

A while later, the door at the end of the cabin opened; a young man emerged. 'My son Hector,' said Monsieur de Bonnetain.

He was tall with tousled hair and a thick black beard. Brown eyes. 'Who are you?' he said through a yawn.

'My name is Gaston. Your papa has offered me passage to Paris. And before you ask, I am a chef and can handle horses.'

Another young man emerged – a little older but almost the same: dishevelled with a black beard and large brown eyes.

'My brother Hercule,' said Hector.

With my hands on my hips, I looked at Madame de Bonnetain. 'Hector and Hercule *and* Achille,' I said. 'I suppose you are Helen of Troy.'

'Cécile, actually' – a grin creased her face.

'You bunk with the boys, Gaston,' said de Bonnetain *père*.

Hercule led me back through a door to a tiny cabin. It smelt of young men. Unwashed clothes littered the floor. Two hammocks suspended from wooden beams. 'You sleep there, Gaston,' said Hercule, indicating the floor.

I dropped my bag, edged some boots out of the way and cleared a space.

'Can you cook?' said Hercule.

'I told your papa I was on my way to a job in Paris as a chef.'

Smiling, he displayed his teeth. 'Good,' he said, rubbing his hands.

Up on deck I watched as Hector harnessed Descartes. Taking up the reins he clicked his tongue. The hawser connected to the barge appeared to stretch, water squirting out of it. 'Made of cotton,' said Monsieur de Bonnetain, his hand on the tiller. 'Sinks when we pass other craft.'

The barge creaked forward.

My spirits soared.

The canal was silent and still. Rooks congregated, hopping and flapping on top of a row of tall, leafless trees. Soon we reached the first of many locks. 'We're moving uphill, lad,' said Monsieur de Bonnetain.

A tedious business, locks. Hercule jumped off the barge to help his brother, who was detaching Descartes from his harness. After spooling a rope round a mooring post, they kept it taut as it slipped, slowing the barge down.

Monsieur de Bonnetain inclined his head. 'Take note, lad.'

Hector and Hercule manoeuvred the barge into the lock with tugs on ropes and prods with poles. The lock-keeper leaned against a lever; the gates to our stern slowly closed. The gates at the upper end of the lock were shut; water gushed in from a sluice at the bottom of them, gradually raising *La Fleur* to the level of the canal upstream. Then it was a matter of the lock-keeper levering open the gates and letting us out onto the higher section of water. With Descartes harnessed again we continued our journey.

Dozing, I was stirred out of my torpor by a series of cracks: *crack-crack-crack* like a gun. Monsieur de Bonnetain was wielding a whip, his pipe clamped between his teeth.

'See that bend, lad? A barge could be coming from the opposite direction.'

'Your whip serves as a warning.'

'You catch on quick, lad. Here, give it a go.'

I tried to refuse – afraid my girlish movements would betray me – but he thrust the thing into my hand. I turned my back – worried he might spot the bulge of my breasts. I flicked the whip several times… nothing.

'Delay the hand movement, flick hard and late.'

I tried several times and eventually produced a crack, albeit feeble. 'You're a small lad, for sure. We'll have to beef you up.'

Early afternoon we reached Pouilly-en-Auxois. The canal was wooded on both sides. Employing the post-rope procedure, the barge came to a halt. Monsieur de Bonnetain lobbed out a rope to Hector. I clambered forward. And when Hector was ready, I threw him a rope. *La Fleur* was docked.

Monsieur de Bonnetain inclined his head. 'Jump off, lad, stretch your legs.'

Hector disappeared into the town. Meanwhile, Hercule tethered Descartes to a rail, plonked a pail of water in front of the horse's nose. I was sitting on the gunwale. He stared at me. 'Where are you from, lad?'

I took my time. '…Gascony, but my family live in Chagny in la Bourgogne.'

'Chagny?'

'Near the Canal du Charollais.'

Hector soon returned, a sack dangling from one hand. Having climbed on board he took out a loaf of bread, a lump of cheese and a *saucisson* – large and knobbly.

'Dinner,' he said, handing me the sack.

Inside a hare – its dead eyes milky blue – carrots and onions.

'We eat early in winter,' said Monsieur de Bonnetain. 'Seven o'clock.'

The idea of skinning and cooking the hare was daunting but I had cooked rabbits for my family.

Forcing a smile: 'I love hare. You have garlic and herbs?'

Rolling his eyes: 'Of course… in the galley. Wine too. Add plenty, lad.'

I stashed the sack near the stove and climbed out topside. The de Bonnetains were dividing up lunch. Hector handed me a battered tin plate. I helped myself to bread, cheese and a chunk of *saucisson*.

'Much better with onion,' said Hercule.

Monsieur de Bonnetain gave me a mug of red wine. 'We allow ourselves a drop at lunchtime.'

Lunch was delicious and is stuck in my memory. Its simplicity, the complementary flavours. The *saucisson* an assault of meat, fat and garlic, the *gros rouge* weak but refreshing, chunks of bread and cheese... and Hercule was right: the onion did cleanse the mouth along with the wine. No one said very much – the odd grunt here and there. And no one was particularly interested in me, though I caught Hector darting looks in my direction.

I cleared away the plates and mugs. And taking them forward I drew water from the canal in a bucket and sluiced them clean. The water was freezing cold but I didn't care.

'Gather in the rope,' shouted Monsieur de Bonnetain, which I did when Hector cast off and we edged slowly away. This time Hercule led Descartes down the towpath.

Inside the cabin I set about preparing dinner. Madame de Bonnetain sat on her bunk – mob cap on her head, blue bow entwined, a cat on her lap. Her colour had improved, pink rather than flushed.

'Good afternoon, madam,' I said, smiling.

'You're the new skivvy? I didn't catch your name.'

'Gaston,' I growled. 'I hope you're feeling better, madam. Your cat, what's its name?'

'Marmalada. She's a *her*, not an *it*.'

I dutifully scratched Marmalada's head.

'You'll find herbs under the sink. Dripping's on the counter in a jug.'

I poured her a glass of water.

She asked about my family and where I was from. I told her the truth – sort of. We talked about my brothers, their patch of land and the vines they planned to plant. She grinned, giving range to her yellowing teeth. 'White. Nay. We don't drink white 'round 'ere. De Bonnetains are red people, drink lots of it too.'

I asked her where I could find the flour.

'Right drawer next to the sink, dear.'

I found a knife. And, after testing its edge, I took the hare topside to the bow, skinned and gutted it. Retaining the heart, liver and kidneys, I tipped the entrails into the canal.

In the cabin I diced the offal. And scraping some onto a saucer I put it on the floor in front of Marmalada. She purred and lifted her tail. I had made a friend.

Madame de Bonnetain chortled. 'Aw, you'll spoil the cat, you will, lad.'

I jointed the carcass, divided the saddle. I was reminded of the jugged hare we had been served at the Girards. The dish was one of Maman's favourites; I had watched her cook over the years. After coating the meat in seasoned flour, I placed the pieces into a skillet together with the dripping. I diced onions and garlic, added sage, thyme, marjoram and two bay leaves. The concoction sizzled. The smell was intoxicating.

Marmalada licked her paws and purred again. 'Cécile' looked on with funnelled lips.

I transferred the browned meat to a large black pot, added stock, made from dripping jelly, and the blood of the hare to thicken it.

I asked Madame de Bonnetain where I could find the wine.

'The floor to the right of the sink, lad.'

I glugged in a generous amount, ensuring it covered the meat. 'Don't be shy,' she said.

I dribbled in more and placed the pot at the back of the stove.

An hour later I stirred the stew and stoked the fire.

'Careful of that, lad,' said Madame de Bonnetain. 'You go topside while I keep a beady eye.'

It was almost dark when we moored at Beurizot, another hamlet with a jetty. Monsieur de Bonnetain squinted at me from under the brim of his hat. 'Dinner in an hour if you please, lad.'

The de Bonnetains sat hunched round the small table, two loaves of bread thereon. I hefted the pot onto one end. The four of them sat there, their eyes intent, not saying a word. A flagon of wine stood to Monsieur de Bonnetain's right hand.

I ladled the concoction into five bowls. Hercule sniffed his helping suspiciously. Monsieur de Bonnetain coughed. Their heads bowed as one. '*Grâce à votre bonté*,' he said.

'*Amen.*'

No one moved; a hush as Monsieur de Bonnetain dispensed the wine into five earthenware goblets. On his nod they were off. No conversation, slurping instead, the occasional murmur, the odd belch. Madame de Bonnetain actually hummed to herself. They tore at one of the loaves, it literally disappearing before my eyes.

'You better get in there quick, lad,' said Monsieur de Bonnetain.

I grabbed the last piece.

They were drinking the wine as though *la France* was about to run dry. Monsieur de Bonnetain offered to top me up. I shook my head. 'Nonsense, lad… puts hairs on your chest.'

If only he knew.

'Not bad, Gasto,' said Hercule, wiping his mouth on his sleeve. 'Could have done with another clove, though.'

The other loaf was left untouched. After an interlude of burping and belching, Madame de Bonnetain tottered to a drawer, returning with a large chunk of cheese. Monsieur de Bonnetain squinted down the neck of the flagon. 'No more wine.' Shaking it at me: 'Come on, lad.'

I stood and went to side of the sink. 'There,' I said, plonking the flagon down in front of him.

He poured more wine. Then they ripped into the bread and cheese. Monsieur de Bonnetain insisted I had more wine. I countered by asking him where it was from.

'Ah,' he said, 'I have a man deliver it to a house in Le Pont d'Ouche. He knows what I want. From Beaune, the Côte d'Or, best wine in all of France.'

I resisted telling him I knew where it was from, especially as it was a rather mediocre Pommard. I didn't want him asking awkward questions. I ate as much of the bread as I could to soak up the wine – not wanting to wake up with a head like a walnut.

The conversation shifted to barges. Hector claimed that horses were on the way out; they were slow and unproductive, that the family had to consider sail or even steam. After a brief silence his father stood up and roared. For a moment I thought he would upend the table. After much puffing and panting he calmed down. 'No one is ever to mention that again. Understood?'

The boys glowered at their father but not for long. Soon they were laughing and drinking again, as though the subject of barge propulsion was but a small passing cloud.

With nothing left on the table de Bonnetain *père* dispensed the last of the wine. Madame de Bonnetain lumbered from the table to return with a large bottle of amber-coloured liquid. Monsieur de Bonnetain poured and handed me a glass. 'Damned fine supper, me lad, for a first attempt, that is.'

Agreement all around. Smiles. A wink from Hector. 'Nearly as good as Maman's,' said Hercule.

'Armagnac or cognac?' Monsieur de Bonnetain asked, handing me a glass.

I took a sip and swilled it around my mouth, pretending to concentrate, my eyes closed, my lips pursed. 'Neither, monsieur, it's a marc de Bourgogne, if I'm not mistaken.' I grimaced. 'A little sharp on the tongue, don't you think, monsieur?'

He glowered at me. Went puce. Looked as if he was about to explode.

Hercule said, 'Huh, I told you, Papa. That Monsieur Lebac is a rogue… Armagnac, my arse. The lad is right.'

Monsieur de Bonnetain huffed and heaved, pulled his beard and twitched. He clapped me on the shoulder, nearly knocking me off my stool. 'How can a stripling like you possibly know!' he roared.

'I know about these things, monsieur, the texture, the colour. It is a little dry' – pulling a sour face.

The brothers were almost on the floor holding their sides, tears rolling down their cheeks. Made all the worse when Madame de Bonnetain tried to console her husband, ridiculous in her mob cap.

Monsieur de Bonnetain filled his pipe, made a business of it. After lighting up, he sucked on the stem. Blue smoke filled the cabin as he puffed away. Madame de Bonnetain opened the window.

After another splash of *marc*, I made my excuses. Blandishments when I staggered to my feet: *have one more, lad* – that sort of thing. I shook my head, went topside and shoved two fingers down my throat. It all gushed out in a sour stream. Wiping the mucus from my lips I breathed in deep. I slapped my face and looked up at the stars. I had done it. I had escaped. Kneeling, I steepled my fingers and thanked Our Lord for delivering me to the de Bonnetain family.

Back in the galley I tried to sneak past the table – more roars for me to join. I pretended not to hear and carried on to the cabin, where I undressed, rewrapping the roll of linen round my breasts to flatten them. With nowhere to clean my teeth I curled up between the blankets. The floor was hard, a minor inconvenience as I was soon asleep.

Later, while it was still dark, I rolled over and almost died of shock – a body was lying next to me. Hector was snoring, his mouth agape. I pulled up the blanket. He was fully clothed. Nothing I could do but go back to sleep.

Next morning when I awoke, Hector was in his hammock and still snoring.

We cast off just before dawn. Everyone seemed rather groggy. Hector was leading Descartes and looked back at me guiltily. I mouthed *EVERYTHING IS ALRIGHT* and held up my hands. He heaved a sigh and smiled.

At midday we docked at Villeneuve-sous-Charigny, another beautiful hamlet. Hercule handed me the inevitable sack with two chickens and turnips inside. 'Dinner,' he said, winking.

I loved the de Bonnetains, but another week of them...?

FIFTEEN

N INE DAYS LATER, on 17 February 1862, we reached the outskirts of Paris. I felt both elated and insecure: my *règles* had not occurred. I put it down to my recent life with its irregularities.

La Fleur de l'Yonne glided past the church of Our Lady, Notre-Dame, as its giant bell rang eleven times. Clouds hung in heavy clumps over the city.

We had been making our way down the Seine since daybreak.

There was a reek to Paris, its own brew: sweet manure, bitter, a concoction – a rank pall from which there was no escape. The tanneries, the cooking fires, the oils, the sweat of human endeavour, the markets, the animals, of human waste – the wash of the Seine.

La Fleur docked at quai d'Orsay. A man in a frock coat stepped on board and shook Monsieur de Bonnetain's hand – a merchant relieved to receive his consignment of coal, no doubt. On the quay, a gang of stevedores alongside two hefty carts.

Time to say goodbye to the de Bonnetains before I got in the way. They had been so honest and I had deceived them. It crossed my mind to tell them who I really was.

On the quay Madame de Bonnetain hugged me to her, handkerchief in hand. I was fighting back the tears. Then Hector and Hercule were shaking me by the hand and slapping me on the back.

'Don't lose touch,' said Hector.

'We'll miss your cooking,' added Hercule.

Then Monsieur Achille de Bonnetain, his huge arms around me, his beard grating against my cheek. 'Well done, lad. We'll miss you. You're one of the best skivvies we ever had.'

The tears fell as he took me aside. 'You're not going to be a chef at Le Procope, are you?'

'No, monsieur,' I said, sniffling.

'You've run away, haven't you?'

I nodded.

'Have you any money?'

'Plenty,' I replied.

Shaking his head, he pressed an envelope into my hand. 'Take care,' he said. '*La Fleur* will be in Paris in a month's time.'

I picked up my bag and walked away, my heart heavy. I opened the envelope... two fifty-franc notes and a letter bound in blue tape.

M Philippe Toussaint
Hôtel de Londres
3 rue Bonaparte

I put down my bag and, when I thought no one was looking, secreted the francs under my blouse. It started to rain. I noticed a café – Café de la Paix – on a nearby corner.

I was glad to be dressed as a youth. I had honed my act on the de Bonnetains. I swaggered in and sat down. The place was crowded, workers mostly – no women – dressed in jerkins like me. Almost all were smoking cigarettes or pipes. A fog hung over the inner reaches.

A waiter attended my table.

'Coffee, no milk, chef,' I growled.

I had to make a decision: remain as a youth or revert to being a girl. I regretted cutting my hair.

And the note addressed to Monsieur Toussaint? He must be a friend of Monsieur de Bonnetain's. I was tempted to read it, shook my head – Monsieur Toussaint would know I had tampered with the tape.

When the waiter arrived with my coffee, I asked him for directions to rue Bonaparte.

'Down the embankment to your right, take the first right towards boulevard Saint-Germain,' he said, pointing.

'How far?'

'Five minutes.'

Boulevard Saint-Germain. Wasn't that where a woman dressed as a man murdered a prostitute, according to Oreste?

Thanking the waiter, I concentrated on the problem of who I was going to be. Although I felt fairly safe, one could never tell – Oreste was a Paris policeman, after all.

I had to be female – remaining 'male' was hard; sooner or later I would be found out. No need to rid myself of my male clothing, though. They would come in handy should I require a disguise.

I needed a name and one that sounded like Gaston. I settled on Gaeta – it was better than the alternatives – and Courlon, after one of the villages on the canal. I had become Gaeta Courlon.

Boulevard Saint-Germain was my first taste of Paris: the sights, the people, the carriages, the cafés, the men handsome in their frock coats and hats. I fizzed with excitement, although the women's costumes disappointed me – long, bulky and layered, not clothes I wanted to wear.

One young woman wore a beret and smoked a cigarette. She exaggerated the way she walked – a strut, more like – placing one foot in front of the other. The pleated blouse under the long-sleeved jacket suited her, as did the A-shaped full-length skirt covering her legs. I thought it unusual, original even.

All sorts of shops, several catering to artists – canvases, brushes and tubes of paint displayed in their windows. Many shops for women – perfumes, shoes, hats and clothes. I entered Marchand et fils, one of the larger-looking establishments.

An hour later I emerged wearing a long white skirt secured with a wide black belt, a grey pleated chemise, a black jacket with padded shoulders, a black beret and a black velvet bow tie tied beneath the high collar of the shirt – somewhat risqué, a tad masculine, but congruent with my cropped hair. A large woollen shawl was double-wrapped round my neck. It was cold but I didn't care – I was fifteen years old and in Paris. The Queen of Sheba redux. The outfit had set me back forty-two francs. But I was Kiki once again, and my black, ankle-length shoes made me feel as though I was walking on air. People turned to look at me, men especially. One beau tried to engage me in conversation. I walked straight past him, my nose in the air.

I entered a leather goods shop and purchased a money belt.

Soon I was outside the Hôtel de Londres. Clad in stone it looked intimidating. Nerves pitted my stomach. After a couple of deep breaths à la Madame Thierry, I made the sign of the cross and walked in.

A man behind a desk was taking details from a gentleman in a frock coat. I took in my surroundings: a fire in the hearth, pictures on the wall, some brass fixtures, wooden beams, lamps and comfortable furniture – cosy and welcoming. A boy in uniform appeared, helping the gentleman with his luggage.

At the counter I waved the envelope. 'A letter for Monsieur Philippe Toussaint,' I said, smiling for all I was worth.

The man stared at me, stroked his manicured beard. He was beautifully dressed: grey frock coat, starched wing collar and cravat. 'Leave it with me, mademoiselle,' he said dismissively.

'Monsieur, if you please, the letter was given to me by a friend of Monsieur's. I was instructed to deliver it to him in person.'

'Monsieur Toussaint is in a meeting.'

'I can wait, monsieur.'

He sniffed. 'Well, if you must... wait over there.'

I sat on a plush red sofa and watched the world go by. An edition of *Le Figaro* was close to hand. Articles apropos the new Paris, the emperor and Baron Haussmann caught my attention. One bewailed the loss of the old Paris: *'Things will never be the same'*. Another complained about the disruption: *'the infernal dust'*, *'the state of the roads'*, *'the traffic'*. A caption referring to Victor Hugo and Alexandre Dumas caught my eye – Dumas wanting to visit Château d'If. And one entitled 'Ballards Parisiennes', a tale about a silly girl called Sophie. An advert for Menier's chocolates.

The back page featured a report on the war in Mexico – more French troops leaving France for Veracruz, reminding me of the debate at the Girards' over Christmas – Sir Reginald Markham, his loud voice. Turning back to the inside pages I noticed a piece that made me gasp out loud.

MEURSAULT DEATHS: SUSPECTS AT LARGE

Mme Christine (Kiki) Monnier – wanted for questioning in connection with the deaths on 9 January of her husband, M Augustave Monnier, and M Guillaume Ligerot – has disappeared. Two mastiffs allegedly under the control of Mme Monnier savaged and killed the two victims at M Monnier's wine estate in Meursault.

Celebrated Paris policeman M Oreste Monnier, 'Le Blaireau', twin brother of M Monnier, is coordinating the search. Rumours suggest that Mme Monnier and M Florian Gaillard – M Monnier's stable hand and son of Marie Gaillard, the housekeeper – have run away to India via Marseilles.

Another rumour has it that Mme Monnier sought refuge at a house in Beaune after the events of 9 January.

Manifests of ships out of Marseilles in the two weeks after the killings have been checked with no evidence to suggest the pair sailed for India.

The police are now concentrating their efforts on France, Paris in particular. Members of the public should report to police should they observe a young couple acting suspiciously.

Both suspects are fifteen years old. Mme Monnier is of less than average height with long dark hair and olive skin. M Gaillard has fair hair and brown eyes.

Fear overwhelmed me. I looked around self-consciously. Then rage: *fifteen years old*. What was the world coming to?

An hour later I was still waiting. Then two men came out into reception and shook hands. 'A pleasure to make your acquaintance, Monsieur Toussaint,' said one.

Monsieur Toussaint turned and disappeared. I followed him, aware I was in a foul mood, in time to see a door close. I entered without knocking. Held out the letter. 'Monsieur Achille de Bonnetain asked me to deliver this to you *in person*, Monsieur Toussaint.'

He looked flustered, angry even. 'That rogue,' he said. 'Can't you wait like any normal person?'

'A normal person would not have been kept waiting an hour, monsieur.'

'Well, you had better sit down' – indicating a chair. 'I don't have much time.'

Monsieur Toussaint sported a waxed moustache and was spotlessly dressed. His hair was coiffed forward in the imperial style. Untying the blue tape, he wrapped on his spectacles. His eyes scanned the letter and, with a wry smile, he handed it to me.

La Fleur de l'Yonne

16 February 1862

My dear Philippe,

I am recommending Gaston to you. He joined us on the Canal de Bourgogne a week ago and has served La Fleur to a high standard. His cooking is good and he has an excellent knowledge of the wines of Bourgogne.

He is honest and diligent to a T. Do not ask me where he is from or what he has done. I suspect he has run away from his family. He has, of course, no papers.

Cécile sends her love.

Your obedient servant,
Achille

I pulled a face – modesty personified.

Monsieur Toussaint said, 'Achille says your name is Gaston and refers to you as a "he". Explain *that*, if you please.'

'Monsieur de Bonnetain is correct… I *am* running away from my family. My name is Gaëtane Courlon; friends call me Gaeta. People are suspicious of girls travelling alone, so I borrowed some clothes and dressed as a young man.'

'How do I know you are who you say you are?'

'Ask me some questions, monsieur.'

Narrowing his eyes: 'The name of the de Bonnetains' barge?'

'*La Fleur de l'Yonne.*'

'His sons?'

'Hercule and Hector.'

'The family horse?'

'Descartes.'

'What can you tell me about them?'

'They're honest as the day and drink like fish.'

He smiled. 'An accurate description. Now, tell me why you have run away.'

'My family. My father abused me, if you know what I mean. And my brothers are pigs.'

'Where are you from?'

'Chagny in la Bourgogne.'

He stood and left the room, reappearing a minute later.

'Do you speak any languages?' he said, sitting down.

'Well, of course I do, sir,' I said in English. 'I have been well educated, sir. Lovely weather, don't you think?'

'Pleasant enough.'

'*Es ist schönes Wetter heute.*'

'English *and* German.'

'To a degree—'

A tap on the door; a waiter entered with a bottle of wine on a tray.

'Achille says you know a thing or two about wine. Please close your eyes, Gaeta.'

I closed my eyes and felt the glass in my hand.

'Take a sip and tell me what you think.'

I was of a mind to tell him it was a bit early in the day but swilled the liquid around my mouth.

'It's a red,' I said. 'A Bourgogne. Rather young.' I swilled again for effect. 'It's a Volnay or perhaps a Pommard...? No... it's a Volnay... without a doubt.' I resisted giving him the particular *domaine* – too clever by half.

'You can open your eyes, Gaeta.'

The waiter was holding the bottle, the label facing me. It was a Volnay, a Domaine de Montille. I should know – the estate was only a short walk away from rue du Moulin Judas.

Monsieur Toussaint dismissed the waiter, a mischievous smile on his face. 'The letter says you can cook, Gaeta.'

'Simple country fare, monsieur.'

'A pity, as we do have an opening for a fully trained sous-chef.'

'I am sure the Hôtel de Londres, its reputation, attracts only the very best.'

'We do have an opening for a chambermaid. You know how to make a bed, I presume?'

'You presume correctly, monsieur. I have a demanding father and two brothers.'

'Can you sew? We like our chambermaids to be able to sew.'

Madame Lonjons appeared in my mind's eye. 'Of course I can sew, monsieur.'

He stood. 'It would be a pity to waste your talents in the kitchen, Gaeta. Direct exposure to our guests is what we require. Madame Boissy will make the requisite arrangements.'

I was churning inside. I couldn't believe my luck. I shook his hand, kept my features even. 'I look forward to that, monsieur.'

I followed him down the corridor to a room where a large woman sat behind a desk. 'Madame Boissy, Mademoiselle Courlon is to be employed as a chambermaid,' said Monsieur Toussaint. 'Kindly inform her, in the usual way, of our terms of employment. She has no papers, by the way.'

Madame Boissy wore a stern expression. Of middle age, she was squat and wore pantaloons and a waistcoat; her hair was cropped and parted to the left. She stared at me in a certain way, at my mode of dress, my hair.

With an insidious smile, she recited the terms of employment: fifteen francs a week for a trial period of a month, rising to twenty if they approved of me. Accommodation was an attic at the back of the hotel, sharing with two other maids. Two sets of uniforms were provided. Training was to commence the following morning.

'There are certain rules in the de Londres,' she said. 'Never be late for your shift and never communicate with a resident unless first spoken to.'

'Oh?'

Clearing her throat: 'Some gentlemen residents may attempt to take advantage of you.'

'Take advantage, madam?'

Turning a shade of red: 'You know… try to persuade you to do something immoral.'

'I think I understand what you are trying to tell me, madam.'

She wrinkled her lips. 'We do not like our maids getting in the family way, Gaeta. If we find that you are, you'll be instantly dismissed. Is that clear?'

I trudged up five flights of stairs, Madame Boissy wheezing behind me. The room was small with a sloping roof. Three cots, clothes strewn everywhere, and one small window. 'There's a bathroom with running water on the fourth floor,' said Madame Boissy.

One cot was unmade, sheets and pillowcases folded thereon. 'Must be yours,' she said, pointing. 'Anyway, sort it out with the other girls.'

'Girls, madam?'

'Yes, Joeline and what's her name?' Screwing up her face: 'And Séverine, yes.'

I nodded.

'They are on duty at the moment. Enjoy your privacy while you can. Staff breakfast is at six thirty in the kitchen. Don't be late. Someone will show you what is required in the performance of your duties.'

Giving me a stare she left, closing the door behind her. I was on my own at last and danced a jig on the spot. I made my bed, yawned, undressed, lay down and fell asleep.

Next thing I knew was being shaken awake.

Joeline introduced herself.

She was comely, brunette, pale-skinned with blue eyes, a delicate chin and a fine nose. She reminded me of Simone. Her hair was done chignon-style. Her ears were neat and cute. She was chatty and, despite all the personal questions she asked me, I immediately took to her. When she told me she was from Alsace I felt I could open up to her.

'I simply had to come to Paris,' she said. 'My bourgeois parents were driving me mad. They wanted me to become a schoolteacher, for God's sake.'

I mumbled something along the lines of my family being insufferable.

'Stand up,' she ordered. 'Turn around.' Rubbing her chin: 'You're a beauty, for sure. Not so keen on the hair, though.'

The door opened; a girl entered. 'Oh, it's Square-Eyes,' said Joeline.

Séverine was gawky and wore glasses. She squirmed when Joeline introduced me, avoiding my eyes. A dark clump of unruly hair daubed her forehead; her teeth were too large for her face. She was flat-chested, a feature not attributable to Joeline, and from Étampes, a town south of Paris. She explained she was studying dentistry – worked in the hotel to help pay expenses, tuition fees. Joeline later told me that Séverine's father knew the owners of the de Londres.

Next morning I rose early, crept down to the fourth floor. Two girls stood outside the bathroom, towels in hand. 'Join the queue,' said one. We chatted amiably between yawns.

It didn't take long before I was washed, dressed and looking my best. Breakfast downstairs in the kitchen was *tartine* and a large dish of coffee. All sorts of people congregated there. I recognised the bellboy from the day before who, through a leer, told me his name was Alain.

Madame Boissy informed me that Séverine had been assigned to me. Upstairs in an empty room we changed a bed together – hospital corners, plumping the bolsters, cushions on top. She showed me where to find supplies: towels, sheets and soap. We cleaned the bathroom – the *toilette* with a brush and sodium chloride.

Séverine said, 'The guests often leave them in a horrid state.'

Every day the rooms had to be aired, the furniture dusted, the wastepaper baskets emptied, the fire grates cleared of ash. 'Cleaning rugs is tedious,' she said. 'Once a week, I'm afraid. We lug the larger ones downstairs, hang them on the line and beat them. The smaller ones we drape out of the window. Most guests leave around ten in the morning, our busiest time.'

Lunch was at noon in the kitchen: cold meats, bread and soup, water to drink. I was on duty at five o'clock. I had four hours to myself.

After lunch, I found the post office on boulevard Saint-Germain and rented a postbox, purchasing writing materials from a shop close by. In my room I wrote to Junius care of École Spécial Militaire de Brest. I explained my circumstances to him, that I had a job in a hotel. Taking a risk, I supplied him with my postbox details.

SIXTEEN

APRIL IN PARIS is meant to be a joyous time: winter forgotten, flowers in the parks, people out and about. But I had missed my *règles* again – three months in a row – and most mornings I was sick. *And* there was a small bump in my belly. I had suspected it for a while, so I finally accepted the fact I was pregnant.

'Accepted'. If I was meant to feel panic, I did not. Fear neither, though it did occasionally grip me in moments of weakness. The thought of having a child thrilled me; as usual I was hopelessly optimistic. My 'bump' was barely noticeable. I could keep it concealed for the time being – relegate the problem to the future. And whose was it? I prayed the baby was Junius's, although it would not be so bad if the child was Monsieur Monnier's – he or she would have a claim to le Merle.

I continued to check my postbox every other day – nothing from Junius.

I also wrote to Anne Lamarck c/o Rennes, the sister of Junius's friend.

'Joelie' and I had become friends. After lunch we had the habit of walking in Jardin du Luxembourg. The lawns were lush and green and surrounded by beds of flowers in bloom, so numerous I was at a loss to know what they were. All winter we had hidden behind our coats but it was spring and now we disported ourselves. Men were constantly approaching us on the most implausible of excuses. Most wanted to escort us round the paths. The more forward ones wanted to take us for a drink and *have a good time.*

Joelie fended them off with an eloquent confidence.

Sometimes she talked of her 'friends' – men, I assumed. On one particular day we were sitting by the lake. 'Forgive me, Gaeta,' she said. 'Please don't take offence but you may be aware that I earn a little money on the side.'

'What do you mean?'

She blushed. 'Men pay me for favours.'

'Favours?'

'Have sex with them, all right!'

'*What?*'

'Calm down, Gaeta. It's not as bad as it sounds.'

'It *sounds* disgusting.'

She huffed and puffed. 'I "do it" about once a week, usually with a guest. Alain and the doorman, Pierre, arrange it for me. The guest pays them their "fee". I vet them beforehand. I insist they use a condom. I use a contraceptive, just in case. I'm in control most of the time.'

'But not all of the time?'

'Only one has got out of control so far. I threw him out.'

'How much?' I couldn't resist.

'One hundred for the night… in *their* room.'

'More than we earn in a month.'

She spread her arms.

'One day the arrangement will go very wrong and you'll be out on the street.'

'That's as may be, but I am accumulating a hoard of cash, enough to support myself for at least a year.'

I was reminded of Oreste, his case of the prostitute found dead in a laundry basket in a hotel off boulevard Saint-Germain.

'Have you ever…?' said Joelie.

'Had sex, you mean?'

She rolled her eyes.

I felt the urge to tell her my story: my marriage with Monsieur, my dalliance with Junius. Instead, I threw her a scrap. 'Joelie, I was married to a man three times my age and had to "perform".'

'That *is* disgusting. Far worse than what I do.' Squeezing her nose: 'Did you *like* him?'

'I hated him.'

'How long did this go on for?'

'Six months.'

'Ah, so you were a whore for six months – a lot longer than a single night. Don't forget I vet my clients. Most are young and rich… in want of a good time. In other words, I enjoy what I'm doing… most of the time.'

I thought of what she had said. In my condition I couldn't have done what she had suggested, even if I had wanted to. 'Forget it, Joelie,' I said. 'You lead your life, but don't try to involve me.'

'You are very attractive, Gaeta. Men, the finest, would be desperate to get you between the sheets.'

'You're not listening to me, Joelie.'

She pouted. I was of a mind to tell her I was pregnant but thought better of it.

One day, a month later, Joelie and I had the night off. 'I know an exciting café in Montparnasse,' she said.

'We can't just go to a bar together. It's unladylike – unseemly.'

'Nonsense, Gaeta, don't be such a prude. We earn our money just like the other man. We are liberated. We live in a new world, or are you deaf, dumb and blind?'

Later we arrived at La Closerie des Lilas on boulevard du Montparnasse, – a statue of a soldier brandishing a sword outside.

The Whore of Babylon squeezed my arm, her excitement infectious, making me giggle. The terrace was open-air, tables and chairs in line in front of a row of flowering shrubs. Despite the early hour there were four well-dressed men at a table, seemingly putting the world to rights. And a man on his own, intent, with his pince-nez and beard, scratching on paper as though his life depended on every written word. No women were about, and we took our seats at the table next to his.

A waiter appeared, a bemused look on his face. 'Yes, mesdemoiselles?' he said, bowing extravagantly.

'A bottle of your house red,' said Joelie.

I held up my hand. The waiter assumed a bored expression. 'It's a little early for red. A white from Bourgogne, perhaps?'

Rolling his eyes: 'Chablis, a Pouilly-Fuissé or a Meursault, mademoiselle.'

'We'll try the Meursault, if you don't mind.'

He swooped away.

'You've got a nerve, Gaeta,' said Joelie. 'Sounds like you know of these things.'

'I do know a thing or two, funnily enough.'

The waiter returned. Pulled the cork. I swilled the liquid around my mouth. 'Delicious,' I said.

'You did that as though you are an expert,' said Joelie. 'As though you actually know about wine.'

'As I said, I know a thing or two.'

'You like to keep your cards close to your chest.'

I pulled a face.

'You haven't even—'

'Excuse me, mesdemoiselles,' said a voice. 'Forgive me, but friends will be joining Émile and myself soon – a lot of us actually. Rather than disturbing you with our chatter, would you mind moving down a table or two?'

He was of medium height, his hair cropped, his skin olive; he wore a moustache. His dark eyes blazed with intelligence.

Joelie tittered.

'Excuse me, but I must join Émile,' he said, taking his leave.

Like good little girls, we shuffled down one table.

Soon, others had joined Émile. Their conversation was intense; the waiter plied them with drinks. From their dress I guessed they were arty/literary types. One, slightly older, kept looking at me. And after having spoken to the man with dark eyes they both stood up.

'Mesdemoiselles, my apologies,' said the dark-eyed man. 'My friend Gustav would be obliged to have a word with you.'

Gustav was short and overweight, but his beard was trimmed. His jacket had wide lapels à la mode. A red tie hung in a lazy loop round the collar of his shirt. 'Forgive Paul,' he said. 'He's more forward than me.' Sighing theatrically: 'Zola and his friends are giving me a headache. I am an artist and would rather be painting.'

Joelie stifled a yawn. 'So why *aren't* you painting, monsieur?'

I leant forward. 'What is your genre, monsieur…?'

'Sorry, how rude. Gustav Bonifay' – tipping his head. 'Anything, really… landscapes, still life, portraits. At the moment I am studying the female form.'

'Most men study the female form, monsieur.'

'Ha, very droll, mademoiselle.'

Joelie came to life. 'Surprise me, monsieur, tell me you are *not* looking for a model.'

Gustav continued to stare at me. 'I *am* looking for a model, matter of fact, a particular type…'

'Really?'

'I am currently studying the old masters – Titian, Raphael, Rubens. I am looking for a petite, dark-haired girl with, how do I say, well-proportioned features.'

'With large tits and a fat backside,' said Joelie.

'In other words, not you, mademoiselle.'

Joeline pouted. An act, of course.

Gustav looked me up and down. 'Um, you would be perfect, mademoiselle.'

I tossed my head. 'Would I by any chance have to disrobe?'

'Only in part. I am trying to fathom the musculature, the shading, the exact proportions.'

'Of what, monsieur?'

'Legs, arms, back, neck. When you look at a Titian, all these features are in perfect harmony, beautifully shaded.'

'What about arse and tits, monsieur?' Joelie again.

I chuckled. Joelie was a gem.

'Yes, I will want to view those as well. Mademoiselle, I will not require all the clothes to be off all the time.'

'More like most of the clothes off some of the time,' I said.

'Or… most of the clothes off most of the time,' chipped in Joelie.

Gustav laughed and produced his card. 'Consider my offer, mademoiselle. As I said, you have what I am looking for.'

I considered asking him his terms of employment – in other words how much and when – but resisted the temptation.

He stood and bowed. 'Excuse me, but I must return to Zola and his clique of bores.'

Next day, while waxing an armoire, I thought of Gustav Bonifay, his proposition. I was over four months pregnant and, although the bump was slight, it would soon be evident to anyone who cared to look. The problem was my job. Last year, apparently, a chambermaid had to leave the de Londres when they discovered she was in the family way.

I knew they liked me at the hotel. I had gone out of my way to be friendly. But would that make a difference? I feared not. It was a cruel world, and to those so-called 'respectable' bourgeois, an unwed and pregnant woman was *insupportable*.

By and large I had conserved the money I had when I stepped

off *La Fleur de l'Yonne* three months ago.

Five months pregnant, I would lose my job in the de Londres in a month – two if I was lucky. Finding another position would be difficult, given my condition. Three months thereafter the baby would arrive, plus time for weaning the child, and recovery would amount to six months without earning a sou. With accommodation, food and clothes for the baby, I would need seventy francs a month to see me through – four hundred in all. Slightly more than the cash I had secreted round my ever-expanding waist. With another month's wages from the de Londres I would be able to survive.

After lunch I checked my postbox – nothing from Junius or Anne Lamarck.

On the way back to the hotel I came to a decision.

SEVENTEEN

AWOMAN OPENED the door onto a courtyard. I asked her for Monsieur Bonifay. 'At the back,' she said, jerking her thumb.

At the back was a door on the left – 'G BONIFAY' scrawled in bold red letters thereon. I knocked. The door opened. 'Ah, the bird has arrived. Come in, Gaeta,' said Monsieur Bonifay, sweeping down an arm.

The room was large, a galley kitchen at the far end, an unmade bed against a wall. No windows, although skylights ran along the entire length of the pitched roof. The walls were covered with canvases. I wrinkled my nose – the smell a not-so-subtle blend of linseed oil, unwashed clothes and the *pissoir* in the Gare Saint-Lazare. A bottle had mysteriously found its way into Monsieur Bonifay's hand. 'Pastis?' he said.

'A little early for me, monsieur.'

'Sorry, the place is a mess.'

'When did you last wash your sheets?'

He hunched his shoulders.

'And the dishes?'

'About a week ago.'

'I'll work for you, Monsieur Bonifay, but I need terms of employment. I have most afternoons to myself, from one to five

172

o'clock. I work fifteen minutes away in Saint-Germain.'

Scratching his beard: 'Can I suggest two sessions a week, Tuesdays and Thursdays, two thirty to four thirty?'

I tapped my foot and gave him a sharp look.

'Oh, money' – more scratching. 'Five francs a session.'

My turn to prevaricate. 'Ten francs,' I said eventually.

We agreed to eight francs. Sixty-four a month – much the same as the hotel paid me.

'One thing before I start,' I said. 'This place is a slum. Have mice, do you?'

He looked fit to burst.

'I won't work in a filthy environment. No' – shaking my head.

I held out my hand. 'Sixteen francs, please, eight for today and eight for cleaning materials, laundry bills, et cetera. I am a chambermaid. I know what I'm doing.'

After rummaging in a niche near the bed he handed me some change.

I took off my jacket and rolled up my sleeves. Stripping the bed I then raked his clothes from all sorts of surfaces, mainly the floor, dumping them inside the sheets. I knew of a laundry close by and, with the bundle over my shoulder, I took my leave.

Not much later, back in the studio, I handed Monsieur Bonifay a piece of paper. 'The receipt for your laundry; it won't be ready until tomorrow afternoon, monsieur.'

'But tonight, what will I do for sheets?'

'Buy another set.'

After an hour there was a semblance of order; the washing-up was dried and stacked in his excuse for a cupboard. I had tidied up as much as I could, dusted the shelves and swept the floor. I noticed a door at the back of the kitchen, thick with old paint. 'This place smells like a sewer,' I said, pointing. 'Open it, if you please, monsieur.'

A while later he wrestled it open.

'Open the front door,' I commanded.

Warm May air flowed into the atelier.

The following Tuesday, and despite my doubts, I returned to the studio on rue Vavin. I had brought with me a change of underwear and a sheet from the de Londres. After knocking I entered. My spring clean had had an effect on Monsieur Bonifay. The place was tidy, with no clothes on the floor. The back door was open.

The obligatory glass of pastis was in his hand. We exchanged pleasantries: the weather, how clean the studio was, him thanking me for my efforts.

Then we looked at each other, me nervously.

'Ah, I am sorry, Gaeta. Um, let me see… I suggest we start with your back. I want to see the back of your head, your neck, your back and the top of your backside.' Pointing: 'That screen over there.'

I took off my clothes, not my pretties, though. And after draping the sheet round my torso I crept from behind the screen.

He indicated a stool. 'Your back, please, Gaeta.'

I draped the sheet over the front of my body, holding it prissily at my neck. It was uncomfortable and after a while I let it go, rendering me virtually naked.

M Bonifay instructed me to do this and that – *turn, raise your chin*, that sort of thing. 'Ah, that's where I want you,' he said. 'Now stay still.'

It was boring, especially for someone like me – constantly on the move. I thought of the money, the baby inside me. Junius and Florian. How I was to survive. My future.

Monsieur Bonifay invited me to view his work. My head, neck and back were shaded in charcoal, smudged at the edges. 'Looks good,' I said.

'You are perfect, as a model, I mean. Well formed. It appears you have led a healthy life. Your skin glows, is lustrous. You are very beautiful, Gaeta.'

'And very unavailable, monsieur.'

He stared at me, did something with his eyebrows. 'Now we need to study your front. Try to relax.'

Nodding, I returned to the stool and draped the sheet round my waist.

More instructions.

I looked down at my breasts and stomach. My nipples were small and erect; my belly had its telltale bulge.

'Titian would have been envious,' he said. 'Rubens too. Perfect.'

An hour later it was over. I dressed and emerged from behind the screen. Inspecting the canvas, I nodded my approval. 'Now I must go, monsieur.'

He handed me eight francs. I smiled, telling him I had enjoyed the session and that I looked forward to Thursday.

Walking down rue Vavin, my head was full of the 'session'. Once I'd become used to posing naked it was not too difficult. It was boring, certainly, but the money. I did the arithmetic again; it made me feel good. And Monsieur Bonifay had not tried to take advantage of me, despite a couple of risqué comments. I was Kiki Vellay, artist's model in *La Belle Paris*.

On Thursday I arrived at rue Vavin ten minutes late. Monsieur Bonifay greeted me at his door. To my surprise two other people were sitting there behind their easels, a man and a woman.

'Three of you,' I said to Monsieur Bonifay.

He squirmed, wringing his hands. 'I-I thought my fellow artists could take advantage of what you have to offer, Gaeta.'

I stared at them, each in turn. 'You wish to avail yourselves of my services?'

The woman smiled and tipped her head.

'If it is convenient,' said the man.

I made a business of rubbing my chin. 'Monsieur Bonifay gives me eight francs a session. Fifteen seems fair; that's five francs each.'

They eyed each other. Monsieur Bonifay clapped his hands. 'Good idea,' he said. 'I was going to suggest it myself.'

Introductions were made: Clara Leyster and John Walter Wynburne.

They talked amongst themselves. Then Monsieur Bonifay said, 'Your back, Gaeta, including your buttocks, if you don't mind.'

I emerged and perched on the stool, presented my back and let the sheet drop. Monsieur Bonifay told me to turn this way and that. I held the pose and contemplated my hands, raw from the carbolic.

An hour or so later Monsieur Bonifay handed me a glass of water. 'Take five minutes, Gaeta.' Then: 'We need to study the front of your body.'

I felt rather silly watching the artists at work. I tried to imagine their lives. I decided that John Wynburne was the most interesting – he was English for a start. Small and neat, he had the habit of chewing the end of his brush while studying me. I wondered how he saw me – a block of animate flesh, perhaps, there to be shaded, rubbed and blown? Or was I something else – an object of sex, something he desired.

At the end of May, the de Londres had paid me eighty-eight francs. The following day I received fifteen francs from my coterie of artists in rue Vavin. I had earned 164 francs in a single month.

I maintained my habit of reading *Le Figaro* every day. The campaign in Mexico dominated the news – the army beaten by the Mexicans at a place called Puebla. One editorial argued that the emperor should commit more troops and do the job properly – establish an empire while the Americans were busily slaughtering each other.

Sunday was our afternoon off. Joelie was usually with one of her 'friends'. Séverine was rarely available for a stroll or something to eat.

Séverine.

I didn't really see her on a social basis – she was either studying or socialising with her fellow students. She had a quick temper and did not appreciate being interrupted while in her books. She had a lot on her plate with her duties at the hotel and her studies. She was always running out of money and, although her parents sent her something every month, she often borrowed from Joelie and me – the only time she deigned to speak to us. She was at a disadvantage with her looks and mangled appearance, whereas Joelie and I could earn 'a little extra on the side' – 'peddle our wares', so to speak.

One of the few times she opened up was when I asked her about my teeth. She sat me down and probed my mouth with two metal prongs, one with a small mirror at its end. 'You're lucky, Gaeta,' she said. 'You have a perfect set of teeth.'

Saturday, 14 June. I felt tired and looked forward to Sunday afternoon on my own. But John Walter Wynburne disrupted my plans, sending me a note care of the de Londres.

> *80 rue de l'Ouest*
> *Paris*
>
> *14 June 1862*
>
> *Dear Gaeta,*
>
> *Mathilde and I would be honoured if you could join us for luncheon tomorrow. My apologies for the short notice given. Were you to be available we are at the above address. Twelve thirty would be perfect or at your convenience. If you are otherwise engaged, we could leave it for another time.*
>
> *Your humble and obedient servant,*
> *John W. Wynburne*

I noted the address – not too far away, close by Jardin du Luxembourg and rue Vavin for that matter.

At just before one o'clock on Sunday I walked out of the de Londres, the small box of chocolates purchased from Debauve & Gallais in my reticule. I walked up rue Napoleon away from the river and past Saint-Sulpice with its crowds. After hurrying through the Luxembourg I emerged onto rue de l'Ouest. Number 80 was closer to Monsieur Bonifay's studio than I had imagined. I rapped on the door with its shiny brass knocker.

Having given her my name, the maid welcomed me in and led me through the hallway. I was pleasantly surprised: the place smelt of fresh paint, the furniture looked new and pictures covered the walls. *There is money here*, I thought to myself. *Perhaps I should be charging Mr Wynburne more than five francs a session.*

The maid opened a pair of doors leading into the dining room. The Wynburnes were seated at the end of a long table. They both stood. John was effusive: 'So pleased you could make it, Gaeta. May I present my wife Mathilde?'

'My apologies for being late, I couldn't escape the de Londres, madam,' I said, handing Mathilde the chocolates.

Mathilde appeared to be older than her husband. She was stout and wore a dress not dissimilar to the one I had bought in Beaune after my wedding: full-length, tight bodice, high neck, buttoned front with low sloping shoulders that flared into wide full sleeves. Her hair was parted down the middle and worn in low ringlets.

'That's all right, my dear,' she said. 'We were just about to start. Please be seated.'

The table was set for three. I sat opposite Mathilde. John rang a bell and took his place at the head of the table. The maid arrived with soup in a tureen – vichyssoise. John ladled helpings into bowls.

Mathilde asked about my family and where I was from. I stuck to my story of the house in Chagny, my abusive father and unpleasant brothers. It turned out she was from Paris and therefore could not ask me questions I might have found awkward to answer.

John did not say much, often deferring to his wife. *Yes, dear. Quite so, dear* – that sort of thing.

Gigot of lamb followed. The maid cleared away the bowls. John carved and served. I helped myself to vegetables. John poured the wine – red from Bordeaux. I rolled it around my mouth – a lot fuller than a Bourgogne. No chance for me to show off.

John told me he was born in Florence and was fluent in Italian and French. He was six years old when his artist parents returned to London. Mathilde entered his life when he wished to view the archived works of Giorgio Vasari in the Louvre, where she worked as an assistant curator. 'My parents were compulsive artists, dreamers, poor as mendicant priests. I had a wonderful childhood, though. Apart from languages, painting was all I knew. Oils are in my blood, so to speak. Canvases and easels dotted our house. An aunt died, leaving my father an inheritance, enabling me to study at the École des Beaux-Arts. That's how I came to meet Mathilde in the dungeons of the Louvre.'

'That was twelve years ago,' said Mathilde. 'John was living in a garret on rue du Montparnasse with two other hopefuls. Thin as a stick, he was. As a woman, I was lucky to work at the museum. Caused a bit of a stir, though. Luckily, my father was a patron of the Louvre, so they had to accept it. John asked to view the Vasaris and I took him down to the "dungeon".'

Further revelations over dessert: her mother's death while giving birth to her, the demise of her father two years ago. 'He left me this house,' she concluded.

'Do you have children?' I enquired.

They exchanged looks – a tremor on Mathilde's bottom lip.

I felt myself blush.

John glanced at his wife. 'Unfortunately, we have been unable to conceive.'

After lunch we took tea with milk and sugar in their flower-filled garden. Afterwards Mathilde insisted I tour 'the estate'.

The house was on three floors connected by a wide flight of stairs – light yet cool with shade. Mathilde talked of her possessions, the pictures on the walls. 'A Corot,' she said, indicating a painting of a horse and its rider walking through an avenue of trees.

'It's lovely,' I said, feigning interest.

There were five bedrooms, all beautifully furnished. One was decorated as a child's room with blue wallpaper, a cot and a rocking horse in front of the fireplace. It smelt stale, made me feel uncomfortable.

'I had a miscarriage four years ago. A baby boy' – dabbing her nose with a handkerchief. 'I couldn't bring myself to redecorate it.'

I glanced at my stomach subconsciously.

I looked up to find Mathilde staring at me intently, our eyes meeting for an instant before she turned away.

She knew.

EIGHTEEN

FOUR WEEKS LATER, in early July, I was nearly six months gone – the bump more a bulge despite the loose clothing I was given to wearing. My pregnancy was no longer a secret at the studio. My artists were loyal and kept me employed. Monsieur Bonifay was his usual jolly self and they made light of drawing a pregnant woman. Clara Leyster said, 'I'll never have the opportunity of doing a Madonna with Child, Gaeta.'

Finding Junius was utmost in my mind. Given my accumulation of francs, I could afford a trip to Rennes – Brest if needs be. So one day after lunch I plucked up the courage to ask Madame Boissy for a few days' leave.

Scowling, she took out a file and made a business of reading it. 'You have worked at the de Londres for less than six months, Gaeta.'

'I need to visit friends as a matter of urgency. Please.'

She looked at her diary and huffed. 'You *have* been diligent in your duties, never late. I am told you are popular with staff. Very well. Five days, starting Sunday, the twentieth. Without pay, though.'

I bobbed and curtsied. Thanked her. Leaving before she could change her mind. It was 9 July – eleven days to go.

The following day I was leafing through *Le Figaro*, trying to find items of interest. On reaching the middle pages I had to prevent myself from falling off my chair.

MEURSAULT DEATHS: BARGE OWNER QUESTIONED

Oreste Monnier, 'Le Blaireau', told our correspondent he has questioned M Achille de Bonnetain, captain of the barge *La Fleur de l'Yonne* concerning a young man he took on board in early February.

Police believe that 'Gaston' was Mme Christine Monnier, wife of M Monnier's twin brother Augustave, who died after being savaged by dogs at his wine estate in Meursault.

The barge was moored at Le Pont d'Ouche on the Canal de Bourgogne when Gaston was invited on board. He alighted in Paris on 17 February.

Sergeant Monnier wouldn't comment as to how he tracked Gaston to the barge, although it is thought that Mme Monnier fled to a house in Beaune after the killings on 9 January.

Sergeant Monnier said the search for his sister-in-law is now centred on Paris.

I forced myself to calm down. Was Oreste aware of the letter to Monsieur Toussaint, its contents? Monsieur de Bonnetain would have hated being questioned. I was convinced of his loyalty, despite him having been deceived by me.

I was of a mind to ask Madame Boissy to bring forward my leave. I had ten days to survive in Paris. Not wanting to appear as desperate, I decided to leave things as they were.

Despite the heat I covered my head with a shawl as I walked to rue Vavin.

At the end of the session, I informed my artists of my unavailability the week after next. John Wynburne asked me what I was doing. I fobbed him off – he did not need to know.

Monsieur Bonifay said, 'A break will do you good, Gaeta. We all look forward to your safe return, my dear.'

Walking back to the de Londres I tried to blend in with pedestrians, keep to the shadows. I knew I should leave the hotel immediately. It boiled down to Monsieur de Bonnetain's letter – had Monsieur Toussaint read the article? I was reminded of Oreste's story of the murdered prostitutes, his knowledge of the hotels of Saint-Germain. He might have an artist's impression of me – his friend who drew sketches to help him identify the murderer.

On Tuesday I decided to buy the train ticket to Rennes. I had read of attacks on single women in parts of the capital – the station area of Montparnasse 'ripe for pickpockets'. I was pregnant, unable to defend myself. Nevertheless, I decided to walk there to preserve my money.

Alone in my room and after extracting one hundred francs, I stuffed my belt in my secret place behind the skirting board beside my cot. I was dressed as a chambermaid, my hair tucked up in my beret – a disguise of sorts.

I was on my guard, sticking to crowds and shadows. The further I walked down rue de Rennes the more I felt free of Saint-Germain, of its artistic and literary pretentions. And free of Oreste. Paris was at its best: people on horses, in carriages and walking their dogs. People doing ordinary, everyday things – things I craved. This life would come to me. I swore it would.

An open-top phaeton stopped at the approach to the embarcadère. A woman stepped out with a Pekinese on a slender lead. Her dress shimmered in front of me. I had never seen anything quite like it. Full-length and peach in colour, it flared from her waist. The bodice was close-cut and buttoned to her neck, covered by a black lace wrap secured in a bow round her midriff. The sleeves were full-length. Her cascade of dark curly hair was topped with a straw hat set at an angle.

Our eyes met. She was older than me, in her early twenties.

She smiled: *I was once like you.*

I smiled back: *I want to be like you.*

The glance was fleeting but intimate. She spoke to the Pekinese – *Mitzi's a good girl*, something like that – and walked towards the Hôtel Marine Terminus. I felt like running after her. But she melted into the crowd and disappeared as though she'd never really existed.

I arrived at the station and searched for the ticket office.

Purchasing the fare took no time, and soon I was back outside with the ticket secure in a pocket of my uniform. Forty-eight francs and ninety centimes for a third-class return to Rennes. The train was due to depart at eleven o'clock, Sunday morning.

An hour later I was back at the de Londres climbing the stairs to the fifth floor. The door was locked. The walk to the station had done me in. Muttering, I walked back down to the ground floor, only to be confronted by Madame Boissy – her arms crossed, her face wreathed with anger. 'My office, mademoiselle,' she said.

Shutting the door behind her: 'Lift your shift, if you please.'

My heart was in my mouth. I knew what was coming. God help me. I lifted my shift.

'I thought so. Why didn't you tell us?'

'I am only four months,' I lied. 'I thought I could work another three.'

'Well, you thought wrong. I explained the rules for this sort of thing.'

Protesting, I asked her how she knew.

She shook her head. 'I have spoken to Monsieur Toussaint. We have no alternative but to ask you to leave.'

Instinctively, I asked her for a glass of water. With a scowl she waddled out of the room. I tried to think… my departure from the hotel was no bad thing considering the *Le Figaro* article.

My immediate concern was my belongings. After the cost of my ticket I had over 650 francs, enough to see me through nine months. I would ask Madame Boissy if I could stay one last night. Something else: the de Londres owed me for days worked in July. I felt better – things were not so bad after all.

Madame Boissy toddled in, glass in hand. I drank deeply. 'I accept what you say, madam. I knew the rules.'

She looked down her nose at me.

I took my time. 'I have nowhere to sleep tonight. I need to make arrangements. Would it be possible to stay the night?' I smiled – not the brightest of my Kiki smiles.

Crossing her arms: 'No.'

Anger streaked through me. I felt like hitting her smug, fat face. Then, for the first time, the baby kicked inside me. I had not expected this. 'All right,' I gasped. 'But I need to collect my things.'

Tapping her foot: 'You have ten minutes.'

We trudged up the five floors, Madame Boissy wheezing behind me. I opened the door. Joelie's cot was in its usual state of disarray – sheets and clothes everywhere. Séverine's bed was made up – no clothes were evident, no books either. I looked at Madame Boissy.

'Séverine left us this morning.'

I implored her with my eyes.

'She's returning home to Étampes... something about needing more time to study.'

'Hmm, if you wouldn't mind, madam, but I have to change... some privacy, if you please.'

She pulled a face. 'Ten minutes, Gaeta.'

With the door closed I was like a thing possessed. My first priority was the money belt. After moving the cot, I extracted it from behind the skirting board and strapped it round my waist. Stripping off my uniform I dressed in my white-skirt, black-jacket combination. Then it was a matter of squeezing everything into my bag, the one from le Merle. The baby kicked again.

Back on the ground floor Madame Boissy almost manhandled me through the front door. 'You have overlooked one thing, madam,' I said.

She looked at me as though I had just crawled from a swamp; her eyes bulged in her fat cheeks.

'Today is the fifteenth of July. My wage is three francs a day. I have worked fifteen days in July including days at the end of June. The de Londres owes me forty-five francs, madam.'

She blustered. Monsieur Toussaint appeared in the lobby, dabbing his brow with a handkerchief.

She apprehended him. 'Mademoiselle wants to be paid for July, monsieur.'

'Don't bother me with this now, madam. An important visitor is about to arrive.' I caught his attention and smiled. Scratching his head, he then glared at Madame Boissy. 'Pay mademoiselle what she is due.'

Stuffing the notes in my bag I walked out onto the street. As I stood on the corner of rue Bonaparte a fiacre stopped outside the hotel. A man stepped out – Monsieur Toussaint's important visitor, probably – of no importance to me until I recognised the movement, the shape of him, as though I had known him a long time. He turned around.

Oreste Monnier.

Monsieur Toussaint bustled out of the hotel and clasped Oreste's hand.

Pulling my beret down over my forehead I crossed the road and ran down a ramp to the river, flattening myself against a wall. I was shaking; sweat ran down my back. I tried to hold back the tears. The baby lurched again.

Once I had calmed down, I realised I had been very lucky. Had I not been relieved of my job, had I left half a minute later, all would have ended badly for me. I pictured the scene in Monsieur Toussaint's office – pleasantries exchanged, coffee served, Oreste showing Monsieur Toussaint his artist's sketch of me. *Have you seen this woman, monsieur?*

It wouldn't take long before Oreste realised I had slipped through his fingers.

What would he do now? Knowing I needed a bed for the night he would check nearby hotels and pensions. Madame Boissy would have told him I was pregnant. It would cross Oreste's mind that the child could be his niece or nephew. 'Le Merle is in need of an heir,' he had said on several occasions.

Where to sleep? Five nights before my trip to Rennes. I could stay with Monsieur Bonifay or the Wynburnes even. But Oreste would likely check these places. Joelie knew I was modelling for artists in a studio near Jardin du Luxembourg. Anyway, it was too much to expect of them – harbouring a fugitive. I thought of throwing myself on the mercy of the church – a nunnery... No. Kiki Vellay was not one to rely on charity.

Then I realised I hadn't been thinking properly – I would change my ticket and go to Rennes tomorrow.

I walked along La Rive Gauche away from Saint-Germain.

An hour later I entered a pension on rue Saint-Dominique in the Seventh Arrondissement. The clerk behind the desk looked at me as if to say: *You're young and desperate. How can a strumpet like you afford a place like this?* His hand was out – he wanted the tariff in advance. I gave him eight francs – three days' wages – for a bed.

The room was small, the sheets clean. It would do. Stripping off my clothes I crawled into bed and fell asleep.

I awoke in the dark – my intuition was screaming at me. Matches and a lamp were at hand, and soon I was unstrapping my money belt, opening the pouches. I took out the two wads rolled up and tied with string. Sighed with relief. Untied the bow to one of the wads. Ten-franc notes enveloped both ends. Something struck me as odd: the sides of the notes were white rather than grey. The blood drained from my face as I flicked through the pile – blank sheets of paper. Panic engulfed me. I gulped for air. Tears stung my eyes. With frantic hands I unravelled the second wad – exactly the same. I rifled through the other pouches: nothing. Emptying my bag on to the bed I rummaged through my things: nothing. Repeated the process: still nothing. I slumped to the ground in a welter of tears and disbelief. I remember beating my fists on the floor. I wanted to murder someone… destroy something… tear my clothes to shreds. I twisted the bracelet round my wrist. I wanted to destroy Junius; I wanted to rip it off and throw it out the window. He had got me into this mess. He had made me pregnant. He hadn't replied to my letters. What was wrong with him? The useless… Words failed me.

I searched my belt and belongings again, knowing it was pointless. I had been duped, robbed. Whichever way I looked at it I had lost my savings. I had to blame someone, something – even the *conard* thieves round Montparnasse. In the end it boiled down to three people: Joelie, Séverine or Madame Boissy.

Joelie was addicted to money, craved beautiful clothes and jewellery. She was ambitious. Her vanity endless. It had to be her. Filthy slut. I seethed when I saw her face in my mind's eye.

Séverine was a shy little mouse, so surely not her? Strange, though, that she should leave the de Londres on the very day of my dismissal. And she never had any money – borrowing from Joelie and me as she did.

Madame Boissy had a key to the room. She could have been aware of the skirting board. *And* she had been reluctant to let me collect my things.

I eventually brought myself under control and checked my resources. I had fifty-one francs and ten centimes left over from the train ticket, forty-five from my wages and the four tens covering the dud wads: 136 francs and ten centimes in all.

Not enough money to go to Rennes.

Not on a fool's errand.

In the morning I spoke to the clerk on reception: 'At what time do I have to vacate my room, monsieur?'

'Midday' – squeezing a spot on his chin.

I had four hours.

I walked down avenue Bosquet, keeping to the shady side of the street. I hadn't eaten for a least a day, so I bought a glass of milk, an apple, a stick of bread and a lump of cheese from a stall on the corner of rue du Champ-de-Mars, a total of two francs and ten centimes. I gulped down the milk and handed back the glass. My head was full of what I should do. Rennes was out the question, as was Meursault, Paris my only choice. I was mindful of Madame Thierry's words: *Paris will swallow you up, Kiki.*

I arrived at the station, hurried to the ticketing office. Fortunately, the same man was behind the counter. Explaining my circumstances, I patted my stomach and gave him a knowing look. Tut-tutting, he asked for my ticket. He took his time but eventually handed back my fare.

I was down to 183 francs. I had to reduce my room rate to at least five francs a night, food to three a day – my expenditure limited to no more than eight francs a day.

Three weeks to sort out my life.

It wouldn't take long before le Blaireau interviewed my rue Vavin artists. Would they be loyal? I believed so. I could creep back to Monsieur Bonifay – all I had were my artists. Except there *was* a darker alternative: Joelie and her 'friends'. But I was too far gone for that sort of thing.

An idea popped into my head as I entered Pension les Charbonnières. The clerk was behind his desk. Smiling brightest of Kiki smiles: 'Monsieur, I have worked for a year as a chambermaid. However, circumstances have led me—'

'Want a job, do you?' he said.

'I *can* start right away.'

'How do I know you are a chambermaid?'

I showed him my hands, raw from the carbolic.

'Where do you think you are going to stay?'

'Do you have maids' quarters?'

He snorted. 'Les Charbonnières is not that sort of establishment, *dear.*'

I took off my shawl and ruffled my hair. 'How much would you pay a chambermaid, if a job were available, that is?'

'Two francs a day for the days you work.'

'My room is eight francs a night.'

He picked his teeth.

'I will pay four francs a day and work for free,' I said.

He shook his head. 'And I would lose two francs a day. Why would I do that?'

'The room would be occupied the entire month. Long-term customers where I used to work received a twenty per cent discount.'

Counting on his fingers: 'I would still be out of pocket.'

'Yes, but I'll be working for free.'

He belched out of the side of his mouth.

'Do you have a smaller room, monsieur?'

Scratching his chin: 'On the top floor.'

'I would like to see the room, if you don't mind, Monsieur...'

'De Goffre.'

Once again, I was trudging up the stairs of a hotel. Monsieur de Goffre was gasping behind me, enjoying, no doubt, the sight of my swaying backside.

The room was minute, smelt stale and was crammed between the eaves. Light strained through a slit of a window streaked with grime.

'This is not acceptable,' I said, my hands on my hips.

He stared at me. I had seen that look before. He was revolting, fat and unshaven.

Repulsion bloomed in my throat as I took off my chemise and 'wrappings'. I sat there and smirked, letting him take it all in.

'Hand only,' I said. 'There are conditions: my existing room for thirty more days, four francs a day paid a week in arrears. And access to your kitchen for food.'

Monsieur de Goffre went red, looked fit to burst. And he was licking his lips, his eyes fixated on my breasts. 'W-we don't serve food at les Charbonnières,' he said, choking out the words.

Rolling my eyes: 'In that case, three francs fifty a day. My hours of work, eight in the morning to one in the afternoon, seven days a week, Sundays off at noon.'

He nodded.

I held out my right hand, rubbing my fingers. 'This happens once a week, the day I pay my tariff. Understood, monsieur?'

He grunted a yes. He hadn't even asked me my name.

I nodded and he unhitched his britches. I sneered at myself as much as I did at him. It wasn't as though I hadn't done this before. After all, I had been Monsieur Augustave Monnier's little whore for six long months.

The Pension les Charbonnières had twenty-one rooms. Magda, from Rhine Province, was my fellow chambermaid. Large-boned and in her late forties, she had the hint of a moustache. She smoked a pipe and spoke little French – a chance for me to work on my German.

We worked as a team: made the beds, emptied the chamber pots, brushed the rugs. Unlike the de Londres there were no uniforms. Knowing I was pregnant, Magda, bless her, did much of the heavy work – turning over mattresses and the like. A 'DO NOT DISTURB' sign was always welcome. Fortunately, it was summer, with no fireplaces to clean or bedwarmers to empty. The standard required was well below that of the de Londres.

I had to supply Monsieur de Goffre with a name, so I became Clara Duroche – Clara of the rock. He didn't bother to ask me for my non-existent *passeport intérieur*.

In my mind I imagined Oreste would think I was six months pregnant. Although my 'bulge' was not that obvious, I decided to give the impression I was eight months pregnant by placing a cushion under my shift.

My hair was dark, curly and long. I decided my new persona would be of a common type – twenty-five years old with henna hair. I had been in Paris long enough to know how market-stall girls spoke – much the same as chambermaids in a run-down pension.

After work I purchased a bottle of henna and two small brushes from the pharmacy on avenue Bosquet, and some lemons from a nearby stall.

Back in les Charbonnières I locked the bathroom door and cut my hair shoulder-length, parting it down the middle. Slicing the lemons, I squeezed the juice into a bowl and added the henna. It was then a matter of applying the concoction to the parting with a brush. I forced myself to be patient, brushing in the mixture thoroughly.

Three hours later I looked in the mirror – ugh, I had aged five years. The reddish hue did not suit my skin. No matter. I had achieved my objective: I *was* Clara Duroche.

Now I had to find a job – afternoons only.

The following day I drank coffee with Magda at a café on rue Cler.

We spoke in German and, of course, she remarked on my appearance.

I shrugged my shoulders. 'Tell me about yourself, Magda.'

She shifted in her chair. 'My husband, Hans, represented companies from the Saar region. We moved here when I was twenty years old. Life was good – we were happily married and had money to spend. But then Hans gets the sniff of the French girls, visits brothels, the money begins to drain away. In the end he left me for a *salope* from Pigalle.'

'Men are much the same, Magda, their brains in their trousers.'

She laughed her guttural laugh and produced a pipe. After thumbing in tobacco and lighting it she heaved out a cloud of smoke. Looking at my belly: '*Ja*, all men are the same.'

'Five months to go,' I said, preserving the lie.

She looked at me from under her brows, blew out smoke.

'Magda, you've been in Paris for twenty-five years, you know the ins and outs.'

'I'm not that old, *liebling*.'

'I need money in the coming months. I cannot continue to stay in les Charbonnières. That pig de Goffre is mean as rat droppings. I need to work in the afternoons.'

More smoke. 'Five months, you say?'

I grimaced.

'So you need something for three months.' She hummed and hawed. 'Are you good with numbers?'

I said a silent prayer for Madame Thierry. 'I am. Test me.'

'How do you mean?'

'Give me two numbers and I will multiply them in my head.'

She puffed away. 'All right – ninety-eight and forty-eight.'

It took me less than five seconds. I halved ninety-eight, added two noughts and deducted 196. 'Four thousand, seven hundred and four,' I said.

'What! I don't believe you.'

I explained how I had worked it out.

Her eyes glazed over. 'Remember I told you… my husband represented companies from the Saar. One imported coal. Still does. I clean their office once a week. Their bookkeeper walked out on them last week. They are very German, don't trust the French, preferring to hire their own. A replacement will arrive from Saarbrücken in eight weeks' time.'

'What will it entail?'

'Oh, I don't know. What is flowing in and out of their pockets, I suppose.'

'Could I work afternoons?'

'Don't ask me.'

NINETEEN

I LOOKED EFFICIENT in my white skirt and black jacket, fresh from the laundry. My hair was a mess, so I wore my beret. And there was no need for the cushion. I felt safe: away from Saint-Germain.

I waited for Magda outside les Charbonnières. She was late. I looked at the hotel signboard and it occurred to me – *charbonnier* meant charcoal burner or coalman. The irony was not lost on me. Had I been the superstitious type I might have thought it a good omen.

Magda arrived. 'A short walk from here,' she said out of breath.

'Société les Mines du Saar' occupied a site on the quai d'Orsay close to rue Malar. The warehouse was constructed of wood and streaked with dirt. Crude plank doors opened onto a yard full of coal separated into large pens. Dust was everywhere, every surface covered in a film of black. A large central yard where men heaved coal on and off wagons; where horses stamped their large hairy feet; where sacks bulged on top of one another in separate piles; where men were covered in muck, their faces smudged. They called them '*les forts*'. I understood why. Stabling was at one end where two lads with pitchforks shifted dung and bales of straw.

I never really appreciated how a city operated – took it for granted. Behind the scenes was the real world: a world of sweat and toil, a world of commerce and numbers, of misery, of survival – there to satiate the great beast of Paris.

Some of the men were staring at me. One bared his teeth.

'Ignore them,' said Magda. 'You'll get used to it.'

We climbed a worn staircase. The front of the building consisted of a mezzanine – the Les Mines office, a squalid space occupied by two clerks and some threadbare furniture. A strange-looking machine sat on one of the clerk's desks. Magda said it was a telegraph – a new-fangled communications system powered by electricity.

At the far end, a section separated by a pair of low swing doors. Behind a large desk sat a large man. 'Herr Friedrich Schiel,' whispered Magda. He was tapping a lever – part of the telegraph – that sprang back into place every time he tapped. He was rough-hewn, his huge shoulders bulging in his ill-fitting frock coat. He wore an off-white, wing-collar shirt *sans* cravat.

He indicated we sit. Clearing papers from a chair I sat down.

Herr Schiel swore and finished his 'tappings'. His head was round and fringed with dark hair, bushy whiskers and a large moustache. Nodding at Magda he then glared at me. 'Tell me about yourself, Madame…?'

'Duroche. I am good with horses and I can sew.'

'Sew…? You can't sew coal, madam.'

I smothered a smile.

'She's good with sums,' piped up Magda.

Herr Schiel scowled. 'Can you audit accounts?'

'I'm good with figures. Accounts are a matter of annotating what comes in and goes out.'

'Annotating, eh? What else can you do?'

'I speak reasonable English, *mein herr*.'

'No good 'round here. We're a German company and conduct our business in France.'

I laughed. 'As you can see, I know some German. I also speak French, monsieur.'

'Are you trying to be funny?'

Magda shot me a look.

'I am a good cook and I know my wines.'

'Were I requiring a sommelier, I would go to Le Meurice.'

'The machine on your desk… it's a telegraph.'

'What's it to you?'

'It operates on a code, Morse, if I'm not mistaken.'

'Morse. Right.'

'Do you have the code, *mein herr*?'

'*Ja*' – opening a drawer in his desk.

I scanned the dots and dashes. 'Please give me a minute to familiarise myself.'

'Well, I'll be' – rubbing his chin. 'All right, sit over there.'

Only Madame Thierry knew I had a memory capable of retaining information by simply reading the text. *Like a photograph*, she had said.

Back in my seat I handed him the code. 'Please write out a message, *mein herr*.'

A smile played his lips. After jotting something down he slid the note across to me: 'TWO TONS OF ANTHRACITE READY FOR DELIVERY', it read.

After writing a series of dots and dashes I drew a line, adding a note of my own.

Handing it back, I looked him in the eye. Grinning, he wrote on the paper and slid it back to me.

Magda was waving her arms. 'What did she say, Freddie?'

'She coded the message correctly and added to it, damn cheek, if you ask me' – handing her the paper.

'I don't understand code.'

'It says, "Now give me the job".'

Magda stared at me. 'How could you, Clara?'

Herr Schiel took back the paper, writing on it before handing it back to me.

I smiled. It was easy to decipher. 'IT IS YOURS', it read.

'Ha ha ha!' Herr Schiel may have been a surly Saarlander, but his laugh made me jump. Then, like the de Bonnetains, he burst into a fit of uncontrolled mirth.

Looking befuddled, Magda started laughing as well.

One of the clerks shook his head and yawned, woken, no doubt, from his afternoon nap.

I sat there calm and under control. 'We need to talk terms,' I said. 'When *mein herr* has calmed down, that is.'

'I'll pay you eighty centimes an hour, six hours a day, starting midday every day, six and a half days a week,' he said eventually.

'One franc thirty centimes an hour, five hours a day, starting at two o'clock every afternoon, six days a week, Sunday off,' I replied.

'*Mein gott*, you're a cheeky one, aren't you just? Ninety-five an hour.'

'One franc ten centimes' – standing and offering him my hand. 'You're bound to squeeze unpaid overtime out of me.'

'She's special,' said Magda.

'She's a special load of shit, for sure.' Herr Schiel vacillated – all 120 kilos of him. Time for my brightest of Kiki smiles. 'All right, all right,' he said. 'One franc an hour, my final offer.'

'Agreed and thank you, *mein herr*. Paid when?'

'Friday afternoon, along with the rest of the staff.'

I stood and shook his hand. 'I look forward to Monday afternoon, Herr Schiel.'

Monday, 21 July. My first day at Société les Mines du Saar. It took seven minutes in my pregnant state to walk from les Charbonnières to the warehouse on quai d'Orsay. I wore my standard attire and resolved to treat myself to some new clothes. I entered the office at just before two o'clock.

My first task was to clear away months, if not years, of accumulated mess.

'What are you doing?' demanded Herr Schiel.

'Clearing away your papers, *mein herr*. "Tidy desk, tidy mind".'

Muttering in German he waved his hand dismissively and stalked back through the swing doors.

An hour later the office had a semblance of order. One of the clerks, Philippe, handed me a ledger and a pile of papers. 'More than a week's worth of business,' he said. 'Frieda departed rather suddenly and without notice.'

Shrugging, I asked him what I was meant to do with them.

'They are invoices, paid and outstanding, and receipts for payments made in the last ten days.'

'I see.'

'At the end of each month we file all the papers in the cabinet at the back of the office.' Wishing me luck, he returned to his desk.

I checked the ledger – a large notebook. Frieda's writing was virtually illegible. On the front cover was scrawled 'SOC LES MINES 1862'. The figures were haphazard but at least the invoices were stacked in date order. There were very few 'interim tallies', one month running into the next. I counted the sheaves, all 309 of them, and created four piles.

– Invoices paid
– Invoices unpaid
– Receipts for bills paid
– Bills unpaid

At seven thirty I decided to go home. I was exhausted. Herr Schiel wished me goodnight, adding, 'I hope you can cope, Clara.'

'Of course I can, *mein herr*. Goodnight to you.'

Next afternoon I had it worked out and stood at the swing doors to catch Herr Schiel's attention. He beckoned me with his finger.

'I require twenty-four box files if you please, *mein herr*.'

'Twenty-four? Do you know what stationery costs nowadays?'

'I have worked out a system that will make Les Mines far more efficient.'

He blustered – Germanic expletives under his breath.

'The present system is a mess. You cannot possibly know your financial situation one month to another. There are currently thirty-three unpaid bills and twenty-four unpaid invoices, Herr Schiel.'

'Madam, this business has been in operation for eleven years. We have never had a problem.' He stood and drew back the filthy flap of a curtain. 'Look down there. They're like rats on a pile of shit. We sell eight tons of coal a week.'

'With respect, *mein herr,* you have been lucky. Do you know how much money Les Mines is owed?'

He shook his giant head.

'Or the money the business owes its creditors?'

'Madam, as our name suggests, we supply our own coal from our mines in the Saar.'

'All well and good, but there has to be a nominal cost for that coal.'

'How do you mean?'

'The coal is not *free*, Herr Schiel. It has a cost of production in the Saar. The mine. There has to be a figure on the books to reflect the costs at the other end.'

He scratched his head.

'Plus, you have transport costs from the Saar to Paris.' I pointed out of the window. 'And you have a large labour force, a fleet of wagons and God knows what else out there.'

He looked at me as though for the first time. 'How do you know all of this? How old are you, Clara?'

'Old enough to know it is impolite to ask a lady her age. "Knowing all of this" is a matter of common sense. I went to a school where the headmistress was a demon for arithmetic. She drilled it into me and taught me how to think on my feet.'

Gawping at me: 'I'll sleep on it,' he said.

Two days later, 24 July. My sixteenth birthday. I felt totally alone. My family in Meursault was uppermost in my mind; it seemed such a long time ago. Alie especially. I felt a surge of affection for her, so strong and sudden that it took me unawares. Tears pricked the back of my eyes.

Apart from my duties in the morning, Sunday afternoon was free. At two fifteen I left the pension, shuffled down a side street and stuffed the cushion under my shift. I had become the common market-stall tabby, eight months pregnant. I decided to risk a walk to Saint-Germain. The weather was clear – sun bounced off the pavements. The air was still and hot. I turned right and headed down rue Saint-Dominique. At Les Invalides people were queuing outside the tomb of Napoleon Bonaparte. Soon I was on boulevard Saint-Germain itself. I was not wearing a hat – my coarse red hair was on display. I exaggerated my walk – lurching from side to side as though my pregnancy was a burden. I was enjoying my freedom – the sights and sounds, the people.

The Carrefour de l'Odéon is at the heart of Saint-Germain and where people placed advertisements on large display boards. A poster with a sketch caught my attention. Then it struck me: I was looking at myself. *Myself*. God! The blood drained from my face and I fought for control. Forced my feet apart automatically, to keep up the pretence. With my hands on my hips I read the words – the feeling I was in a trance, somehow disembodied.

WANTED BY GENDARMES

Madame Christine Monnier
Aka: 'Kiki'
'Gaston Artagne'
'Gaëtane (Gaeta) Courlon'

Aged 17 with long dark curly hair
Petite in height and pregnant
A Reward — Contact nearest Préfecture

Fear twisted through me – my name was in print for all to see. I chanced a look at the people around me. No one was looking at me. Madame Boissy or someone at the hotel would have supplied the name. 'Aged 17' – they had that wrong. My artists, had they questioned them?

Despite my anonymity I felt I had to get away and collect my thoughts. Hurrying, I turned right down a narrow street. After a short walk I entered Saint-Sulpice, where I prayed for Alie, Junius, Florian, Madame Thierry, my unborn child – that Jesus would protect me from Oreste Monnier.

I then ambled through Jardin du Luxembourg, where I bought myself a *glace*, which I slurped, acting out my role. I felt safe.

A young woman stood and pirouetted for the amusement, no doubt, of the gallant who was lying at her feet. I recognised her... it was Joeline. What to do? I was torn, riven with indecision. I liked Joelie. Although older than me she was good company, a friend. And, when I thought of it, the only real friend I had in Paris – until she had stolen my francs, that is.

Deciding to risk it I walked over to her and looked her in the eye.

'You are staring at me, madam?' she said.

'Joelie, it's me, Gaeta.'

'Gaeta!' The gallant stirred. 'Oh, don't worry about him.' Clasping my hands: 'Where have you been? The police are looking for you. I've been dreadfully worried. And what do you think you look like?'

I placed my hands on her shoulders and shook her. 'Joelie, listen, there are many things I want to explain to you, but I have to know... my savings. Was it you?'

'Savings? I am not aware you had sav—'

'Someone stole—'

'Not me! I might be a flibbertigibbet, but I am certainly not a thief, especially where my friends are concerned.'

'Oh, so you *are* a thief?'

'Not from someone like you, Gaeta, whatever your name is.'

'What do you mean?'

'I've seen the wanted posters.'

I pulled a face.

'They are all over Saint-Germain.'

'And the police are offering a reward. You love money, Joelie. Can I trust you? *Can I?*' I shook her again.

'*I did not take your money*, understand? On the Holy Book, I swear it.'

'Prove it, Joelie.'

'How can I? *Merde.* All right, be like that!' she said, stamping her feet and turning to go.

'Sorry, Joelie. Sorry. I just can't afford to trust anyone.'

'If you want my opinion that mouse Séverine stole your damn money. Remember, she left the very day you were fired.'

'Or that cow Madame Boissy?'

'No, I don't think so. Where was the money hidden?'

'Behind the skirting board below my cot.'

'Stupid girl. Don't you wear a money belt?'

'Of course I do. All the time.' I explained my reason for not wearing it that day. 'The one day I didn't wear it, my money was stolen.'

'Gaeta, what are you doing?'

'Now?'

'Yes, now.'

'The day is mine.'

Pulling her nose, she looked in the direction of her gallant. 'Give me a minute.'

The man stood, his hands thrashing up and down, then gathering the blanket he stomped away.

Joelie skipped back to me. 'Don't worry about him. Rodrigo will come begging later.'

Rolling my eyes: 'You haven't changed, Joelie.'

'But you have, Gaeta. Come. I know a small place.'

The 'small place' was on rue d'Assas, close to the park, away from Saint-Germain. 'VINS' on a board outside proclaimed its *raison d'être*. It *was* small. The men drinking there gawped at us as we searched for somewhere to sit.

We settled in at a vacant table at the back. A waiter appeared. Joelie ordered a carafe of *gros rouge*.

I clasped Joelie's hands, brought my head close to hers, staring her in the eye. 'If I find you have stolen my money or you betray me, I will hunt you down and kill you. Is that understood?'

'What...?'

'You saw the poster. I am wanted for murder. I *am* capable.'

'Gaeta, I don't believe you killed anyone.'

I felt myself relax a little. 'Between you and me I *did not* kill anyone.'

The wine arrived. Joelie poured, clinked my glass and looked at me expectantly.

I told her as much as I dared without mentioning names and places: my family, my education, my family's betrayal, my marriage to an older man, the 'arrangement', the dog fight, my confinement in my own home, my tryst with a naval cadet, our attempted escape, the fight, his injury, the dogs attacking my husband, my ride (into Beaune) and how I was sheltered by an older friend.

I did *not* mention the brand close to my vagina.

I told her of my journey to Paris by barge.

She said, 'I remember reading a newspaper... a policeman – "Le Blaireau" – something about the skipper of a barge. That's right, a man killed by his dogs.'

I pulled a face.

'Huh. What are you going to do, Gaeta? This Blaireau will catch up with you eventually.'

'I know nothing of this… of this Blaireau.'

Rolling her eyes she sipped her wine.

'Enough of me, Joelie, what about you?'

'Me…? I have quit the de Londres.'

'Oh?'

'I told you I had friends – friends willing to pay me for "favours". Alain and the doorman Pierre, well, they put me in touch with guests requiring "you know what".'

'And I told you I thought it was disgusting. I remember you trying to involve me. You should be ashamed of yourself.' I tried not to blush, mindful of Monsieur de Goffre.

'Gaeta, don't play high and mighty with me.' She showed me her hands. 'No longer red and raw. See? Oh, yes. The de Londres pays a miserable three francs a day to clean up other people's shit. I can earn a month's wage in a single night.'

Shaking my head: 'It's your life.'

She drank deeply and helped herself to more of the wine. 'Three girls work for me. Apart from the de Londres, there are four other hotels whose doormen and bellboys supply me with clients. My girls are the best. I insist they use the latest contraceptive devices. I also supply them with gentlemen's accoutrements – condoms, matter of fact.'

'Condoms?'

'You know what I mean.'

'I'm very happy for you, Joelie, but your point…?'

'This is something you could do, once you've had the baby and tidied yourself up, that is.'

The bile of hypocrisy rose in my throat. 'I will never do this.'

She huffed. 'Suit yourself. No skin off my back.'

I poured more wine and asked her where she lived. Delving into her reticule she handed me a card. 'Not far from here,' she said. The card was stiff and scripted in immaculate copperplate letters. The address: I couldn't help but smile.

We gossiped a while – the unfairness of life, especially for women, especially those pregnant and without support.

She asked me where I lived and how I survived.

I chopped my hand à la Madame Lonjons. 'You don't need to know, Joelie.'

We parted on friendly terms, sort of – a peck on the cheek, hands lingering on sleeves. We wished each other luck. Walking back to les Charbonnières I wondered if I had been a complete fool.

Wednesday. I had been in les Charbonnières for two weeks; time to pay my tariff and perform for Monsieur de Goffre. After work the pig was in my room, red and sweating. I felt like an idiot kneeling there doing what I had to do. I could have been working for Joelie. A minute later, though, it was all over. He hitched up his britches and I handed him twenty-four francs and fifty centimes, my tariff for the week. He left and I wiped away the mess. I felt ashamed. Fought the tears, but the tears fell.

Later, at Les Mines, a pile of files lay on my desk. 'Twenty-four as requested,' said Claude, one of the clerks.

I applied myself to the reorganisation of the accounts. Three hours later I had filled five of the files with payments received and bills paid in the first five months of 1862. At the front was my summary for the particular month. I filled five other files with invoices rendered but remaining unpaid; likewise for billings received but not yet paid. I created another file, 'UNPAID BILLS 1861', applicable to the eleven unpaid invoices that year.

Les Mines' debtors owed twenty-two thousand francs, the company owing fifteen thousand, approximately. The first six months showed that if all invoices and billings had been paid or received the business would have produced a profit of about fifteen thousand francs a month.

I concluded that the only reason the business had not suffered an accounting problem was because the cost of the coal had not been factored in. I remembered Herr Schiel's explanation that Les Mines sold eight tons a week. The cost of that coal had to be included to produce the true profitability of the enterprise.

I asked Claude if he had an idea of the costs – he shook his head.

Next day I spoke to Herr Schiel about the 'notional cost'. Waving his hand he dismissed me, but I stayed put. 'Very well, you're as bad as my wife. Claude!' he shouted across the room. 'Just give Madame Duroche what she wants,' he said as the clerk scurried through the swing doors.

TWENTY

WEDNESDAY, 27 AUGUST. No need to check my cash; I knew what I had down to the last sou: eighteen francs and forty-four centimes.

Desperation swamped me *and* I was starving. My belly was distended and yet my ribs poked out. I had survived on scraps from storekeepers I knew on rue Cler. And food in the office – cakes most days, coffee, sugar and milk.

My tariff at the pension… I was due to be paid by Les Mines on Friday afternoon – thirty francs for the week. I had two weeks before my replacement arrived. Herr Schiel informed me I could stay a further week. *To help Gretchen with your systems.*

I couldn't pay Monsieur de Goffre. I had run out of money and was eight months pregnant.

The baby thrashed inside me. I had to think of something while I was able.

Monsieur de Goffre was behind his counter smoking and reading a newspaper.

'Morning,' I said. 'I am due to move out today.'

He thumbed a page and turned his gaze on me. 'You can stay if you continue to pay your tariff, if—'

'I have run out of money.'

He picked at a scab on his chin. 'You owe forty-nine francs, two weeks in arrears.'

I fluffed my hair, looked at him lasciviously and kneaded my right hand.

'*Merde.* Go to your room... ten minutes,' he said.

I trudged up the stairs. He duly arrived, out of breath. His hand was shaking; ash spilled off the end of his cigarette.

'I owe the tariff and I intend to pay. Thirty francs will come my way on Friday afternoon.'

'You sure?'

'I have a job. How do you think I've been paying you?'

He shrugged, his hand fumbling with his belt.

'I need one more week' – lowering my chemise to reveal my breasts.

On the way to Les Mines, I stopped at rue Cler. It had been on my mind – the shop with three balls suspended on a wire outside. I entered. A man wearing a skullcap was perched behind a screen. I handed him Junius's bracelet.

He shrugged and applied a loupe to his eye, turning the bracelet over several times.

'Eight francs,' he said eventually.

'Let me see,' I said indicating the loupe.

He slid the items through on a tray. I made a business of inspecting the bracelet with the glass. 'Pure gold,' I said after a while. '*And* there's a hallmark, turn of the century, if I'm not mistaken. Thank you, but I'll take it elsewhere. Good day.'

I turned to leave.

'Fifteen, madam.'

I took my time. 'How can eight become fifteen? You're not trying to cheat me, monsieur?'

He pulled a lazy face and opened his palms.

'Thirty francs. Not a sou less.'

We settled at twenty-two. He handed me two greasy notes and some coins.

Three weeks earlier I had urged Herr Schiel to employ a debt-recovery agent to collect monies applicable to invoices more than thirty days unpaid. He had railed against the idea on the grounds of cost. Eventually, he agreed when I showed him a list of the amounts due.

While discussing the recoveries with Monsieur Bailleau of the agency there was a commotion at the front of the office. Mein Herr's face clouded over. I looked up to witness a woman the size of a Holstein bull barge her way through the swing doors.

I had Friedrich Schiel down as the archetypical dominant male type – assertive, strong, not given to fools. But now he was a quivering blancmange as the woman I assumed to be his wife stood before him.

'Have you forgotten, Schiel?' she said. 'We are travelling to Saarbrücken this afternoon.'

She was sweating like a sow; hardly surprising given the weather and her clothes: a dress akin to a wedding cake where all the layers had fallen on top of one other. She looked at me. 'Who are you?' she huffed.

I stood and offered her my hand. Her eyes went to my stomach. 'She's a slut, Schiel. What is she doing here?'

Herr Schiel mumbled something about Frieda's replacement… Clara's doing a good job… Gretchen will be here soon, dear. Platitudes.

'Clara, aha. I see.'

I waited my turn and spoke softly. 'You don't see, madam. You see what you want to see, otherwise you are blind. I am pregnant, yes. Have you ever been pregnant? If so, after eight months, you would know how it feels. Not very comfortable, I can tell you, especially when one is trying to hold down a job.'

A prayer for Madame Thierry. *Always confront a bully, Kiki*, she had told me many times.

Frau Schiel's mouth worked akin to a freshly gutted fish in Les

Halles. 'We need to go *now*, Schiel,' she said at length, glaring at her husband.

After mouthing me an apology Mein Herr followed his wife through the swing doors. The office was silent. Monsieur Bailleau gave me an embarrassed smile.

On Sunday I had the day off. Despite the francs for the bracelet and my wages I still had an accommodation and money problem. I ventured into Saint-Germain. My feet were taking me somewhere and soon I found myself outside number 8 rue Vavin.

I was in my 'disguise' but no longer in need of a cushion. Standing under a tree on the other side of the street I looked about me, checking for suspicious-looking characters: police waiting for Mademoiselle Gaeta Courlon to reveal herself. Satisfied the building was not being watched, I crossed the road and walked through the courtyard. A moment's hesitation before I knocked on the door.

Monsieur Bonifay opened up. His artist's smock was daubed with paint – an old master redux. Paint smeared his chin.

'To whom do I have the pleasure, madam?' he said.

'It's me. Gaeta.'

'Gaeta.' Taking my hand and peering at me: 'My God, Gaeta, is that really you?'

'Yes, Gustav, it is I.'

He spluttered. 'Where have you been? We have been so worried. We could not understand why you had not been in touch.' Sweeping down an arm: 'Come in, my dear.'

We were alone.

'I wouldn't mind a pastis.'

'Sit, sit,' he said. 'Sit, my dear.' He busied himself in the kitchen.

A glass of pastis found its way into my hand. I took a sip. 'The police, have they been here asking questions about me?'

'No' – arching an eyebrow.

'Have John and Clara mentioned anything to you?'

'No. Except how much they missed you.'

I tried not to show it but I heaved an internal sigh of relief.

'Are you in trouble, Gaeta?'

'Sort of, Gustav' – aware I had used his Christian name.

His eyes searched my face. 'Do you want to tell me about it, my dear?'

I felt a surge of affection for this jolly little man and related my story for a second time that week – again leaving out names and places.

His facial expressions darted and dived at every change in my fortune – every twist and turn – a pastiche of *Um*s and *Ah*s and *You didn't, did you…? You couldn't have…? That is unbelievable… No?*

When I related the tragedy of my money belt, he held my hand. 'That's terrible,' he said. And of being relieved of my duties at a well-known hotel, he went puce. '*Conards*,' he said. 'How could they?'

'Without your generosity, Gustav, life would have been very difficult for me.'

Patting my hand: 'You are worth it, Gaeta.'

Guilt crept up on me – the feeling I was manipulating him. 'I am currently employed. I cannot tell you by whom or where. Ends in three weeks. I have no money. I live in a pension, but at least I have a room to myself. I could move into lodgings, share a room with people I don't know.'

He waved his hand dismissively. 'Gaeta, stop, you don't have to explain yourself to me. I know what it is like out there.'

'Do you, Gustav?'

'Yes. My parents sent me to Paris to study architecture. I was a year into my studies when my dear father died. He controlled the purse strings but didn't leave a will… His brother claimed the family assets. The estate was in limbo, my mother left with no money to speak of.'

'Oh dear.'

'I didn't want to return to Orléans, so I abandoned my studies and stayed with friends. I spent two weeks sleeping in a park, living off scraps.'

'Then what happened?'

'The uncle died. Fortunately, he had never married so no children were involved. My dear mother had money again. *Et voilà*.'

'What happened to the architecture?'

'Paris happened. And while I realised I enjoyed drawing, it was people, not buildings or bridges, that intrigued me.'

His eyes went to my belly. 'What about you, Gaeta?'

'I am eight months pregnant.'

'You poor thing.'

Monsieur Bonifay paced the studio, kneading his chin and mumbling to himself. 'I may have a solution, my dear. Return in two days, before lunch. I need to speak with someone.'

I explained I had two jobs – the only time I could see him was at one thirty.

Dipping into a pocket he pressed a note into my hand, folding my fingers around it. 'It's not much but should tide you over for a few days.'

'I can't.'

'Let's just say it's an advance on your next modelling session.'

About to leave I turned to him. 'Gustav, I have told you my story… known to only one other person, by the way, and cannot be imparted to anyone. My life depends on it and that of my baby. Imagine if the police were to lay their hands on me.'

'No, no, rest assured, my dear, your secrets are safe with me.'

I kissed him on the cheek, whispered my thanks.

Outside, I opened my hand: twenty francs.

Tuesday. After work I struggled my way across Paris. It's a long way from rue Saint-Dominique to rue Vavin when heavily pregnant. After knocking on Monsieur Bonifay's door, he waved me in.

'A pastis, my dear?'

'Water, please.'

He smiled. 'I have good news, Gaeta.'

I leant forward.

'I have had a word with John Walter. He and Mathilde would be delighted to take you in.'

I forced a smile. I felt a certain joy, relief, of course, but foreboding as well. There was something strange about the Wynburnes, especially Mathilde whom I found rather sinister – the blue room for the baby boy she never had.

I forced myself to my feet and tried to enthuse. 'Thank you, Gustav, how can I ever express my gratitude?' I kissed his cheek.

He batted me away, making excuses. 'It was nothing, my dear, really.'

'You are very kind, Gustav, but I must go. I am running late.'

'Of course, my dear.'

'Can I suggest I meet John and Mathilde on Sunday, my afternoon off?'

'Good idea. At what time?'

'Here, at one?'

My mind was racing as I waddled my way to quai d'Orsay. The Wynburnes knew me as Gaeta Courlon – one of my wanted poster aliases. They must have seen the poster. Living with the Wynburnes would entail huge risk; changing my name would look very strange. Or was I to tell them everything?

I had five days to make up my mind.

Wednesday, my tariff was due. Monsieur Bonifay's charity would see me through. On the way to work I handed Monsieur de Goffre twenty-four francs and fifty centimes.

'You're still a week behind. And what ab—'

'I haven't got time for that now.'

He huffed. His face puce.

A customer walked in.

I walked away as fast as I was able, away from the loathsome de Goffre.

Sunday, 7 September. After a moment of hesitation, I knocked on Gustav Bonifay's door. He smiled and waved me in. John Walter Wynburne was reclining on a divan, a cheroot in his hand. He stood, the way Englishmen do when a woman enters a room, and bowed. Gustav handed me a glass of water.

John held up a hand. 'Gaeta, please. Mathilde and I are very happy for you to share our humble abode. You must never feel as though you are not entirely welcome.'

'John, that is very kind of you. Really it is. I will try to help about the house. I am trained as a chambermaid and can sew.'

'We have a maid and a cook, but thank you all the same. We want you to feel at ease, have a successful delivery. Childbirth is hazardous, sacrosanct – you should avail yourself of all the rest you require, before and after the birth.'

I smiled. 'Very kind. Thank you, John.'

He bowed again.

'I am over eight months pregnant. The birth should occur at the end of the month. I would hope to be out of your hair by mid-November at the latest.'

'Entirely your choice, we are happy for you to stay until you are fully recovered, the baby weaned.'

I thanked him again.

'Gaeta, when did you want to move in?'

I was prepared for this question and explained I had a job as a chambermaid 'mornings' and as a clerk in the afternoons. 'I propose giving up my morning job immediately and moving in at your convenience.'

'And your job as a clerk?'

'I have two weeks before I am replaced.' I shook my head. 'I cannot let them down.'

'Admirable,' he said in English. 'Working afternoons should not be too much of a strain?'

'I can cope.'

'Then can I suggest you move in tomorrow evening?'

'That would be perfect. My job finishes at seven. I need to leave my accommodation, pack and pay the bill.'

'Then it's settled.' John Walter Wynburne rubbed his hands. 'Mathilde and I look forward to your safe arrival.'

Gustav Bonifay beamed.

I decided to take the risk. 'John... Gaeta Courlon is not my real name.'

His eyes crinkled, the slightest of smiles.

'I used it, um, as my artist's-model name. My *nom d'art*, if you will.'

'*Nom d'art*. How droll. So how would you prefer to be known?'

I was prepared. 'Lucia d'Arnay.'

'Anything else you feel you ought to tell me, *Lucia*?'

I looked at John and Gustav in turn and took my time. 'I was forced to marry a man nearly thirty years older than me. He abused me, treated me as his slave. I ran away.'

'Oh, I am so sorry. Is he by any chance the father?' said John Wynburne.

I shrugged my shoulders.

TWENTY-ONE

NEXT DAY I packed, squeezed my clothes into my battered bag. Magda chatted as we went about our routine. I would explain my move to her later. I just made it through the morning – the baby inside me making his or her presence known.

At just before two I lugged my case down the stairs and presented myself to Monsieur de Goffre. 'Monsieur, I am leaving les Charbonnières,' I said, handing him an envelope.

He opened it, counted out the francs with a dirty thumb. 'And my little bonus?' he said, leering.

'I haven't time for that today. You'd better do it yourself.'

I picked up my bag. And, with Monsieur de Goffre shouting abuse at me, I walked out onto rue Saint-Dominique.

I struggled my way to Société les Mines du Saar. Monday, 8 September and Herr Schiel was still on holiday with his heifer of a wife. I busied myself finalising the July accounts. Not such a good month, being summer, with sales to domestic users almost non-existent.

At seven o'clock I wrote out the summary page. Having checked the figures one last time, I locked the door and struggled down the stairs to the street with my bag. I allowed myself the luxury of a fiacre. Half an hour later, with doubts crowding my head, I rapped the knocker to number 80 rue de l'Ouest.

The maid opened the door. 'Mademoiselle d'Arnay, we have been expecting you. Please come in.'

The Wynburnes stood when I entered the salon. Mathilde enthused, draping her arms around my shoulders and kissing my cheeks. John clasped my hand, welcoming me to their 'humble abode'.

I mumbled my thanks.

'Oh, one thing, Lucia, we only speak English in this house, except to the servants, of course.'

I silently thanked Madame Thierry and replied in English: 'Suits me, John. I think I am, how do you say, a little out of habit.'

'Out of *practice*,' said John.

Mathilde took my arm. 'Let me show you to your room.'

She nattered as we trod the stairs to the second floor: *John did this. We did that.* All was neat and tidy. Paintings and engravings lined the walls. One I recognised as being by John Walter Wynburne himself. But not of Kiki displaying her breasts, or any other part of her anatomy, for that matter. Mathilde would surely not have approved.

Mathilde opened a door. The room was of a decent size. For once I would sleep in a place without a sloping roof. She opened the full-length curtains, revealing a large window with views from the back of the house – Jardin du Luxembourg and the garden below where we took tea.

The single bed was covered with a quilt. The sheets had been turned down in a neat fold – crisp and white. On either side of the bed was a small table, each with a lamp. A fireplace, framed with rose-patterned tiles and a black mantelpiece, was set in the wall opposite the bed. A wardrobe stood left of the fireplace, away from the window. Beside the window were shelves full of books above a desk and chair.

'I hope you will be comfortable, Lucia. Blankets are in the wardrobe should you feel the need.'

I patted the bed. 'I haven't slept on something like this for a long time.'

'All that has changed now, Lucia.'

She lingered a while, admiring the view, a smile plastered to her face. Despite her welcome, her overt friendliness, I felt a distance between us. Would we be friends? Would she reveal her inner thoughts to me?

'Breakfast is at eight,' she said, unexpectedly. 'Lunches are informal, except Sundays. Dinners are at seven thirty. Avail yourself of the whole house. Wander as you please. The garden is lovely at this time of year.'

I smiled, thanking her again.

'There is a running-water bathroom down the corridor on the right.'

I thanked her again.

'The maid Lili and our cook Georges have been told you will be living here, that you are pregnant.'

My jaw ached from smiling and I thanked her again. I nearly said that my being pregnant was obvious but held my tongue.

'In other words, make yourself at home, Lucia.'

I thanked her *again* as she closed the door quietly behind her.

I slumped on the bed. Mathilde might have a mask, but I could feel mine slip away. Exhausted, I lay on my back. *So Kiki is now a pregnant bird in a gilded cage.* The baby kicked – reminding me of why I was there.

I must have dropped off – the light outside was faint when I awoke. I was starving, not having eaten since daybreak. The last thing I wanted was to go downstairs, have to smile again. Had it not been for the minute heart beating within my womb, I would have stayed put.

Lili the maid was sitting at a large table and yawned when I entered the kitchen. 'I know how you feel, Lili,' I said.

She liked to talk, did Lili. Her name was Lillian Soulignac from Évry, a town to the south of Paris (where *La Fleur* had moored for a night). She was fifteen when her mother had arranged employment for her as a nanny to a family in Bercy. Four years later she had sought another position. 'Three wretched kids, they drove me insane,' she explained. 'I had to leave. I got lucky and found a job with the Wynburnes.'

I nodded and took the opportunity to speak. 'Excuse me, Lili, I'm pregnant. My baby needs food.'

She stared at my stomach. 'Oh, me and my mouth, mademoiselle. I'll fix you something right away.'

Lili fetched me a slice of chicken pie and a slab of cheese. I found it hard to maintain my manners, such was my hunger. She poured me a glass of milk. 'That'll feed the little 'un,' she said.

I asked her about the Wynburnes.

'They are a good lot,' she said. 'She's a bit la-di-da, if you know what I mean. Tragic about her little boy.'

I nodded sagely.

'Poor thing had a miscarriage. Five months gone, she was. Distraught. Taken her years to get over it.' Tipping her head at the ceiling: 'Still hasn't, really. That room upstairs.'

'I heard her father had something to do with the Louvre.'

'Monsieur Bertot. Oh my, rich as anything, he was. I remember him. Died a couple of years back.' Lili leant forward and whispered, 'He left her this house, he did. And others, so they say.'

I bade Lili goodnight. I had recruited a useful informant. Climbing the stairs, Madame Thierry's words came to me: *We'll make a spy out of you yet, Kiki.*

The following morning I luxuriated in the snugness of my bed – pulled the sheets round my shoulders. The clock on the mantelpiece told me it was eight fifteen.

I availed myself of the bathroom, filled a basin with cold water from the tap. Stripping off my night shift I washed myself with soap, shivering as the water ran down my back. On a shelf a hand mirror. I angled it so I could inspect my vagina. The scar had healed and was pinkish, the letters **AM** as clear as they could be, considering the circumstances in which they were wrought.

A jar on the basin surround, the words *Crème Dentifrice* on its lid. *Better than soap*, I thought, as I dipped my much-used toothbrush in the powder and scrubbed away. My mouth felt fresh and clean. I resolved to buy myself a new toothbrush on the way to Les Mines.

Downstairs all was quiet. I wandered into the salon. No one was there. Then the kitchen – no one there either. The pantry was full, food under lace and mesh covers, bottles and jars *and milk*.

I drank deeply – imagined every drop feeding my baby, making his or her bones strong. Fruit was plentiful, apples and pears in season, grapes as well. I felt a compulsion to eat – I wanted my baby robust.

'Good morning,' said Mathilde in English. 'I trust you slept well.'

She had caught me unawares; grape juice dribbled down my chin. 'I did, Mathilde, thank you,' I replied in English.

'The bed was comfortable?'

'It was, and thank you.'

'Are you sure you want to go to work today? You are eight months pregnant…'

Reverting to French: 'I have to. As I told John, my replacement arrives in two weeks. They can't do without me.'

'If you must, Lucia.'

I felt she wanted to interrogate me – my arrival in Paris, where I was from. My family. And my ex-husband – particularly my ex-husband.

Her expression gave her away. She was struggling because of her upbringing – asking personal questions, especially of a stranger. I had only spent one night under her roof and she would, no doubt, defer her interrogation to another time. 'Is there anything you need, Lucia?' she said.

I was tempted to ask her for all sorts of things. 'No, thank you, Mathilde.'

I changed my mind: 'My night soil, where do I put it?'

'My dear, I should have told you… a water closet on the first floor. Feel free to use it.'

'A water closet.' I was about to add, *We had them in the de Londres*, but held my tongue.

More pleasantries: 'You must sit in the garden… There's a small terrace on the roof… The shops on rue de Vaugirard are close by.'

I looked blank at her remark about the shops.

'Oh, Lucia' – looking embarrassed. 'I forgot… money, eh? You don't need any, do you?'

'Not for the moment, Mathilde.'

'That's good. If you ever feel…'

I sighed. The baby kicked. Mathilde left the room. I drooped then toiled up the stairs to the second floor.

Friday, 19 September. My last day with Société les Mines du Saar. At close of business, a surprise: the staff gathering round where Claude presented me with a cake, my name on it: 'CLARA'. Philippe handed me a slice. '*Voilà*,' he shouted. Magda clutched a handkerchief. Herr Schiel popped the cork on a bottle of champagne. I didn't feel like drinking but raised my glass. Herr Schiel coughed for silence.

'Some weeks ago Magda introduced me to Clara as someone who could keep our books, albeit temporarily, while we waited for my niece Gretchen to arrive,' he said, beaming an avuncular smile. 'I don't know where Magda found her… I don't care. Clara insisted I test her. She had a minute to memorise Morse code. I wrote out a message in code. Straightaway she handed it back to me, translated, but with an addition, also in code. "Give me the job", it said. I was dumbfounded.'

Polite laughter.

'I coded a reply: "It's yours". What else could I do? Throw her out on her ear?'

More laughter.

'She had the cheek to ask me for twenty-four files. Twenty-four! She wanted me to accept her new system of bookkeeping. What nerve. I don't know where she got it from. But it was, how should I say, *wunderbar*. Now I can tell my credits from my debits.'

Polite laughter again.

He turned to me. 'Clara, thank you very much from Les Mines and from me. We are a more efficient organisation because of you. I'm sure I can say for all of us that we will miss you.'

Hear! Hears! all round – Magda snuffling in her handkerchief.

'One last thing before I bore you all to death. As you know Clara is very close to giving birth. How she struggles to work every day is a mystery to me. Anyway, we hope all goes well, the child healthy, and if it's a boy she will call him Friedrich.'

Even I laughed at this one. Claude had tears streaming down his cheeks. Philippe was doubled up. And Herr Schiel was looking very pleased with himself – his little joke.

The baby lunged again, forcing me to sit down.

While the staff was tucking into cake and champagne, Mein Herr invited me to his office. 'Please sit,' he said, sliding an envelope across the desk. 'I meant everything I said out there, Clara. *Danke schön.* You are always welcome to return. I am sure we can find something to employ your considerable talents.'

I pocketed the envelope, tottered to my feet and thanked him as best I could.

'Oh, and one thing, Clara, don't let anyone know of my present. Our little secret, eh?'

On my bed in rue de l'Ouest I opened the envelope – six twenty-franc notes inside. I would have danced a jig if I were able. Herr Schiel, bless him, had been very generous.

It crossed my mind I could leave the Wynburnes, but I dismissed the idea out of hand. What could I be thinking? Return to les Charbonnières? I had enough money to last two months.

Although I could hardly move, the thought of not returning to Les Mines filled me with dread. I could just about endure the Wynburnes for breakfast and dinner, but lunch – cooped up all day long?

I needed something to do. I hadn't had time for the shelves full of books. To my dismay, most were written in English. *Wuthering Heights* by Ellis Bell, for example. I had already read *Jane Eyre* by Currer Bell. Strange, these English names: two books written by people with the same surname. I leafed through *Wuthering Heights* to see if I could fathom the English. I could – just – but some of the words I didn't understand. There would be an English-French dictionary in the library downstairs.

Archibald Fullarton & Co's Atlas 1860 caught my attention. I flipped through the pages – at the front was a map of England. Turning to France, I traced my finger from Paris to Rennes. I searched for Brest. I knew it was in Brittany – 'on the end' – and found it. I mouthed a curse. The naval town was a good distance from Rennes. Madame Thierry had been right – Junius had given me the impression the cities were not far from each other. *We will see each other every weekend*, his very words.

At seven I hobbled downstairs. John was in the salon and asked me to join him. I patted my stomach, shook my head when he offered me something to drink.

'John, my English has progressed since I moved here.'

'Your English was certainly not bad then. You remember I corrected you from time to time.'

'I am determined to read a book in English. My shelves are full of them.'

'Ah, I remember leaving *Wuthering Heights* up there.'

'Yes, that's one of them. I skimmed through it. I need a dictionary – English into French.'

'There's one in the library. Mathilde struggles with a word once in a while.'

'Would you mind if I borrowed it?'

Rising from his seat: 'My pleasure, Lucia.'

Returning from the library he handed me *Nugent's Pocket Dictionary 1856.*

Over dinner we discussed *Wuthering Heights.* John said, 'The Bells are the Brontë sisters, Charlotte and Emily.'

' "Currer" and "Ellis" sound male,' I said.

'Deliberately so. The Brontës wanted to separate themselves from the negative association female writers have with the public.'

'That is ridiculous.'

He held up his hands. 'It's to do with perception – the reading public is predominantly male. Male means outgoing and worldly. Female is associated with the home – cooking and raising children.'

'That is absurd. Giving birth, I am told, is the hardest thing on earth.'

'Mathilde, what do you think, dear?'

'You know what I think, John. Women should be educated, even have a job as I did. Their primary function, though, is to bear children and serve their husbands and, ultimately, the family prosperity.'

'That's all very well, Mathilde,' I said, 'but what if a woman has brains? God forbid.'

'She should apply her intelligence to the betterment of the family.'

'Ignore half the world's intellectual capacity in exchange for the upbringing of children. Seems like bad arithmetic to me.'

'Children need to be nurtured.'

'That goes without saying. If I give birth to a girl, I will educate her to the highest standards and teach her independence in both thought and action. If it's a boy the same principles will apply.'

TWENTY-TWO

O N 8 OCTOBER 1862 I gave birth to a baby boy. The Wynburnes provided me with a midwife. Although it hurt like nothing on earth, the delivery was without complications.

Propped up in bed I searched his eyes for the umpteenth time; they were brown, as were Junius's. Augustave Monnier's eyes were a yellowy hue of blue.

Mathilde was especially excited – insisted on holding him and making silly gurgling noises. She clung to him longer than was necessary. I felt my hackles rise and asked her, in no uncertain terms, to hand him back.

John said, 'Have you thought of a name?'

'I have. Lucien.'

'As in Lucia. A fine name.'

'My grandfather on my mother's side was a Lucien,' piped up Mathilde.

At last they left me in peace. Lucien was swaddled in a woollen shawl which I took off several times – to convince myself that nothing really was missing.

Lucien had a sheen of fair hair. Both Augustave and Junius had brown hair. Was his face pinched or round? I could not decide. I lopped out a breast when he started to cry; he suckled greedily, making little slurping sounds. His eyes were closed.

The happiest days of my life.

My Lucien.

The Wynburnes, give them their due, left me alone most of the time. One afternoon, downstairs reading, I yawned when Mathilde entered the room. 'Sorry, Mathilde, I had a bad night. Lucien kept me awake.'

Folding her skirts she planted herself next to me. 'We could engage a wet nurse, Lucia.'

'Have someone suckle my baby?'

'Everybody does it. She could move into the room on the first floor.'

'The blue room?'

'If that's what you call it…'

'But my room is on the second floor.'

'Lucien would move to the "Blue Room"… to be with his nurse. No more sleepless nights, Lucia.'

I knew where this was going and stared her down. 'No. I will feed my baby. Me alone. Lucien and I will not be separated. Is that understood, Mathilde?'

The next few weeks I worked on my fitness – my feet-under-the-end-of-the-bed routine. Walks in Jardin du Luxembourg, Lucien in his baby carriage, a strange contraption with four spindly wheels – the ones at the back larger than those at the front, reminding me of the berlin. My hair had grown out its awful henna stain and was long, dark and lustrous again. Men tipped their hats, turned round when I passed them by. At meals I often caught John Walter Wynburne sneaking looks at me. Not unsurprising given the shape of his wife.

Sometimes, Mathilde accompanied me. I could hardly refuse – she *was* my host. We chatted amiably enough and she liked to wheel the carriage, an annoying experience given she mewed incessantly at Lucien as though he was a cat.

I struggled through *Wuthering Heights* with the aid of the dictionary. A plot not dissimilar to *Madame Bovary*. The heroine Catherine Earnshaw a victim because of men. She married the wrong man (of course) and suffered when her animal instincts for Heathcliff overpowered her. I was drawn to Heathcliff – could see him in my mind's eye, feral yet romantic. Not unlike Junius, but wilder and certainly not spoilt. The Lintons reminded me of the Wynburnes: their dress, their genteel manners.

Mid-November, the weather had turned; leaves clogged the Luxembourg. The air was damp. Mathilde had a habit of taking Lucien out of the carriage and wrapping him in more shawls. Her trite comments infuriated me: *Might catch his death of cold* and *Snug as a bug in a rug* among her favourites. She always held him longer than was necessary. I was constantly having to bite my tongue.

The subject of my departure was never raised. I was aware I had become used to the comfort and lack of expense, and realised I couldn't live off the Wynburne's charity indefinitely. They had been very generous, providing baby clothes and a new outfit for me – layered as it was.

The police would now be looking for someone with a baby and *long dark curly hair*. I felt relatively safe in the Luxembourg but stuck to the Montparnasse end, away from Saint-Germain. I had eighty-four francs and sixty-two centimes, enough to last a month with a baby in tow. I could revert to modelling in rue Vavin but discounted the idea. I didn't want John Walter staring at my backside; anyway, the police could visit Monsieur Bonifay any time. I could work as a chambermaid in one of the best hotels, with my Kiki charm, knowledge of languages and wine. But it held no appeal: the pay, the carbolic, the chores and emptying other people's chamber pots.

I was aware of Joelie's card in my reticule. It lurked there – a temptation into a world in which I couldn't allow myself to sink.

My postbox had remained unopened for three months. The more I thought of it the more urgent it became. A tingle went down my spine at what I might find there. No point in taking Lucien. Lili would keep an eye on him.

I decided to wear the layered dress, portray myself as slightly pregnant. A small cushion did the job and I hid my hair under my mob cap. I stuck to crowds and shadows. It felt good to be on the boulevards again; the atmosphere was palpable even in autumn – the cafés, people everywhere, carriages thronging the streets and the smells…

I entered the post office, turned the key in the lock and prayed. Nothing.

What had I expected?

Outside, my head down, I found myself mumbling angrily. *Junius, where are you and why are you ignoring me?* Over ten months had passed since our 'tryst' in rue Paradis. At that time, he had a year to complete his training. He would be in Rennes or Brest, surely. I felt a want, a need bloom inside me. I had to find Junius – find a path to Lucien's future. The eighty francs would buy me a third-class return to Rennes and a couple of nights in a pension. After that I would be down to my last centimes.

Back at rue de l'Ouest I hurried upstairs to find Mathilde rocking Lucien in his cradle, humming a lullaby. Despite my presence her eyes never wavered from his face. 'I will attend to him now, madam,' I said somewhat brusquely.

'He was crying, Lucia. I thought to soothe him.'

Before dinner I was in the habit of reading the newspapers in the salon. *Le Figaro* was in its usual place together with an edition of *The Times* of London. I scanned *Le Figaro* for news of 'le Blaireau'. Nothing. In fact there had been no reports on the Meursault deaths in the weeks I had been at the Wynburnes'.

A piece on the cotton famine: prices had doubled in a year. The Yankee blockade of Confederate ports… workers in the mills of France laid off. A paragraph on trade: *Le Figaro* urging the government to intervene in the war in the United States to ensure the trade, not only in cotton but also in wine, brandy and silk, continued to flow. The government took the Confederate side. Trade was king. Meanwhile France was still at war in Mexico. I tried to fathom what it all meant.

The same in *The Times* of 14 November – the war in America. 'The appeal of the French emperor... supporters of Mr Lincoln', et cetera. Another: 'Mediation in America... opportunities for an armistice'. On another page a report of skirmishing at a place called Phillipmont... 'Confederate prisoners captured'. 'The Confederate steamer *Alabama* capturing eight more American vessels'. It struck me as strange that the first three pages of a newspaper contained nothing but advertisements. 'Lost, a Brown Leather Portmanteau' said one. 'Found, an Italian Greyhound' another.

I closed the paper. The world and the greyhound would sort themselves out. I leant back and shut my eyes. John walked in. 'Ah, Lucia,' he said. 'You like to keep yourself appraised of the latest news.'

'Hmm. Although women play a minor role in history, it is our responsibility keep up with current events. Europe is feeling the consequences of the war in America... affecting our workers in the cotton trade. Women will be married to those workers and affected as well.'

'Where do you get all this, Lucia? You seem very well informed.'

Without mentioning names, I told him about Madame Thierry. 'She made me read *Madame Bovary*.'

'A salutary tale, for sure.'

'Especially for us women.'

'Lucia, I don't wish to pry, but do you know the whereabouts of Lucien's father?'

'Sort of... he has connections in Rennes.'

'Forgive me, but why don't you go there, contact these "connections"? It's a simple trip on the train. Eight hours or so.'

'Two reasons, John. I haven't the resources and Lucien's too young to travel.' I omitted telling him that I didn't know where the Lamarcks lived.

'Ah, good reasons indeed, Lucia' – kneading his chin.

Next day the three of us were breakfasting in the morning room. John wiped his mouth with a napkin while glancing at Mathilde. Clearing his throat: 'Lucia, our conversation last night… you mentioned Lucien's father, his connections in Rennes.'

I nodded.

'And that, how do I put it, you do not have the resources to make the trip.'

'And that Lucien is too small to travel.'

'You will remember what we said when you moved in, that we were happy for you to stay until you were fully recovered.' He smiled. 'You are fully recovered, I believe. No, don't concern yourself, Lucia' – patting the air. 'I have discussed it with Mathilde. We are happy for you to continue to live here.'

'We would be delighted,' said Mathilde.

I gushed my thanks. 'But I can't stay here ad infinitum. I have to get on with my life.'

'Quite so,' said John. 'And in that regard, we would be very pleased to sponsor your trip to Rennes.'

I am a cunning little vixen, for sure, this time entirely by default. Without realising it, this was what I had been aiming for. 'John, that's very generous, but as I said Lucien is just too young to make the trip.'

TWENTY-THREE

ONDAY, 24 NOVEMBER. I was on a train bound for Rennes, travelling third-class despite John's insistence I travel in second. The wooden seat was uncomfortable. Fortunately, my seat was on the end of the row, affording me a view from the window.

The Wynburnes had 'bribed' me into going to Rennes – talked me out of taking Lucien when he became colicky, crying all the time. Mathilde had been persuasive: *If Lucien were taken ill, there would be no doctor readily available. Anyway, you'll be back in a couple of days.*

The excitement of travelling by train for the first time had paled, such was my guilt at leaving my son.

I attempted to read *Wuthering Heights* but couldn't concentrate.

The train pulled into Rennes late afternoon. I prayed *la poste* was open. A porter pointed me in the direction of place de la République. The sun strained through light cloud. I wrapped the shawl around my shoulders. There was a pension on rue Duhamel off l'avenue de la Gare where I installed myself for the night. At seven francs the room was adequate, the sheets clean.

A while later I arrived at *la poste*. It was closed. The notice on the door told me it opened at nine and closed at four. I returned to the pension, determined to lighten my mood. I tried *Wuthering Heights* again, took it with me to the small dining room on the ground floor. A dish of fish for dinner followed by cheese, a *demi* of Muscadet to wash it down. I only managed a few pages, such was my apprehension.

Next morning, I screamed myself awake from a horrible dream where a ferocious-looking Sir Reginald Markham offered me and Alie a ride in the berlin: Markham pulling Alie onto his lap, his huge member bearing down on her; me attacking Markham, the carriage spinning out of control.

After breakfast I walked to *la poste*, arrived early. After a short wait the doors opened. A middle-aged gentleman in uniform was seated behind a desk. Smile firmly in place, I asked him if I could locate the address of persons living in Rennes.

Looking down his nose: 'We sell stamps, not addresses, mademoiselle.'

'Monsieur,' I said, looking sweet and innocent. 'My elder sister, Louise, lives in Rennes. Two weeks ago our father died.' Sniffing into a handkerchief: 'There is the question of his estate. My sister is entitled to her half, modest though it is.'

'But surely you have her address, mademoiselle?'

'If I had I wouldn't be troubling you, monsieur.'

He sighed. 'Excuse me, mademoiselle.'

After walking over to a counter, he spoke with another man. 'Come,' he said, waggling a finger at me.

I repeated my story to a Monsieur Veraque, using my handkerchief to full effect. 'Louise went away with a man named Pierre Lamarck. They eloped. Broke my mother's heart. We were given to understand that she was living in Rennes, monsieur.'

'We are a sorting office, mademoiselle, not a repository for people's addresses.'

'Oh dear.'

'Please don't worry, though. The place for your enquiries is the Hôtel de Ville. Ask for a friend of mine, Monsieur Levanson, of the tax office. Tell him I sent you.'

Fifteen minutes later I presented myself at the Mairie de Rennes. A woman directed me to the tax department on the first floor. After a brief wait, I faced a middle-aged balding man with a goatee and pince-nez. He reminded me of one of 'Émile's' arty friends at La Closerie des Lilas. He was unsmiling until I told him that his friend Monsieur Veraque of *la poste* had sent me.

I repeated my story for the third time, handkerchief in hand. 'Lamarck,' he said. 'Pierre, you say. A bit irregular but for a good cause. If you would kindly wait, I'll see what I can dig out.'

Monsieur Levanson eventually re-emerged, a piece of paper in his hand. 'The address, mademoiselle,' he said with a bow.

Thanking him, I asked for directions to rue des Dames.

Leaving the Mairie, I prepared myself for disappointment. At least Pierre Lamarck was not a figment of Junius's imagination. Would they welcome me as a friend of his or treat me as another abandoned mistress in a long line of abandoned mistresses? Or try to get rid of me, fob me off? I prayed Junius was there.

I arrived at the entrance to the cathedral. Rue des Dames was straight ahead, number 17 a short walk away. Not much sign of life – hardly surprising: the Lamarcks would be out at work. I rapped on the door, held my breath.

Nothing.

I rapped again, rather impatiently. Again, nothing.

I peered through a window. The floorboards were exposed, although there was a chair in a corner, somewhat forlorn, though.

I thumped on the door with my fists. Close to tears I tried to reason with logic: *The Lamarcks were out at work.*

A voice behind me. 'Can I help you, dearie?'

I turned around. A woman of a certain age was leaning on a stick and wearing a mob cap, missing teeth revealed when she smiled at me. 'They left two weeks ago,' she said.

I breathed in deeply. 'How do you mean, madam?'

'We used to chat Mademoiselle Lamarck and meself. Lovely,

she was, 'er brother too. I used to mind their 'ouse, when they was away.'

'Away…? Maybe they will return, Madame…'

'Duval, and a pleasure too' – sticking out a hand. 'I can't see them returning, though, mam'selle. Lovely pair…'

I found myself agreeing with Madame Duval despite my churning insides. 'A pity. Where do you think they have gone?'

'He was something to do with the navy, so she said. Must 'ave been called away to his ship, like. On manoeuvres, per'aps.'

Disappointment dug a pit in my stomach. And after a feeble attempt to thank her, I sloped away. I tried to clear my head. My trip had been a waste of time. I would take the first available train back to Paris.

Then it occurred to me: I was halfway across France. The opportunity would not present itself again. That the train service terminated at Rennes was inopportune. The journey by post-chaise might take a day. I would be in Brest tomorrow evening at best. I would make enquiries, stay the night and return to Rennes the following day – back in Paris on Friday night.

Lengthening my stride, I crossed the river. Walked by the side of la Vilaine, then down l'avenue de la Gare. The station clock told me it was just before noon. The clerk behind the desk informed me the train to Paris left at ten past.

I was tempted to take it – abandon my things in the pension and my ridiculous notion of travelling to Brest. The next train was at eight the following morning.

I was in two minds. I could hear Madame Thierry: *Never be indecisive, Kiki. Indecision will kill you.* Shaking my head, I asked the clerk where I could catch the post-chaise to Brest.

Soon I was queuing for a fare, in front of me some young naval types who gawked at me. I smiled blankly, tried to ignore them. One tried to engage me in conversation, a tall fellow in a blue tunic with its white flap collar and starched white belt. Some joshing from his friends: 'Renaud is trying to get lucky again,' one quipped. 'Leave her alone,' said another.

I decided to talk to him. 'Monsieur, you're on your way to the academy at Brest?'

Renaud nodded. 'I've just spent two weeks' leave, mademoiselle.'

'How long does it take to get there by coach?'

'Depends on the weather. If it is dry, over a day and a half. If it's wet, well…'

'When's the next post-chaise?'

'Two o'clock.'

'Do you think there will be space for me?'

'No chance, I'm afraid. We're all trying to buy fares as well.'

'You'll be lucky to get one tomorrow,' said one of Renaud's friends.

'I'll try my luck all the same.'

'Why are you going to Brest, might I ask?'

'To see a friend.'

'Lucky man,' said Renaud's friend.

'They won't let you on board,' said Renaud.

'The commandant is a stickler for these things,' said the friend. 'Women are taboo.'

'The commandant?'

'The officer in charge, the big cheese that runs the place.'

'So whom would I speak to if I wanted information?'

'Why, may I ask, mademoiselle?' said Renaud's friend.

'As I said, I'm looking for a friend.'

Someone whistled. 'I'm looking for a friend as well.'

'Shut up, Arnaud,' said Renaud. 'Who, may I ask, mademoiselle?'

'Junius Girard.'

'Anyone heard of this Girard fellow?'

After some discussion, Renaud shook his head. 'I'm afraid not, mademoiselle. Hardly surprising, though, as we are relatively new Bordaches.'

I felt myself sinking but carried on. 'Bordaches?'

'Yes, the academy is housed in an old ship – the *Borda*.'

'How quaint.'

'When did this Girard fellow become a cadet?'

Racking my memory, I make a guess: 'Early last year, late 1860, perhaps.'

'Ah, that's a long time on the *Borda*. We all joined in September. The older cadets tend to shun us newbies.'

'And there is the war,' said one of the others.

'In Mexico,' I said. 'How do you mean?'

'Our navy is a massive support operation, men and supplies. Your friend might have left the *Borda* before completing his training.'

I clung to straws. 'How long does the training take?'

'Two years, mademoiselle.'

I thought to myself… if Junius had commenced training in late 1860, he would be close to completing the course. He could be back in Meursault or in Mexico or still in Brest?

I had no alternative: the Wynburnes were driving me mad and Meursault was out of the question. Although I loved Paris it was a dangerous place for me to be. Anyway, I had no money. There was always Joelie and her disgusting proposal. No, I had to find Junius.

The cadets had reached the front of the queue. Arnaud turned to me: 'We're on the two o'clock tomorrow afternoon. No more seats, I'm afraid.'

My turn at the front of the queue. I asked the ticket man the time of the next available coach.

'Six o'clock Thursday morning, mademoiselle.'

'Arriving when?'

'Eight at night the following day.'

I hesitated. I was in a fluster. 'Hurry up,' someone behind me said in a loud voice. I would not be back in Paris until Monday at the earliest. I couldn't leave Lucien that long and shook my head. As I turned to leave, a man barged in front of me. He was in a sweat, despite the weather. 'I am unable to travel to Brest,' he said to the ticket vendor. 'Family circumstances... I wish to cancel my fare and receive a refund. Please.'

The vendor rolled his eyes.

'Monsieur,' I said, tapping the man on the shoulder, 'at what time is your post-chaise?'

'Two o'clock tomorrow afternoon, mademoiselle. What's it to you?'

'I will buy your fare.'

'Hold on,' said the vendor.

'Please' – giving him the sweetest of smiles.

'Bit irregular.'

'Go on, let her have it,' said the man with 'family circumstances'.

I clutched the ticket. Renaud and Arnaud and the other cadets were drinking at a nearby bar. 'Any luck?' said Arnaud as I passed by.

'I'm on the same coach as you, believe it or not.'

'What a relief. You are welcome to join us, mademoiselle.'

My mood had improved. What did I have to lose? I would be kicking my heels for nearly a day. 'My pleasure,' I said.

Five of them: apart from Renaud and Arnaud, there was Jean-Antoine, Hippolyte (Hippo) and Roland. They competed for my attention – teeth and sparkling eyes in abundance. They were a little younger than me, and certainly a lot less mature. Renaud was their leader, Hippo their undoubted clown. After treating me to a glass of wine I agreed to meet them for supper at a café on rue de Coëtquen.

The following day I woke up late. My head told me I'd had too much to drink. After breakfast I idled round town window-shopping. Just before two we boarded the post-chaise. Apart from the coachman and his relief the carriage had a capacity of ten: six people inside with four on the roof. The cadets offered me the best seat, by the window, facing the direction of travel. Arnaud and Hippo were in the carriage with me, along with a young couple and a gentleman who was travelling alone. The other cadets were on the roof – not so bad, the weather sunny but cool. Hippo kept me entertained with his mimicry and silly faces, the gentleman shooting him sour looks from time to time. Eventually, he quietened down.

Wuthering Heights was a struggle – keeping the book still as the coach rumbled along the road was a challenge. I enjoyed looking at the countryside but fell asleep. I awoke when the coach rattled to a halt. Night-time swathed us in darkness. We had arrived at Broons. 'We spend the night here,' said Arnaud.

Departure the next morning was at six o'clock. Someone knocked on my door. Another night with the cadets was taking its toll. I managed to board the coach with only minutes to spare.

Renaud and Jean-Antoine's turn in the carriage. I dozed, worked out when I would be back in Paris. At eleven we stopped at Saint-Brieuc – a bowl of soup and a chunk of bread while the horses were being changed. Late into the night we arrived at Morlaix. Before dawn we were back on the road. I had Arnaud, Hippo and Roland for company as well as the couple – the gentleman having alighted at Morlaix. Arnaud said Brest would take six hours. We settled in. Now the question that had been vexing me: finding someone at the academy to speak to.

I discussed my problem with the cadets.

Roland said, 'The commandant won't see you, for certain. I could speak to Captain Colinet, the friendliest of our officers.'

'Good idea,' said Arnaud.

'A damned good idea,' mimicked Hippo.

The young wife nudged her husband.

He leant forward: 'Mademoiselle, forgive me, but I could not but overhear your conversation. I might be able to help you. My name is Pierre Massignon, secretary to the commandant. It would be my pleasure to assist you where I can.'

'Monsieur, you are very kind. I am looking for one of your cadets, a friend of mine – Junius Girard.'

'Girard' – shaking his head. 'No, I haven't heard of him. Not unsurprising, though, as I have only been stationed in Brest for three months.'

'Forgive me, but I need to find him as a matter of urgency. I have to return to Paris as soon as possible.'

'Pierre,' said his wife, 'please help mademoiselle as far as you are able.'

'Of course, my dear.'

Monsieur Massignon stared at me. 'You realise that the academy is a ship? You will not be allowed on board. But we do have an office on shore. I will deliver a message there by six tonight. Junius Girard, you say?'

'Yes. I'm very grateful to you, monsieur.'

Taking out a pencil and a notepad he wrote something down and carefully tore out a page. 'The address, mademoiselle.' Handing me the notepad: 'Write down your name, please.'

Madame Massignon smiled at me.

We arrived in Brest before noon. Excited chatter among the cadets as we thanked the coachman and his relief. We hauled our luggage down a long, steep flight of steps to the quayside. Jean-Antoine took my bag.

Activity everywhere: men crawling over a ship under construction, huge ribs of wood sticking out from its keel. 'The *Valeureuse*,' Roland assured me. Rows of cannon and piles of wooden beams littered the quay, as well as chunks of masonry and sundry boxes. A narrow stretch of water, sailors crossing what appeared to be a half-submerged walkway to the bank opposite.

Arnaud said, 'The Pont de Recouvrance, it opens like a door.'

The place churned with noise – seagulls diving and screeching.

Madame Massignon, her face ruddy with cold, appeared ready to leave and tipped her head at me. 'Pierre will keep his word, mademoiselle,' she said. I squeezed her hand and thanked her. A nod from her husband and they were away.

My cadets, all five of them, gathered round me to say their goodbyes. They all kissed my hand. Jean-Antoine smuggled a fold of paper into my palm. I wished them *all the best* and curtsied as they took their leave.

I was freezing and climbed back up the steps somewhat mournfully. With six hours to spare, I found the post-chaise booth to book my return trip to Rennes. A place on the six o'clock next morning was available and I paid the fare.

I found somewhere to eat. It *was* lunchtime. All sorts were about: fishermen sucking on pipes, two gentlemen in frock coats, a gang of rowdy stevedores. I was the only woman in the place. The smell was intoxicating – steamed fish and the aroma of *soupe des poissons*.

I was starving – the sea air – with only a mug of tea for breakfast. I checked my purse – forty-five francs and a few centimes. A blackboard told me the *plat du jour* was fish stew and bread: one franc and twenty centimes. The waiter arrived. After ordering the *plat* and a glass of Muscadet I took Jean-Antoine's note out of my reticule.

Morlaix

27 November 1862

Dearest Mademoiselle Lucia,

Sorry to write to you like this, but I really enjoyed the time you spent with us cadets on the way to Brest. It was good for our esprit, especially mine, as we return to the Borda after leave. I find it difficult returning to my studies, dread it in a way, and I miss my family, especially my sister, Louise, who reminds me of you (she is very beautiful).

I know it is presumptuous but I would like to see you again. Should you wish to write, my address is c/o Brest Naval Training Centre. My surname is Anquetil.
    I am lonely and not cut out for all-male company.

In hope,
Jean-Antoine

The *plat* was placed on the table. I dunked bread in the stew, took a couple of mouthfuls, reread the letter. I couldn't help but smile – so sweet he told me I was beautiful, likening me to his sister. And missing his family as a well-brought-up young man should. He could be no more than sixteen years old – same as me, although a lot less worldly. It weighed on me… I had grown up too quickly. I could thank my family for that.

I wolfed down the stew and prayed Lucien would turn out as daring and well-mannered as Jean-Antoine Anquetil. My cynical side wished Jean-Antoine could have supplied his family's address. I might have thrown myself on their hospitality.

I checked the address Monsieur Massignon had given me. The waiter informed me the office was down the steps on the quay. I paid my bill and asked him where I could stay the night: 'Not too expensive, though.'

On leaving the café, I trudged back down the steps to the office. A beefy seaman, with two chevrons and an anchor on the arm of his tunic, informed me they closed at six thirty. I asked him to keep an eye out for a letter addressed to Lucia d'Arnay from Monsieur Massignon, beaming my brightest of smiles.

Next stop was rue Neptune. Back up the steps again. The building looked well kept. Madame Denemet showed me to my room. I whiled away the time with *Wuthering Heights*, then returned to the quayside. The petty officer waved at me. 'Your letter, mam'selle.'

I gushed my thanks and opened it – my hands shaking.

Brest Naval Training Centre

28 November 1862

Dear Mademoiselle d'Arnay,

I have checked the status of ex-Naval Cadet Junius Girard. I can inform you that he left the training centre on 31 August this year having passed out with distinction as a marine.

Sub-lieutenant Girard was posted to the Redoutable in Brest to join the fleet in Campeche on the Gulf of Mexico. I can inform you that the Redoutable continues in active service.

I hope this letter provides you with some comfort.

Je vous prie d'agréer mes salutations distinguées,
Pierre Massignon

Rereading the letter, I didn't know what to think. But I did feel a glow of pride. Strange. The news did not help my immediate plight – it made it worse: I had no one to rely on except myself.

I asked the petty officer if he knew the *Redoutable*.

'Fine ship, mam'selle. She sailed for Mexico, if I recall.'

'Someone I know is serving on her. A sub-lieutenant, a marine.'

'A marine? They are special… an elite, so to speak. Would you mind giving me his name, mam'selle?'

'Junius Girard.'

'Girard… yes, I remember him. That's right… he returned two weeks late for the start of term in January. Injured, he was. The commandant was most put out. In fact, Girard would have been discharged but he made his excuses – his injuries – and persuaded the commandant to let him stay. A charmer, he was.'

'You said he was injured?'

'His face was covered with bandages, his eyes black and blue, and he walked with a limp. I remember… yes, he said he'd been attacked by dogs.'

The whole grizzly scene in the winery was there in my mind's eye. My last sight of Junius: lying there on the straw, his clothes soaked with blood.

Three days later I was on the train between Rennes and Paris. Despite my failure to find Junius I was in a fever of excitement. Lucien. I had not seen him in seven days. He would have changed – certainly bigger and his hair would have grown. A tooth may have appeared.

The ticket inspector worked his way through the carriage. I searched for my ticket. At the bottom of my reticule was Joelie's card with its copperplate lettering. I couldn't help but smile: the address. The inspector asked for my ticket and clipped it. 'Have a good journey, mam'selle.'

December 1, 1862. It was dark when the train pulled into the station at Montparnasse. I walked as fast as I could up boulevard du Montparnasse, weaved through the streets and arrived at rue de l'Ouest. Few people were about. Fine beads of rain hung in the still night air. The pavements were glassy – light in gleaming pools below the gas lamps.

I felt my confidence rise with every step. I could hardly contain myself.

On arriving outside the house, I noticed the shutters were closed. Fear hammered through me. I rapped the knocker, quietly at first; soon I was pounding the door.

Nothing. I squinted between the shutters – inside was dark with no sign of life. Then I was blubbering and tearing at the door with my nails, sinking to my knees. Despite my frenzy I sensed a presence behind me. A pair of hands grabbed me, forcing my arms behind my back. Something was wrapped round my wrists and I started to scream.

'Madame Monnier,' a voice said, 'you are wanted for

questioning. Do not struggle, it will do you no good.' Instinctively, I lashed out with my feet. A grunt from behind: '*Putain de merde.*' Someone slapped me. There were two of them. I felt their grip tighten, the sensation of being pulled backwards, my feet bumping down the steps, across the cobbles. A wagon, a pair of black horses waiting, their backs slick with rain. For a moment I was on my feet, but not for long before I was lifted and bundled into the back. I screamed for all I was worth and then a rag was stuffed in my mouth. Someone pushed my head down to the floor, holding it there. I wriggled but couldn't move.

I fought for self-control as the carriage rattled over cobblestones. I tried to focus on Lucien, his face, his nose, his bonny smile when he wrapped a pudgy hand round my fingers, his milky warm smell when he nuzzled at my breast, the marks on his body, peculiar only to him. It didn't take me long to work out I'd been betrayed – betrayed by the Wynburnes. I cursed them to eternal damnation, the fires of unremitting hell. Apart from Gustav Bonifay no one knew I was living with the Wynburnes. It *had* to be the Wynburnes.

It had to be Mathilde.

Her face when she rocked my baby. All she wanted was one of her own. *To hell with Lucia, it doesn't matter about her. She's a salope anyway, disposable and incapable of bringing up a child.*

And John Walter Wynburne: *Yes, dear, certainly, dear, anything you say, dear... what about Lucia? No, dear, she'll survive, dear... relieved we took the baby off her hands, dear.*

TWENTY-FOUR

I REMEMBER BEING rough-hauled out of the carriage into a large building, my bag and reticule being taken from me, a large man in uniform taking imprints of my hand, signing a paper, being searched by a woman with missing teeth, being thrown into a cell containing several other women. Catcalls. The door clunking shut behind me.

I looked around, wild-eyed – a large cell with six other women inside. A single window with vertical iron bars was the only ventilation. A cold draught pervaded the place. Bunk beds were arranged along the walls. The women stared at me. One said, 'What 'ave we got 'ere?' Another: 'A proper little madam.' Another: 'Aw, leave 'er alone, can't you see it's 'er first time?'

One darted forward and fingered my dress. I was confused and gathered my senses as best I could. My instincts told me that I needed to lash out, make my presence felt, and so I kicked her away. 'Anyone else want to have a go?' I said coolly, staring each in the eye, my arms akimbo. One woman started to stand. 'Don't,' I warned her.

More staring, but I felt I had the situation under control. 'Where do I sleep?' I asked.

'Can't you count, *dearie*? There are six bunks. You'll 'ave to wait your turn. Ha! Dead men's shoes, if you know what I m'ean.'

Someone threw me a blanket.

The thing was clammy and smelt. Lying down between two of the bunks I made myself comfortable as best I could, despite the freezing floor. I closed my eyes. My hate for the Wynburnes was so intense that sleep was impossible. I tried to calm myself – images of Lucien, prayed he was well cared for. Though I was sure he was – Mathilde would be doting on him, spoiling him, kissing him.

I must have drifted off until a man nudged me awake, dragging me out of the cell and down a series of passages to a dark, windowless room. Forcing me to sit he bound my arms to the back of a chair. I protested. He told me to shut up and left.

A while later Oreste Monnier walked in carrying a lamp. 'Ah, Kiki,' he said, 'you have proved elusive. My brother was murdered a year ago. Where have you been?'

'None of your business, monsieur. Why I am here? I've done nothing wrong.'

'Then why did you run away?'

'Your brother was abusing me, as you are doing.' I strained against the rope.

'By running away, you have implicated yourself.'

'Implicated myself in what, Oreste?'

'The murder of my brother.'

'Murder? I learnt of his death from a newspaper.'

'Then you should have come forward, explained yourself, availed yourself of the French justice system.'

'Justice system, bah. Look at me, Oreste, in your filthy prison, snatched off the street. Restrained while you interview me. Is this how justice treats people?'

'All right,' he said, walking behind me and untying the rope. 'Now, tell me what happened?'

'Augustave confined me to my room after I discovered his dogfighting activities, his gambling. You saw it with your own eyes, Oreste. At Christmas.'

He shook his head. 'Continue.'

'I decided to escape. I had no choice.'

'Junius Girard helped you.'

'Have you questioned him?'

'I am asking the questions.'

'Well, have you?'

He shook his head again. 'By the time I arrived in Meursault he had disappeared.'

'You never thought of visiting him in Brest?'

'That's enough. I want your version of events.'

I told him what had happened, omitted the part about being branded. I was *not* going to tell him *that*. 'The dogs were out of control and attacked Guillaume. They turned on your brother as I was leaving the winery with Florian.'

'Madame Gaillard and Guillaume's father, Benoît, say you encouraged the dogs to attack Augustave.'

'Humph. They would, wouldn't they? Remember, the dogs weren't mine. That they turned on their masters is hardly surprising given how badly he treated them.'

'You were pregnant, so I am told.'

I was prepared for this question. 'I was,' I whispered.

Irritation marred his face. 'Well?'

'*Well*, I got rid of the thing.'

'*The thing*, you realise what you have done?'

'The idea of having Augustave's brat was repugnant to me. Anyway, how could I support it, on the run and hounded by the likes of you?'

That rocked him. I could see the guilt in his eyes. 'That's ridiculous,' he said.

'The facts of life on the Paris streets, monsieur.'

'How did you find your way to Paris?' he muttered.

'No, monsieur. My travel arrangements are my business.'

'Are you Gaston Artagne?'

Rolling my eyes: 'Do I look like a boy?'

'My men in Beaune questioned Madame Thierry, you know.'

This stopped me in my tracks, but I forced myself not to blink. 'My old schoolteacher. Lovely woman. Taught me everything I know.'

'So you're not going to tell me, Kiki?'

'Tell you what?'

'How you arrived in Paris.'

'As I said… none of your business. Of course, the Wynburnes know all about me.'

'Oh, them.'

'Ah, so you know who they are?'

Oreste avoided my eyes and turned away.

'They betrayed me, admit it.'

He reddened. 'I ask the questions, Kiki.'

'What's going to happen to me? How will this French *justice* of yours run its course?'

'You have been uncooperative, Kiki. It will go against you. You will be tried for the murder of Augustave.'

'Good, the truth will come out. I can't wait.'

'Don't be so sure. You're forgetting the witness statements – Madame Gaillard's and Monsieur Ligerot's.'

'Huh, those two frauds.'

'Oh, you think so?'

'They hated me.'

'They both say you yelled at the dogs, encouraged them to attack Augustave. That you often visited the dogs' enclosure, fed them scraps.'

I closed my eyes. 'They are lying. I certainly felt sorry for the dogs once I knew they were being abused.'

'Abused?'

'They were fighting dogs, Oreste. I witnessed one of the fights. Sir Reginald Markham was there. Ask him, he should know. He sold your precious brother the dogs. And he was taking bets with Augustave, winning money off him. Augustave couldn't even afford to pay his taxes. Don't tell me you don't know about *that*.'

'Their statements were taken under oath.'

'You are not listening to a word I've said.'

He rolled his eyes.

I decided to mention Florian. 'Florian, Madame Gaillard's son, knows exactly what happened.'

'So why did he run away? He's not been seen since.'

'Because he cut off Guillaume's hand defending me.'

'Guillaume's hand?'

'Don't tell me you don't know about *that* as well, Oreste. Le Blaireau overlooking a major detail. Tut-tut. You imagined his hand was bitten off by one of the mastiffs, or you simply didn't notice? God…'

He blustered. 'I was not at the scene of the crime. The local sergeant—'

'Huh, there you are. It's all supposition on your part.'

'The report… don't presume to tell me how to do my duty, madam.'

'Your duty is to ensure justice is done.'

He looked fit to explode and rubbed his chin as though he was about to say something. Then, appearing to have changed his mind, he stomped out of the room.

Five days later I was charged with the murder of Augustave Olivier Baptiste Monnier and Guillaume Ligerot. My trial was set for Monday, 22 December 1862.

Three of the six original women had left the cell and were replaced by three others. I was now accepted, to the extent that I considered myself their leader. You make friends and enemies quickly in those places, and Brigitte had become a friend. She told me we had no chance of escape, but not to give up, that justice would be done. She was trying to lift my spirits, bless her. *That justice would be done* – nonsense.

I remember us indulging ourselves, working out how we might escape, from seducing the guards and taking the keys to escaping through the latrines. We knew the guard roster off by heart: three shifts of eight hours each, two guards per shift. Changing at six in the morning, at two in the afternoon, at ten at night – our way of telling the time. They were all male. One drooled over us. I was sure he was 'abusing' himself behind the door.

Food was pushed through the grille at the bottom of the door at eight in the morning and five in the afternoon. Mostly bread and water but sometimes a foul-tasting porridge or a chunk of mouldy cheese. As top dog I separated the food into six portions – a little extra for Lottie, who was nine months' pregnant.

She was our latest intake and was allowed visitors. She admitted to being a prostitute but told me that Maurice, the father of her child, loved her. His daily visits sparked an idea in me. One morning I asked Lottie if Maurice wouldn't mind doing something for me.

My conundrum: who on the outside could help me. Herr Schiel had money but was plodding and wouldn't be able to react quickly enough, to say nothing of his wife. Monsieur Bonifay, whom I trusted, was also a plodder with a tendency to panic. And he knew the Wynburnes, so not him. I boiled it down to Joelie who, though resourceful, was not entirely trustworthy. Would she help me? Why would she? She *had* to help me. I had no other choice. Her address? Her card was in my reticule; I had found it there while rummaging for my train ticket. Remember smiling when I read it. I racked my brains… then it came to me: number 12 rue Madame.

Next day my *avocat commis d'office* paid me a visit – a gaunt, middle-aged stick by the name of Bernot Grasse. Our interview was held in a small, windowless room. He appeared in a hurry and waved me through my story. 'Yes, yes,' he repeated with impatient flicks of his hand. He didn't appear shocked by what I told him. I omitted telling him about my brand and Lucien.

'Has Florian Gaillard been found?' I enquired.

'Not that I am aware,' he said, taking notes. 'I'll check with the police, though.'

'And Junius Girard?'

'You have just told me he is a marine in the navy, with the fleet in Mexico. Not much use to us there, is he?'

'What is the basis of our defence, monsieur?'

He shrugged. 'We will concentrate on the dogfighting aspect, although there is no proof that Monsieur Monnier and his "assistant", Guillaume Ligerot, were, in fact, dog fighters.'

'Oh, for God's sake, everyone knew. Whose side are you on? Go to Meursault and find out.'

'I don't have the t—'

'Your laziness will result in my execution' – fighting to control my temper.

'I am an *avocat commis* paid by the state who will not sanction a trip to Bourgogne. The cost.'

'Madame Gaillard and Benoît have to attend the trial. You must insist. Under oath they w—'

'Your trial is in Paris – impractical for those two to attend.'

'That is outrageous.'

'We have their statements, madam.'

I huffed. It was clear I was a nobody to Monsieur Grasse. I tried another tack. 'There were witnesses to the dog fight, *paysans* mostly. But one person in particular: an Englishman, Sir Reginald Markham, a *négociant* here in Paris. His firm is Markham père et fils. Well known in the wine trade and very well known in dogfighting circles, I assure you.'

Monsieur Grasse continued making notes. 'I'll try to find him,' he said with an impatient brush of his hand.

'Yes, *do* try.' Then: 'By the way, can I borrow a pencil and paper?'

Scowling, he tore a couple of pages out of his notepad, handing them to me together with the pencil.

'Mind if I keep the pencil?'

'Very well' – scraping back his chair.

'What will happen to me if I'm found guilty, monsieur?'

Shaking his head: 'I believe you know the answer to that, Madame Monnier.'

Maurice visited Lottie the following day. Passing a note to him was child's play.

The night before I had discovered a louse in my hair. I remember pulling it out, squashing it between my fingernails, a minute, grey slug – its goo on my fingers. I banged on the cell door and called for the guard. Didn't let up, and my cellmates joined in. The guard rattled the bars with his nightstick, shouting at us to shut up. I explained the louse problem to him, made him agree to reporting it to the proper authorities.

Three days later, before the two o'clock changing of the guard, Lottie received a visitor – a nun, a Carmelite. She went about her business inspecting Lottie. When least expecting it, I heard 'Psst, Gaeta' from her direction. I stared at her intently. To my astonishment, it was Joelie. I resisted the temptation to shout when she stopped me with a discreet slash of her hand. She ignored me and continued to administer to Lottie, but my eyes were fixed on her. When she stood to leave, she dropped a ball of paper on the ground, edging it towards me with her foot.

No one appeared to have noticed. The light was poor.

G,

M has told me of your plight.

He tells me the guards change at 2pm every afternoon.

I intend to arrive at the prison at 1pm on Sunday and gain entrance to your cell before the guards change.

I will be dressed as a nun.

I have paid M, with promises of more. So don't worry about him.

Destroy this note.

Courage,

J

Sunday, 14 December. I was unable to stay still, such was my trepidation. At about one thirty, two large women entered the cell and ordered us to hand over our blankets – 'Now!' We all did as we were told: stripped our bunks. This done, the women proceeded to heft our mattresses out of the door.

Brigitte kicked up a fuss.

'Fumigation,' said one of the women.

Amid the confusion, two 'nuns' entered. With the guards distracted, one of the nuns reached beneath her robe and tossed me a loose assemblage of clothes. She ignored me, tended to Lottie. By the time the women had removed the last of the mattresses, I was dressed in the tunic and scapular of the Carmelite order – wore them below my everyday clothes, having stuffed the cowl under my shift. A wink from Joelie told me I had done the right thing.

The cell door clanged shut. My face dropped; I was close to tears.

Joelie took out her pocket watch, looked at it though she had not a care in the world, nodded to her fellow nun who then rapped on the grille to be let out. The door opened and she was gone.

At two o'clock, the guard changed. A nod from Joelie and I stripped off my shift, stuffing it behind a bunk. Draping the cowl over my head, I joined Joelie who was still fussing over Lottie. A minute later she stood and headed towards the cell door. I followed. She told the guard that we had finished our business and that Lottie *must* be provided with better food. 'A disgrace. You don't want a dead pregnant woman on your hands, do you?'

The door opened – two nuns had entered and two had exited – and we walked through the Conciergerie, the humble servants of Our Lord.

Outside, we gathered our habits and ran, turning right and crossing the Seine via the Petit Pont. 'Sanctuary,' Joelie gasped when we entered the church of Saint-Séverin. We adopted the prayer position on pews to the side and the back. I was about to talk but she shushed me. Half an hour later she stood and, taking my arm, led me out onto the backstreets of Saint-Germain. Not a word passed her lips until we were on the Sorbonne side of rue des Écoles where she proceeded to jump up and down. 'We did it, Gaeta! *We did it.*'

I flung my arms around her. 'How can I ever thank you, Joelie?'

'Oh, I'll find a way. Don't you worry, dear.'

At her apartment on rue Madame, she handed me a glass of cognac as I stripped off my disguise. I drained it in a single swig, luxuriating as the liquor seemed to burn to the very ends of my fingertips.

Joelie walked behind me, stroked her chin. 'Still beautiful,' she said. 'A bit scrawny, and your hair, tsk-tsk. Won't do. No, won't do at all. We need to fatten you up. And plenty of sleep.'

TWENTY-FIVE

THE FOLLOWING MORNING I was pleasantly surprised at not waking up in my cell. The bed was soft; the pillows smelt of lavender. I stretched like a cat and scratched my head – the lice a reminder of my time in the Conciergerie.

Joelie walked in with a cup of something. 'Sleep well?' she said.

'Like the dead,' I said, scratching my hair.

'Head lice?'

'Afraid so.'

'I know all about lice. They love clean hair but hate oil of anise. A couple of treatments will see you right. I suggest you get up and wash. I've heated water like the good chambermaid I was.'

In her bathroom she tipped boiling water into a basin. 'Don't wash your hair, not yet anyway,' she said.

I lathered the carbolic into my skin as hard as I could.

'Just popping out,' she said, dumping clothes onto a chair.

I was immediately on my mettle; my instincts were shrieking at me. *Is Joelie after the reward?* She would have spent money on my escape, run a huge risk. No, I was being stupid, surely? I was worried, nevertheless.

Soon I was dressed and ready for a fight, a kitchen knife to hand. Joelie entered the apartment with a bag on her arm. 'Sit down,' she said, glancing at the knife. 'You once told me you would kill me if I betrayed you. Thought I would hand you in, did you?'

I pulled a face, mumbled an apology.

'Gaeta, take off your top.'

I stripped to my waist and sat down.

'Oil of anise,' said Joelie.

I remember the feeling: the heat as the oil permeated my scalp, a soothing yet burning sensation. I shivered, the hairs on the back of my neck erect, my nipples hard. 'You have a good touch, Joelie.'

'That's what they all say' – wrapping a towel round my head. 'You must leave this on for at least half an hour.'

Later we were tucking into one of her famous omelettes – garlic, onions, bacon and parsley, washed down with a red wine I didn't recognise.

'A Chinon,' she said, raising her glass. 'The last time we met you told me your story – the old man you were forced to marry, the dog fight, some beau, your escape to Paris… on a barge, I recall.'

I mopped my plate with bread.

'Come on, Gaeta, or whatever your name is, you can tell Auntie Joeline.'

I exhaled and sipped my wine. Feeling light-headed, an urge got the better of me – I needed to tell someone the truth. 'My name is Christine Vellay. Friends and family call me Kiki. "The old man", my husband, was Augustave Monnier.'

Joelie pursed her lips.

'I was forced to marry him in exchange for a piece of land. The Vellays have been vineyard labourers for generations and wanted to grow their own crop. I met someone… a navy cadet, who helped me escape. But the escape went wrong and my husband was killed by his own dogs.'

'Like Actaeon.'

'Actaeon?'

'Who spotted Artemis in her bath. Her modesty assailed, she turns him into a stag, which his hounds proceed to rip to shreds.'

'Seems a little extreme.'

'You said you made your way to Paris on a barge.'

'A wonderful family saved me.'

'I remember mentioning the newspaper article to you. Where a well-known policeman, Le Blaireau, questioned the skipper of a barge about someone on the run.'

For some reason I did not want Joelie knowing about Oreste. But she had me cornered. 'Le Blaireau is Oreste Monnier, Augustave's twin, the policeman who captured and imprisoned me. I was supposed to go on trial just before Christmas.'

'For a murder you did not commit.'

'I didn't know Augustave had been killed until I read it in *Le Figaro*.'

'You said you were protected by an older friend.'

'I was, but there's no point in telling you her name.'

Joelie pouted – gave me the eye. 'So what happened to your *beau*?'

'I went to the Naval Academy in Brest but, too late, his ship had already sailed for Mexico, the war there.'

'That folly.'

I shrugged.

'Anything else you want to tell me?'

I shook my head – she did not need to know about Lucien and the Wynburnes, or about the brand next to my vagina.

'How were you captured?'

'Funnily enough, I had just returned home from Brest, and two policemen were waiting for me.'

'So once again you are on the run for murder.'

I shrugged again.

'We will have to give you a new name and change your appearance, create a new world for you, Kiki.' She smiled. 'Incidentally, I like the name "Kiki".'

'More's the pity we can't use it.'

The next day we repeated the anise-oil treatment. Joelie insisted I follow a strict diet: milk, lean meat, fruit, vegetables, infusions of *verveine*, mint and sage, wine limited to two glasses a day. She ordered me to wash my hair with a light application of soap. Then we proceeded to the next phase of 'my hair': Joelie's not-so-secret formula of egg yolks, olive oil and water, left to soak for half an hour.

Joelie was away most of the day 'on business'. One night after supper, a knock on the door. Joelie sighed, an anguished look on her face.

A girl tottered in – beautiful despite her tangled hair, her smudged lipstick, her puffy eyes. Joelie manoeuvred her onto an ottoman. The girl was bawling her eyes out, clenching and unclenching her fists.

'Calm, Babette, calm,' said Joelie. 'What did he do to my baby? Aw, you'll be all right, girl. Couple of days and rest, and you'll be as right as rain.'

She turned to me. 'She'll have to have your room for the night.'

After draping towels over the bottom sheet, we put her to bed. Joelie spooned a tincture from a blue bottle into her mouth and soon Babette was asleep.

Next morning, there were three of us for breakfast. Babette was smiling despite her bruised face. 'Who are you?' she said, pouring herself coffee.

'A friend of Joelie's, from our days as chambermaids.'

'Do you have a name?'

'I prefer not to mention my name, if you don't mind.'

Joelie was cagey too. 'Babette, life has been difficult for my friend here. Like you, she needs to recover from an unfortunate episode.'

Babette was tall, skinny and blonde, her hair a tangle of ringlets, her ears cute. She had a birthmark to the side of her mouth. Her eyes were blue but hard. Her beautiful teeth showed to advantage when she smiled, though I *was* reminded of a shark. She liked to talk and told us of the night before with her client in the Pavillon de la Reine. 'He attacked me once he found out I was having my *règles*. Went mad and demanded I return his fee, kicked and punched me. If I hadn't smashed his head with a lamp—'

Joelie stood and screamed at her. 'Never engage with a client when you have your *règles*! How many times I have I told you? Ruins my reputation. Word gets around. Get out! I can't stand the sight of you.'

Babette gathered her belongings, muttering apologies. Joelie slammed the front door behind her.

'She is beautiful. The clients love her, but her brains are between her legs. I meant the bit about my reputation… later today the client will be asking me for a refund, then he'll denigrate me 'round town. *Merde.*'

'Not clever.'

'No, and that's why I look forward to working with you, Kiki. You have more sense.'

'Working with me?'

'Don't act the naive little mam'selle with me. You saw Babette. You know what she does. And *you* will do the same.'

'And if I don't?'

'I will go straight to the police – Oreste Monnier – to the very top.'

'I—'

'You have a short memory, Kiki. Not long ago you were a lice-ridden baggage in the Conciergerie without a sou to your name. Now you are living in the lap of luxury, rent-free, I might add. And talking of money, your escape cost me a pretty packet. Fanny's services—'

'Who's Fanny?'

'The third "nun", the one who left the cell before the guard had changed. She took a big risk, did Fanny. Cost me a fortune. And Maurice, Lottie's excuse for a man, did not come free.'

'Oh, I worry about Maurice. He has your name and address.'

'I told him there are people I know who would be very upset if I was compromised.'

'But—'

'It won't be as bad as you think, Kiki. Christmas is upon us and I want you to complete your beauty rest. You won't have to start until early in the New Year. So you can relax and enjoy my hospitality. I will be here most of the time.'

'All right, tell me about it. There's no harm in hearing your terms.'

'My standard fee is a hundred francs, of which you receive fifty. What the client pays as a bonus is your business. Oh, I insist that you subject yourself to a medical examination every month, on your account, by the way. A doctor I know specialises in these matters.'

'Where do the clients come from? How can you guarantee their provenance?'

'I can't. But most are regulars. As you know, I have people in certain hotels who supply me with "gentlemen", for a fee, of course. Most are well-heeled: from good backgrounds, aristos, bankers, industrialists, soldiers of rank and fortune, scientists in the case of the de Londres, the occasional artist or actor, though I don't really favour this type.'

'All right, Joelie, I do owe you, perhaps with my life.' I hesitated. 'I will go along with your plan, but I want the best of your clients, known to you personally, those that don't attack the Babettes of this world. I will only work three days a week, one client a day.'

She smiled. 'That's better. For what it's worth I actually "work" myself, two "regulars". The men are my friends: they value my company and they take me to lovely places.' Pianoing her ring-bedecked fingers in my face: 'They indulge my desires – material and physical. I also happen to be fond of them, the sex they provide.'

'You make it sound easy.'

'Because it *is* easy, Stupid. I'm not some madam who runs banged-out whores in a brothel, five-times-a-night *cocottes* who'll get the pox and die in penury. No, mine is a bespoke, top-of-the-line operation.'

'How many girls work for you?'

'Five, including Babette. All are as beautiful as her but not as foolish. You will be my "sixth". My best, Kiki.'

'Your best?'

'I have watched you. You know things most other girls don't – including me – wine, languages, the affairs of the day. Some men, believe it or not, love to converse with an intelligent woman and will pay for the privilege.'

I retreated to my room, lay on my back and stared at the ceiling. I had accepted Joelie's proposition, disgusting though it was. I could always change my mind… knew I wouldn't… I had no alternative. I needed money – not centimes from a hotel or a franc an hour from Friedrich Shiel – and protection from the police. And time and money to find Lucien. It boiled down to Lucien, *my* darling son. I tried to block him from my mind. Impossible: he was with me every minute of the day. He would be three months old. Was he teething? Had his hair grown? I imagined him with Mathilde, swaddled and swamped by her, drowned in love. The bloated cow. I prayed she was riven with guilt. It was all her fault.

Or was it? Was I to blame? If I hadn't been so wilful, so selfish, just accepted my lot, my loss of Lucien would never have happened.

I knew I was thinking nonsense. An excuse, if you will. I had done the right thing by running from Augustave Monnier. I put it down to bad luck.

Henceforth, I would not allow myself to wallow in self-reproach. I had to do what I had to do – Joelie was the only way out.

TWENTY-SIX

ARLY IN THE New Year 1863, I was readying myself for my
first 'assignment'.

My 'professional' name was Monique Langeron, after
Louis Alexandre Andrault de Langeron, a Royalist soldier who
left France at the beginning of the Revolution. Joelie's idea: some
nonsense to do with the subconscious effect the name would have
with clients, despite the fact that de Langeron fought on the losing
side at the battle of Austerlitz. I actually liked the name, more for
its titillation factor – sounded like 'lingerie'. That's right... in my
mind I was Mademoiselle Lingerie. *Quelle bêtise.*

Joelie advanced me one hundred francs to buy clothes. The
long nights played to my advantage, with people cramming the
streets over Christmas and the New Year. And dark – easy for me
to remain concealed. I visited Carrefour de l'Odéon – the wanted
poster of Christine Monnier, *also known as...* was no longer
there. Maybe Oreste and his police were ashamed of my escape –
disinclined to advertise their stupidity.

Parisians were still gripped by their cover-women-from-head-
to-toe chapter. Necklines, though, had dropped and more of the arm
was exposed, but skirts still billowed and were worn full length.

One evening I crossed the Seine and made my way to rue du
Faubourg Saint-Honoré and its shops of haute couture.

I perused the window displays. One dress caught my eye – décolleté, the straps on the rounds of the shoulders rendering the arms exposed and secured with buttons at the back, the skirt full. I entered Purcell's and asked the assistant if I could try it on.

I was in a bustle of excitement as I changed. The assistant guided me to a mirror. The dress didn't fit but nevertheless suited me – showed my cleavage to my advantage, my olive skin and my arms.

A man emerged from the back of the shop and clapped his hands. 'Lovely, mademoiselle, but too large.' Shaking his head: 'Alterations are out of the question. Hmm, if you prefer, though, we can make one to fit mademoiselle like a glove. And we can choose a material, how do I say, more suitable to mademoiselle's complexion.' He bowed. 'Clément Purcell at your service.'

I inspected my back in the mirror. Monsieur Purcell was fussing, paying me compliments. 'How much, monsieur?' I enquired.

Looking embarrassed, he coughed. 'Eighty francs, mademoiselle, but for you, ahead of the sales, sixty-five.'

I prevaricated. Eventually, Monsieur Purcell wrung his hands. 'All right, fifty-five francs were you to purchase a pair.'

I shook my head. 'I have to buy shoes and undergarments, monsieur.'

We agreed fifty-five francs for a single dress.

'I will return if it proves a success. I must have it by the tenth of January.'

Monsieur Purcell was full of joy and flattery. 'I adore dressing beautiful women' – running a tape around my hips.

January 10. I was plumped like a goose in Monsieur Purcell's creation. Joelie told me I looked sumptuous. Rubbing her hands: 'The client will be pleased.' After removing my silver 'Florian' necklace, she strapped a single strand of pearls around my neck. 'On loan for the night,' she said.

I was to meet my client at Hôtel Le Meurice on rue de Rivoli. Joelie had hired a cab. She kissed me goodbye. 'Play this right, Monique, and the world is yours.'

As the cab rattled over the cobbles I grew in confidence. The woman in the phaeton crossed my mind as I walked into Le Meurice – putting myself in her place, imagining I owned the hotel. I felt especially brazen when I told the receptionist I had an appointment with Monsieur Fabry.

'An appointment?' he said.

'Yes. And hurry up, I'm not accustomed to being kept waiting.'

A wry smile as he clicked his fingers – a bellboy appeared, seemingly out of nowhere.

According to Joelie, Jacques Fabry was a 'regular' and known to be generous. When I entered his room, he bowed, helped me out of the coat Joelie had lent me, draping it over the back of a chair. He was 'youngish', dressed *à la mode*: dove-grey frock coat, white shirt, winged collar and blue cravat. I remember his shoes shining like jet.

'Champagne, Monique,' he said.

'That would be very agreeable, monsieur.'

He handed me a flute. I'm no aficionado of champagne but knew that the grapes employed were the same as for the wine of Meursault.

We chatted amicably. He was an industrialist from Metz. Steel. And very busy, he explained: the expansion of the railways, the huge demand for track. 'I can't produce enough of the stuff,' he said.

He asked me if I was hungry.

'Starving,' I replied, somewhat unladylike.

More conversation. The food arrived: *soupe aux artichaut* and a dozen oysters from the Belon estuary in Brittany, *and* a Meursault: not a le Merle or an Oubliette, but one I knew. I decided not to show off.

Strange bird, Fabry. He didn't seem to lust after me, no gawking down my cleavage or piercing my eye with a noble look.

After dessert of spiced pears, I was wondering where the evening was leading. A lull in conversation. 'Umm, Jacques, is there anything you want me to do for you?'

'There is, Monique, if you don't mind. I will prepare myself for bed, then issue you with your instructions.'

A spasm in my gut. I prayed something unpleasant was not about to unfold. 'Would you like me to prepare, Jacques?'

'When I give the word.'

Leading me into the bedroom he then disappeared, soon to re-emerge dressed in a nightshirt, nightwear I hadn't seen since my days with Monsieur Monnier. Climbing into bed he propped himself up with pillows as though he was about to watch a play or some such. Lanterns glowed in every corner of the room.

'You are very beautiful, Monique,' he said. 'Please don't mind, but I want you to undress very slowly.'

I smiled. It was a matter of projecting myself into the exotic fantasy I imagined he wished to indulge himself. I wriggled out of my 'Purcell' dress, as smoothly and fluently as I was able, raised the hem of my slip above my waist, looping it over my head before I let it slide to the floor. I felt faintly ridiculous, there in my pretties and 'bindings', so I started to sway, curvaceously, lasciviously, suggestively.

Jacques blinked his eyes.

I turned away from him, unwound my bindings, covered my breasts with my hands, pivoted to face him again. I forced my breasts upwards, exaggerated my cleavage. An intake of breath from Jacques as I took my hands away, one by one. I remember enjoying myself, moving my hips from side to side as I started to lower my pretties, teasing them downwards ever so slowly, turning around several times, shaking my backside at him.

'Come,' he gasped.

I took my time. Trailed my pretties in my hand and slunk into bed. He murmured endearments, told me he loved me – and so forth. I murmured as well. Felt a twinge of guilt when I asked him if he had any protection.

'Do I have to?' he said.

'You do, Jacques.'

A lull in the proceedings. He reached somewhere – some fumbling as he put the thing on. I felt 'down there'; he was wearing a slippery type of glove. Soon he was on top of me, trying to get inside me. I lent him a hand, so to speak. He was surprisingly large for such a small man. I was only half acting when I gasped. And when he came, a ripple of what I felt when Junius had made love to me.

He insisted I stay the night. 'Of course, Jacques,' I purred.

Squeezing himself close to me, we soon fell asleep.

The following morning we had sex one more time. Breakfast of eggs, toast and coffee as we sat there prim and proper in our nightclothes. Not much conversation, though the odd conspiratorial leer from Jacques. Then it was time for me to go. When I was dressed and ready to leave, he bowed and slipped me an envelope – asked me to present his compliments to Madame Joeline. A fleeting kiss and I was out of the door.

Downstairs I found my way to the ladies' and opened the envelope: five crispy twenty-franc notes.

A month and eleven clients later, I was breakfasting with Joelie and cracked: I told her about Lucien and the Wynburnes. I *had* to tell someone; I couldn't keep it bottled up. I made a fool of myself, breaking down in tears – part act, part self-pity. I wanted her to do something for me – walk past the house on rue de l'Ouest, check for signs of life. Explained that I'd rather not risk going myself in case a policeman was there to apprehend me.

At the time I admired Joelie; you asked her to do something and she did it. She went out, soon to return only to tell me news

I expected: that the house was unoccupied, its shutters closed. 'A neighbour informed me the Wynburnes had moved out at the end of November,' she concluded.

'They didn't say where?'

'I'm afraid not.'

As I prated on about Lucien and the Wynburnes, Joelie appeared to be working herself up to something. 'Monique, now you have settled your accounts with me and have established yourself, I'm going to have to ask you to leave.'

'I have already given this some thought, my dear. You have been very generous. God knows where I'd be if you hadn't come to my rescue.'

'I hate to say, but I do regard you as an investment. Well, not quite, that's unfair. I consider you as a friend, a friend who has paid her way. And I do enjoy your company.'

'The feeling is mutual. It *has* crossed my mind to rent a studio. I can't depend on your generosity ad infinitum.'

She suggested I find a place in the streets behind the Sorbonne – rue Mouffetard specifically. 'Overlooking the square would be pleasant.' Then: 'About tonight's client.'

'Tonight is one of my nights off, you know that, Joelie.'

'A special case, Monique. One that will need your special touch, an aristo – a baron, no less – whose wife has just died.'

'So not a regular?'

'No, but he comes highly recommended. The concierge of Hôtel Beaujon is reliable.'

That evening I entered Hôtel Beaujon wearing my second creation by Monsieur Purcell. Despite my nerves I felt self-assured. People smiled at me. The dress was an improvement: the skirts less billowy, the neckline more risqué. And, oh, the colour – dark red and opulent like a Pinot Noir. My hair was drawn back in a chignon, my ears *mignon* with their single pearl earrings. Florian's cross hung daintily above my cleavage.

The bellboy gawped as he ushered me to the second floor. I tipped him a couple of francs, told him to get lost then knocked on the door.

He was tall and thin, in his mid-thirties. His hair was short and dark, his features unadorned by facial hair. The cut of his frock coat was longer than what would be considered fashionable. His jaw dropped, his face a contortion as he struggled to invite me in. The obligatory bottle stood in its crystal cooler. 'Champagne?' he croaked.

'Monsieur.'

He handed me a glass. 'I-I have never done this before. My wife died ten months ago. She was so full of life. The women I've met since simply don't match up to her. Sorry, I must sound such a fool. M-maybe I expect too much, move in the wrong circles – my friends too genteel. I feel in need of excitement with someone I don't know – outside the clique, so to speak.'

'I understand…'

'Armand. Sorry, how rude of me.'

'Armand, my name's Monique. I'm here to make you happy.'

'Happy? I hardly know the meaning of the word anymore. Look, I don't want to impose myself, Monique, so can I suggest we go downstairs and avail ourselves of something to eat?'

We were installed at our table. Admiring glances. Waiters fluttered around us, one poured from a bottle of brut. We clinked our glasses. Silence. Armand rescued by the waiter taking our orders. He deferred to me, and so I chose for both of us, the wine too.

It came out in a torrent; he was desperate to unburden himself: his Virginie dying of the cancer in early 1862; his children, a boy and a girl – Arnaud and Céleste – their devastation; his mother-in-law, the Comtesse Something-or-Other, distraught.

I tried to empathise: 'Oh dear'… 'No'… 'Poor you'… 'Life is cruel, Armand.'

The food arrived – sole meunière, *pommes vapeur*, parsley and capers. The wine, Muscadet Sèvre et Maine sur lie, goes well with fish.

The waiter refilled our glasses. I toasted Armand with a smile. I believed his never-done-this-before story.

'Enough of me, Monique, tell me about yourself, if you want to, that is.'

This often happened and I had it off pat. It was usually followed by, *Why are you doing this, Monique, one so young and intelligent?*

I sipped the wine and reeled off my tiny white lies: escaping the poverty of Chagny for the promise of Paris. Usually I omitted the part where *I was married to a foul old man*. But there was something trustworthy about Armand, so I told him of my marriage without supplying names.

His turn to empathise: 'Women are treated like dirt. There'll be a revolution, mark my words. The wives of my friends talk of suffrage.'

'Suffrage?'

'The vote for women, Monique. Imagine that.'

'The age of consent in this country is thirteen – *thirteen*.'

'A disgrace.'

Dessert was served – crêpe Suzette. The conversation turned to horse racing: Armand's family amateurs of the sport with horses in training, but not anymore. 'Too expensive,' he said. 'And too many losers. My father had a bad run of luck.'

'Oh dear.'

'Have you ever ridden, Monique?'

I looked at him as though he was an idiot – rolled my eyes.

He grinned. 'Tell you what… do you want to go riding? I have access to some horses in Bois de Boulogne.'

'I would love to.'

'Are you free tomorrow?'

I thought about it. 'Umm, I need to buy some kit – boots, jodhpurs—'

'Jodhpurs?'

'I don't favour side-saddle. Restricts movement, with poor control of the horse. I thought you were one for suffrage, Armand.'

'Ha, you have me there. What an old stick-in-the-mud you must think I am.'

'Quite the contrary, monsieur. The fact you haven't pooh-poohed the idea leads me to the notion you might in fact be civilised.'

'Or civilisable, at least.'

After dinner we decided to take the night air. I welcomed a walk – the effects of too much wine and rich food. Outside was biting cold. Curious, but I remember the wind billowing my dress. Armand took my arm. Stars sprinkled a crystalline sky. We walked as far as the Arc de Triomphe, strode round it, returned the way we had come, fighting against the wind. Not much was said; I didn't feel the need to converse. Passing under a gaslight I studied his profile – his aquiline nose, the swept-back hair – dashing and similar to Junius in a way, but devoid of vanity. A 'night' with him would not be so onerous. I felt somewhat let down, therefore, when he failed to invite me to his room.

And no money passed hands, either. The whore in me was disappointed, albeit fleetingly. Instead, he was organising a cab with the doorman. He squeezed my hand when it arrived – telling me how much he was looking forward to seeing me again.

Sunday, 8 February. My boots hurt a little – they *were* brand new. My jodhpurs fitted like a glove, though my backside did look rather large. My tweed jacket, neatly buttoned, did, however, compress my breasts. My rider's cap was decidedly male – one can never be too careful when riding a horse. My stash of ill-gotten gains was 110 francs and forty-six centimes to the worse. Joelie told me I looked ridiculous and not to get carried away. 'Hubris is followed by nemesis,' she reminded me.

Allowing myself the luxury of a fiacre, I arrived at Hôtel Beaujon. Armand was waiting in the foyer. Soon we were trundling down avenue de l'Impératrice in a calash. Despite the rugs covering our legs it was freezing cold, but at least last night's wind had blown itself out. The promise of a beautiful winter's day – the sun's low rays pale through the leafless trees. Not much traffic; the clip-clop of the bays was clear and rhythmic. Armand was silent and looked the very model of an equestrian: tweed hacking jacket, cream shirt and, unusually, a tie, not a cravat, a steampunk hat on his head. *Very stylish*, I thought.

Handing me the hip flask: 'I always stay at the Beaujon to be close to the Bois.'

After driving through porte Dauphine we arrived in the Bois de Boulogne. I was given to flights of fancy – was this really happening to Christine Vellay from Meursault?

The carriage dropped us off at a cobbled courtyard alongside a row of stalls. The smell of manure, leather and horse reminded me of Lapin. I approached the nearest stall, scratched the muzzle of a gorgeous bay colt.

Armand appeared to be discussing me with the head groom. I wandered back over to them.

'I understand mademoiselle has ridden before,' said the groom.

'A little.'

'I suggest you try Tetra, she's "fifteen eight", seven years old and used to race the jumps. Gentle as a kitten, mam'selle.'

Tetra was led out of her stall; she was a good hand taller than Lapin.

Soon I was in the saddle – it had been over a year – and felt as though I was born to it. 'Come on,' I said to Armand, urging Tetra into a trot.

He yelled and thundered past me, scuds flying.

We were in a race. The path was a mush of vegetation, trees on either side bereft of their leaves. The smell of decay. I breathed it in. Armand was thirty metres ahead, so I tapped Tetra's flank with my crop. Surging forward like the good racer she was, we quickly narrowed the gap.

A bend. I was on the inside – the side with the taller trees. Armand's horse drifted towards me and soon we were level. Something was blocking the path and coming up fast. Armand swerved away from me, yelling at the top of his voice. It was all or nothing. I have jumped before, but never over a tree with its branches sticking out. Leaning forward, I urged Tetra who jumped for all she was worth. Then the feeling of time suspended until something slammed into my leg. I heard myself scream. We crashed through the tangle of branches and landed on the other side. Tetra slowed. By some miracle, I managed to jiggle the stirrups free before crashing to the ground.

I forced myself to a sitting position, gasping at the pain in my leg. I can still see Armand's face as he ran towards me, one of utter shock, guilt even.

'My God, are you all right, Monique?'

'My leg,' I groaned.

He undid his tie. I hardly dared look… the gash in my jodhpurs, blood oozing through.

'How is Tetra?'

'She's unharmed. Now, let me see. Ah.' Ripping my jodhpurs, he took the handkerchief from his top pocket; spitting on it, he then gently wiped the wound. 'Does that hurt?' he said.

Through clenched teeth: 'You could say that.'

He undid his tie and wound it round the back of my thigh. Folding the handkerchief, he kept it in place by knotting the tie over the wound.

'Can you stand?' he said, offering me his arm.

I shook him off – stubborn little bitch that I am – and struggled to my feet.

'Can you ride, Monique?'

'I think I've already answered that one, Armand.'

Tetra was cropping on grass. I took her reins and tried to mount her. Two strong arms propelled me upwards and once again I was in the saddle. I muffled down a cry.

I was cosseted in Armand's room in Hôtel Beaujon. A man with a sallow complexion was sitting on the bed and asking me to show him my thigh.

'The last time a man said that to me, monsieur, I slapped his face.'

A sheepish smile as he folded back the sheet. With utmost care he undid Armand's knot and coaxed off the bloody handkerchief. Warm water to hand, he bathed the wound. 'You're lucky,' he said. 'Not too deep. A few stitches will see you right, mademoiselle.'

I grimaced as he dried the wound. Armand was pacing the room and looking noble. 'Will she be all right, Doctor?' he kept repeating.

The doctor threaded a needle. 'Mademoiselle, this may sting…'

TWENTY-SEVEN

THREE YEARS SINCE my accident in Bois de Boulogne. Somewhat wistfully I inspected the scar on my right thigh: it was banana-shaped and gleamed white against my skin.

I felt as though it had happened yesterday: Armand telling me how brave I was, insisting I stay in the hotel in a suite of my own and waiting patiently – our meals taken in my room. After a couple of days I was back on my feet.

I can take mollycoddling, but not to excess.

And visits from Joelie.

I was aware of discussions between Joelie and Armand at the time. Turns out they were debating my 'price'. Armand then told me he had 'paid off' Joelie, that I was free to come and live with him. Again I was being 'traded'. I lost my temper: *How dare you arrange my future without telling me? I may not wish to live with you* – words to that effect.

In the end I relented – no easy decision leaving Paris and Lucien. And did I love Armand at the time? I used to think about it. I did in a way but not in a Junius way: all lust and infatuation and the way he had made love to me. Oh my!

I had grown to love Armand, but in a different way. He was a gentle and considerate lover, no great Lothario, though. Our love was based on respect and kindness and generosity of spirit.

And I lived in luxury, at Château Bèze in the Touraine, close to the village of Monteaux and the river Loire. I knew he couldn't afford an allowance, but he managed to give me a hundred francs a month.

I said 'in luxury' – the place was falling to pieces. Most of the west-facing rooms were affected by damp – tiles missing from the roof. I asked Armand where the money came from... Transpired the family owned farmland near Montargis rented to farmers for the cultivation of wheat.

Château Bèze encompassed ten hectares. Most was given to orchard: apple, pear and cherry. An upper slope was embedded with old, straggly vines, the land clogged with weeds. Armand was embarrassed when I raised the subject. Originally the family had eight hectares under vine, but his father sold them to settle debts, leaving only Corbeau ridge.

The ridge was just over a hectare, the grape Chenin Blanc and Pinot Noir. I reminded Armand I was from la Bourgogne and knew about Pinot Noir, and that one hectare, properly cultivated, could produce as much as forty hectolitres – about five thousand bottles a year.

I remember Armand becoming excited. Me calming him down by telling him the existing vines might be 'irrecoverable'. If so, new vines would have to be planted – five years before we could harvest a meaningful crop. The same problem my brothers had had.

I employed Honoré, who came recommended. The vines *were* recoverable. We hired a labourer. The following year we produced our first crop: thirty hectolitres. A friend of Armand's took it off our hands for a hundred francs a hectolitre. Three thousand francs in total: a profit of 2,360 francs after expenses.

I remember Armand taking me in his arms and kissing me when I told him the business would cover my allowance. And repeating: *What would I do without you, Monique?*

That was at the end of 1864. And now I have a horse, Leveret, my 'baby hare'. She was fifteen hands, six years old, and I don't know how I would cope without her.

Life is never easy, though; there was always a Madame Gaillard character. This time there were two of them: Armand's children, the younger Armand, aged sixteen, and Céleste, aged fourteen. They both detested me. I tried to ingratiate myself by making myself useful. But when they saw me, they sidled away, shunning me at every turn. Not once did they initiate a conversation. Instead, they answered me with grunts while avoiding my eyes. Armand told me he felt very awkward.

I have thought about it. Virginie, damn her, was a goddess. Her portraits dotted the walls. No one could ever match up to her, especially a little trollop from Paris. The children must have been worried about their inheritance – that Kiki, the whore-leech ineluctable, would bleed their father white. And jealous. Armand loved me, for sure. Maybe they felt his love for them was somehow diminished. I don't know, but I certainly felt uncomfortable. It wasn't as though I hadn't tried. So I gave up. Good riddance to them. Not that they were at Château Bèze much of the time: Armand attending Saint-Cyr Military Academy and Céleste a *pensionnat* in Orléans.

Early April 1865. I was pining for Paris; it was spring, after all. A letter arrived: Joelie telling me she was tired of the city and in need of some country air. Armand indulged me when I showed it to him.

A week later I drove the brougham to Tours and met her off the train. She had visited us before, but now she really was the grande dame – the Whore of Babylon in all her finery.

Looking me up and down: 'My, you look wonderful, Monique. The country air must be doing you good.'

'You forget I'm from la Bourgogne, Joelie.'

I asked her for news.

'I have bought my own place near Jardin du Luxembourg, a three-bedroom apartment overlooking place de l'Estrapade.'

'How many girls do you employ?'

'Ten, and that's quite enough. Something is always happening to one of them. You remember Babette?'

The drive back to Monteaux was agreeable. Cattle grazing, the world swathed in green, men fishing on the Loire. I was reminded of the de Bonnetains, God bless them. Barges. Some belched smoke. I prayed they had survived the change to steam.

We talked of Paris.

Joelie was the only person who knew of Lucien. 'I am desperate to find him,' I told her.

'Have you told Armand?'

'Of course not, though he knows I was married.'

'Silly girl, hiding the truth will come to no good.'

'He doesn't even know my name.'

Joelie shook her head. 'You're in a tricky situation name-wise. You're still wanted by the police.'

'Of *that* I'm well aware.'

'Hmm, your name actually doesn't matter. That you haven't told him about Lucien worries me. It means you have kept secrets from him, that you don't really trust him.'

'I will tell Armand about Lucien once I find him.'

'The sooner the better, Monique. You explain he was taken from you, that you have a duty to find him. Or you don't tell him and leave Lucien to another day.'

'Are you mad, Joelie? Lucien is my son. My blood.'

'Armand is reasonable, he would understand.'

'I am wanted by the police, for goodness' sake. *And* I escaped from the Conciergerie. God knows how he would react.'

'Visit Paris for a couple of weeks. Hire a detective… track down the Wynburnes. You would stay with me, like old times.'

'Thank you, Joelie, but Armand is possessive.'

The conversation see-sawed to the subject of wine. 'Next year we may bottle our crop,' I said.

Joelie was very nosy and winkled it out of me: the du Plessis finances, my allowance.

'I pay for myself, Joelie. The business covers my expenses.'

Taking my arm: 'You say you will produce your own wine next year?'

'I hope so.'

'You will need a *négociant*?'

'Of course.'

'A Parisian *négociant*, Monique. Think about it.'

'You mean I have an excuse?'

'You do, *chérie*. This is what we'll do.'

A couple of nights later we were discussing wine over dinner – what the beau monde in Paris was drinking. Joelie expounded on the power of the *négociants*. *The market drinks what the négociants want it to drink.* 'Monique tells me you will produce your own Pinot Noir next year, Armand.'

'That's the plan, Joeline. She has handled the business in such a way that we are able to afford some plant and machinery.'

'That's as may be, Armand, but you will need a *négociant*. The wine will not sell by itself.'

'A *négociant*?'

'And one you can trust. They don't grow on trees, you know.'

I kept my mouth tightly shut.

She continued, 'Takes time to secure a good one.'

'So we should get on with it?'

'Well, it's Monique's business. She should make the choice.'

Joelie and I resisted looking at each other.

'Monique, why don't you stay with me, defray expenses? Armand could visit you. Yes, that's a good idea.'

'So it's settled,' said Armand.

Ten days later Joelie and I were bound for Paris, travelling in first class. Joelie wouldn't have it any other way.

I told her again how guilty I felt 'playing' Armand.

'Shut up, Monique. Say that one more time and I will scream.'

I smiled. Despite my misgivings I was in a jumble of excitement. I would walk the boulevards again. But I did need to find a *négociant* – returning to Château Bèze empty-handed was not an option. I had promised Armand I would be away no longer than two weeks and would write to him daily.

Joelie picked up on my thoughts. 'I have some ideas about *négociants*,' she said. 'Incidentally who are you going to be?'

'How do you mean?'

'What is your name?'

'Ah. As you know Armand and I are not married. Some people, however, address me as Madame la Baroness.'

'Very grand, I'm sure. And very useful. We will need to produce cards for you. The Baroness Monique du Plessis has a ring to it. I know the very man.'

'I will have to change my appearance. *Sergent-de-ville* Monnier will still have an interest in me.'

'More so since you escaped from him.'

'I need a wig and a good one.'

'Blonde – but not too blonde. Again, I know the very man.'

Porters took our luggage when we alighted from the train at Montparnasse. What Joelie and I must have looked like I can't imagine. One porter hailed a fiacre and soon we were rattling down rue de Rennes. It felt like a triumphal return. The streets thronged with people. And, oh, the smell – intoxicating: manure, smoke, garlic and a pungent vinegary waft.

Joelie's apartment was spacious, as was my bedroom. Her maid was welcoming. Turning down the sheets on my bed, she told me her name was Lily.

Lily? At first her name didn't register with me.

After strolling in Jardin du Luxembourg, Joelie and I retreated to our small place on rue d'Assas where we shared the inevitable bottle of wine.

We walked back to place de l'Estrapade with a spring to our step. Joelie cooked one of her famous omelettes. More wine. Reminding her that we had a busy day ahead I retired for the night.

I climbed into bed and mouthed a curse – I had forgotten to bring a book – lay on my back, left with my thoughts. Then it came to me: Lily. The Wynburnes' maid was also a Lili. We had become friends, tacit partners in crime against Mathilde.

She was one of those 'gnacs', as in Armagnac.

Then I remembered: Lillian Soulignac from Évry.

TWENTY-EIGHT

TWO DAYS LATER I boarded the train at Gare d'Orléans. I had taken the precaution of wearing a disguise. The prêt-à-porter wig purchased the day before was honey-blonde and worn beneath my hat. The pair of plain-glass spectacles and dark suit completed my resemblance to a governess on her way to the *environs*. Paris to Évry takes an hour. I remembered spending a night there with the de Bonnetains. The Seine flowed to my left, light rippling off its surface in the late April sun. At the station I sought out the stationmaster.

'The Soulignacs,' he said. 'She was 'ere, not 'alf an hour ago.'

'Madame Soulignac?'

'Lovely lady is Madame Soulignac.'

My brightest of smiles: 'Can you tell me where she lives, monsieur?'

'Who wants to know?'

'I have news of her daughter Lili.'

'Lili? Nothing serious, I 'ope. 'Aven't seen 'er round these parts for some time.'

'Lili is well, monsieur.'

He gave me the address. 'Up there,' he said.

After a short but steep climb I knocked on the door of a small terraced house.

A slight, middle-aged woman with grey hair eventually opened up. Her gloves were covered in mud.

'My name is Lucia,' I announced. 'A friend of Lili's.'

'Lillian's? Oh, do come in. Sorry. I was in the garden.'

We sat outside. Madame Soulignac placed an infusion of *verveine* on the table in front of me. Sitting down she leant forward expectantly. 'Please, Lucia,' she said with a nod.

'Lili and I were friends. I met a man. We married and lived in the country. When he died earlier in the year I moved back to Paris.'

'Oh dear, poor you.'

'With few friends in the city I decided to re-establish contact with those I was fond of.'

I remember squirming in my seat as she ran her eyes over me.

'You came all the way here to… to find out where Lillian lives. Surely?'

'I was passing – on my way to Sens. I thought…'

'Why don't you tell me why you are really here, mademoiselle?'

'I can't, madam… All right, I have not just *passed by*. I have a reason, one I cannot disclose. Of a highly personal nature, madam.'

'In other words, I should mind my own business.'

'Quite.'

She topped up my *verveine*.

'She worked for the Wynburne family.'

'She left the Wynburnes some time ago.'

I tried to hide my disappointment. 'No matter. I would be grateful if you could give me Lili's address.' Urging her with my eyes: 'It's very important to me, madam.'

She hummed and hawed, appeared to make a decision, stood and went inside – soon to re-emerge with a piece of folded paper. 'I hope you find whatever you are looking for, Lucia.'

Outside on the street, I felt thwarted. But when I thought about it, why would Lili still be working for the Wynburnes? I opened the note.

18 rue de la Victoire

'I have an address,' I told Joelie on my return.

'The Wynburnes?'

'Their ex-maid.'

'Bah, you're wasting your time. You should hire a detective.'

Next day I walked to the Ninth Arrondissement in my 'governess' clothes. I felt safe as I crossed the Seine onto Île de la Cité. The sight of Notre-Dame sparkling in the morning sun filled me with joy and I upped my pace.

Soon I was passing through Les Halles, with all sorts of activities there – mainly food, vendors of various hues bawling out their wares. Meat hanging in chunks from grisly hooks, a welter of fish displayed on trays. Cheeses of all descriptions, the smell… garlic and onions piled high. Olives. Fruit stacked on counters. I bought an apple and crunched down into it. The streets were narrow, though. And, wary of pickpockets, I was relieved when I emerged at Saint-Eustache.

On rue Montmartre, my optimism succumbed to doubt. I was on a fool's errand, surely? Maybe Joelie was right?

As I crossed rue Réaumur, a banker type in a top hat clambered out of a cab. Consumed by impatience I took his place. Ten minutes later the driver dropped me off at the top of rue de la Victoire at its junction with rue la Fayette.

Walking down the odd-number side I found a café from where I could observe number 18. Having purchased a copy of *Le Siècle*, I settled at a table outside. The air was clear, the sky an iridescent blue, and although I was wasting my time I might as well enjoy myself. A waiter took my order – *café au lait* and a tranche of brioche.

I scanned the front page, not really concentrating.

A couple of hours later I was bored and ordered another coffee, asking the waiter the time. 'Eleven fifteen, madam,' he said just as the door to number 18 opened. I held my breath. Lili emerged onto the street carrying a basket. Handing the waiter some centimes I told him to forget the coffee. Lili was walking in the opposite direction to the rue la Fayette junction. Feeling rather naughty I tracked her to a market in front of the church of Sainte-Trinité.

She was annoyingly slow in making her purchases, chatting with storekeepers, her head bobbing up and down. After drifting through a few more stalls she sat down outside a café. While she made herself comfortable, I made my move.

'Mind if I join you?'

'There are plenty of other tables, madam.'

'Lili,' I whispered. 'It's me. Lucia – Lucia d'Arnay.'

'What?'

'Please calm yourself, my dear. No ill intentions on my part.'

'Is that really you, Lucia? How—?'

'I visited your mother two days ago.'

'My mother?'

'I wanted your address. I followed you here.'

The waiter arrived and took our order – *petits cafés*.

'She said you no longer worked for the Wynburnes?'

'They fired me the day they left rue de l'Ouest.'

'They took my baby. I think about Lucien every day.'

'What they did was disgusting, criminal. I was of a mind to report them.'

'Why didn't you?'

'I just didn't.' She leaned towards me. 'Although they paid me off, I thought about…'

'Yes?'

'I thought about making money from them.'

'Blackmailing them?'

Lili squirmed. 'In the end I decided not to. I was worried she might do something to me.'

'She did something to me.'

'I tried to find out where they went. I spoke with friends, other maids. Then a friend of a friend told me.'

I averted my eyes, held my breath and prayed.

'Rue du 29 Juillet.'

I exhaled. 'The number?'

'I don't know. It's off rue de Rivoli, in one of those *beaux quartiers*.'

'Thank you, Lili,' I said, dipping into my reticule.

'Hope you find your Lucien,' she said. 'Bring those *conards* to justice.'

I dangled twenty francs in front of her. 'Not a word to anyone, Lili. *Understood?*'

'Not a word,' she said, taking the note.

On leaving Lili, I walked down rue de la Chaussée-d'Antin. A huge construction site to my right: the new opera house, one of Baron Haussmann's madcap projects, no doubt. Crossing boulevard des Capucines I turned left down rue de la Paix and walked past its shops. Place Vendôme was ahead, its dazzling column resplendent in the spring sunshine. From its base, I gazed up at the first Napoleon then crossed the square onto rue de Castiglione where I asked for directions. Soon I was on rue du 29 Juillet. Despite my disguise I pulled my hat down over my forehead. At the end of the road I reached rue de Rivoli. A café on the corner: the Welcome, where I installed myself with a view up rue du 29 Juillet. I prayed the Wynburnes would approach from the direction of Jardin des Tuileries. I opened *Le Siècle* and waited.

Not much later a small boy and his maid emerged from the direction of the Jardin. He looked about three or four years old and wore a short coat. He was laughing and waggling a toy in his hand, a tin soldier. They passed by my table. I glimpsed into his eyes: they were brown. Junius's eyes were brown; Monsieur Monnier's a yellowy blue. I was tempted to snatch him there and then – my baby. Instead, I followed them. A hundred metres or so further up the street the maid stopped and opened a door: the door to number 6.

There was no café from where I could observe, so I walked up and down the street, my eyes focused on the door. In the early afternoon a man slowed down and took out a key. He looked up and down the street, his face revealed: the face of John Walter Wynburne.

At place de l'Estrapade Lily informed me that Joelie was not expected until seven o'clock. I heaved a sigh of relief. Although I had made progress I needed to think. She poured me a coffee and I settled myself on one of Joelie's comfortable ottomans.

How to rescue Lucien? I pictured one scene where I am snatching him off the street, another where I am in court surrounded by lawyers. I yawned.

The next thing I knew, the front door was being slammed: Joelie in a huff and looking as though she wanted to kill someone. Lily hovered in attendance.

'Don't just stand there,' Joelie told her. 'Fetch some wine.'

'You look frazzled,' I said.

'That stupid cow Babette has done it again – on the rags with a client. I could strangle her. And Josette has managed to get herself beaten up.'

'Josette?'

'You don't want to know.'

Lily poured two glasses. Joelie drained hers in a single draught. 'That's better,' she sighed. 'How was your day, Monique?'

I recounted my adventures.

'No? But that's good news. Well done' – pouring another glass. '*Now* what are you going to do?'

'I—'

She held up a hand. 'Stop. I need to take a bath, soothe myself. I don't know about you but I fancy a night out. I know an interesting place. We'll discuss Lucien over drinks.'

An hour later we were sitting in Café de la Renaissance off boulevard Saint-Michel. Joelie ordered pastis. Saturday night and people were letting off steam, shouting and laughing. The atmosphere was dense, smoke from pipes and cigars. Men made drunken attempts to join us, Joelie batting them away with disdain. Later in the proceedings a man stepped forward and started to hector the crowd.

'Raoul Rigault,' whispered Joelie.

He was young, squat and wore a vast beard. I remember shivering with repulsion.

'He's a rabble-rouser, atheist, hates Louis-Napoleon, *detests* the police.'

People were cheering, though a few were booing.

'The government is corrupt!' roared Rigault, stabbing the air. 'Napoleon and his overfed cronies are living off the fat of the land while people starve *not very far from here*. The police are in the pockets of the politicians while the clergy do nothing, cowering in their churches. I tell you, my fellow *citoyens*, there will be a day a reckoning. And soon.'

One man stood and told Rigault to shut up and sit down. Rigault responded by sticking his nose in the man's face and shouting, 'One day I'm going to have you shot!'

More hectoring. I turned to Joelie. 'I think we should leave.'

We dropped coins on the table and walked out. Soon we were on rue des Écoles, a café on a corner. After ordering a bottle of wine I told Joelie how I had found Lucien.

'Through the maid?'

'Yes.'

'You sure it was him?'

'Of course... I told you, both Lucien and John Wynburne entered the same house.'

I outlined the alternatives for taking back my son.

She pulled a face. 'You can't go through the courts – you're wanted by the police. Anyway, it would be very expensive and you would probably lose.'

The waiter filled our glasses.

Joelie took a sip. 'Snatching Lucien from the street, umm… I don't know. You'll be in disguise, though. You would have to leave Paris immediately afterwards, your escape route planned military-style.'

'A carriage would be standing by to take me to the station at Montparnasse.'

'Where you would have to wait for a train… No, I don't like it.' Shaking her head: 'You would have to take the carriage as far away from Paris as possible, take a train from there.'

'And how will Lucien react, being grasped by a woman he doesn't know?'

'He's a three-year-old and will adjust to his change of circumstances.'

At Joelie's I drafted a letter.

Place de l'Estrapade
Paris

27 April 1866

My darling Armand,

I am missing you.

I have to tell you that something strange has happened to me of a personal nature (nothing to worry about), which I will explain to you in person. It means I will have to go to Bourgogne and will therefore be away from you longer than I expected.

I am well cared for in Joelie's comfortable apartment.

Your adoring heart and with kisses I love you,
Monique

TWENTY-NINE

ONDAY, I PACKED sparingly – wore my governess's outfit. At the last minute I changed into my riding boots, stuffing my shoes and jodhpurs into my bag. After taking a fiacre to Gare de Lyon, I caught the ten o'clock to Dijon where I stayed the night. The following morning I took the train to Beaune.

I was in a rash of excitement as the train trundled into the station. The sky was clear, the air like champagne. And it was warm. Tuesday was a school day. If Madame Thierry was not languishing in a gaol somewhere, there was no reason why she wouldn't be at the school.

Usually, she returned home at around five in the afternoon. With three hours to myself I walked up rue du Château towards the centre of town. Everything appeared smaller, including place Saint-Pierre where I entered a wine shop. I searched the Meursaults – Domaines le Merle and de l'Oubliette in particular. One rack contained a few bottles of Oubliette, but there were no le Merles. And just when I was taking one of the Oubliettes off the rack a man sidled up to me. 'May I be of assistance, madam?'

'Monsieur, I was in Beaune some time ago and shared a bottle of le Merle with a friend. I enjoyed it so much I thought I would avail myself of a case.'

Rubbing his hands: 'We haven't sold le Merle in over three years.'

'Really?'

'The owner died four years ago. Savaged by his dogs. Made the Paris newspapers. A pity, the wine was popular with clients.'

'So, they no longer produce?'

'Alas. Otherwise I'd be selling it.'

'I was also partial to the Oubliette.'

'Oubliette's not bad, good soil, a tad tight when young – lemon curd, apple and honey – but as it unwinds with age the flavours build, intensify.'

'A typical Meursault.'

'Yes, and managed by a woman, madam.'

'A woman? No? Really, monsieur? How unusual.'

'A Madame Girard.'

'Surely there must be a *man* involved. A woman on her own in the *wine* business, monsieur?'

'There was – is – a Monsieur Girard. He joined the navy. Sailed to Mexico, so I'm told.'

'Never to return,' I intoned theatrically.

Eventually I purchased two bottles of the Oubliette, informing the proprietor I would pick them up later.

I left the shop deep in thought. *What had happened to le Merle? And Oubliette managed by Eloise.*

I booked a night at the Hôtel de Chevreuil. Just past four I collected my bottles and walked down rue des Bouchers on my way to Faubourg Saint-Jacques. Halfway across a bridge I stopped and looked down at la Bouzaize. I shivered at the thought of that terrible night, pictured myself in the water. With time on my hands, I checked the outside of Madame Thierry's house. Ambling back towards town I spotted her crossing place Saint-Jacques. I decided to follow rather than surprise her in the street. She walked at a good pace, her back straight and proud. I was filled with joy:

Madame Thierry appeared to be in rude health, not pallid and wasting away in some prison.

She entered her house. I felt jumpy, could hardly contain myself. Rapping her door I held my breath. Despite my disguise, she knew who it was. 'Come in,' she said, closing the door firmly behind me.

We threw our arms around each other, the tears rolling down. Nothing said for a while. Then she stood back, inspecting me. 'My, you've changed, Kiki. You left as a girl and return as a woman.'

'Ah, Saint Ignatius of Loyola.'

' "Give me the boy and I will give you the man." Now sit down and tell me all.'

Handing her the bottles she winked at me conspiratorially. Uncorking one, we sat down. I raised my glass. 'Before I start, Mad—'

'Delphine.'

'Delphine, please tell me what happened after I left.'

'They were quite livid, knowing full well I had harboured you. They insisted on searching the house. I saw them off – told them they needed a warrant. They returned in due course, by which time I had brushed away all signs of Christine Vellay – telltale hairs in your room, that sort of thing. They had me watched for at least a month.'

'I had visions of you languishing behind bars somewhere.'

'You have an overactive imagination, Kiki. Always did.' She sipped her wine and looked at me as though to say, *Well?*

I told her everything, from the de Bonnetains to my life as a prostitute, and Armand. 'Although we are not married, people refer to me as—'

'Stop. Please do not tell me your name... I do not need to know. That I know him as Armand will suffice. There are many Armands in France.'

'None quite like my Armand.'

'So, you have a child with no idea who the father is?'

'As I said, he could be a Monnier or a Girard.'

'It's important. Lucien could be the heir to Domaine le Merle.'

'I don't care if he's the Dauphin. He's mine and I want him back.'

'Why are you in Beaune, Kiki?'

'To seek your advice.'

'All the way from Paris?'

'All right, I was missing the place where I grew up. But I *did* want to see you, make sure you were all right. And to see my family.'

'Careful, show your face and the police will get a sniff.'

Touching my wig: 'As you can see, I do have a disguise of sorts.'

'Of sorts. You'll have to lie low. Someone might spot you in the street – a shopkeeper or some such.'

I pursed my lips.

'Have you thought of where you will stay the night?'

'I have booked a hotel.'

'Nonsense, you'll stay here with me.'

'I can't… really… I mean.'

'I don't think you take your situation seriously, the chance of someone recognising you.'

I exhaled somewhat theatrically. 'All right, I'll cancel it right away.'

'Oh no, you won't. I'll do the cancelling. I don't want you on the street. Which hotel?'

'The Chevreuil, although I will go there tomorrow to hire a horse.'

'Tomorrow will take care of itself' – putting on her bonnet. 'I'll be back in half an hour. Make yourself at home. Use the top room. The linen's you know where.'

Dinner was Jambon à la Chablisienne – a casserole, chunks of ham in a sauce, boiled potatoes on the side. Madame Thierry handed me a bottle of *vin de pays*.

I didn't realise how hungry I was. Soon my plate was clean.

Madame Thierry topped up my glass.

'You said you wanted to talk.'

I outlined the choices that faced me.

She took her time, placing small rounds of goat cheese on the table together with a loaf of bread. 'The courts are not a good idea. The process will be drawn out and very expensive. Unless Armand has deep pockets.'

I shook my head.

'Anyway, you are wanted by the authorities, to say nothing of your escape. You will be exposed. The Wynburnes know this, of course.'

'They have the advantage of me.'

'Abducting Lucien from the park…?'

'He goes there daily with his maid.'

'Every day?'

'All right, I don't know.'

She rolled her eyes. 'You would have to be highly organised, leave Paris as soon as you have done the deed.'

'That's what Joelie said.'

'I like the sound of this Joelie.'

'Despite what she is… does?'

'We all have to survive, my dear.'

'So, is there an alternative, Delphine?'

'Yes, you could leave him with the—'

'Impossible, he's my son, for God's sake.'

'Yes. And not even four years old, to be taken by a woman he doesn't know.'

'He will adjust to his change of circumstances.' I used Joelie's exact words.

We went round in circles. She racked her brains for an alternative. In the end we said goodnight and retired to bed.

I awoke in a sweat. A terrifying nightmare where I was in a coach with Lucien being chased by mastiffs, careening off a bridge and being washed out to sea; a boat, its bow bumping through the waves; handing Lucien to a faceless sailor; me trying to climb the gunwales and slipping back into the sea time and again; the current carrying the boat away; the sailor looking back and smiling – John Walter Wynburne – his teeth like a shark's. Me sinking down and down.

I wobbled out of bed, washed and dressed in my riding kit, the dream still in my head.

Breakfast was set out: brioche and apricots, a pot of coffee.

I asked Madame Thierry if she had seen Alie.

'Aliette? No. Not since you were both removed from the school.'

'Domaine le Merle, any news from your "busybody"?'

'In a bad state by all accounts… since your husband died.'

'And Madame Gaillard?'

'No idea. Hanging on, I suppose.'

'Hanging on?'

'You know, keeping the place going.'

An hour later, with all of Madame Thierry's warnings banished, I trotted out of Beaune astride a small chestnut mare.

The sun was out, the air crisp, the vines vast carpets of green. Birds in profusion. Starlings weaving patterns in the sky. Workers toiling in the fields, most in their *bleu de travail*. Passing Monsieur Blanc's orchard I recalled the day I accepted the ride from Augustave Monnier. Leaving Volnay I glanced at the *cabotte*. It seemed a long time ago.

Riding into Meursault I grappled with my emotions. Joy certainly – I had been away for over four years. Triumph, perhaps. Nostalgia certainly: the streets where I had played as a child, the fountain I had paddled in. Simple things. Turning right I prodded the mare into a trot towards Domaine le Merle.

I passed the main gate; the yard was littered with weeds. Stone tiles were missing from one of the roofs. I was tempted to walk round the back and look into the courtyard. Instead, I continued on the road to Auxey-Duresses. Spotting a path on my left I urged the mare up the hill.

Soon I was looking down on the back of le Merle, the courtyard. Tethering the mare, I walked through the vines towards the *domaine*. A sad sight: chickens scratching at the earth, holes in all of the roofs, lopsided shutters, a barrel, its staves splayed. The place looked deserted, tempting me to poke about. Thinking better of it I trudged back up the hill. Weeds were strewn in profusion – dandelions and daisies everywhere. Desiccated grapes sagged in bunches from tangled vines.

Mounting the mare I looked back down the hill. A lone, bent figure shuffled across the courtyard in her black skirts. She appeared to be scattering scraps for the chickens. Madame Gaillard – I could just make her out.

Strange, but I remember feeling nothing but pity for her.

I was tempted to confront her. Thought better of it – the risk it entailed – and decided to inspect the half-hectare of land instead. I tethered the mare again and, treading silently through a small copse, I came across a man wielding a pickaxe.

Salvat.

I considered my next move. Should I speak to him? He was my brother, after all.

The vines would have been planted four years ago; now they were lush and green. Salva was stripped to the waist, his torso honed by years of toil. Sweat matted the dark thatch of hair on his chest.

I had to admire what they had done, despite what they had done to *me*.

Someone grabbed my shoulder. I screamed.

'I wondered when you would turn up, Kiki. Spying, are you? Oi, Salva, look what we have here?'

I was tempted to lash out and run. Then Dago grabbed my arm, twisting it down, shouting at me. 'Father's dead, did you know that?'

'Let go,' I cried, struggling.

'You're wanted for murder, your husband, for Christ's sake. I have a good mind—'

'Let her go,' said Salva.

'Shut up, Salva.' Dago looked at my boots, my jodhpurs. 'Proper little lady, aren't you?'

'When did Father die?' I said, my voice steady, despite my churning insides.

'Three years ago' – releasing his grip.

I didn't know what I felt. I couldn't quite take it in – my fear of what Dago might do. 'A shame,' was all I could manage.

' "A shame" – *a bloody shame*!'

'Leave her alone, Dago. You threatening her does no good.'

'I said shut up, Salva.'

I removed my hat and my wig, my hair spilling down – Kiki in all her glory. I put my arms around Salva's neck, kissed the stubble on his chin and fought to keep the lie out of my voice. 'It's been a long time, Salva. I've missed you.'

Salva turned a shade of red and grinned.

'Come on, Dago,' I said. 'It's been over four years.'

'Don't try to soften me up, Christine,' he said, stepping away from me.

We glowered at each other. I was sure they were surprised at what they saw – a woman of substance and worldliness, perhaps. Their minds may have been alive with supposition – how their younger sister had turned out and what she had achieved. When Salva asked me about my life I fobbed him off with generalities, avoiding details: my life as a mistress to an aristo. I was conscious of how I looked and acted. Regretted having taken my wig off. I knew Dago was riven by greed and jealousy – especially jealousy – and so I pandered to him, telling him how wonderful his vineyard looked and talking 'grape' with him: hectolitres, terroir, schist, Pinot Noir, nodding attentively at his remarks. And, of course,

I never mentioned Corbeau ridge. It was all about them – their success.

I made my excuse to leave: I would be dropping in on Maman and looked forward to seeing them later.

As I rode down the hill, I prayed I had mollified Dago, prayed he wouldn't do anything rash such as blabbing my presence round town. I put nothing past him. Setting my anxieties aside, I couldn't but help feel the thrill of anticipation when I knocked on the door of the house on rue du Moulin Judas.

A young girl opened up; her thumb stuck in her mouth as she stared at me with her large blue eyes. 'Remember me?' I said, picking her up. 'It's your sister Kiki.' She wriggled so I put her down.

Alie rushed out and threw her arms around me. We were both in tears. Standing back, we looked at each other. She had aged well. And although we were talking at the same time, she managed to tell me she was going to be married.

'When?'

'In the autumn after *vendange*.'

An old woman hobbled into the room. Struggling to conceal my shock I put my arms around her. 'It's Kiki, Maman.'

Alie pulled a face while twiddling her forefinger around her temple.

Maman's eyes were rheumy and unfocused. She tried to say something – my name, perhaps. Her lips were chaffed, some of her teeth were missing. Her breath stank.

I remember feeling a welter of affection – intense and overwhelming.

I turned to Alie and told her I had met Dago and Salva, that I was worried about Dago reporting me to the authorities.

'He won't. I run this house and he does some work for Antoine.'

'Who's Antoine?'

'My fiancé.'

'Does Antoine know about me?'

'Of course, you're notorious, a husband murderer.'

'Do you believe that?'

'Persuade me otherwise.'

Anger stabbed at me. Taking a breath, I related the story of my escape. I questioned her about Junius... had he been seen?

'No, nothing. In the navy, I suppose. Rumours he was in Mexico.'

'And le Merle?'

'Gone to rack and ruin. I'm surprised the bank hasn't stepped in.'

While Alie prepared lunch I played with Arlette, pulled faces. When I swung her round, she squealed with laughter. Again I told her my name was Christine and that I was her sister.

'Kikine, Kikine,' she squealed.

With lunch on the table I continued my story – my life in Paris. Alie appeared disinterested until I told her about Lucien. She insisted I take him back: 'In the park, on the street, wherever you can.' When I told her I didn't know who the father was, she wagged a finger at me. I also let her know I was happily 'married', only mentioning Armand's first name and that we lived in the Loire.

I changed the subject: 'Le Merle, Alie, what is really happening there?'

'After Augustave died, the place went into decline, the vines untended, the buildings as well. Benoît is still the winemaker. A couple of workers harvest a small crop, a hundred hectolitres or so sold to local producers.'

'And Madame Gaillard?'

'A broken woman by all accounts.'

Any satisfaction I may have felt was non-existent. 'A broken woman?'

'Cooking for Benoît, laundry, everyday tasks. They make a sad pair. I hardly ever see her in town. Her son Florian...'

I tried to keep my voice even. 'Florian?'

'He disappeared after the killings, has not returned since.' She gave me a blue-eyed stare. 'Rumours at the time suggested you had run away with him to Marseilles, India even.'

'Completely unfounded, I assure you.'

'Broke Madame Gaillard's heart, so I'm told.'

'Serves her right. She hated me the day she laid eyes on me.'

'Antoine saw her in the market recently. He said she was a mess, her clothes ragged, her hair unkempt.'

On the point of asking her if I could meet Antoine, I changed my mind, aware of the risk I would be taking. The less people who knew of my visit…

On leaving, I was tempted to give Alie some francs but held back, knowing how proud she was.

On the outskirts of Meursault, I stopped and reapplied my wig. I remember exploding with happiness, despite the death of my father and my mother's decline. Arlette was a delight. And Alie – the way she had turned out, her happiness, her upcoming marriage.

Her comment was lodged in my head: 'I'm surprised the bank hasn't stepped in.'

I described my day to Madame Thierry.

'Your family,' she warned me. 'Small towns have large ears.'

I changed the subject. 'Tell me about mortgages, Delphine.'

'You're talking about le Merle?'

'Of course.'

'The wine business requires a lot of capital before any return flows back to the producer – equipment, vats, presses, bottling, et cetera. The mortgagee lends funds secured against the title to the property. The mortgagor, or borrower, if you like, must repay the loan at an agreed date; meanwhile, interest has to be paid.'

'And if the loan is not repaid on time?'

'The mortgagee can take possession of the property.'

'And do what with it?'

'Sell it to recover the monies lent or run the place as a going concern.'

'Le Merle might not be mortgaged. After all, it has been in the Monnier family for generations.'

'New equipment is needed from time to time, new vines as well.'

'But you know what I mean.'

'And we both know that your husband had a gambling problem.'

'He had trouble paying his taxes. The mayor told me himself.'

'Well, there you are. Le Merle will be mortgaged to the rafters.'

'You said something about interest.'

'Yes, and usually paid every quarter.'

'So why hasn't the mortgagee taken possession? Augustave died over four years ago.'

'Either they are very slack or the mortgagor continues to pay the interest.'

'The mortgagee is not being slack. That's not the way of business. Anyway, the mortgagor is my husband and he is dead. Someone else has to be covering the cost.'

Delphine pulled a face. 'You could be right.'

'Who are mortgagees, typically, Delphine?'

'Banks usually.'

'In the case of le Merle?'

'The mortgage deed will be registered against the title.'

'Available for public scrutiny?'

'At the Hôtel de Ville.'

Next day was a Thursday, a school day for Madame Thierry. Just after five she was back for the day. 'I've checked the Land Registry. Banque Villiard is the mortgagee,' she said, removing her bonnet. 'The loan amount is seventy thousand francs.'

'Banque Villiard. Makes sense. It was – is – my bank in Beaune. A Monsieur Tausend the manager.'

'He is still there. I also checked the title deeds – Domaine le Merle sits on 22.8 hectares of land, of which 14.6 are cultivated for grape.'

I reached for a pencil and paper. 'And who is registered as the borrower?'

'Your husband.'

'But he's dead.'

'Therefore, his estate will be paying the interest… Oreste Monnier, his twin, perhaps?'

'You may well be right, Delphine. By the way, do you know a competent lawyer?'

'I have the very man, Kiki. But I worry, the more people you meet the more danger you're in.'

'Then can I suggest you see him? You know what I want… to pay off the mortgage and take possession.'

'Where will you find the money?'

'Armand. Where else?'

'You told me he is…'

'He is, but we'll find a way.'

THIRTY

S UNDAY, 6 MAY 1866. Back in Joelie's apartment. A letter from Armand, nothing out of the ordinary – him wishing me bon voyage and looking forward to my safe return.

Next day I felt compelled to go to Jardin des Tuileries. I took a book from Joelie's shelf – *La Confession de Claude* by Émile Zola – to pass the time.

Zola? *Zola and his clique of bores at La Closerie des Lilas.* It must be the same person – Zola an unusual name.

At Debauve & Gallais I bought a bag of bonbons. After walking down the rue des Saints-Pères I crossed the Seine and entered the Jardin. On rue de Rivoli I checked where it intersected with rue du 29 Juillet and positioned myself where I thought Lucien and his maid would likely enter the park.

I sucked on one of the bonbons and opened the Zola. The park was alive: babies in carriages, maids, tots with hoops, people walking their dogs. Some older children were floating their boats in the pond. One young man was flying his kite.

Before long Lucien and his maid entered with a terrier straining on its lead. I checked my timepiece: just past eleven o'clock. The tin soldier was not in evidence, the dog his preoccupation as he chased it round the paths.

I was spellbound: *my* flesh, *my* blood were there for me to see.

Hiding my face behind the Zola, I tried to breathe him in, inhale his very essence. The animal scent between mother and child is ingrained, known only to them. Indelible. Could he, would he pick up on me? I doubted it – running around as he was in pursuit of his dog.

The terrier sniffed one of the legs of the bench I was sitting on. Ready with the bonbon I dangled it down in my left hand. It almost bit my hand off as Lucien ground to a halt in front of me.

'Your doggy's sweet. What's his name?' I choked out the words.

He twisted, stared at me unblinkingly. 'Pogo,' he said. I studied his face… a trace of me, perhaps. His smile. Yes… the way his mouth crinkled at the corners. His ears were like mine, oval and neat with small lobes. His teeth were white and even, as were mine.

I tried to capture the moment: graft it, file it, sear it into my brain. 'What a nice name,' I managed to say as I ruffled Pogo's head.

I was about to ask the boy his name when the maid arrived.

I nodded, avoiding her eyes.

'Come on, Lukie,' she said.

Then he was gone, off chasing Pogo.

I kept my head down in the Zola, the words a blur. I wanted to draw it out, savour the moment. Pogo sniffed my hand a few times before they finally left the park.

'Lukie,' the maid had said. Lukie. My Lucien.

I meandered back towards Saint-Germain in a daze. Halfway across Pont du Carrousel I stopped and gazed down on the river, its immemorial flow. I felt the tears. I had seen my son, his face indelible. My tears were tears of pure joy.

A week later I returned to Château Bèze having accomplished my objectives, including the appointment of a *négociant*, Dent, Urwick & Co. Armand was effusive in his welcome and we went straight upstairs. His passion was intense. Mine too, despite my fear of how he would react when I told him about Lucien.

The following morning I woke him up, straddling him, making sure he could not see the brand. I moaned, clawed his back and nibbled his ear.

I bided my time, waited for the opportunity. Over lunch he mentioned my trip to la Bourgogne.

I explained that I had wanted to see my family and view le Merle, the property of my late husband. 'It's in a poor state and mortgaged to the hilt,' I added.

'Oh dear.'

'*Chéri*, there is something you should know… I have a child by my late husband.'

'What?' he said, standing up, glowering at me.

'A boy.'

'A b—'

'He is nearly four years old and lives in Paris. I saw him during my trip there.'

'Why didn't you tell me this before, Monique?'

'I was afraid. I thought you might think the less of me.'

'Nonsense. But you should have told me. Where is he?'

'He lives with the Wynburnes.'

'Who in God's blood are they?'

'I was eight months pregnant and without money, and knew John Wynburne, an Englishman. He and his wife Mathilde gave me a room and the run of their house so I could deliver my baby.'

'Then what happened?'

I squirmed. I couldn't tell him about Junius – not yet, anyway. 'I was visiting friends in Brest. Lucien was too small to travel. When I returned to the Wynburnes' he was gone, the house shuttered up.'

'Why were you visiting Brest?'

'A childhood friend was at the Naval Academy there. I was desperate. I thought he could help me.'

'Hmm, but he wasn't there.'

'No. He'd sailed for Mexico, the war there.'

He looked as though he was going to say something provocative but changed his mind. 'So how did you find your way into Joelie's clutches?'

'With no money and nowhere to live, I threw myself on her generosity. As you know, we were chambermaids together.'

'Yes?'

I couldn't bring myself to tell him of my escape from the Conciergerie. 'Joelie was very good to me, but I had to pay my way, and that's how I met you, Armand.'

'What do you propose doing about Lucien, the Wynburnes?'

'I thought of applying to the courts, but as you know I'm wanted by the police. I would be too exposed. The only real choice open to me is abduction.'

'Abduction! Umm, that's rather extreme and will add to your list of, how should I say, "crimes".'

'Crimes! How dare you? Augustave was savaged by his dogs. The Wynburnes stole *my* child.'

He pulled a face and tried to hold my hand with a '*sorry, chérie*'. I brushed him away. 'You have no idea what I've had to endure, do you, Armand?'

Armand, bless him, eventually agreed: 'abduction' was the only solution and Lucien would live with us. At times, I sensed he was on the edge of saying something – how Armand and Céleste would react, perhaps – but he managed to hold his tongue.

'Rescue Day' was decided: Tuesday, 5 June. I wrote informing Joelie of my impending arrival.

THIRTY-ONE

I ARRIVED AT the station in Montparnasse wearing my governess disguise and took a fiacre to place de l'Estrapade.

Joelie was her formidable self, her eyes bright, her hair up chignon-style in ringlets, exposing her neck and beautiful ears. The lace headdress, though, made her look faintly ridiculous. After hugging me she handed me a box – my custom-made, honey-blonde wig inside. I tried it on as she held a mirror. 'Perfect,' she said.

I looked at my reflection. 'Not bad, makes me look like someone else.'

She winked. 'My clients would love it.'

I laughed. 'You forget, I'm a respectable "married" woman.'

'Wanted for the murder of her husband, escape from prison and, as of this time next week, kidnap.'

Next day over breakfast I returned *La Confession de Claude* to her.

'Did you enjoy it?' she enquired.

'It was hard work. I feel Zola is indulging himself. The juxtaposition of wealth and poverty, I can relate to that. Although I thought he over-romanticised the poverty part. Do you remember him at La Closerie des Lilas? "Émile" on the table next to us, scribbling away, his friend asking us to move.'

'Where you met your artist friend…'

'Gustav Bonifay.'

A change of subject: Joelie was worried about Lucien's dog.

The next four days I found ways to pass the time. Walks – my new wig in place on occasions – in the Luxembourg, along La Rive Gauche, half-expecting to see *La Fleur de l'Yonne*. I bought clothes for Lucien: three shirts, a pair of shorts, a jumper and two pairs of shoes. And toys: a tin soldier and a wooden train. Pogo the dog was a worry. Wicked thoughts in my head – a knife, poison…

Joelie was adamant: 'Stabbing Pogo is a very bad idea. The thing will make a din – attract attention. No. Poison is the far better option.'

I reminded her of the terrible risk she'd be taking.

'My role will be to a minimum. The carriage will be waiting on the Rivoli. I will be disguised and leave you once it has left the immediate area.'

It was agreed. I would enter Jardin des Tuileries at ten thirty and leave at noon should Lucien fail to 'turn up'.

'Lucien's maid,' she said. 'There may a tug of war – you on one arm, her on the other.'

'Other people may join in.'

I revisited the Jardin two days before Rescue Day. A bench was positioned close to the rue de Rivoli exit. I rehearsed the manoeuvre, acted it out in my mind – the timing, the actions. I imagined luring the terrier with a treat and waiting for it to die. And where would Lucien be? I would need to get him in close before I made my move.

Walking back to Joelie's, I purchased a stout cane from a shop on boulevard Saint-Germain.

The sequence was in my head: treat to Pogo, wait twenty seconds, grab hold of Lucien's hand while beating back the maid, out of the entrance and into Joelie's waiting carriage.

The night before Rescue Day I could not sleep – reviewing the plan again and again. I decided against poisoning the dog. I loved animals, and killing Pogo would reduce me to the level of my late husband. Joelie had 'acquired' a potion: extracts of camomile and lavender as well as a hypodermic. For my part I had purchased a bag of bonbons from Debauve & Gallais.

The following morning I awoke feeling exhausted. I washed and packed, breakfasted with Joelie. Lily was not there – dispatched on leave to her family in Meaux.

I held the bonbon while Joelie filled the hypodermic. 'Not too much,' I said.

After securing the bonbon between a pair of nutcrackers, she injected the liquid then sealed the small hole with a sticky, dough-like concoction.

Just before ten I handed my valise to Joelie. We kissed and wished each other luck; then I was on my way in my disguise and with my cane. With every step towards the Jardin, I felt I was walking towards my fate. I felt like a criminal, tried to justify what I was about to do. But I was on the right side of my conscience. I wasn't the wrongdoer; the Wynburnes had abducted my child for their own selfish ends.

And what of Lucien? While the Wynburnes were evil, they would have been devoted 'parents'. Mathilde had doted on him in front of my eyes. Would he be distressed? Almost certainly but, once ensconced in Château Bèze, he would recover, with me there to love and adore him. Armand would fall into line and play his part. Anyway, living in the country was a healthier place to rear a child than Paris.

After crossing the river, I walked past Notre-Dame. I couldn't help but stop. Making the sign of the cross I found myself mumbling a prayer to Our Lord.

On entering the Jardin, I realised I had nothing to read – to hide behind – so I purchased a copy of *Le Monde* on quai du Louvre. Back in the Jardin I sat on *the* bench.

The park began to fill – the usual assortment of prams, maids, children and dogs. No Lucien. Not yet. I stood up and fingered the bonbon in my pocket. Felt compelled to walk and check that Joelie was in place – she was, in a calash with the hood up.

A man checked his pocket watch. About to ask him the time I pulled back, wishing to remain unobserved. Back on the bench I hid behind *Le Monde*. Not long to wait before Lucien bowled in, followed by Pogo and the maid.

Odd, but a feeling enveloped me – one of detached calm. I had rehearsed the scenarios, and bided my time. Patience was essential – this I knew.

After a while Pogo drew close to the bench, canine memories of bonbons past, perhaps. I dangled the sweet in front of his nose. I remember feeling mortified. Soon Pogo was panting, his tongue lolling out of the side of his mouth. Lucien raced up and stopped in front of me. 'Something is wrong with your doggy,' I said, standing up and closing my hand round his. 'Come, Lukie, let's find someone to help him.'

To my horror the maid was hurrying towards us. 'What are you doing? Let the child go. Immediately. Now!' she shouted. When she took Lucien's free hand, I rapped her on the wrist with the cane. Howling, she let go. An old man joined in – stretching out his arm which I thwacked away. The man swore. Lucien started to cry. Tightening my grip, I dragged him stumbling towards the exit. The gateway was clear. I spotted Joelie in the corner of my eye. And just when I thought I was going to make it, an apparition in blue blocked my way – Mathilde looking vast, angry and hot.

'What are you doing? Let go of my child!' she said, lunging her bulk at me. I said nothing – relying on my disguise – and beat her away with the cane. Somehow my hat fell off, the wig askew. I can see her face as though it was yesterday: the piggy-blue eyes – the shock, the realisation – shot with instant hate. 'You!' she screamed, lunging at me again. Lucien was shrieking and I clung onto his hand. Meanwhile the old man had recovered and was at me again. Others joined in and I flayed away with my stick. Then Joelie appeared and dragged Mathilde away. At the same time the maid wrenched Lucien free.

'It's too late!' shouted Joelie. 'Out of here! Now!' Lucien was nowhere to be seen. I lashed out at the arms grabbing at me and suddenly I was free.

I remember Mathilde on the ground, her legs scrabbling in the air. The door to the calash was open. I jumped in before it rattled away. Joelie was telling the driver to hurry, waving a wad of francs in his face. I was in a daze of rage and tears. I was vaguely aware of Joelie's arms around me. 'There, there,' she repeated. 'Everything will be all right, *chérie.*'

I clenched my teeth, forced myself to calm down. I recognised the Champs-Élysées. Joelie said, 'We have to change carriages and disappear. This fellow's taking a huge risk.'

The driver dropped us off at rue Balzac. More francs changed hands. At least I had the wit to hold on to my valise. Joelie clasped my hand and, after a short walk, we entered a large church, of Sainte-Sacrement, on avenue de Friedland.

We found some pews at the back and I sat there blubbering. Joelie slapped my face and shook me. 'Stop it! You're drawing attention to yourself. For God's sake, calm down.' I sagged against her, my head on her shoulder.

Armand. He was waiting for me – relying on me. 'I must be going. Armand,' I wailed.

'That's better, now you're thinking straight. Eat these,' she said, handing me the bag of bonbons, the ones I had purchased what seemed eons ago.

Outside the church Joelie waved down a fiacre, instructing the driver to take me to Café de la Comédie in Versailles. More francs. Her eyes bored into me. 'Kiki, listen. You will recover. Do you understand? And you *will* recover your son.'

The fiacre pulled away. I was on my own. 'Kiki?' Joelie hadn't called me Kiki in a long time.

A month later. The day in Jardin des Tuileries was in my head most waking moments, the nightmares over and over again. I came to realise that my penchant for caution had caught me out. I should have been more brazen – employed a couple of 'toughs'. Or I should have been more patient: gone to the park every day, spoilt the dog, built up trust, become 'that kind lady'. But how could I? I didn't have the time. Anyway, the rescue would have succeeded had Mathilde not been in the way.

Each day I had to force myself out of bed. Armand was patient but I sensed his unease – him making faces, sucking the air between his teeth. He kept telling me that everything would be all right, but I knew he was churning inside. And intercourse, I felt like a cow – the 'desire' just not there.

One morning he entered the bedroom and handed me an envelope. The writing told me it was from Madame Thierry.

Faubourg Saint-Jacques

25 June 1866

My Dear,

I hope all is well with you.

Reasonable news: your avocat's letter is enclosed. You'll note it's addressed to me. He does not know who you are, although I think he can guess. Don't worry, Monsieur de Gaalon is discretion personified.

Please let me know how you wish to proceed.

All my love and good wishes,
Delphine

'Anything interesting, *chérie*?' said Armand.

'From my old schoolteacher in Beaune with an attachment from a lawyer there.' I waved the letter at him.

François de Gaalon, Avocat
23 rue de la Charité
Beaune

21 June 1866

Dear Madame Thierry,

Further to your instructions I have spoken with Banque Villiard, the manager M Tausend, who confirmed that the outstanding balance of the mortgage is seventy thousand francs. He also confirmed that interest on the loan was payable at the end of each quarter.

Although he refused to disclose the payer of said interest, he intimated that the payment emanated from Paris. When I mentioned the late M Monnier's brother, Oreste, he neither confirmed nor denied it. But thirty years' experience leads me to believe that the payer is indeed M Oreste Monnier.

M Tausend informed me that the mortgage was for a term of five years expiring on 31 December of this year, 1866, when repayment of the loan is due in full.

I ventured to M Tausend that I represented a party who wished to acquire the property, thus relieving the bank of any risk of non-repayment.

I took the liberty of reminding M Tausend of the rumours currently in circulation: of an insect plaguing crops in the south; that my client was aware of the problem.

M Tausend said he was aware of the threat. In fact he visibly blanched, suggesting to me the bank's mortgage book is full of wine estates in la Bourgogne.

We left it that he would consider what I had said. My guess is that he will prevaricate, wait for the mortgage-expiry date and pray the loan is repaid.

Je vous prie d'agréer mes salutations distinguées,
François de Gaalon

Handing the letter to Armand I thanked God I'd had the good sense to have mentioned my idea to him. 'This insect scare, Armand, what do you think?'

'It's in the early stages. They have no idea what it is. In the south, for the time being.'

'This is the first I've heard of it.'

Scanning the letter: 'I don't know where you think the money's coming from, Monique.'

'Let's worry about that if and when the opportunity presents itself.'

'What do we do with Corbeau ridge?'

'Let me think about it.'

He nodded.

'Armand, *chéri*, let's celebrate with a special dinner tonight. I feel I'm on the mend.'

Armand grinned the way he used to. 'Thank God for that, Monique. I was beginning to worry.'

'I have been guilty of ignoring what I have… you, Armand, and this wonderful place we live in.'

We dined outside on the terrace overlooking the orchards. The cook, sensing perhaps a lifting of a cloud, outshone herself. Fat pigeons stuffed with breadcrumbs, sage and other delicacies; a *jus* flavoured with cognac. The wine a Gamay.

'I've thought about Corbeau ridge,' I said, slicing into the pigeon. 'Bèze has a total of ten hectares, whereas Corbeau ridge, given to the grape, is only 1.2 hectares. Last year we sold forty hectolitres for 125 francs per hectolitre – five thousand francs – a profit of about four thousand francs.'

Armand refilled my glass.

'This insect threat is in the early stages. We are a long way from the south. It's warmer down there, more open to disease. We may have three, five years of productivity. More. Anyway, it may never reach here.'

'The oidium fungus spread here in the forties.'

'Understood. But even if it did arrive it would be no great disaster for us. The value of our vineyard today is seven, maybe eight thousand francs. Infected with "the insect" it might be worth one… two thousand. So, if we didn't sell, we'd be out of pocket by five, six thousand francs, nothing in the greater scheme of things. *And* we miss out on the profit in the years waiting for the insect, or whatever it is, to arrive. If we sold the land and it goes away, we'll have to start again – clear a new parcel, plant new vines, then wait four to five years before producing a crop for sale. Anyway, the best piece of land is Corbeau ridge.'

'It is not as though we have all ten hectares given to the grape.'

'We are very small *vignerons*.'

'So you're against a sale?'

'There's no business case for it.'

'I am glad you came to that conclusion, Monique. Makes absolute sense.' Taking my hand: 'You're wasted, you know, you should be out there changing the world.'

'Sweet words, *chéri*, and thank you. If we had the resources we could take advantage of the insect – buy mature vineyards at giveaway prices.'

'Alas, we have no money. Well, not enough to buy more land.'

'And there is no point in producing our own wine as we had planned.'

'Therefore, no plant and machinery, and no *négociant*.'

'And no expense. We carry on as we are. Take the money, cut

costs and ride out the storm if and when it arrives.'

After dinner, upstairs, I undressed him, not a word said. I slipped out of my clothes and shook my head when he tried to snuff out the candles. I was in control. When he rolled onto his back I teased him, his erection rock-hard. Then I mounted him. We rocked and swayed for a while. Bliss. I screamed when he turned me 'inside out'; my fists clenched as I rode the wave. I lay there afterwards, counting my blessings. Lucien would have to wait another day.

That was my life and yet I wasn't even twenty years old.

The following day I drafted a letter to Madame Thierry.

Château B

6 July 1866

My Dearest Delphine,

I hope all is well.

> *So much news: my attempt to rescue Lucien failed and I am back with Armand. It was terrible and Mathilde was there, blocking my way. I spent a month moping but feel on the mend. My husband is a dear and very supportive. I am very fortunate. I would love you to meet him.*

> *This 'insect' threat puts the acquisition of le Merle in a different light. Please instruct M de Gaalon to break off contact with M Tausend... let him stew.*

> *Please also ask M de G to give an estimate of what le Merle is worth per hectare in 'normal' times and if there has been any panic selling.*

> *Enclosed is two hundred francs to cover his fees.*

My love and good wishes to you,
K

I showed the letter to Armand. 'Exactly the right approach, *chérie*,' he said. Then: 'Who is "K"?'

'Delphine's nickname for me.'

Mid-December. Our crop was unaffected by the insect, as was most of France. The pest was confined to the lower Rhône, a long way from Bourgogne and even further away from the Touraine.

I received a reply from Madame Thierry. A letter from Monsieur de Gaalon enclosed.

F de Gaalon, Avocat

5 December 1866

Dear Madame Thierry,

I bumped into M Tausend, who informed me the interest payments are continuing to be made. He also told me the mortgagor has requested a one-year extension of the existing arrangements and that the bank has agreed to said extension.

In answer to your question: land values. Recent sales indicate the value of land with mature vines thereon in Meursault is in the order of ten thousand francs per hectare. Domaine le Merle is in a poor state of repair: the vines, plant and equipment as well as the buildings all requiring attention. I would therefore value the domaine at eight thousand francs per hectare, a total (rounded down) of one hundred thousand francs.

The insect scare has not gone away. In my opinion most vignerons in Bourgogne are in a state of denial. It is also my opinion that the renewal of terms is good news for our mutual client – in a year's time the insect problem may be better understood.

Je vous prie etc,

François de Gaalon

I felt disappointment but also relief: for the moment there was no need to bother Armand as to where the money was coming from.

When I arrived at Château Bèze four years previously, the place was in a state of disrepair, the west-facing roof so dilapidated that the rooms on the second floor were damp, the walls streaked with stains. In one room, plaster had crumbled away from the ceiling.

The Château contained eight bedrooms with three reception rooms on the ground floor. Art littered the walls. I counted over a hundred pieces in the reception rooms alone. Three years ago, I managed to persuade Armand to move the paintings out of the affected bedrooms. He insisted on supervising the transfer and hanging the paintings himself.

I also persuaded him to list the pictures and have them valued. Many of the pieces came from Virginie's family – always a sensitive subject with Armand. I remember one of our rare arguments. *If you think we're going to sell some pieces to pay for repairs...* In the end I convinced him to sell some of the lesser pieces, enough to fix the roof. *It's what Virginie would have wanted...*

Marriage. The subject was rarely discussed. The problem was, of course, Armand *fils* and Céleste. We both knew they did not approve of me. Armand was clearly embarrassed, but I saw no point in exerting pressure on him.

I was content for our life to continue as it was.

THIRTY-TWO

WO YEARS LATER, October 1868. They say the devil makes work for idle hands. Boredom was my enemy. Once I had shaken off my failure to recover Lucien, I had set myself some tasks.

Late in 1866, I had purchased a Singer sewing machine and made a dress – three of them, in fact – which I wore around the house. No hoops, crinolines or corsets; no full-lengths covering me like a Bedouin. Made from wool, it was more a skirt than a dress – hanging loose from the waist to below the knee. With the use of pleats, it flared from the hips. A cardigan fastened with buttons and hugging the torso added to the overall effect, flattering the female form with the addition of a belt. Pinning a brooch to the cardigan made me look 'modern', as did the beret, especially when I wore it at an angle.

Armand said I looked gamine. 'Try it out on your friends,' he suggested. I took him at his word and wore it at a get-together. Strange looks from the guests. Although one of the wives – Marceline Lamartine – told me how lovely I looked.

I continued to work on Armand's artworks – had every painting professionally photographed. I itemised the details in a file: the size, a brief description, the artist's name and dates. I knew nothing about art at the time, although I was aware of the masters: da Vinci, Rembrandt – those types.

There were 151 pieces in all. I didn't recognise any of the names: Corot, Turner, van Ruisdael, amongst others. Determined to attain some knowledge, I stayed with Joelie so I could visit the Louvre and other galleries.

On one trip Joelie advised me to make the acquaintance of an art dealer she knew. 'Monsieur Durand-Ruel on rue Laffitte has a good reputation,' she assured me.

Armand's collection included two portraits by Philippe de Champaigne of a cardinal dressed in his magnificent red robes. 'Cardinal de Richelieu is a distant ancestor,' said Armand, giving me a look as if to say, *Forget it, they will never be sold.*

'De Richelieu. Ah, one of Dumas's villains in *The Three Musketeers*.'

'Quite.'

As for the grapes, the 1866 and 1867 crops were plentiful – about forty-five hectolitres' worth. There was no sign of 'the pest'. I made a habit of reading the journals on wine and horticulture. *Le Messager Agricole du Midi* provided me with an answer. The insect had been identified as an aphid: *phylloxera vastatrix* – the dry-leaf devastator. Although it was still confined to the lower Rhône, our determination not to produce our own wine held fast. Meanwhile, I hatched an idea – a plot, more like.

Marceline Lamartine had become a good friend. Adolphe, her husband, was a well-known *vigneron* and a friend of Armand's. In 1866 we sold the bulk of our crop to the Lamartines. After the 'presentation' of 'the dress', Marceline invited herself to a morning at Château Bèze. With her compliment in mind I wore the latest version of my 'Kiki Combination'.

Marceline turned up in an absurd concoction – all frills and layers, full-length with billowing sleeves. Her hair was done up in a lace headpiece. I remember feeling embarrassed – a dove to her peacock. It was summer and hot. Marceline appeared uncomfortable, fanning herself much of the time, while I sat there cool as you like.

Marceline was, give or take, the same height as me and opulent despite her age – her figure, the bumps and curves in all the right places.

We talked couture. And soon she was standing there in one of my combinations. I handed her a beret.

She giggled like a thirteen-year-old, blushing as she inspected herself in the full-length mirror. More giggles as she flounced and adjusted the beret. Curtsies. 'I love it,' she proclaimed. 'A bit tight, though.'

'Let me take your measurements.'

A month later I presented her with my creation: a peach-coloured combination that complemented her complexion. She changed behind a screen. I told her she looked wonderful. She didn't know where to put herself, such was her joy. I handed her a beret. '*Voilà*, Marcy,' I said.

She was worried what Adolphe would think. 'Just hit him between the eyes,' I said.

'Or the legs,' she replied naughtily. She insisted on paying me, taking notes from her reticule. I refused... all part of my wicked Kiki plan.

Armand returned home earlier than expected. Marcy squirmed when he entered the room. 'Who is this stranger in my house?' he said, a mischievous gleam in his eye.

I looked at him, my hands on my hips, my mouth agape. Marceline continued to squirm.

I remember Armand breaking into a smile. 'Why, Marceline, ha. I have to say you do look lovely, my dear.'

A year later, with the *vendange* under way, I persuaded Armand to ask Adolphe if he could produce some wine made exclusively from grapes on Corbeau ridge.

'I'll try,' he said. 'But you have to realise that Adolphe is a hard-headed businessman.'

'Hard he may be, but he has a wife.'

'Oh, now I understand. You clever girl.'

Next day I took coffee with Marceline, quietly letting her know that Armand would be in touch with her husband: 'On matters concerning the grape.'

Earlier that year I took delivery of fifty cases of Corbeau Ridge, Chenin Blanc. The label designed by me was affixed to each bottle. I had to pay Adolphe, of course – one franc per bottle for expenses incurred. We retained two cases for ourselves. The rest we sold to local shops and restaurants and to people we knew – a profit of three francs a bottle. This together with the sale of our crop meant that 1868 was a very good year.

Not an hour went by when I didn't think of Lucien. I imagined all sorts of tortures to inflict on Mathilde, from pulling out every one of her fingernails to boiling her alive. I can still see her, clear as day, standing there in all her bulk, blocking my way. I was minded to try to rescue him again – a gang of thugs in tow – knock down the Wynburnes' door in the dead of night, stomp in and take what is mine, smashing everything of theirs in my wake, furniture, their precious paintings – *every damn thing*.

Just a silly notion, of course. Lucien would be guarded more closely than the Man in the Iron Mask.

At the end of November, I received a letter from Madame Thierry, a letter from Monsieur de Gaalon enclosed.

F de Gaalon, Avocat

24 November 1868

Dear Madame Thierry,

I thought I should update you regarding a conversation I had with M Tausend of Banque Villiard. The last time I wrote (5 Dec 1866) I informed you that the mortgage arrangements re Domaine le Merle had been extended to the end of 1867.

These arrangements have been extended (again) to the end of this year.

 Several of the mortgage payments have been in arrears and the mortgagor has asked for a further extension of one year. M Tausend has asked me if my client would be interested in purchasing the estate were the bank to foreclose. In my last letter I indicated a value of one hundred thousand francs. Despite the phylloxera scare, prices have not declined in Meursault. If anything they have risen. However, Domaine le Merle is in a further state of decline, offsetting any rise there may have been in land value.

 I look forward to our mutual client's instruction (if any).

Je vous prie etc,
François de Gaalon

Excitement churned within me. I felt light-headed; I didn't know what to do with myself. But once I had settled down, I knew I had to go to Beaune. Besides, I had been cooped up in Château Bèze for nigh on six months and was in need of a trip.

A week later I was sitting in Madame Thierry's parlour in my new governess's outfit. Two bottles of Corbeau Ridge stood on her kitchen table. She looked her usual healthy self despite the dusting of grey at her temples, the filigree lines round her eyes. A feeling of deep affection welled inside me, such that I had to wipe away a tear.

 'Are you all right, Kiki?' she said.

 'Sorry. It's nothing. Just seeing you again, I suppose.'

 'Why are you here, dear?'

 'Le Merle. The letter from Monsieur de Gaalon. I need to meet him.'

 'Do you have the means to acquire le Merle?'

'Not at the moment.'

'We don't want to waste his time.'

'I know… there must be another way.'

Crinkling her eyes: 'Another way… how, Kiki?'

'I haven't thought of it yet.'

'I can't think of anything apart from borrowing the money.'

'Difficult given my situation.'

'You could incorporate a company.'

'True, but any self-respecting banker would want to know who is concealed behind the "veil".'

'I am sure you are right.'

'On the other hand, Oreste wouldn't know who is behind it – the company, that is.'

'Let's see what Monsieur de Gaalon has to say.'

'Can you arrange a meeting?'

'Of course. Though he should come here.'

'My husband died seven years ago, Delphine.'

'Yes, and people haven't forgotten. Only the other day one of my "parents" mentioned you. "I wonder what happened to her?" – words to that effect.'

Monsieur de Gaalon was close to what I'd imagined he'd be: small, in his late fifties, bald and neatly dressed in a black frock coat and cravat. His facial hair was restricted to a goatee. He sported a monocle.

I was dressed in my governess garb and wore my 'long' wig.

He introduced himself.

'Please refer to me as Madame du P, monsieur.'

The pleasantries exchanged, he afforded me a grim smile. 'The bank will require a conditional agreement for sale and purchase to be signed by you before they foreclose on the mortgage.'

'One moment,' I said. 'How do we know the mortgagor, threatened with foreclosure, will not produce the requisite funds?'

'We don't, madam…'

'Or sell the property and redeem the mortgage from the proceeds of sale?'

'Ah, good questions, madam. This is one of those cases where the value of the property and the loan are quite close. And banks don't like to be seen to foreclose… bad for business. And, of course, there's still the threat of *phylloxera*.'

'What is le Merle worth, monsieur?'

He sighed. 'A lot of work needs to be done. Two years ago, I suggested a hundred thousand. Now… about the same, a little less, perhaps.'

'Ninety thousand?'

'Maybe. You'll need at least twenty thousand to effect repairs.'

'The outstanding mortgage is seventy thousand francs, so if the bank foreclosed and sold to a third party, they would gain twenty thousand.'

'Less expenses, Madame du P.'

'Thing is, monsieur, I don't want to take possession of le Merle. I don't want the responsibility or the costs.'

'Then we're in a bind,' said Madame Thierry.

Monsieur de Gaalon stroked his beard. 'Hmm, not necessarily, Delphine.'

'How do you mean?'

'We could acquire the mortgage from the bank.'

I scratched my chin. 'How would that work, monsieur?'

'You would pay the bank its seventy thousand and become the mortgagee. "Oreste", for want of a name, would be obliged to pay interest to *you* and would continue to be responsible for the property.'

'What is the interest rate?'

'Five per cent.'

'Three thousand five hundred francs a year.'

'Eight hundred and seventy-five a quarter,' piped up Madame Thierry.

'How can a policeman afford that?'

'Am I correct in thinking he's not married?' said Monsieur de Gaalon.

'Oreste always told me he was a committed bachelor.'

'So low domestic expenses.'

'The property does produce *some* income.'

'True,' I said. 'This arrangement would suit me, monsieur. I would have control of sorts and an income.'

'Forgive me, madam, but do you have seventy thousand francs available?'

'Not at the moment.'

Madame Thierry said, 'Madame's husband is from the landowning aristocracy, François.'

It was settled. Monsieur de Gaalon would speak to Monsieur Tausend right away.

The following day I hired a mare from Hôtel de Chevreuil. I'd had the sense to pack my boots and jodhpurs. Madame Thierry lent me some warm clothes. The sky was a pale winter blue. A chill wind rolled down the Côte d'Or.

On my way to Meursault I tried to rationalise my obsession with le Merle. By the time I reached Pommard I had worked it out: my family. I was desperate to outdo my brothers – teach them a lesson for selling me for a piece of dirt. Generations of Vellays had been little more than *paysans*, struggling to survive by working someone else's land. It was time for a change, not with a measly half-hectare but with an entire *domaine*.

I always thought that one day I would return to Bourgogne. Why? I was 'married' to a man whom I adored but whose family despised me. Armand would always choose his children over me; they would inherit Château Bèze and the land in Montargis. Armand was fifteen years older than me. I would likely outlive him. Then what?

The world of wine excited me. I knew I had a head for business – my experience with Les Mines du Saar and Corbeau Ridge. I wanted to battle with the *négociants* of Paris, be part of that world, bargain and haggle with the best of them.

Lastly, Monsieur Oreste Monnier. Having some sort of control over him made me feel vengeful. I could feel the thrill, the blood coursing through my veins. Oreste was better than his twin. But he was smug and had refused to listen to me in the Conciergerie – I was guilty in his eyes and *he* felt vengeful. He knew Augustave was abusing me, an innocent fifteen-year-old, yet he had stood by, done nothing.

As for the wine, I wanted to produce the best. The 'science' fascinated me: *terroir*, *vendange*, the fermentation process, barrels – choosing the right wood. And the selling process: I felt the position of *négociants* was too powerful. There had to be a way of selling wine without the use of an intermediary. The idea of dealing with the likes of Sir Reginald Markham was anathema to me.

The dream of buying le Merle outright had paled: borrowing money, paying interest, the responsibility and the cost – all those repairs. *And* having to deal with Madame Gaillard and Benoît who were welded to the place. Could I throw them onto the street? I'd love to, especially Madame Gaillard. But could I? Would I…?

There were risks, of course. What if Oreste redeemed the mortgage? Paid me back? What if he stopped paying the interest? I would have to foreclose, take control, assume responsibility. Ah, but I had a backup plan: Alie and her husband, Antoine, could manage the *domaine*. Meanwhile, I would be in the background. And one day I would surely clear my name.

Arriving at le Merle it struck me how large the buildings were. Some windows at the front were cracked. Shutters hung off their hinges at odd angles, the wood bleached by the sun and in need of paint. Tiles were missing from all of the roofs.

I urged the mare up the hill, tethered her, then walked down through the vines. The grapes remained unharvested, furred with mildew, hanging in desiccated bunches. Weeds were everywhere.

This time Madame Gaillard did not appear – too cold, perhaps. I imagined her huddled by the fire. Again, I could only feel pity for her.

I decided to avoid the centre of Meursault and rode up the hill into Monthelie and down the other side to Volnay. I found Domaine Albert Bouzereau et fils up beyond the chapel. Giggling with excitement, I knocked on the door. Alie opened up. My blonde wig fooled her for a moment and then she wrapped her arms around me – though at a stretch since her belly got in the way. I stood back. 'How many months?'

An embarrassed look then she grinned. 'Eight months, Kiki.'

'Are you happy, Alie?'

She smiled again.

'Where's Antoine?'

'Nurturing his beloved vines.'

'Sorry I could not attend your wedding – too much of a risk.'

'I missed you. Now tell me all, Kiki.'

I had to fight myself not to tell her about le Merle. I couldn't. Even to Alie, who might let it slip to Antoine. The fewer people 'in the know' the better. Instead: 'I was bored with life in the Touraine and in need of a break. And I wanted to see you, Alie.'

She asked me about my husband. I replied in generalities… that I loved him and was happy. We discussed wine – the barrels I had produced.

Alie said, 'We Vellays are always drawn to the vine.'

'How are Dago and Salva doing?'

'They sold their first crop two years ago.'

'Good,' I heard myself say. 'What's Antoine's view on *phylloxera*?'

'He thinks it will arrive here. For the moment it's confined to the Rhône, although there are one or two outbreaks in Bordeaux.'

'Strange, the Rothschilds purchased Château Lafite this year.'

'Antoine thinks people have their heads in the sand.'

'Perhaps he's right. We just don't know, do we?'

She narrowed her eyes. 'Why are you really here, Kiki?'

I took her hand. 'I can't tell you, Alie. Please don't ask me again.'

Wrinkling her lips: 'How is it with you and the authorities?'

'That's why I'm here,' I lied, hating myself.

I asked her about Florian. Same answer as two years ago: no one had seen him since the night he disappeared.

'His mother must be very upset.'

'People say she's lost the will to live, hanging on by a thread. I occasionally see her shuffling through Meursault. Very sad.'

I asked her about Junius.

'As you know he went to Mexico and has yet to return. People assume he must have died there.'

I experienced a pang, a void of sorts – nothing more. I was surprised how dispassionate I felt.

I stayed for tea. She talked about Arlette, her intelligence. And Eloise – how she was coping with Oubliette. She appeared to be doing well, despite Junius's absence. I stood and said goodbye. 'No one should know of my visit to Meursault. No one, including Antoine.'

I rode away shrouded in regret. Alie with the child inside her, a child she would keep – not have taken from her. Lucien and the child would be cousins.

By the time I reached Pommard I was having serious doubts. Were my ambitions getting the better of me? Was I aiming above my station? Why couldn't I settle for something more modest – as Alie had? No, no and no. I gritted my teeth – if Eloise could do it, I could do it.

The following morning at Madame Thierry's, Monsieur de Gaalon came straight to the point: 'Madam, I spoke with Monsieur Tausend at some length. He said he would put the mortgage idea to his co-directors.'

'When will we have an answer?'

'A week, madam.'

'I can't stay here a week, monsieur.'

'I can't hurry them. We don't want to appear too keen.'

'Hmm, you're right.'

'Madam, forgive me, but I have gone out on a limb – the money, I mean. He asked me if my client had the means. The cash. I told them it was not a problem.'

I had anticipated this. 'Monsieur, if they say yes to our proposal would they take a deposit of, say, ten per cent, pending completion of the transaction?'

'Not an unreasonable request.'

'Could we sign a *compromis de vente* with completion three months thereafter?'

'It will be an assignment, not a *compromis*. I can but try, madam.'

'Offer them six months to start with, please, monsieur.'

He shot Madame Thierry a look. 'As I said, I will try, madam.'

'I will need to form a *société*.'

Wiping his monocle, he agreed to draw up the papers. Madame Thierry would have power of attorney to sign the mortgage-assignment deed on behalf of the *société*.

'One question, monsieur, could a minor be added as a shareholder without his knowledge or consent?'

'The age of said minor?'

'Six years old, monsieur.'

'Not a problem. The minor's name, if I may enquire?'

'He is known as Lucien Wynburne.'

'"Known", madam?'

I looked at Madame Thierry. 'Lucien is my son, monsieur, taken from me just after he was born. Delphine knows the details. Suffice to say that he lives with John and Mathilde Wynburne of number 6 rue du 29 Juillet in the First Arrondissement, Paris.'

Monsieur de Gaalon made notes. 'Shocking, if I may say so, madam.'

'Monsieur, by now you will have guessed who I am.'

He spread his hands. 'Madame Monnier.'

'Yes, and wanted by police for questioning in connection with the death of my husband. The irony is that Oreste, my husband's twin, is or was leading the search for me.'

'The likely mortgagor, madam – ironic indeed.'

'Who when he finds out who the mortgagee is…'

'Will double his efforts to track you down.' He arched an eyebrow. 'You are playing a dangerous game, madam.'

'He will be apoplectic. His incentive to put me away will be enormous. Is there a way I can remain in the background, not appear on any of the documentation, Lucien as well?'

De Gaalon rubbed his chin. 'You could hide behind the société. Highly irregular… Nominee directors would be required.'

'Yourself and Madame Thierry?'

He nodded. 'Delphine?'

'Yes, provided I have no financial obligation or liability.'

Monsieur de Gaalon said, 'Have you considered a name?'

I grinned. 'Société Vins du Cluvé.'

'Cluvé?'

'Christine and Lucien Vellay,' said Madame Thierry. 'Sounds like "cuvée". Clever.'

'Ah, that's good, madam. It doesn't give you away and yet it's there, hidden.'

'Precisely.'

'Then it is settled. It will take me three days to draft the documents. Then it's up to the bank.'

THIRTY-THREE

FIVE DAYS LATER I was back in Paris with Joelie. The weather was fine but cold, the sun low in the sky.

I wore a heavy coat together with my long wig and beret as I walked to rue du 29 Juillet. Joelie had lent me a pair of gloves.

I crossed the Seine via Pont des Arts, taking care to look left and right down the flow, but *La Fleur de l'Yonne* was not there. Skirting the Louvre, I reached the Jardin and entered rue de Rivoli through the exit where Mathilde had blocked my path. I could see her standing there as though it was yesterday.

I walked up and down the 29 Juillet several times on the side opposite to number 6. Aware I might have looked suspicious, I entered the Welcome café and sat at a table by the window. I stayed there for some time, ordered coffees as well as an omelette. And although number 6 was some way away, it appeared that no one had entered or emerged from the property. At four, it was becoming dark. After settling *l'addition* I walked up and down the street until it was too cold.

Two days later I returned to Château Bèze. Armand was not looking well and complained of stomach pains. I ordered him straight to bed then asked the cook to make her special chicken broth.

'Just a winter's cold, ma'am,' she said. 'Couple of days in bed, he'll be as right as rain.'

Upstairs I fussed round Armand, plumped his pillows, tucked him in, added another blanket, poured him a glass of water. 'Cook's making chicken broth, *chéri*,' I told him.

Barely able to utter the words he asked me how my trip had gone. I omitted telling him of the mortgage idea – not the time to burden him.

He asked me the date.

'Saturday, 12 December, *chéri*.'

'Céleste and Armand will be home soon,' he croaked.

'That will be pleasant,' I lied.

I was determined to make an effort, make Château Bèze welcoming. Over the next three days I helped the maid prepare the children's bedrooms. Pleasant touches including candles and sprigs of holly here and there. Downstairs in the main room I placed a small fir tree, dug from the garden, in a corner close to the hearth, decorating the branches with lace and more holly. I made a small crib, the figures contrived from old cork *bouchons* and covered with material from my sewing kit. I was proud of the donkey I had made from a log, his head fashioned from a cork. A spray of mistletoe, lopped from a tree outside, was suspended beneath the arch separating the main salon from the dining room. I rummaged in the cellar, chose the best wines, stood the reds up, put the whites and two bottles of champagne in the icehouse outside.

Armand made an effort as well: tottering downstairs and telling me how lovely everything looked. But it was too much for him and he had to return to his bed. He refused to see a doctor, of course. But the day before Céleste was to arrive, I put my foot down and walked into Monteaux to find Dr Péguret.

In the afternoon the doctor attended to Armand. I insisted on being present, at a discreet distance, though. After examining him thoroughly, Dr Péguret handed Armand a glass bowl and a small bottle. Armand shuffled to the bathroom, emerging grim-faced minutes later.

'Is your husband eating, madam?'

I shrugged. 'A slice of toast for breakfast, broth at lunch, a little something in the evening. Hardly two square meals a day.'

Dr Péguret examined the stools, turning them with a spoon. 'They are a little pale,' he said looking up. 'Apart from that they look normal.'

'Please explain?'

'No traces of blood or discolouration, madam.'

By the window he squinted at the bottle of urine. 'The colour is a trifle dark. I'll take it to the surgery for analysis.'

Dr Péguret patted Armand on the shoulder. 'Bed and rest for you, Baron du Plessis. You are well cared for by your lovely wife, that much I can see. I'll return in a week's time or earlier if needs be.'

Outside I clasped the doctor's arm, asked him if everything was all right.

'It's probably a severe bout of influenza, the time of year. Your husband needs plenty of rest. Make sure he eats regularly.'

The following day Céleste arrived. She was pretty with dark hair like her father's. I tried to make her feel comfortable. She looked down her nose at me. 'Your father is unwell,' I told her.

Instead of asking 'How is he?' as a normal person might, she shot me a look as though *I* had made him ill. She ran up the stairs. The last I saw of her until the evening.

Dinner was a monosyllabic affair. I attempted conversation. Asked Céleste about school. 'It's fine,' she replied. And about her friends: 'They're fine.' She was fourteen years old to my twenty-two – old enough to be my sister. At her age I was as good as married. I couldn't imagine the next seven years would tangle her life the way it had mine. I felt relieved when she announced she was going to bed. There was no *thank you for the lovely dinner, Monique. And by the way the Christmas decorations are delightful* from this little chit. I just managed to hold my tongue.

Two days later Armand's son arrived. Tall with long dark hair he cut a dash in his cadet's uniform. I made a fuss of him, took his hand, even flirted a little – after all, he was only three years younger than me. He glanced at his sister, his hand limp in mine. 'I must see Father straightaway,' he said as though I wasn't there.

The evening passed as it had with Céleste: terse in answering my polite enquiries – lively whilst talking among themselves. I felt like an intruder and bid them goodnight as soon as I had finished the main course. Again, I had managed to hold my temper.

With Armand ill, I slept in a separate room. After preparing myself for bed I went to kiss him goodnight. I found him sitting up in bed and looking a little better. When he asked me how it was going with the children, I told him the truth: 'I've been with you for six years, *chéri*, yet they still ignore me. They take me for a whore, whose only interest is your money and estate.'

He looked at me with rheumy eyes. 'What money? I'm sorry, but what can I say? I've tried. God *knows* I've tried. I've had words with them. But, like me, they are stubborn.'

I held his hand. 'I don't know how long I can last without losing my temper.'

'They are only here till early January. Try to stay calm, for my sake.'

'You look better, *chéri*.'

'I'll be up and about for Christmas and the New Year.'

I kissed him goodnight.

Armand was out of bed to celebrate Christmas. We all attended mass on Christmas Eve in the church at Mesland, returning to Château Bèze for the traditional feast – crevettes and foie gras from a farmer friend of ours.

The occasion proved too much for Armand. He managed to eat some bread before retiring for the night. Once again, I was left with the children and made my excuses to go to bed before I said something rash.

I kissed Armand goodnight and retreated to my room. Once in bed I buried myself under the blankets. I forced myself not to cry… They were not worth crying for.

Christmas Day. As the staff had been given the day off, it was left to me to prepare lunch – a goose with all the trimmings, a ham and a Christmas cake. I half-expected Céleste to help me. No such luck. Instead, she was in the salon cavorting with her brother – often whooping with laughter. I could feel my temper rise with every dice of a vegetable, every dash of this and that, every stir. I hid my anger when Armand handed me a glass of champagne. I could see the strain in his face: his eyes were sunken; his skin was pallid. 'Time to hand out the presents,' he said.

We were gathered in the salon by the tree, the logs in the fire aglow. In time-honoured du Plessis tradition Armand handed out the presents. For me a single strand of pearls, which I still occasionally wear. I giggled and wrapped them round my neck, having removed Florian's cross. There was what I took as a jealous look from Céleste.

I had made an effort: three beautiful silk ties for Armand *fils*, a pair of jodhpurs for Céleste. I remember them looking at each other as though my gifts were unsuitable: cravats the neckwear of choice; side-saddle the way a woman rode a horse.

Their gifts to me were disappointing, as they were every year: six cotton handkerchiefs from him and a lace headdress from her – as though she knew I loathed headdresses. I made the best of it – fluttering one of the handkerchiefs and trying on the headdress. Armand looked bemused.

With no help from Céleste I wrestled lunch onto the table. Armand *fils* was at least doing something – decanting a bottle of red wine. Céleste sat straight-backed, expecting to be waited on hand and foot. Armand made a valiant effort in carving the goose, but he was struggling – beads of sweat on his brow.

The conversation was pleasant enough until Céleste pushed

her plate away. 'The fowl is undercooked,' she declared.

'If you had helped me in the kitchen, I might have had more time to concentrate on the *fowl*.'

'I don't know how to cook' – to no one in particular.

'It is a matter of helping. You know how to boil water, I suppose.'

Armand ran a finger under his collar. 'Please,' he said.

'No. I'm fed up with your children, Armand. They have done nothing to contribute. They won't even talk to me.'

'My dear.'

'They haven't once said how lovely the decorations are. Instead, they complain.'

'I haven't complained,' said Armand *fils*, addressing me directly for once.

'Yes, but you sit there eating the food I have gone to a lot of trouble to prepare and yet not a word. You're an ungrateful brat.'

He stood. 'Father, are you going to let this woman speak to me like this, in *my* house?'

'It's not your house *yet*.'

'Armand, sit down,' said his father. 'Now calm down, everyone, it's Christmas, a time for fam—'

'Don't talk about family, Armand, these two haven't said a kind word to me in six years.'

Armand *fils* stood again.

'I thought I told you to sit down.'

'No. We all know what this woman is—'

'Is what?' I hissed.

'A *cocotte*. A whore, come to steal you away, Papa.'

'Sit down. I won't have you speak to Monique in that way. Apologise immediately, do you hear?'

My turn to stand. Scowling at them one by one, I took my time.

Armand wiped his brow with a napkin, his eyes beseeching me.

I shook my head. 'Yes, I was a *cocotte*, as you call it. Do you think I wanted to be? No, I was forced into it. My baby was stolen

from me when I was sixteen. I had no money and nowhere to live.'
Staring at Céleste: 'I wasn't much older than *you*.'

'So why didn't you get a job?' said Armand *fils*.

'Get a job, huh, in the middle of winter? I didn't have a sou. Easy for you to say "get a job". My problem was there and then, you have no idea – the realities of life.'

'The econ—'

'Don't talk to me of the economy. In places like Belleville, the north-east *arrondissements* – places where you have never been – people are trying to survive on two francs a day. *Two francs*. Alcoholism is rife. People are living in squalor. Rats. Disease. Again, you have no idea.'

'Huh, what's that got to do with me, Monique, if that is indeed your real name?'

Armand *père* staggered to his feet, wiping his brow again. 'Enough, I told you not to speak to her like that.'

Armand *fils*' comment had me rocked on my feet, but again Armand came to my rescue. 'I met Monique through a mutual friend. Yes, I paid for her company. I was desperate to meet someone, your mother long in her grave. I was blessed when Monique entered my life. Look what's she's done with this house, the wine business.'

'For her own ends,' said Céleste.

'It might have escaped your notice,' I said, 'but your father and I are *not* married.'

'You'll find a way,' said Armand *fils*. 'Your type always does.'

'"Type"? And what type are you, Armand? I'll tell you. You're an idler, playing soldiers, waiting for your father to die so you can live off the fat of the land. You're far worse than me. At I least I did something, rather than hanging round like the vulture you are.'

I remember him glowering at me. For a moment I thought he was going to attack me.

Céleste stood. Dabbing her eyes with a napkin she announced she was going to her room.

'Good riddance,' I muttered under my breath.

The following two weeks were hell. The children avoided me, moped about the place with sullen faces. The only good moment was when Dr Péguret informed me that Armand's urine test was favourable, that there was nothing to worry about.

Early in the New Year of 1869 the children departed, leaving Armand and me to ourselves.

A letter from Madame Thierry arrived, a letter from Monsieur de Gaalon enclosed.

F de Gaalon, Avocat

16 December 1868

Dear Madame Thierry,

Indifferent news, I'm afraid. The directors of Banque Villiard have decided not to assign the mortgage to our mutual client. I will continue to monitor the situation.

Je vous prie etc,
François de Gaalon

THIRTY-FOUR

IN OCTOBER 1869 Armand suffered a relapse. This time Dr Péguret had bad news for me: Armand had cancer. We sat in the salon.

'Is there any chance of recovery?' I said, fighting back the tears.

'I am sorry, madam, not when the cancer affects the pancreas.'

'How long…?'

'Three, six months at most.'

I was at Armand's bedside when the doctor informed him of his condition.

'So, they're coming for me,' he said.

'They take us all in the end,' said Dr Péguret.

'Well, they haven't got you yet,' I said. 'We'll make the best of it.'

'Armand and Céleste will be devastated.' A tear ran down his cheek. 'I'll write to them without delay.'

Caring for someone is a full-time occupation. I fed him broths and boiled vegetables but to no avail: the loss of weight, the mottling of his skin. He rallied occasionally, enabling him to hobble round the grounds.

On one such day in the spring of 1870 we were sitting in the sun when he grabbed my hand. 'Monique, you have looked after me. What would I have done without you?'

'With your looks and charm, a flock of women would have vied to attend to your needs.'

He laughed. Then he looked at me, his eyes locked on mine. 'Monique, I have been very selfish.'

'Selfish, surely…?'

'We are not married. The law will not provide for you when I die.'

'Don't worry your—'

'We should become man and wife, Monique.'

'Is that a proposal, *chéri*?'

'Of course it is. And I haven't told you how much I love you recently. Well, I love you, have done from the day I first clapped eyes on you.'

'Armand, I love you too, you know I do, but I have to reject your proposal.'

'Why? Think what will happen to you.'

'*Chéri*, your children hate me. The law means I would share your estate with them. This I will not do.'

'Why?'

'Think about it… the three of us would be locked together for years, a war of attrition, inexorable, wearing us all down. No. I have other ideas.'

'Ah, last year, just before Christmas you returned from a trip to Beaune. I was ill. We never really talked about it. Selfish of me.'

I explained there was a chance of buying Domaine le Merle or at least having the mortgage assigned to me.

'Why didn't you discuss it with me?'

'You were ill, my love.'

'Nonsense.'

I explained how it could have worked. 'But the bank was reluctant to foreclose. Bad for business, they said. My lawyer in Beaune informed me the bank was not interested in the mortgage idea.'

'Damn fools, what with *phylloxera*.'

I shrugged.

'You don't want to marry me and you've explained why. Tell me what you do want.'

'For you to get better, *chéri*.'

'You're playing with me.'

'You have art on the walls, 151 pieces.'

He arched an eyebrow.

'This year we sold all our own wine. The Lamartines produced four barrels for us. The account has a balance of over fourteen thousand francs.'

'You have done well, *chérie*.'

'Before you, well, pass away I would be happy if the Corbeau Ridge account transferred twelve thousand francs to my account.'

'I will arrange it immediately. It's yours anyway. You deserve it.'

'It would also make me happy if I could have one or two of the paintings. Were you to agree, I would be willing to sign a piece of paper that says I have no claim on your estate.'

Armand rubbed his chin. 'No, Monique, I have another idea.'

I ignored him – ploughed on. 'You forget that aged fifteen I was exchanged for a piece of land and forced to marry a man I loathed.'

'How could I forget?'

'I know the wine business and I want le Merle. I was born in Meursault and wish to return there one day.'

He nodded.

'Armand, there's something you should know.'

'Are you sure you want to tell me?'

'My real name, you deserve to know who I am.'

'Monique, don't.'

'I have to. I've held on to it for too long. I'm doing this for me rather than for you.'

'If you must,' he sighed.

'My name is Christine Vellay – family and friends call me Kiki.'

'Kiki? Ah, the K in your letters.'

'My younger sister had a problem pronouncing the word "Christine".'

'Kikine.'

I laughed. 'Exactly.'

'Well, "*Kikine*", I am happy to give you some of the paintings, subject to a condition.'

My turn to sigh.

'That you marry me.'

'Armand…'

'For your own good, Monique. Once I am gone, you will have cash and some silly paintings. The most valuable thing I can give you is my name. Think about it… many doors will open for a baroness. *And* the authorities are looking for you… your disguise will be complete. No false names, you'll be able to prove who you say you are.'

'The children know who I am.'

'No, they don't. I'm certainly not going to tell them. And they don't know your history.'

'They know who Joelie is, that I worked for her.'

'True, but beyond Joelie they know nothing about you. So don't worry. I will ensure their discretion.'

'Armand, you are not listening to me – your children and I will be at war. I want them out of my life, do you understand?'

'And what you don't understand, my sweet, is that my lawyer will draw up a *contrat marriage* – the francs and the paintings will be legally yours before I die. However, once I have gone you will have no rights or access to my estate.'

I was overcome, buried my head in his shoulder and cried unashamedly. A short while later: 'Nothing would give me greater pleasure than to be your wife, Armand.'

Three weeks later we were married in the small chapel attached to Château Bèze. The Lamartines and Dr Péguret attended as witnesses. Armand had rallied, looking gaunt but handsome in his army uniform. We signed the marriage certificate. 'Don't lose this, Baroness du Plessis,' he said, handing it to me.

Twelve thousand francs was credited to my account. Fifteen paintings were taken off the walls and packed in wooden crates. The problem: where to store them. I was keen to avoid any confusion when Armand died: Armand and Céleste taking everything, including what was legally mine.

Wednesday, 1 June 1870. We were gathered at Armand's bedside: Armand *fils*, Céleste and myself. Dr Péguret at the foot of the bed looking suitably grave.

Armand had not wanted a priest. At the last minute he changed his mind.

'I'm Father Michel,' the priest said to me upon entering the room. 'I officiated at your wedding, Baroness. I would be obliged if you allowed me time alone with your husband.'

We retreated to the back of the room. Father Michel administered the last rites. Céleste quietly wept into a handkerchief. I reached out and took her hand. She didn't resist and gave me a small look. Both children were beautiful in their grief. I could see traces of their father in them – a rueful look, a mannerism, the way Armand *fils* stroked his chin.

Father Michel stood and made the sign of the cross, muttering things that priests mutter on the occasion of death. He took me aside: 'Madam, my sympathies are with you on this day. Your husband is a good man and, although not inclined to religion, it must be of joy to you that he sought the sacrament in his finality.'

Before I had time to answer, Dr Péguret called for the children. 'Your father is asking for you.'

Either side of the bed they each clasped a hand, Céleste burying her head in the nape of her father's neck. After a while Armand *fils* stood. 'Father wants you, Monique.'

I sat beside the man who had rescued me. He tried to lift his head as though he wanted to say something to me. I lowered my head. 'My *chérie*,' he wheezed, 'I am leaving you soon. You have made my life so wonderful. I don't know what I would have done without you. I want you to understand that you have exceptional gifts. You're the most talented person I know.' Fighting for air between his lips: 'I have told the children to respect you, to treat you fairly. They are stubborn, just like me.'

The tears welled. I tried to whisper 'I love you' but the words caught in my throat.

'Lucien,' he said. 'I pray you find your son.'

'I will,' I choked. 'My darling.'

'I love you. Have I ever told you?'

'Many times, my love.'

I held his hand. He was smiling. Time stood still. I felt the ghosts in the room – the spirits. After a while I beckoned the children and we knelt by the bed. He was still smiling, my wonderful Armand. Wind rattled the windows. The room went dark as though a cloud was passing and his hand slipped away.

We prayed. I could hear their breathing and the ticking of a clock. After a while, the priest leant over the bed and closed Armand's eyes. 'He died in peace,' he whispered.

The next day at breakfast, an uneasy silence, stolen looks between the children. Armand coughed, not quite looking me in the eye. 'Monique, our father's final wish was that we be friends with you,' he said. 'We are, of course, aware of your marriage to Papa and the arrangements made between you.'

I remained silent.

A glance at his sister: 'Céleste and I need to take control of our lives, face up to our responsibilities. This place' – spreading his hands. 'I hope you will understand.'

'Monique, what my brother is trying to say is that we need to agree a date for your departure.'

I shrugged.

'Hmm, today is the second of June,' said Armand. 'A month… how long do you need?'

I took my time. 'Your father wanted us to depart on good terms. A pity we couldn't have been friends, much easier for all of us.'

Céleste said, 'I may have judged you unfair—'

'Please, can we stick to the matter in hand, Celly?'

'No, Armand, it has to be said. Monique made Father a happy man. She cared for him while we were away. She's performed wonders with the house and the vines. We should be thankful to her.'

Armand flexed his fingers, his face contorted. 'Yes, we judged you unfairly, Monique. I'm sorry.'

'It's rather late for apologies. Such a waste of eight years.' Gritting my teeth: 'Apologies, however, are accepted. You both know that I loved your father. But now I need to organise my life.'

'Where will you go?' said Céleste.

'Paris.'

'Tell us how long you need?'

'Let's say the end of July – gives me two months.'

Céleste stood and, leaning down, brushed her lips against my cheek. 'Thank you, Monique, the end of July is acceptable to me.'

Monday, 6 June. Monteaux to Tours takes five hours on a horse, a long way but pleasant in summer. Leveret trotted at a steady pace. The Loire flowed in its timeless tilt towards the sea; buttercups and daisies filled the meadows; cows grazed. The vines were lush and green. The threat of the *phylloxera* aphid felt as remote as ever.

Despite my sadness, the world was mine. I was a woman of means, sufficient to establish myself in Paris, rent an apartment and gain employment. Become a dressmaker if I so chose. I had almost given up on le Merle, having heard nothing in eighteen months.

Lucien was constantly in my thoughts. In Paris I would be close to him. He was nearly eight years old. That I had missed out on his boyhood cut me to my very soul.

One thing I had brushed aside was the police. Wishful thinking, perhaps, but in the countryside the threat was as remote as *phylloxera*. Although Augustave had died nearly nine years ago I'd be naive to imagine that Oreste had forgotten my so-called crime.

How to clear my name? Only Madame Gaillard and Benoît knew what had really happened that night – as did Junius and Florian. But what good were they, long gone from Meursault? Madame Thierry's 'busybody' was still alive, as far as I was aware. News of any significance would have filtered back to me. The war in Mexico had ended three years ago. It was likely that Junius had perished. And what of dear Florian? I saw him in my mind's eye and felt the cross at my breast. He could have been anywhere, India, perhaps, far away from tiny Meursault. He too might have perished, God forbid.

In Tours I stabled Leveret at a hotel. My bank manager didn't keep me waiting. *Baroness this, Baroness that. Sorry about your husband, et cetera.* My account balance was 14,751 francs – much as I had expected. I asked him about my paintings. A proprietorial thrill as he led me down a flight of stairs and past two guards. Elaborate arrangements in the opening of the vault: several sets of keys involved. My fifteen boxed-up paintings were stacked in a corner. 'THE PROPERTY OF BARONESS DU PLESSIS' in black letters on each box.

After a light lunch I collected Leveret and rode back to Monteaux. 'A woman of means'… I felt excited. Next month I would be twenty-four years old. I thrilled at the thought of Paris. Seeing Joelie. Celebrating my return with her. I wondered if I could afford a studio in Saint-Germain, close to her. My head was so full of dreams.

THIRTY-FIVE

T EN DAYS LATER I returned from a trip to Paris having viewed several properties. One had taken my fancy: a second-floor apartment with a bedroom, a kitchen and a salon leading to a small terrace overlooking the square at the junction of rue Mouffetard and rue Lacépède. What's more, it was only three minutes' walk from Joelie's.

The asking price was eleven thousand francs; redecoration works were required. After haggling I agreed a price of 10,500. The *compromis de vente* was to be signed the following week on my return.

A letter was waiting for me at Château Bèze. I recognised the writing: Madame Thierry. The sense of foreboding as I slit open the envelope, a letter from Monsieur de Gaalon inside.

F de Gaalon, Avocat

                                          7 June 1870

Dear Madame Thierry,

I have to report that M Tausend of Banque Villiard came to see me yesterday. He wanted to know if our mutual client was still interested in assuming the Domaine le Merle mortgage.

I replied I would seek my client's instructions. I would remind you that the mortgage amount is seventy thousand francs with an interest payment of five per cent per annum, payable in advance every quarter.

I enquired as to why the bank has not foreclosed. He reminded me they were not in the habit of foreclosing unless there was no alternative.

I also enquired as to the regularity of the interest payments received and took the liberty of stating that payment of the interest was of importance to my client. M Tausend assured me the payments were continuing to be made. I feel what he says is true but that the payments are late (as they were eighteen months ago).

I was in Meursault last week and noted the property was in further decline – holes in all of the roofs as well as many broken windows. A viticulteur I know tells me the crop is not fully harvested, grapes left rotting on the vines.

I would advise that affairs there are in such a state that the value of the property and the mortgage amount are not that far apart.

I look forward to our mutual client's instruction (if any).

Je vous prie etc,
François de Gaalon

Hell! I did not want this, not at this particular time in my life. I stuck the letter in a pocket and went outside. I needed to think clearly – impossible, such was my turmoil. I walked through the orchards up to Corbeau ridge. A warm summer wind wafted the vines, swaying them, caressing them. A strange feeling – as though I was on the hill overlooking Meursault where my brothers had their parcel of land.

I walked back towards the Château. Paris. I wanted to live in

Paris, live life as a woman of worth, of character, of substance, in my pretty little apartment overlooking the square. The Quartier Latin at my feet, the cafés, the artists, the writers, the frauds, the *flâneurs*, the beau monde, the demi-monde, fine clothes, the best cuisine in the world, with Lucien just a short way away.

Four days later I was with Madame Thierry in her house in Beaune. Eighteen months on she was little changed, more streaks of grey in her hair, perhaps. I explained my dilemma to her.

'The sensible option is Paris. You have money. You are a woman of the world and one with a title, the Baroness du Plessis, no less. How old are you, Kiki?'

No one had called me Kiki in a long time. Made me smile. 'Twenty-four next month.'

'You'll find something to do in no time. Dressmaking, a *négociant* even.'

'A *négociant*. I hadn't thought of that. Problem is it renders me exposed. I *am* still wanted by the police.'

'Of that I am all too aware.'

'Any news from your busybody?'

'If you mean have either Junius or Florian returned, then no.'

'How will I ever be able to clear my name, Delphine?'

'A problem, certainly, and made more onerous were you to buy le Merle.'

'I will not be *buying* le Merle but controlling it through the mortgage. Something I can do remotely from Paris.'

'And if Oreste stops paying interest?'

'I would have to foreclose.'

'And then you will have to support the place. Repairs, taxes, people to run it, money frittered away unless you have the means. Excuse me for asking, my dear, but *do* you have the means?'

'Although Armand was not a wealthy man, I have funds for a small apartment in Paris.'

'But not enough to acquire a seventy-thousand-franc mortgage?'

I told her about the paintings. 'They will only sell in Paris. I'll put them on the market one by one, extract the best price.'

'Enough for the mortgage?'

'Delphine, I have done my research. They're by well-known artists – Turner, van Ruisdael, Corot. Others. It won't be a problem.'

'You will have to rent an apartment in Paris.'

'I was about to buy one before this cropped up.'

'Oh?'

'But were I to receive a sufficient amount from the paintings, I could perhaps have the best of both worlds.'

Madame Thierry pulled a face. 'I hope you're right, my dear.'

Midsummer Day 1870. Monsieur de Gaalon arrived at Madame Thierry's house. He came to the point: 'Monsieur Tausend assures me the directors of the bank will agree to an assignment of the mortgage in the amount of seventy thousand francs.'

I thanked him for his efforts on my behalf and explained my financial situation: fourteen thousand francs in the bank and fifteen paintings by well-known artists.

'Fourteen thousand, twenty per cent.'

'Neat and tidy, eh?'

'The paintings?' – rubbing his chin. 'You have a list?'

Digging into my reticule I handed it to him. He hummed and hawed. 'May I ask how you came by these, madam?'

'My recently deceased husband gave them to me, part of our *contrat marriage*, monsieur. I have the document.'

'When and where did your husband acquire them?'

'My husband was an old-fashioned aristocrat. They have hung on the walls of his ancestral home for years – family heirlooms, monsieur. Although some were "brought in" by his first wife.'

'Provenance is important in these matters, madam. Are they still on the walls?'

'No. In my bank, the Banque Touraine, their vault in Tours.'

He eyed the list with his monocle. 'An amount has been allotted to each piece?'

'I am in touch with Monsieur Durand-Ruel, the Paris art dealer. He has the list and was especially keen on the Turner. He asked me if it was for sale. "One day," I replied. He told me what he thought the paintings could fetch if they are genuine. You'll see that the Turner is valued at eight thousand francs.'

'A total of eighty-five thousand for the whole lot.'

'Enough to cover the fifty-six thousand, monsieur.'

Removing his monocle, he buffed it with a handkerchief. 'I suggest we offer seventy thousand for the mortgage, fourteen thousand francs down, the balance payable within three months… enough time for you to sell your art, madam.'

'Six months, if you please, monsieur.'

Squinting at me: 'I can try. They will almost certainly require a guarantee for payment of the balance.'

'I could deposit the paintings with the bank here in Beaune.'

'You would have to transport them here… entailing practical difficulties and a degree of risk.'

I pondered Monsieur de Gaalon's wise words. I had not thought of the 'practical difficulties'.

Madame Thierry said, 'There could be an agreement between the two banks.'

'There could,' said Monsieur de Gaalon. 'Let me see… along the lines of a staggered release of the paintings to our client.'

'Ah, for example, were I to take two of the pictures, sell them, repay the bank part of what I owe them, I could take possession of the next two pictures and so forth.'

Monsieur de Gaalon had another go at his monocle. 'Unconventional, certainly, but I can't see why it shouldn't work. Complicated paperwork, though.'

'A lot of toing and froing,' said Madame Thierry.

'More fees for you, Monsieur de Gaalon.'

A wolfish smile. 'Indeed. If the bank goes for it, that is, which I very much doubt, madam.'

'Use your considerable persuasive abilities, monsieur. Remind the bank of the *phylloxera* threat, the condition of the *domaine*.'

Despite my bravado, I was churning inside. Fourteen thousand francs to Banque Villiard meant a paltry six hundred francs left to my name. Less – once I had paid Monsieur de Gaalon's fee. Leaving me with a sufficiency of francs to feed and house myself in Paris for six months.

'Today is Tuesday,' said Monsieur de Gaalon. 'I will convey your offer to Monsieur Tausend this afternoon. We should have an answer by the end of the week.'

I thanked Monsieur de Gaalon and handed him an envelope. 'A modest amount, monsieur, sufficient to keep you going, I trust.'

He bowed, pocketing his fee. Madame Thierry saw him to the door.

Once he was gone, I stared at Madame Thierry. 'Can you bear to put up with me until the end of the week, Delphine?'

Reaching for the sideboard she handed me a book. 'This will help keep you occupied.'

I read the cover: *Moby-Dick; or, The Whale* by Herman Melville. It was long and in English. I turned to the first page. *Call me Ishmael…*

Saturday, 25 June. Monsieur de Gaalon was flushed, clearly excited, a condition I wouldn't have imagined of him. He sat. I leant forward. He spread his hands. 'They've agreed, madam,' he said, 'subject to the painting-release mechanism we discussed. And…'

'Yes?'

'They retain the interest payments until such a time as you have paid the balance in full.'

'And if Oreste fails to pay the interest payments?'

'That is entirely a matter for the bank, nothing to do with Société Vins du Cluvé.'

I bit my lip. 'Sounds reasonable to me.'

He stood and bowed. 'Congratulations are in order, Madame du P.'

I remember feeling stunned, tried to mask my emotions – both joy and fear at the same time.

Madame Thierry shot me a look. 'Congratulations are indeed in order, my dear, but are you sure this is what you want? You are not obliged to go through with it, you know.'

She had me – I didn't know what to say. I could be putting my head in a noose. Monsieur de Gaalon looked deflated.

'François, would you mind giving me and Delphine ten minutes?' I was aware I had used his Christian name.

'I'll take a stroll.'

Once he was gone: 'What do you think, Delphine?'

'Kiki, we've been through this so many times.'

'I'm sorry. But now it's a reality and I have to make a decision.'

Clasping my hands: 'Is this what you really want, Kiki?'

I explained my motives to her – my brothers, getting my own back for what they had done to me.

I could see she did not approve.

'In the short term I will go to Paris, start a career. Not easy for a woman, especially one wanted by the police.'

'As a baroness it will be a lot easier. Doors will open for a widowed aristocrat.'

'That's what Armand said.'

'But a problem were you to occupy le Merle.'

'That's why I favour the mortgage route… I can live in Paris, in the background, hidden, so to speak.'

'You hope.'

'*And* I will be close to Lucien.'

'And getting him back? Impossible, until you have cleared your name.'

'I feel we are going off the subject, Delphine. In the long term le Merle will provide me with an income and something to do, excitement, the rough and tumble of the wine business. And something I can pass down to Lucien.'

'You're highly eligible, but you know that, of course. Twenty-three years old, beautiful, intelligent, a baroness with money and an art collection.'

'Eligible… Armand died a month ago. I'm not ready to be tied down. I don't want to be beholden to any man, at his beck and call.'

Madame Thierry wrinkled her lips.

'Ignoring le Merle is the easy option, Delphine. I've never been one for easy options. I know it will cause me many headaches. But that's life and it's what I want in the long term.'

A few minutes later a knock on the door – Monsieur de Gaalon back from his stroll.

He sat down and scrutinised me from under his brows.

'I wish to proceed, François.'

'I will draft the documents; incorporate Société Vins du Cluvé. Please let me have the name of your account manager at Banque Touraine. I will contact him via the telegraph.'

Two weeks later I was back in Beaune to sign the papers and put in place banking arrangements. Lucien and I now controlled the fate of Domaine le Merle.

THIRTY-SIX

T HURSDAY, 14 JULY 1870, Bastille Day. I was back in Paris having breakfast with Joelie. She scowled and handed me a newspaper.

EMS TELEGRAM: AFFRONT TO FRENCH HONOUR

I read the article. Something to do with Wilhelm the Hohenzollern, King of Prussia, Otto von Bismarck, Louis-Napoleon and the vacant Spanish throne. The French ambassador had rudely intercepted Wilhelm while he was taking the waters in Bad Ems, a spa town, demanding he commit to never again back a Hohenzollern candidacy to the Spanish throne. The telegram rejected the French demand – the king having 'refused to receive the ambassador again, and had the latter informed by the adjutant of the day that His Majesty had no further communication to make to the ambassador'.

I shook my head. 'What does this mean, Joelie?'

'I have no idea. A diplomatic spat. France trying to intimidate the Prussians. It will blow over.'

A few weeks earlier I had managed to lease the apartment on rue Mouffetard. Apart from organising a plumber and decorator I had a lot on my mind: moving my belongings to Paris together with two of the paintings.

The following day I made my way to rue Laffitte. On entering the gallery I presented my card: Baroness Monique du Plessis embossed in black italics. While waiting I perused the paintings on the walls. Several were by new artists – one by Édouard Manet, of whom I'd never heard. The shapes and the colours flowed; the brushstrokes were applied without inhibition – representing an impression rather than an exact reproduction of the subject matter.

Paul Durand-Ruel was middle-aged and exquisitely dressed in a grey frock coat, winged collar and blue silk cravat. Of medium height, he wore a full beard and was handsome despite his receding hair. He leant forward and stared at one of the paintings. 'By Auguste Renoir,' he declared.

I made a pretence of looking at it. 'I've come about the Turner. It'll be here in two weeks' time,' I said, aware of sounding impatient.

'And not a minute too soon, Baroness. You've read the newspapers, presumably?'

'The Ems telegram.'

'Friends of mine believe there could be a war. Napoleon thinks he can win, as he did against the Austrians in '59. He needs a victory – the saviour of the nation. Muffle the discontents of the left, prolong the life of his corrupt regime.'

'Corrupt?'

'Of course. The rich are favoured, the poor downtrodden with no justice for the lower orders. The police do as they're told. And no one has faith in the Church anymore. Have you been to Belleville recently, madam?'

'How does this affect my paintings, monsieur?'

He sighed as though I was a child. 'If there is a war and were Napoleon to win, the value of art will continue to rise. Were he to lose…'

'… Prices will fall?'

'Dramatically. My advice is that you bring in the Turner as soon as you can. I have a particular collector in mind.'

I left the gallery, my head held high. Outside I pretended to look at shoes in a window, but my head was in a spin. I felt faint. How could a telegram start a war? And what had I done to myself with all those commitments, a mortgage and a lease? I felt my confidence ebb. By the time I was back in Saint-Germain, however, I had convinced myself that everything would be all right. Selling the Turner was imperative.

Tuesday, 19 July. I arrived at the station in Montparnasse, hailed a porter and retrieved my paintings from the luggage car. I heaved a sigh of relief: they had survived the journey – not been stolen. The porter waved down a cab. With the pictures safely on board I instructed the driver to take me to number 16 rue Laffitte.

Monsieur Durand-Ruel ushered me into his office. An assistant carried in the paintings.

'I have instructed Charles to unpack your paintings, Madame Baroness,' said Monsieur Durand-Ruel.

I rubbed my hands.

'Have you heard the news?'

'I've been travelling all day.'

'Charles, please fetch a glass of water for Madame.' He looked at me. 'Something stronger?'

I shook my head.

'On Saturday the National Assembly voted to declare war on Prussia. The government is expected to inform the Prussians today.'

Over the years I'd become adept at disguising my feelings. This time I held on to Monsieur Durand-Ruel's desk.

'Are you all right, madam?'

After a supreme effort of will, I managed to arrange my features. 'It's been a long day, monsieur.' Mercifully, Charles set a silver tray with its glass of water next to me. I took a sip. 'Should be over in a couple of months. Napoleon's a great general.'

'Don't be so sure, madam.'

'We have a new musket, the *Chassepot*.'

'True, but they have formidable artillery, from the factories of Alfred Krupp, a customer of mine, matter of fact.'

A polite cough from Charles. Each picture was set on an easel. Hands on hips, Monsieur Durand-Ruel viewed the Turner from a distance – umming and ahing to himself. Without warning he darted forward, magnifying glass in hand. Turning the painting over he examined the back of the canvas and the frame, taking his time, scratching here and there with a fingernail. He turned it over again.

The painting was an outline of a ship at sunset, bare masts, smudges of red and orange sandwiched between a white and brown churning sea, beneath a multicoloured sky. What looked like links of a chain and stretched-out arms. I wouldn't say it took my breath away.

Monsieur Durand-Ruel took out a loupe, knelt and inspected the signature. He rose to his feet. 'Appears genuine,' he said.

'And worth the eight thousand francs… your estimate, monsieur?'

He stroked his beard. 'As I said I have one customer who might be interested, if you can leave it with me for a couple of days…?'

'And the other painting?'

'The Daumier… you can take it away with you.'

'I'd rather not. I'm on the move with nowhere to store it. I will make arrangements and take it when I return, if you don't mind, monsieur.'

He bowed. 'A pleasure, madam.'

'Please let me have a receipt.'

He nodded to Charles.

Ten minutes later I was back on rue Laffitte. Odd, but as I walked through the streets it felt strange, the atmosphere – something had changed, as though Paris was especially alive. How to describe it? Like a gathering, a fiesta – some cheering as I walked down rue de

Seine. At the Saint-Germain end of the street a couple of drunks held one another up, shouting, 'À *Berlin*. À *Berlin*.'

Despite my worries and the heat, I upped my pace. The excitement fizzed within me too.

I arrived home to find Joelie counting money on her dining table.

'For me?' I joked.

'Love to, dear. Business is good at the moment. The town seems to have lost its mind. My girls are flat out. Literally.' She laughed. 'We're at war, it appears.'

'That's what I've heard.'

'Men lose their brains when war's afoot, as though there is no tomorrow. Girls too.' She looked as though she was on the verge of suggesting something but kept it to herself.

I recounted my meeting with Durand-Ruel – his interest in the Turner, not the Daumier.

'Careful, dear, they are all snakes. His real interest could be the Daumier.'

'He tried to get me to take it away.'

'Exactly.'

Three days later I felt I had to return to Château Bèze, sell Leveret and gather my belongings. Instead, I held on for Monsieur Durand-Ruel. I considered visiting him in his gallery. Thought better of it: he might take advantage of me. Meanwhile, I checked on the workman in rue Mouffetard – all looked spick and span. I handed him two hundred of my precious francs.

A day later a letter from Monsieur Durand-Ruel. To my relief he wanted to see me at his gallery on Monday morning, first thing.

Sunday, 24 July. My birthday: I was twenty-four years old. Joelie was in a cheery mood, as was the rest of Paris. We strolled through Jardin du Luxembourg in the sweltering heat, but we didn't care. Many soldiers were about; some tried to engage us in conversation.

One young captain persisted: 'I will be fighting for *la France* next week, mademoiselle.'

Joelie handed him her handkerchief. 'I will think of you, monsieur.'

Students were splashing in the pond and shouting. A band was playing 'La Marseillaise'.

Joelie had booked lunch at La Closerie des Lilas. People stared at us as we crossed the terrace to our table. The usual arty literary cliques were there, as well as groups of army officers, dashing in their uniforms. One stood shouting for champagne. His friends cheered. I looked for Gustav Bonifay. He didn't appear to be there – thank God. Joelie ordered a bottle of Meursault. For a moment I was back in my hometown, outside the house on rue du Moulin Judas. My reverie was shattered when the waiter arrived, uncorking the bottle with a pop. I took a sip and nodded my approval. Joelie raised her glass, wishing me *joyeux anniversaire.* In that moment I knew everything would turn out for the good: I would sell my paintings and one day I would return to where I was born, with my son.

Monday morning, rue Laffitte. Monsieur Durand-Ruel made his announcement. 'Good news, Baroness, my customer has agreed to purchase the Turner for eight thousand francs.' He smiled. 'Ah, six thousand after the deduction of my commission.'

I bit my tongue. I had not factored in the commission. 'Any interest in the Daumier?' I said after a while.

Shaking his head: 'You can take it away or leave it here, hope a collector will buy it off the wall.'

'Paul, I'm very fond of the Turner, as was my husband. I am prepared to accept your customer's bid and pay your commission… subject to you purchasing the Daumier for three thousand – your valuation. That's nine thousand in all.'

His eyes twinkled, reminding me of Joelie's warning about 'snakes'. He pulled his nose. 'There's a war on, madam.'

'So what? As you said… if Napoleon wins, prices will rise.'

'Eight thousand two hundred and fifty, that's three thousand for the Daumier minus my commission.'

'Your commission for the Turner almost covers the cost of the Daumier… Nine thousand, Paul.'

An audible intake of breath through clenched teeth.

'I have thirteen more paintings for sale, including the van Ruisdaels.'

He stood and beamed at me. 'You're quite right. Nine thousand it is. This calls for a glass of champagne. Charles…'

I left the gallery as if floating on air, a cheque for nine thousand francs in my reticule. Charles flagged down a fiacre, instructing the driver to take me to Gare Montparnasse.

After spending the night at a hotel in Tours I entered Banque Touraine, first thing. Having presented the cheque to Monsieur Lagarde, I instructed him to send the entire amount to Banque Villiard in Beaune. Tempted to 'syphon off' an amount for myself I resisted, intent on paying down the debt as soon as possible. I reminded Monsieur Lagarde that under the terms of the 'arrangement' I was permitted to take two more of my paintings away.

'Once I have telegraphed Banque Villiard,' he said. 'Would you mind returning in an hour, Madame Baroness?'

I made my way to the booth and bought my fare to Monteaux. After browsing some shops I returned to the bank. Monsieur Lagarde informed me all was in order; then I descended into the vault to choose two of the smaller paintings: the Caspar David Friedrich and one by Théodore Rousseau.

I boarded the noon poste-chaise. At Château Bèze I dashed off a note to Marcy Lamantine, handing it to the stable boy for delivery.

I had five days to pack and leave.

Next morning Marcy paid me a visit. 'I will be sad to see you go,' she said.

'Would you mind taking some of my clothes, Marcy?'

'I'd be delighted.'

Handing her one my creations: 'I've only worn this once.'

'I love it' – holding it up in front of herself in a mirror.

'My parting gift. You have been very generous, Marcy.'

'Think nothing of it, my dear.'

'We should go riding before I leave.'

She pulled a face. 'Alas, Puck is lame.'

'Oh dear, poor Puck.' I felt guilty but I found myself saying, 'Marcy, Leveret needs another home. Do you know of—?'

'Say no more. I'll take her, subject to Adolphe's approval.'

Two days later, she handed me two hundred francs – enough to cover five months of rental payments for my apartment.

Armand *fils* arrived on 30 July and offered to drive me to Tours. He had business in the city. An excuse, no doubt. I was sure he was trying to part with me on good terms.

At supper he was positively jovial, telling me he couldn't wait to join his regiment 'to have a go at Fritz'. We shared a bottle of Corbeau Ridge. He was charming and courteous, reminding me of his father. He complimented me on the wine. 'We couldn't have created this without you, Monique.'

I was tempted to ask him how he would run the business, especially with a war about to erupt, but I kept quiet.

Next day he supervised the loading of my luggage onto the brougham. When we were ready to leave, the maid, the cook and the stable boy as well as Honoré, my vineyard man, were lined up outside the Château. Tears from the maid and the cook – myself too.

I knew it would be difficult: I was leaving Armand behind forever. Halfway down the drive I asked Armand *fils* to stop at the chapel. One last time I knelt at my husband's grave. My flowers had wilted – the petals splayed on the ground. I said a prayer to Our Lord, as much for Armand as for myself. I brushed away a tear. Strange to think of him rotting down there, a man of flesh and blood. I prayed his soul had gone to a good place, if indeed there was such a thing as a soul.

At Tours, Armand loaded my not inconsiderable amount of luggage onto the train. When done, he looked at me the way his father used to. 'I'm sorry,' he said.

I couldn't help but put my arms round him. 'It's all right. Take care, Armand.'

I remember him walking down the platform, tall, his back straight. It was hard to imagine he would be fighting a war soon. I prayed God would protect him.

THIRTY-SEVEN

I REMEMBER THE thrill when I opened the door to the second floor of number 16 rue Mouffetard – the smell of fresh paint, the brightness of the rooms. The driver helped me with my belongings. I paid his fare plus a tip and closed the door. I had done it: I was living in my own place in Paris. I threw open the doors to the tiny terrace and breathed in the air.

The next two days I occupied myself with chores: buying utensils for the kitchen – cutlery, pots and pans, et cetera. I stocked my larder from a market in nearby place Scipion where the prices seemed reasonable: eggs at 1.80 francs a dozen, a wedge of Beaufort cheese for two francs, a slab of butter for 1.60 francs. I flirted with the butcher and came away with a strip of brisket for my dinner. The wine shop was close by, where I bought a flagon of *gros rouge* poured from a tap. No need for bedding and towels as I had brought ample supplies from Château Bèze.

Thursday, 4 August. I wrestled my two paintings down the stairs and hailed a cab. 'Rue Laffitte in the Ninth,' I told the driver.

'I know where rue Laffitte is, ma'am.'

Strange, but despite the early hour the streets were busy. Soldiers and gangs of youths were about, one lot singing 'La Marseillaise'.

I tapped the driver's shoulder. 'What's going on?'

''Aven't you 'eard, ma'am? We've taken Saarbrücken.'

My thoughts turned to Herr Schiel. 'No?'

'*Mais oui*, the emperor's done it again. We'll be in Berlin in no time.'

Outside the gallery he helped me with the paintings. Charles was on hand and carried them inside.

Waiting for Monsieur Durand-Ruel to arrive, I perused the paintings on his walls – a couple by Eugène Delacroix and one by Caspar David Friedrich. *Friedrich?* One of mine was a Friedrich. I asked Charles the price. 'Monsieur Durand-Ruel will let you know,' his reply.

'Oh, come on, Charles. How long have you worked here?' – fixing him with my eyes.

He squirmed. 'Six thousand five hundred, Madame Baroness.'

Monsieur Durand-Ruel arrived. 'Ah, Madame Baroness, so soon after the sale of the Turner?'

'I have eleven more, monsieur.'

He ushered me into his office. Charles stood the paintings on easels.

Monsieur Durand-Ruel sprang forward. 'A Friedrich, wonderful.' He completed his routine, examined the Rousseau. Murmurs of satisfaction. 'They appear genuine, madam.'

'Your valuation, Paul, three thousand for the Rousseau, 4,500 for the Friedrich.'

He made a business of consulting his notebook. 'That is correct, madam. Seven thousand five hundred for the pair, less my commission, let me s—'

'Five thousand six hundred and twenty-five, Paul.'

'Quite.'

'And not acceptable.'

He arched an eyebrow.

'Two things, Paul... Napoleon has captured Saarbrücken... *and* I believe the Friedrich is worth more.'

'Oh, really?'

'You have a Friedrich on your wall outside – smaller and of a later date than mine. And you might agree that the subject matter of mine is superior to yours.'

'That's as may be, madam, but how do you know the price of the one on the wall?'

Charles was wringing his hands.

'I don't, monsieur, but no doubt you will elucidate me.'

He looked at Charles. 'Well?'

'S-six thousand five hundred, monsieur.'

'Speak up, man.'

'Six thousand five hundred, monsieur.'

Monsieur Durand-Ruel glowered, and lifting up the Friedrich he carried it outside. Bidding me to follow him he leant my Friedrich against the wall below his. 'The dates are irrelevant, you know that, don't you, madam?'

I sniffed. He bobbed up and down. 'Yours is slightly bigger. The quality is about the same.'

'Mine is more interesting, don't you think? Lovers gazing at a night moon, rather than yours, a pile of broken ice.'

'Quite… Mine is retail and hanging on my very expensive wall. I have overheads, madam.'

'Adequately reflected in your commission, Paul. Let's stop wasting our time. Compared with the one on the wall, mine is worth, say, eight thousand minus your commission. Six thousand francs.'

Stroking his beard: 'Five thousand five hundred, madam.'

I ummed and ahed. Pouted. 'The Rousseau at three thousand minus your commission gives me 2,250, plus the Friedrich… Why don't we say eight thousand the pair?'

He sighed and scratched his head. 'I've met many women owners in my time but none as tough as you. Very well, eight thousand it is, madam.'

He offered champagne. I declined: 'A little early, Paul.'

Next day I travelled to Tours and went through the whole rigmarole again, returning to Paris with two more paintings, including the larger van Ruisdael. Worn out, I went straight home without visiting the gallery on rue Laffitte.

People on the train, the cabbies, everyone was talking about Saarbrücken. A familiar refrain: *We shall be in Berlin in two weeks.*

Despite my exhaustion I was feeling celebratory, and having washed and changed into fresh clothes I decided to drop in on Joelie.

Lily welcomed me, uncorked a bottle of something as Joelie flounced in. We chattered. She enthused when I told her about the paintings, my success. In a more serious vein, I told her I needed something to do – a job. She gave me that look again. Ah, I understood – her girls were busy.

'Joelie, forget it,' I said.

'I didn't say a thing.'

'I can read your thoughts, dear.'

'Become a seamstress, then, at three francs a day. See if I care.'

I asked her what she was doing later on. Shaking her head, she told me she was out for the night. 'I am very busy at the moment.'

'I thought you were beyond that sort of thing.'

'You know I have my favourites. Jacques is at the Brighton for a week.'

After we finished the bottle, I wished her luck and headed home. I decided to amble in the direction of the Panthéon. People thronged the bars on place Sainte-Geneviève; gaiety abounded – laughter and drinking. Plenty of students, with their long hair and down-and-out but flamboyant clothes. I joined a group. They were only a few years younger than me. A youth in a beret poured me a glass of wine. I was reminded of the naval cadets. War dominated the conversation. One of them – a 'Red', I suspect – was vehement to the point of being objectionable.

'The government is corrupt. The army is a shambles. If Napoleon fails, the people will not stand for it. The *Garde Nationale* will rise up. Mark my words, my friends,' he declared.

The others told him to shut up. 'Napoleon will win,' said one.

I soon tired of these juveniles and left. Walking home, the student's words stuck in my head.

Monday, 8 August. Again I visited Monsieur Durand-Ruel and again we haggled. I walked away with a cheque for eleven thousand francs. I took the train to Tours and repeated the whole process, like a hamster on a treadmill, returning to Paris the following day.

On the embarcadère, my porter hunted for a cab. Something felt wrong – people were avoiding each other's eyes. Fear spiralled down my spine; I remembered what the student had said only two days ago. Despite my apprehension I knew that selling my paintings as quickly as possible was the sensible thing to do.

A landau arrived. The porter loaded the paintings on board. We drove up rue de Rennes, crossed the river via Pont du Carrousel. People walking the streets looked dejected, their heads hanging down. 'What's wrong with everyone?' I asked the cabbie.

''Aven't you 'eard, ma'am? The army's been smashed at a place called Spicheren.'

We arrive at rue Laffitte. Paul Durand-Ruel greeted me. Frowned: 'From what I hear, the battle was not decisive, with high casualties on either side. Not good news, though, madam.'

We haggled. The 'valuations' totalled nine thousand francs. This time I had to accept a lower price. 'I'll take them off your hands, my dear – five thousand francs.'

Next day I forced myself to go to Tours. After paying the money into my account I returned with two more paintings – a Corot and one by Christoffer Wilhelm Eckersberg. I decided against visiting Durand-Ruel in the hope the army would recover from the calamity of Spicheren.

The routine was wearing me down, but at least the debt had been reduced to twenty-three thousand francs.

In rue Mouffetard I drafted a letter.

Société Vins du Cluvé

11 August 1870

Dear Monsieur de Gaalon,

This letter will reach you via Delphine.

I have sold eight of my paintings for a total of thirty-three thousand francs. The amount has been paid into my bank account in Tours and remitted to Banque Villiard.

In your capacity as director of Soc Vins du C, please check that the bank has received said amount.

I feel a degree of confidence I will sell some of my other paintings, cover the balance due of twenty-three thousand francs. However, the fact we are at war makes me nervous. I am conscious the amount has to be paid by 8 January.

Je vous prie etc,
Madame du P

I wrote Madame Thierry's address on the envelope and enclosed a note to her.

The following morning I posted the letter and bought food. People were looking worried. Two women were talking in place Scipion: *The Prussians are coming. There might be a siege. We'll run out of food.* I could hardly believe my ears and rushed back to rue Mouffetard to gather my paintings.

Paul Durand-Ruel looked grim. 'All sorts of rumours,' he said. 'Napoleon is not what he was. His heart isn't in it.'

I was of a mind to mention the siege, food and the Prussians, but kept quiet. Meanwhile Charles had stood the paintings on easels. Monsieur Durand-Ruel was not his usual jaunty self as he made his examination, despite taking his time over the landscape by Corot: straggly trees torn by the wind; a small, lonely figure under a desolate sky. Strange, but I imagined the figure was Lucien. Then feelings of rage when I remembered Mathilde's painting by Corot on the wall of her house in rue de l'Ouest.

'Both works appear genuine,' he said. 'But I can't match the valuations, not with the current uncertainties.'

I shrugged. 'Please give me your figures.'

'Madam, we have dealt together for nigh on a month. You have brought me some delightful pieces. I respect you. You are shrewd, an excellent negotiator. I do not want to insult you, but the Daumier and the Rousseau are on my wall and remain unsold.'

I smiled, tried to hide my inner turmoil.

'Madam, forgive me, but why are you selling these wonderful pictures?'

I trusted Paul Durand-Ruel. 'I have purchased a vineyard in la Bourgogne with the aid of a loan and need to pay off the debt.'

'Ah… art for wine. Both will appreciate over the long term. Wine's a lot harder work, though. You're aware, of course, of the *phylloxera* threat. Art hangs on the wall and increases in value… in times of prosperity, that is.'

I sighed.

'Where is this vineyard of yours, might I enquire?'

'Meursault.'

'Ah, one of my favourites. Look, I want to help you. I really do. Can I suggest you leave them with me? I'll hang them on my wall and we'll see what comes along.'

Stroking my chin: 'How would it work, Paul?'

'You give me the minimum price you're willing to accept, after the deduction of my commission, that is.'

'Or I visit Monsieur François Petit.'

He looked at his shoes. 'If you must.'

I took my time. 'Paul, your suggestion is generous and appeals to me. Before I agree to the arrangement, I shall visit Monsieur Petit. See what he has to offer.'

Twenty minutes later Charles waved down a cab and placed the paintings on the front seat.

I thanked him for all the help he had given me.

'My pleasure, Baroness. A pity. The Corot is especially fine. *Bonne chance.*'

Number 7 rue Saint-Georges was close by: 'GALERIE FRANÇOIS PETIT' in black letters above the display window.

Monsieur Petit was short with a thick but neatly trimmed beard. Not as beautifully dressed as his rival because of his figure. I handed him my card. He bowed, exuded charm. Armand was right: a baroness did open doors. His assistant was a lad of fourteen or so. 'Georges, my son,' Petit proclaimed. Georges hung my paintings on a wall.

'A Corot,' piped up Georges. 'And an Eckersberg, Papa.'

'Forgive Georges, Baroness, he's precocious, a prodigious memory for paintings and dates. Incredible. He must get it from his mother.'

He inspected the paintings minutely, as did Georges. Murmurs of what I took as approval. After a while he turned to me, magnifying glass in hand. 'The Corot is wonderful, madam. But the market is, how should I say, over anxious at the moment. Do you have a figure in mind?'

'For the Corot, monsieur, five thousand francs.'

He looked at his son. 'Please do not be insulted, but we are prepared to pay two thousand only. My apologies, madam, but the war...'

'And the Eckersberg?'

More looks between *père et fils.*

'Three thousand, madam' – wringing his hands.

I tried to mask my anger, assess the situation dispassionately.

The combined valuation was thirteen thousand francs, less commission – just under ten thousand. They were bidding five thousand. 'Eight thousand,' I said at length.

François Petit spread his hands and shook his head. 'My humble apologies, madam.'

I looked at the Corot and realised I'd become rather fond of it – Lucien leaning into the wind. 'I am sorry, but I cannot accept your bid. I understand… the unfortunate circumstances.'

More wringing of hands: 'W-we could hang them on our wall in the hope that someone will purchase one or both, even.'

'You have been very kind to view my pieces. Perhaps another time, monsieur.'

I returned to Durand-Ruel. The paintings would hang on his wall. After payment of his commission he had the discretion to sell the Corot for three thousand francs, the Eckersberg for five thousand.

Disappointment leached into me as I walked down rue Laffitte. As I pondered the possibilities, my legs took me to rue du 29 Juillet. I made my way towards the Jardin des Tuileries, keeping my eye on the door to number 6. The door failed to open and I reached the rue de Rivoli. Crossed the road and ventured into the park. Cast an eye. Nothing. I walked up and down the 29 Juillet one more time then gave up.

It didn't take me long before I realised I'd been a complete fool. I should have accepted the Petits' cash and returned to Tours.

Bah! I knew my financial situation down to the last sou: 384 francs and twenty-three centimes – enough to last me four, perhaps five months.

I thought of turning round, grovelling to the Petits. But my pride and innate stubbornness prevented me from doing so.

Hard to believe, but Napoleon handed control of the army to Marshal Bazaine. On 16 August there was an insurrection in La Villette in the north-eastern suburbs. The city was in a state of madness; drunkards were everywhere, people shouting. Tittle-tattle in place Scipion: *We're going to be under siege. We'll run out of food. We're all going to starve to death. We this. We that. Putain de merde. Sacré bleu. Bismarck's three metres tall with two heads and eats babies.* All sorts of nonsense.

Joelie was in her element – her girls never busier. She had ten of them on the go, her coffers overflowing. 'Paris has lost its brain and discovered its dick,' she declared when I visited her one evening.

'Found a job?' – giving me *that* look.

I told her to get lost.

THIRTY-EIGHT

THE FOLLOWING DAY I was walking along boulevard Saint-Germain. A poster at Carrefour de l'Odéon.

WANTED: SEAMSTRESSES

The address given was in rue de Vaugirard. Number 14 overlooked Jardin du Luxembourg, not far from rue Mouffetard. The building was institutional – large blocks of stone – with two guards outside. 'I'm here as a seamstress,' I told them. One indicated where I should go. To my dismay there was a queue of other women there.

One said, 'I never thought I would have to do this. Needs must.'

Another: 'I learnt how to sew as a maid but that was ten years ago. My husband forced me to apply, dear.'

The women entered one by one; ten minutes later they came back out, most with a smile on their face.

Then it was my turn. Two men sat behind a desk. 'Please sit,' said one.

'Name?' the other.

'Monique du Plessis.'

He sniffed. 'Address?'

'I'm living with a friend,' I lied, giving him Joelie's address.

'Can you sew?'

'Of course, monsieur,' nearly adding, *I wouldn't be here if I couldn't.*

One of them handed me a needle and thread and a strip of cotton. 'Sew a hem,' he said.

My skills had improved since the days with Madame Lonjons – the work I had done on *my dress.* I handed it back to him almost immediately.

'Can you use a sewing machine?'

I nearly said, *of course.* Instead, a demure 'I can'.

'You're hired, madam,' he said. 'Three francs a day. Seven in the morning to seven at night. Six days a week. Sunday off. Forty-five-minute break at midday. Starting tomorrow. Sign here,' he said, sliding a paper and pen towards me. I signed. I was now an employee of Société des Drapes et Matériaux.

I'd wager there was not a baroness in all of France being paid three francs a day, employed as a seamstress.

I rose at six. Mid-August, it was uncomfortably hot. After a cold wash I dressed in my dullest of day clothes: grey and loose with black shoes, a beret. I wore a wig, my short-cut redhead version. Breakfast was milk and fruit. After a pleasant walk across Jardin du Luxembourg, I arrived at the building on rue de Vaugirard, along with thirty or so other women. At seven sharp the doors were opened and we all streamed in.

The workroom was huge: a high-beamed ceiling, wooden floor, windows on two sides, good natural light. My supervisor showed me to my workbench, a Singer sewing machine thereon and various needles and threads – Berthe was large and similar in scale to Frau Schiel. 'We'll start you off with pantaloons, easier than tunics,' she said. 'The component parts are in the baskets behind you – top side, underside, crotch point, et cetera.' She showed me the process: *you do this, this and then this.* 'You're making these for our boys at the front, so do a good job. We expect you to complete a dozen pairs by the end of the day.'

I was assigned a corner table. The girl to my right was Amélie

– a shy-looking creature, about eighteen years old. She was one of those bookish types and wore glasses, reminding me of Séverine, the shrew who stole my francs in Hôtel de Londres.

I set about the task. Felt energised despite the process: legs first, crotch, pockets, waist belt, and finally belt loops and fly piece. My thoughts ranged from when I would next see Lucien to tortures for Mathilde. And arithmetic – 7,667 days' working to pay my debt to Banque Villiard, over twenty-five years based on three hundred days a year.

Amélie appeared to be struggling. I showed her how to keep the material taut as she fed it through the Singer.

By lunchtime I had completed eight pairs to Amélie's four. Food was provided – a square of bread and a bowl of watery soup. With twenty minutes to spare we decided to walk in the Luxembourg. She talked about her brother, with the 1st Corps under General MacMahon. His letters to her told of the inefficiencies, the lack of equipment and rations. 'He was lucky to survive Froeschwiller,' she said, crossing herself.

By the end of the day there was a pile of seventeen pairs of trousers beneath my bench. Berthe counted them, inspecting the work. 'The seams are straight and neat,' she said. 'We'll move you to tunics right away.'

For two weeks I kept my head down. News of the army deteriorated: defeats at Rezonville and Gravelotte-Saint-Privat. General Trochu was appointed by Napoleon as governor of the Paris region. Apparently, he had a steady head, was experienced, having served in Algeria and the Crimea. We prayed that Trochu would save us.

Saturday, 3 September. Hallelujah. Joelie was free and available for a night out. After work I returned to rue Mouffetard and, after washing and dressing, I stepped onto the street. The atmosphere was febrile: people were shouting, a man was spilling his guts against a wall, drunkards were weaving everywhere. Someone barged into me, apologising.

'What's happened?' I asked him.

'Haven't you heard? The army's been massacred at Sedan.'

Fear in its multiple dimensions twisted within me. My stomach felt like blancmange; my thoughts scattered in all directions. What next? How to pay the bank? The value of my paintings? Siege? People had been talking of siege for two weeks, gossip rife in place Scipion.

Tucking my head down I hurried to place de l'Estrapade.

Joelie wrapped her arms around me. 'I'm so glad you're here, Monique *chérie*.'

I indicated the half-empty bottle on her table. She handed me a glass. '*Santé, chérie.*'

'What's going to happen, Joelie?'

'The Prussians will encircle this town and we'll be under siege. They are filling the Bois de Boulogne with sheep, apparently.'

'Sheep. Are you sure?'

'Yes, dear. Oxen too.'

'It's dangerous down there.'

'On the street?'

'Do you still want to go out?'

'And miss the fun. Are you mad?'

We walked to the side of Jardin du Luxembourg, turned right down rue de Tournon and made our way to boulevard Saint-Germain. It was warm and still light. The streets were as full as I'd ever seen them. Drunkenness everywhere, people waving the *Tricolore*, people shouting, '*À bas l'Empire!*' '*Vive la République!*'

Joelie and I clung to each other.

'The world's gone mad,' I said.

A gleam in Joelie's eyes; I could see she was excited. 'I smell opportunity,' she said, a touch arrogantly.

The scene at Le Procope was chaotic: people trying to gain admittance – two bruisers on the door.

I shook my head. 'Forget it, Joelie.'

'No, we'll go inside, I know the owner.'

It was packed. Smoke everywhere. Laughter. Some space at a table – I asked the people sitting there if they wouldn't mind us joining them.

Eventually we were served – Joelie an absinthe, myself a beer, not very ladylike, but I was parched. The man next to us said to no one in particular: 'Napoleon is finished, the Empire is finished, *la France* is finished.'

'Rubbish,' said Joelie. 'How can you finish fields and mountains and rivers and people? Stiffen your back, monsieur.'

He grumbled into his drink. 'The Reds will take over this town, mark my words. Have you any idea how they feel in Belleville and La Villette?'

'Murderous, I suspect.'

'Damned right you are, madam.'

'Forty-eight all over again,' I said.

'Worse. Last time we had only ourselves to contend with. This time we have the *putains d'allemands* to aid us in our folly.'

'There'll be food shortages,' said one of the others.

Joelie and I looked at each other. Although her eyes were mocking, I could tell she had taken the comment on board.

We finished our drinks. And with no chance of being served food we stood to leave.

'*Bonne chance*,' said our cynical acquaintance.

Outside, the light was fading so we decided to return to the Mouffetard quarter where there would be plenty of places to eat. Walking back it was hard to believe we could be facing the catastrophe everyone was talking about.

As we crossed boulevard Saint-Germain a group of young men were shouting, '*Dé-ché-ance! Dé-ché-ance! Dé-ché-ance!*' Abdication! Abdication! Abdication!

The following morning, Sunday, 4 September 1870. Mindful of the 'food shortages' I rose early and made my way to place Scipion. The sky was relentlessly blue. Despite the early hour plenty of people were about. Most were queuing; almost all were women. Many had a determined I-will-not-budge look. The line at the cheese stall was the shortest. Twenty minutes later I received my reward: a block of Comté, a hard cheese that would last me three weeks. The fruit and vegetable stall took longer. Forty minutes later I was loaded with potatoes, carrots, apples and pears – basics that would last me a long time. At the meat counter I had to wait half an hour. When it was my turn to be served no chickens were left, so I settled for lamb kidneys and a hock of pork. A *saucisson* hanging down. 'I'll take that too, monsieur.' When it came to paying, I was surprised by the amount and questioned the butcher. 'Don't you read the newspapers?' he said. 'Things will be more expensive tomorrow. Count your blessings, madam.'

Later, I walked through the Luxembourg. Despite the sunshine the atmosphere felt subdued – the way people looked at each other, the shift in their eyes. And a hum from the direction of Saint-Germain – more a low, continuous roar. Another demonstration, perhaps – hard to believe…

Walking through the narrow part of the Jardin away from Saint-Germain, I did the arithmetic. My cash stood at 280 francs; the eighteen francs a week from my job helped. With rent and food, I was spending five francs a week more than I earned. I cursed myself for being so stupid, not retaining some of the francs I'd received for my paintings.

Something Joelie said yesterday stuck in my head: *I smell opportunity*. What did she mean by that?

Surprise. I was given the job of supervisor, with an increase in pay to four francs a day. Berthe was nowhere to be seen – I had been given her place. I was flattered and welcomed the extra money. I was responsible for twenty women, including Amélie – spent my time ensuring the daily quota was achieved.

By lunchtime everyone had heard the news of Louis-Napoleon's abdication. One of the women said, 'Eugénie has gone as well. Good riddance if you ask me.'

'So now what?'

'General Trochu is in charge.'

I could hardly believe it: one day the crowd was baying for Napoleon to abdicate; next day he was gone.

After lunch, per my custom, I snatched a walk in the park. Men in uniforms were on display, including a group of marines in their blue and white get-up. I was of a mind to ask them if they knew of Junius Girard, but I didn't have the time.

After work the following day a colleague joined me. Sybille was tall and jolly, comely, a real woman, and naughty – always up to mischief. I had taken to her. She linked her arm in mine, telling me we were going to the Champ-de-Mars, a large park in the Seventh. 'It's where the soldiers are,' she said, winking.

We knew we were headed in the right direction: the smoke, the susurration of many voices and, finally, the sight of tents in serried rows. A clamour as supper was being prepared – great pots suspended on triangles over fires. And men: some lying on pallets of straw, some standing, others attending to their horses, some sluicing themselves. One hobbled towards us with the aid of a stick. A bandage, stained with blood and covered in flies, was clamped round his thigh. His hand was out. I gave him some change and after a '*merci, madam*' he limped away.

'We should do something, Sybille.'

'Such as?'

'Become nurses, *do* something.'

She grabbed my arm. 'Don't be daft, Monique. You are making uniforms. *That* is doing something. *And* you're being paid.'

We stood there mesmerised as soldiers marched in from many

directions. Sybille tugged my elbow. 'Look, Zouaves from North Africa.'

They were dashing, those Zouaves, in their embroidered tunics, balloon pantaloons, their red fez-like headdresses. One was stripped to the waist and performing exercises with his *Chassepot*, grunting as he stabbed the air with a bayonet. He was young and clean-shaven except for the slash of his dark moustache. I remember the feeling of lust as it swamped me, a rage – prickles of sweat on my back, breathlessness. It had been a long time – two years, with Armand being ill. Had the man ordered me to a nearby tent I would have gone with him there and then.

A glance at Sybille told me she was in a similar state. We looked at each other with inane, lopsided grins. She breathed in deep and closed her eyes.

THIRTY-NINE

ONDAY, 12 SEPTEMBER. An atmosphere in the workroom. I told the women to stop talking and get on with their work. They fell silent for a while and then started up again. They couldn't help it – the excitement – Paris in thrall to itself, its frenzied activity. I had seen it for myself – soldiers everywhere and so many wagons, some full of vegetables; and women and children wheeling carts of every description to the forts circling the city. I crossed the river to Jardin des Tuileries in the half-expectation of seeing Lucien. Instead, the place had been given over to cannons, horses and men. On my way down boulevard Raspail, a triangle of land where cattle were grazing on hay.

Although food seemed plentiful, I made sure I had enough fruit and vegetables to last two weeks.

Next day, Sybille and I skipped lunch – rumours of a vast military parade. We jostled our way across the river via Pont Neuf. Multitudes of people on the other side, some waving flags, children running everywhere. The crowd was shouting '*Vive Trochu*' and '*Vive la République*'. On rue de Rivoli, troops were marching in massed ranks – horses pulling gun carriages; bands playing, the rat-tat-tat of their drums, their brass instruments sparkling in the late-summer sun. Then rumbling sounds.

'They're blowing the bridges!' someone shouted.

Early evening, I returned home and checked my postbox – a letter from Paul Durand-Ruel. I tore open the envelope.

16 rue Laffitte

13 September 1870

Dear Baroness du Plessis,

With regret I inform you that I will be closing my gallery in rue Laffitte.

I therefore humbly request that you remove your paintings with immediate effect.

I am relocating to London for the time being and would hope to return to Paris when this war is over.

My business is reduced to a standstill, with no bids for your beautiful paintings.

I enjoyed our dealings together and wish you the very best and hope we can continue our association once this dreadful business is over.

Je vous prie d'agréer, Madame, mes salutations les plus cordiales,
Paul

Next day I took a cab to rue Laffitte. Charles was on hand. 'Monsieur Durand-Ruel is occupied, Baroness. I'm very sorry,' he said.

Crates littered the gallery; paper, balls of twine and pale patches on the walls where paintings used to hang. An end-of-an-era feeling, or was it the end of the world? Charles apologised for the umpteenth time before loading the waiting cab with my pictures. I thanked him then returned home.

The two parcels lay on my floor. I was tempted to open the

Corot, take a look but could see no point, so I hid them under my bed.

At eleven I slunk into work. Sybille wanted to know where I had been. 'My *règles*,' I hissed.

The supply of material dropped to the extent our seamstresses could only produce six pairs of pantaloons a day each. Louis, one of the men who had interviewed me, informed me that half the workforce had to be 'let go'.

Next day there were only twenty of us, all working hard, all trying to stay employed. I was the only supervisor. Sybille was still there, thank God. She was good at raising morale, singing out loud and telling lewd jokes. The problem was the factory in Oise, unable to produce the material because of the war. At the end of the week, Louis announced they were shutting down production and handed us our pay.

Sybille and I walked out onto rue de Vaugirard. 'Time for that well-earned drink,' she said, taking my arm. Soon we arrived at Joelie's 'small place' on rue d'Assas. It was crowded, soldiers everywhere. When a couple stood to leave, Sybille elbowed her way to their table.

A *pichet* of red soon arrived. We clinked our glasses.

Sybille said, 'They treated us like a load of shit, didn't they? Didn't tell us till the last minute. Typical.'

'At least we were paid.'

We talked about our past. Sybille was from Montélimar in the Midi, *where they make nougat, dear*. Same old story: she was bored, craved excitement; her father knew someone and she travelled to Paris and a job as a nanny.

'You were lucky. When I arrived, I had no job.' As soon as I opened my mouth I regretted it – Sybille insisting I tell her my story.

'Do I have to?'

'You intrigue me, Monique. You appear to me to be hiding something, your beauty for a start, your skin, your manners, the way you talk, and concealed under your dowdy clothes. Somehow that shit Louis picked up on it – made you a supervisor. And you can sew.'

The first part was easy: the well-trodden Chagny tale. 'I arrived in Paris by train,' I lied, 'and found employment as a chambermaid.'

'Where?'

'Oh, somewhere in the Quartier Latin.'

She eyed me, folding her arms in the expectation of a name.

'It didn't work out so I became an artist's model.'

'*Ooh là là*. Anyone famous? One of those new types? Cézanne? Monet?'

'No one famous.'

She sighed. 'Then what?'

'I met a man who owned a vineyard in the Loire. He died in June.'

'My dear, poor you, how awful.'

'We were together, eight happy years…'

'And?'

'We lived well, but he had no money.'

'Any children?'

'His first wife died. He had two children by her, who would have nothing to do with me. Once he was dead, they wanted me out of their lives.'

'So, no children of your own?'

'No,' I lied again. I wasn't going to tell her about Lucien – not yet anyway. I changed the subject: 'Where are you living, Sybille?'

'In a *pension* off rue de Turenne in the Marais.'

'A room of your own?'

Shaking her head: 'I share with three other women.'

'And the rent?'

'Eighty centimes a night.'

'Leaving you with just over two francs for food and clothing.'

She stared at me, her lips a tight straight line. 'There's a man I see once a week. We have an arrangement.'

'Which allows you to survive.'

'It's not that bad. He's older than me. We've become sort of friends. He's a baker, brings me nice things to eat.'

'A cake for a fuck.' I laughed.

I immediately regretted my vulgarity. To my relief she laughed as well.

I felt compelled to tell her a little of myself. 'I was hardly a day over fifteen when I married my first husband. He was nearly three times my age, forced on me by my family. I hated him. *We* also had an *arrangement* – twice a week. It was hell.'

'Poor you.'

'I escaped. I couldn't take it anymore.'

'Did he—?'

I held up a hand. 'Sybille, please, I've told you more than I wanted to.'

'Sorry.'

We sipped our wine, watched the world go by. Then: 'What are you going to do now, Sybille?'

'I have enough money to last two weeks. I will find a job. I may have to ask my baker for a raise. He's mean as pigeon shit, though.'

'How much, may I ask?'

'He pays me ten francs a "cake".'

'Ten francs… bah. Who does he think he is? You're pretty, funny and good company. A friend of mine might be able to help you.'

'Really?'

I told her about Joelie and her girls, without mentioning names.

She asked for my address. Again, I regretted opening my mouth. 'I can't give it to you, Sybille.'

Irritation marred her face. 'Well, how am I going to stay in touch, then, meet your mysterious friend?'

We agreed to rendezvous at the small place the following evening.

Next day I woke at seven, snuggled down in my sheets knowing I didn't have to go to work. I dozed a while. Sunlight streamed through the window. Feeling guilty I dressed and walked to place Scipion. A queue at the egg stall. Eventually I was served and asked for half a dozen. The stallholder knew me. 'You're lucky, I'm about to run out,' he said, putting the eggs in a bag. 'That'll be two francs, madam.'

'Two francs? They're usually ninety centimes.'

'Blame that *conard* Bismarck. As I said… you're lucky.'

I checked my purse – six francs – bought cheese and milk while I had the chance. Both items had doubled in price.

After breakfast of one, not two eggs, I decided to visit Joelie.

On the way to place de l'Estrapade, queues outside the shops, sullen looks on the faces of the women standing there. Two francs for half a dozen eggs – what would they cost next week or in a month's time?

I spoke to one of the women. 'Versailles has fallen,' she replied. 'The Prussian armies have "joined hands".'

'Joined hands?'

'Paris is encircled, dearie.'

I arrived at Joelie's. As she poured coffee, I told her about the eggs.

She pulled a face. 'I bought a chicken two days ago, twelve francs… double what they usually cost.'

We talked about the Prussians.

'We are like rats in a trap,' she said. 'Trouble is, the trap is running out of cheese.'

I told her about Sybille. 'She is tall, well proportioned and entertaining.'

'Has she got big titties, a shapely backside and a pretty face?'

Joelie could be crude sometimes.

'How old is she?'

'About my age, slightly younger, perhaps. I'm meeting her at our place on rue d'Assas tonight.'

'All right, I'll meet her. No promises, though.'

'Good.'

'Monique… um, while we're on the subject I wonder if—'

'No, Joelie, I'm past all that.'

'Three hundred francs.'

'Three hundred francs what?'

'The amount you'll receive *after* the deduction of my fee.'

'I said no, Joelie.'

'You're not getting any younger.'

'Nonsense.'

'He's English, an aristocrat, comes recommended, something to do with coal.'

'Recommended by who?'

'Ah, so you are interested?'

We were ten minutes late. Sybille was sitting outside. A soldier was pestering her. Joelie was her regal self and, standing tall, she told the man to *get lost*.

After introducing them I took my leave. 'I'll be back in half an hour. No need for me to listen to your chatter.'

Joelie shooed me away dismissively. 'Go if you must.'

I turned right, up rue de l'Ouest. Number 80 was close by. I had an aversion to the place – imagined police leaping out of the bushes and arresting me. But I needn't have bothered – the windows were still shuttered. With time on my hands, I entered Jardin du Luxembourg. Soldiers in drill formation by the pond, commands bellowed, the stamping of feet. I walked to the nursery end of the garden where fruit trees were cultivated, some espaliered on walls, others in rows. Some of the fruit was ripe and, after looking round, I picked four apples, stuffing them in my pockets. For a moment I imagined I was Eve in the Garden.

Back at rue d'Assas I found Joelie and Sybille, laughing at one of Sybille's jokes, no doubt. I put two of the apples on the table. 'They're yours,' I said.

'Where did you find them?' said Sybille.

'The Luxembourg… the section bordering boulevard Saint-Michel.' Tapping my nose: 'Our little secret.'

After a while Sybille stood and made her excuses to leave.

Once she was gone Joelie said, 'She's good fun and quite worldly. Some men like that sort of thing.'

'Did she tell you about her baker "friend"?'

'Yes, ten francs a "go", bah. She's not worth three hundred, though.'

'All right, tell me about the Englishman.'

'He's an aristo, the Earl of Bradley or Bradfield, or some such, and staying at the Brighton. In coal, so the concierge tells me. Rich beyond the dreams of Croesus, apparently,' she said, filling my glass.

I rolled my eyes. Then a strange feeling: a sensation on the back of my neck, creeping up on me unawares, of a memory trying to insert itself. 'Bradfield, you say?'

'Something like that.'

She ordered more wine, Nuits-Saint-Georges, with cheese and gherkins – delicious – reminding me of Augustave Monnier, our trip to Dijon eons ago.

We chatted amiably in the autumn sun. In the end I agreed to her proposition. Englishmen were gentlemen, after all. And I was mindful of the three hundred francs, equivalent to a hundred days of sewing. 'Just this once,' I told Joelie.

FORTY

I TRIED TO work out my emotions as I prepared myself. I felt nervous but excited. I hadn't done this for eight years. Armand was my last 'client', and look what happened. I knew I was fooling myself: the notion the Earl of Bradbury would be an English version of Armand – Kiki, lady of the manor in the English Midlands, disporting her equestrian skills to the local hunt. But life wasn't like that.

What to call myself? Certainly not Monique, Baroness du Plessis. So, for that one night, I was Lucia, one of my former aliases.

What to wear? Almost all of my clothes were acquired when I was a respectable married woman. I was twenty-four, not sixteen. I had no alternative but to dress in what was available in my wardrobe and picked out a pastel-olive creation, cut low to show my cleavage. I decided against wearing Florian's necklace, too prim, and opted for the diamond pendant that once belonged to Virginie. My hair was up chignon-style, emphasising my neck and ears with their teardrop peridot and diamond earrings. I kept make-up to a minimum – a dab of rouge on my cheeks, some eyeliner.

I arrived at the Brighton and walked in as though I was the Baroness du Plessis. None of the usual knowing looks as I was escorted to the fourth floor. The bellboy indicated a door at the end of a corridor. From a previous assignation I knew it opened into a suite reserved for the hotel's wealthier clientele. A note was wedged in the door's jamb.

Make yourself comfortable. Back soon.

The suite was opulent: velvet everywhere, Persian carpets, Louis XV-style chairs, two ottomans, exotic lampshades with tassels hanging down, the whiff of petroleum, a bucket with a bottle of champagne wedged in ice, two flutes. I helped myself. And hors d'oeuvres displayed fan-shaped on a platter and set on a low table together with a bowl of caviar from which I scooped a splodge with my forefinger, licking it languorously. Sipping champagne, I felt my confidence soar.

The door burst open. At first, I didn't recognise him – the black sideburns tinged grey, the pallid skin, his height and lack of flesh, the bony outcrop of his head, his Adam's apple.

Sir Reginald Markham.

Such was my shock I dropped the glass. All I could think of was, *Why didn't I wear one of my wigs?*

The glass was not broken, its fall cushioned on the rugs. I bent down, apologising while I concealed my face.

'No, no, let me clear that away,' he said, bending down, his voice slurred.

He appeared not to have recognised me so I decided to brazen it out.

'Fucking Prussians,' he said in English. 'Making everyone's life a bloody misery.'

I looked at him full on, replying in English. 'Food prices have doubled in a week.'

'Your English is very passable, mademoiselle.'

I saluted him with my glass. 'I heard you were something to do with coal.'

'Who told you that?'

'The lady who arranges these liaisons for me.'

'Through that buffoon of a concierge downstairs, no doubt.'

'I used to work in the coal business as an accountant.'

'Did you now? Fascinating. Yes, I own some collieries in the Midlands, centred on Bradford.'

'Bradford?'

'Yes. Matter of fact, I am the Earl of Bradford.'

I inwardly cursed myself but more especially Joelie. Stupid cow had got his name wrong: Bradford the name I had heard at dinner with the Girards many Christmases ago. Had I known...

'Do you have a first name, my lord?' I said, playing it up.

A deep and guttural laugh, followed by a staccato 'ha, ha, ha'. Glugging down the remains of his glass: 'Reginald, mademoiselle, at your service.' He looked at me directly as if for the first time. 'Have we met... I could swear?'

'No, Reggie, although I do tend to get about.'

'Reggie... my brother used to call me Reggie.'

'Oh?'

'He's dead now, thank God. That's how I inherited the title. More champagne?'

'Let me serve you, kind sir. Caviar as well?'

'Please, my dear,' he said, unfurling his cravat.

I busied myself with the caviar – spooning it onto small round pancakes. My mind was churning: were he to remember me, I was done for. He would, of course, know how Augustave had died. He would surely hand me over to the police. *And* he knew Oreste.

Reggie was half drunk. I'd handled drunks before... usually ending in a 'fumble' before they passed out. I would help him on his way then make my escape.

I placed the caviar on the table in front of him and then plied his glass with champagne.

'My dear, what's your name?'

'Lucia, sir.'

'Lucia, ah, well, perhaps you'd like to make yourself more comfortable. Warm in here, don't you think?'

I slipped off my shoes.

'You can do better than that.'

I knew where this was going – that was why I was there – and lowered the top of my dress.

'Let me help,' he said, getting to his feet and standing behind me.

I smiled demurely as he unbuttoned my dress. He stank of alcohol and cigars. I made the appropriate noises when he began kissing my shoulders – licking them, more like. My skin literally crawled.

I stepped out of my dress and was down to my bindings, my pretties, my silk stockings. I was aware of him kicking off his shoes. A brief pause before he undid my bindings, leaving my breasts bare and bobbing below me – not for long, as he wrapped a giant hand round each one, pulling me backwards towards him.

'Mmm, you're beautiful, Lucia,' he said, panting, his breath hot on my neck.

More appropriate noises from me. Then one of his hands made its way down the front of my pretties to my womanhood. I squirmed. 'Mmm, that's nice.'

'Lucia,' he said, 'I'd like to play a game.'

'Tell me, Reggie.'

'Turn around.'

He was naked apart from his socks and, taking my hand, he led me to the bedroom. I remember feeling nauseous – his sinewy body was covered with lank black hair. He loomed above me, his eyes the darkest eyes I had ever seen. My eyes were drawn to his 'parts' – his dangling manhood with its gnarled brown foreskin. I tried to squeeze the panic out of my face. A brief respite when he reached down the side of the bed to produce four strips of a black silk-like material.

'Ooh, I don't do that, monsieur,' I said, reverting to French.

'Well, you do now. What do you think I'm paying you for?'

Before I knew it, he had grabbed one of my wrists and wrapped a strip round it.

'I said no, monsieur!'

'You'll do what I tell you, missy' – cuffing my face with the back of his hand.

For a moment I was so shocked I didn't know where I was, but reality soon reasserted itself when he jumped on top of me, binding the strips round my flaying limbs. He was too heavy and too strong and turned me over so I was face down in the sheets. By this time I was screaming and then something was roughly shoved in my mouth.

I was naked, unable to move. I was a slave, a mute one at that, and tried to cough out the gag. Nothing had prepared me for this. I cringed and waited, expecting to be taken in the roughest of fashions. Instead, he was licking me again, caressing me – running his hands up and down my thighs. Then he started rubbing me – probing my vagina with his fingers.

'What have we got here?' he said after a while. 'A wee scar of sorts, if I'm not mistaken.'

More probing. Vomit gorged in my throat and after retching into the gag I began to choke. I screamed as soon as he took it out so he shoved it back in.

'A…M,' he said contemplatively. 'A…M? Hold on. Let me see.' Grabbing my hair, he turned my head roughly towards him. 'I *have* seen you before. I'll be damned. AM… Augustave Monnier. Yes… By Jove, you're Augustave's bint. Thought I recognised you. A cold little piece, if I recall… always on the make. Made a fool of me at that dog fight. Always a clever remark. Pretty, though, very pretty for a common slut.'

All sorts of things were storming my head. Murder at the top of the list. And fear, not of what was about to happen to me, but of the future, what this creature could do to me, what he had over me – my secret, my darkest shame.

He continued talking to himself, to such an extent I thought him mad, prating on about Augustave and *his pretty little piece.*

He was still chattering when he started probing me again. Then shock – he was suddenly inside me. He was huge and lunged slowly at first, and then it went on and on as he upped his pace. I thought it would never end. At times, I felt myself blacking out and shook my head. I did not know what to do. One minute I was consumed by indescribable rage, the next with sullen acceptance of what was happening to me. I tried blanking my mind but still he went on relentlessly, noiselessly. In the end I must have fallen unconscious.

I woke and moved my head. Markham lay asleep on his back with his legs wide apart, his member lolling to one side. Although he was nearly bald he had hair everywhere, including his shoulders, like the pelt of a great ape. I was still tied to the bed and facing downwards. I struggled as quietly as I could but gave up – with no chance of escape. My body ached all over, especially my vagina. I must have drifted off again.

Next thing I knew he was at it again. I tried to scream, to buck him off like a wild horse. Failed, then he started again. When would it ever end? Eventually and with a grunt he ejaculated. The room was no longer pitch black. I twisted my head – light framed the curtains.

I must have blacked out again, only to be woken by a slap to the back of my head. 'I'm going to remove the gag,' he growled. 'Make a sound and I'll stuff it back in.'

He removed the gag. I screamed and he tried to shove it back in. I was prepared, however, and bit into his fingers as hard as I've ever bitten into anything before. He bellowed and punched me with his spare hand. I gasped, allowing him to remove his fingers. I could taste his blood on my lips and spat it away. Then he clamped my head with a pillow. 'You fucking bitch, you'll fucking pay, I'll be bound.'

He eased the pressure. 'Scream and you'll regret it,' he said.

I was determined not to cry. I had to improve my situation. There was no point in swearing or trying to gouge out his eyes.

'We need to talk, Kiki,' he said.

'Once you have released me.'

Sighing, he undid the strips from the corners of the bed, retying my hands behind my back. Then he released the strips from my ankles. 'Turn over,' he growled.

Now at least I could see him. He was dressed and lit the cigar that was clamped between his teeth. The flame bloomed and he sucked away. 'Tell me what happened, Kiki, after you murdered dear Augustave.'

'You *conard* bastard! I'll—'

'We could be here all day, Kiki' – puffing out smoke.

I sighed. The sooner I was out of there the better. 'I escaped, travelled to Paris, had various jobs and here I am, unfortunately.' I wasn't going to tell him about Armand.

'Is that it? Eight years in Paris and you're still a fucking whore.'

'I have also modelled for artists.'

'A job for a whore.'

'If that's what you think.'

'Gagnon, downstairs, tells me you work for Joeline Lambert, a madam of repute, that she arranges your "nights".'

I nodded.

'Second floor, 23 rue des Fossés-Saint-Jacques, overlooking place de l'Estrapade.'

I didn't know where this was leading, but the eels of fear writhed again. He had Joelie's address

'It means I know how to get hold of you. To be more precise, where the police will know how to *get hold of you*, Oreste Monnier in particular. Matter of fact, I had dinner with him recently. He couldn't stop talking about his brother, you as well, for that matter. He told me he arrested you and that you escaped. Highly embarrassing for le Blaireau.'

'What's it to you?'

'To me…? Oh, Kiki, dear, I'm interested in seeing justice done. As an upstanding citizen, mind, one's obligations to society, for the common good, that sort of thing.'

'You bast—'

'Kiki, I want to know where you live.'

'Why would I tell you *that*?'

'I want to stay in touch.'

'Oh?'

'I could, of course, ask my friend le Blaireau to squeeze the answer out of Madame Lambert. It shouldn't be too difficult.' Popping his lips, a ring of smoke emerged, to hang fleetingly in the air.

'What do you want from me, Reggie?'

Unfolding his legs: 'I want you to be available, Kiki.'

'Available for what?'

'Never you mind. Your address, if you please.'

I sighed again. 'Number 16 rue Mouffetard.'

'Any particular floor?'

'The second.'

'That's better. You can avail yourself of the bathroom. I want you gone in twenty minutes.'

FORTY-ONE

As soon as I was home, I stripped off my clothes and went to bed, from where I did not emerge for at least a day. On Friday morning I crawled from under the sheets and stared in the mirror – not a pretty sight: my hair tangled, dark smudges under my eyes.

I was on the edge of tears, my bottom lip aquiver. 'No, Kiki, not now, not from you,' I said to my reflection. I had been through awful times before and had survived. I had to survive. One thing I knew for certain – Sir Reginald Markham, the Earl of Bradford, was a dead man.

After washing myself I realised I was famished. *Two* eggs and a slice from the dwindling hock of pork. The bread was stale and I dunked a chunk in a glass of milk on the turn. A knock on the door, I edged it open: Joelie. 'Where in heavens have you been? I've been worried,' she said, curling her lip. 'You look a mess, by the way.'

Handing me an envelope: 'Three hundred as agreed. Are you going to tell me about it?'

I had decided not to tell her – that and the fact Markham knew of her address. I told her that I'd had a difficult evening and that I would never 'work' for her again.

'You're not telling me everything, are you, *chérie*?'

I shook my head, glowering at her.

'So you won't tell your Auntie Joelie?'

'You're not my aunt and I would be obliged if you left.'

'Be like that,' she sneered, slamming the door behind her.

The weekend was spent sleeping and shopping for food. Long queues in place Scipion. My 'regular' gave me three eggs for two francs – the price had doubled again. As coffee was readily available, I bought five hundred grams. And a queue at the butcher's – and, when it finally came to my turn, his trays and hooks were bereft of meat. Despite my attempt at a smile he reached under the counter – scrag-end of mutton at triple the pre-siege price.

I had reserved the depths of hell for Reginald Markham. Memories of the night in the Brighton refused to go away. What I recognised as depression leached into me. I had difficulty getting out of bed. Try as I might I succumbed to it, sinking into the darkness of my blankets and sleep.

By midweek I had just about pulled myself together. After washing my hair and dressing in clean clothes I tried to start a new book: *Les Misérables* by Victor Hugo. But I couldn't break into it, dozing fitfully until a knock on the door brought me half awake. *What does Joelie want?* I thought to myself.

I inched the door open: a man stood there. I tried to slam it in his face – too late, as he forced his way into the room. He smiled. 'Forgive me, Kiki, I won't occupy much of your time.'

One look told me he was vain to the rooftops. The way he stood there, looking sleek yet overfed, like a seal. He probably imagined the small but neat scar on his right cheekbone was dashing – something the ladies would admire. The whiff of the military about him: his highly polished boots; his tight, exquisitely tailored trousers; his cutaway dove-grey frock coat. His cravat was black and glossy, reminding me of Markham's silky strands. Removing his top hat he bowed. His face was open and clean-shaven except for his ridiculous moustache – waxed and sticking up at both ends.

The way he bore himself suggested something of the foreigner about him.

I was about to tell him to go away, but he spoke first: 'Kiki – if you don't mind me calling you Kiki, that is – Reggie sent me.'

'Get out!'

'We can play this your way or mine. Your way will lead to Oreste Monnier of the Paris Police, your incarceration and execution. In troubled times, justice tends to be abused.'

I huffed. 'Do you have a name?'

'Moritz.' He bowed again.

'Jacques Moritz? Pierre Moritz? Moritz Duval?'

'Just Moritz.'

'You have the look of the military.'

Twisting one of his waxed outposts: 'Served my time for a while.'

I studied him – yes, there was something strange about 'Moritz'; his French was perfect and yet…

'*Guten morgen, herr Moritz*,' I said suddenly.

A flicker of hesitation. 'Hah, you think you can catch me out, do you?' he said, grabbing my arm and twisting it violently downwards, pulling me off balance. Once I had steadied myself, though, I kicked out at his knee as hard as I could. Then he was on top of me, pinning my arms down.

'Huh, good try. I admire spirited women, especially beautiful ones. Fury enhances beauty, the fire in the eyes, the raven hair.'

I struggled – bucked and writhed. He sat there smiling. 'My, you're strong, Kiki, where did that come from? The stronger the better.'

This was getting me nowhere. 'All right, let me go and tell me what you want.'

'That's more like it,' he said, standing up and straightening his clothes. 'Incidentally, I have a gift for you' – conjuring a tin container from somewhere and handing it to me.

I opened the top – inhaled. 'I don't want your cocoa, Moritz.'

'Suit yourself.'

He shook his head as I tried to hand it back. 'Kiki, the Prussians and their German allies surround Paris. Comestibles such as cocoa are almost impossible to get. I represent people who want information.'

'You want me to spy for you.'

'You catch on quickly, Kiki. Beauty and brains combined.'

'Who *are* your people?'

'You don't expect me to tell you *that*. Really, madam.'

'Spying for the French is one thing. Spying for the enemy is, well, something else. No, I will not spy against my country, monsieur.'

'You leave me no alternative but to hand you over to Sergeant Monnier.'

'Ah, so I would not be spying for France.'

'Kiki, your window,' he said, pointing. 'Look onto the square below.'

I looked.

'You see that rather unpleasant-looking fellow standing there, the large one with the ginger beard?'

I couldn't miss him, lounging against a wall as he was, tapping the side of his leg with a cudgel.

'He and his cohort will know where you are day and night. Any thought of escape would be futile, my sweet.'

I opened my mouth to protest.

'Can you sew, Kiki?'

'Sew?'

'Needle and thread, *dear*.'

'Of course I can sew.'

'Excellent,' he said, extracting a fob watch. 'Time's eleven fifteen. Hum. I want you to go to Gare d'Orléans *now*. It's not far from here. You're to sign on as a seamstress – the balloon factory there.'

Balloons…?

'Those round things that float in the air.'

Forty minutes later I was walking down rue Lacépède. Glancing round, I spotted 'Redbeard' fifty metres behind me, twiddling his cudgel. I dared not think what Moritz had in mind. I was not one to dwell on the past, the "what ifs": what if Armand hadn't died; what if I hadn't spent a night with Reginald Markham. Strange, though, the further I walked towards the station the less glum I felt.

The streets were quiet. The populace going about their business. Although there were more beggars than usual. Some were soldiers – one with a hideously burnt face. I dropped fifty centimes into his kepi. Soon I was walking by the side of Jardin des Plantes down rue Buffon. I chanced a glance: Redbeard was still in tow.

Plenty of activity at Gare d'Orléans. Soldiers patrolling outside. 'The balloon factory, I hear they are looking for seamstresses?' I asked one of them.

'Over there' – pointing to a small brick building.

Inside, a sergeant who appeared to be in charge. 'How did you hear of us?' he enquired, when I told him I was looking for a job.

'Through a seamstress friend of mine.'

'You are here at the right time, madam. We are ramping up production. Can you sew?'

'Sergeant, I was a supervisor at Société des Drapes et Matériaux at their workshop on rue de Vaugirard, before they closed us down, that is.'

'Making uniforms?'

A man entered – middle-aged and distinguished with his goatee-moustache combination, swept-back hair and kindly blue eyes. 'This woman, has she come for a job?' he said, addressing the sergeant.

'Claims she's a seamstress, monsieur.'

'And I told him I was a supervising seamstress at Société des Drapes et Matériaux.'

He tugged at his goatee.

'I design and make my own clothes, monsieur.'

'Hmm, what else, if I may enquire?'

'I have worked as an accountant, monsieur.'

'All right,' he said to the sergeant. 'Subject to the usual security questions, employ this lady immediately. Then bring her to me.'

Smiling, I thanked the man and asked him his name.

'Eugène Godard, aeronaut, madam.'

The 'security questions' were more detailed than I had expected. Luckily, I was carrying my lease as well as my final wage statement from Société des Drapes et Matériaux. The questions unnerved me, though. It meant security was an issue, ramming home the danger of what Moritz had in mind for me.

Guilt suffused me when I was escorted into the station; soon forgotten, however, when I looked around. The structure was immense, huge with its glass and iron roof, and devoid of trains or passengers. Splayed across the tracks was a single balloon, half-inflated. Men were pulling it with halyards, reminding me of Moby Dick.

Monsieur Godard introduced me to his wife. 'Madame Godard is supervising our seamstresses, Madame…?'

'Du Plessis.'

She acknowledged my presence with the curtest of nods.

'We will be building a fleet of balloons for the distribution of letters to the outside world during the siege.'

I was reminded of the letter I had sent to François de Gaalon… as yet unanswered.

'Madame Godard will show you what to do.'

'Come with me,' she said. 'Eugène tells me you design your own clothes.'

'I made a dress that is easy to wear, practical for daytime use. One not constricted by crinolines and bustles, or hoops for that matter.'

Looking me up and down: 'Good for you,' she said with a hint of a smile.

We reached a long trestle table, several women working either side. 'A balloon, its envelope, is made from 120 pieces of percaline,' said Madame Godard. 'Three pieces form a single section, top to bottom, so forty sections in all.'

'I heard that balloons were made of silk, madam.'

'They are but silk is not available. Your job will entail cutting the pieces and sewing the sections together.'

'What stitch do we employ?'

'A fell stitch, it—'

'I am familiar with the fell stitch, Madame Godard.'

'The stitch work has to be very accurate. The aeronauts' lives depend on us.'

Three large, flat pieces of wood of varying sizes lay on the table together with pencils and pairs of scissors.

'I touched one. A template, madam.'

'Exactly, Madame du Plessis. How did you know?'

'Common sense, madam.'

Back in the brick building, the sergeant handed me a *laissez-passer* – asking me to sign it. Then he stamped, signed and dated it. 'You are required to show this every time you enter the building.'

Thursday, 29 September. No sign of Moritz, although when I walked onto the street there was a large man with a black beard slapping a cudgel against his palm. Touching the brim of his hat he then followed me when I made my way down rue Lacépède. Again, I persuaded myself that my situation could have been a lot worse. *And* I would be paid three francs a day for doing something worthwhile.

That morning six of us were gathered round one of the trestle tables. Madame Godard stood at one end.

'Ladies,' she said, 'France is depending on you. You will have the honour of building the first balloon. *Le Washington* is set to sail in twelve days' time, giving us nine days to complete our work on the envelope. I have spoken to you all individually, so you know what to do. We work in pairs. Madame du Plessis will supervise the pairings.'

Once Madame Godard had left, the team turned their eyes on me.

'My name's Monique. Your names, please.'

'Marie,' said one. 'Claudette,' another. 'I'm Suzanne,' another. 'I'm called Francine,' another. The last one said, 'My name's Cécile, I worked for Charles Worth, the couturier.'

'Well, good for you,' said Claudette.

Smiles all round.

I said, 'All right, I'll team up with Madame Charles Worth, here. Marie and Claudette will work together, leaving Suzanne and Francine as a pair.'

Large sheets of red and white percaline hung on lines – soaked to leach out the dyes and rid them of stiffness. Once they were dry, a coat of varnish was applied. 'Madame Worth' knew what to do, placing a template over the cloth. I carefully drew lines on the material then cut out the shape while she kept the material taut. The others followed our example.

By the end of the first day the team had cut out all 120 pieces – sixty red and sixty white – separated into six piles according to colour and size.

'Blackbeard' appeared to know my working hours and stood at the station end of rue de Buffon at seven fifteen, making eye contact when I passed him by.

My supplies. I was down to my last egg and decided to save it, settling for leftover stew and a knob of stale bread. I had plenty of wine, though, and glugged out a large glass. Just when I was about to tuck in, a knock on the door: Moritz, looking pleased with himself.

He took a seat and crossed his legs. 'Well, Kiki, how did it go?'

I was tempted to tell him to get out. Instead, I gave him vague details of my day.

'You've worked out what we want you to do?'

'We?'

'What *I* want you to do.'

'Of course… report on the production of balloons… spy for you.'

'Very dangerous work. Caught and you'll be shot. You'll need eyes in the back of your head, your wits about you every second.'

'Huh, don't worry on that score.'

'Of course. Silly me. You've managed to evade Sergeant Monnier for eight years.'

Moritz took out a pencil and paper. 'This is how we'll communicate. I'm not interested in the name of any particular balloon, only the time and date of its flight.' Writing something down he turned the note to face me.

930am

'What does this mean?'

I rolled my eyes. 'Nine thirty in the morning.'

'Correct.' He wrote on the paper again.

9am3

'What does this mean?'

'Same thing.'

He nodded and wrote again.

3a9

'And this?'

'Abbreviated and reversed.'

'You catch on *rapido*, Kiki. Write down four in the afternoon.'
I picked up the pencil.

0p4

'Right, now substitute the "a" for a "b" and the "p" for a "q".
Write down five fifteen in the afternoon.'
Again, I wrote.

15q5

'Excellent. One last addition… the date, not the month as that
will be obvious, only the day. Try the twenty-fourth at twelve thirty
in the afternoon.'
I wrote.

3q12

Then.

43q122

'There,' I said.
He smiled. 'What languages do you speak, Kiki?'
'French, monsieur.'
'Really, Kiki, do we have to…?'
'*Mein herr, ich spreche ein wenig Deutsch.*'
He shook his head, a mischievous look on his face. 'What does
that mean?'
'Monsieur, I speak a little German.'
'Your accent's not bad… anything else?'
'Jolly nice weather, don't you think? I speak a little English.
Incidentally, how do I get the messages to you?'

'I was just coming to that. Never go to work with a pencil and paper on you. Write the message in the morning before you go to work and drop it off on your way in.'

'Where?'

'Your route is rue Lacépède, rue Geoffroy-Saint-Hilaire, rue Buffon, Gare d'Orléans. There are four wastepaper bins. Day one you use the bin on rue Lacépède, day two the one on rue Geoffroy-Saint-Hilaire, and so forth. Tomorrow is day one, Friday, the thirtieth of September.'

'What if I don't have any information?'

'You drop the message in the next designated bin. Days one, five and nine and so forth are always a Lacépède bin day.'

'What if I need to contact you?'

'Do you wear bonnets?'

'I prefer berets.'

'What colour are they?'

'Blue and red, monsieur.'

'Wear the red beret when you need to make contact. Write a note saying what you want. Someone will knock on your door that evening, slip the note under the door when you hear the knocks. Do not open the door.'

'The knocks?'

Moritz knocked out a rhythm on the table: *rat-tat-a-tat-tat, tat-tat.*

My turn to knock – repeating what he'd done.

'Good,' he said. 'Oh, and for the time being you'll not see me again.'

'What a shame, Moritz.'

With a sly look he dug in a pocket and produced a *saucisson*, placing it on the table.

After supper I could not fall asleep, my head full of balloon construction and Moritz's code. Moritz, whoever he was, knew what he was doing – a professional and a mystery. And what of his connection with Sir Reginald Markham?

Bizarre, but when I woke up next morning I couldn't wait to go to work. I was part of an important enterprise and played a central role. My team's performance was of national importance. That I could destroy something I helped create was abhorrent to me.

Before leaving home, something made me wear the short blonde wig. A foreordination if you will.

On my way to Gare d'Orléans I noted the position of the four bins: on rue Lacépède, on the corner of Lacépède and Geoffroy-Saint-Hilaire, on the corner of Saint-Hilaire and rue Buffon and at the station end of rue Buffon. That particular day was day one – a Lacépède bin day. Halfway down rue Lacépède I stole a glance – Redbeard was fifty metres behind me.

I was reminded of the *cabotte* – the tin concealed behind the stone. Junius. A lifetime ago.

Inside the brick annex the sergeant on duty inspected my *laissez-passer*.

The station reminded me of a huge aviary. I was early – not many people there except Monsieur Godard, his neck craned, gazing up at the roof. I checked my piles of cut-out shapes.

Just before eight o'clock the team was assembled, Madame Godard at the head of the table.

'Today you will sew the three pieces together to form a section,' she said.

'What stitches do we employ?' said Claudette.

'Fell – also known as double lap. Anyone familiar with fell?'

Madame Worth said, 'Also known as French fell. We employed it at Worth, where extra strength was required. To do it properly the fold has to be shaped then flattened. We'll need hand irons, madam.'

Madame Godard stroked her chin. 'I will speak to Monsieur Godard straightaway.'

The irons arrived just before lunch – the latest model, with detachable wooden handle.

Madame Godard presented me with a youth: 'Your ironing assistant is Paul, the brother of Albert Bertaux, the aeronaut who will fly *Le Washington*.'

We soon had a system. Cécile Buffet, nicknamed Madame Worth, folded the edge of one of the middle 'white' pieces, and after securing it with pins she flattened the fold with an iron supplied by Paul. She repeated the process with a bottom piece. We then slotted the shapes together before ironing the joint flat. Double-threading a needle, she stitched the sections together down the fold but to one side, allowing for a second row of stitches. Half an hour later she had completed both rows.

We held up the combined pieces and tried to pull them apart. They held firm and tight.

'Applause, please, for Madame Worth.'

The sewing was the hard part – bent over the table – so we changed tasks every half an hour or so. Meanwhile Paul kept us supplied with hot irons. Madame Worth was a better sewer than me, her fingers digits of repetition, putting me to shame.

I checked the work of the other pairs. Marie and Claudette were working well together. But Suzanne and Francine were struggling – especially Suzanne. After a while I swapped Suzanne with Madame Worth to balance the teams, have them working at the same pace.

Suzanne was clumsy, her stitches not straight. And she was always apologising.

By noon Madame Worth and Francine had almost completed their section. Madame Godard examined the seams, complimenting Madame Worth.

She took me aside. 'Good work, Madame du Plessis, except the section you are working on.'

I explained that I had swapped Madame Worth for Suzanne. 'Cécile's an excellent seamstress, she used to work with Charles Worth.'

'The couturier?'

'Quite so.'

'And Suzanne?'

'Not so good, I'm afraid.'

'Madam, *Le Washington* is scheduled to fly in ten days' time. This factory is of vital national importance – balloons the only way Paris is able to communicate with the outside world. Our work has to be of the highest quality. Our aeronauts will be taking huge risks. A blown seam would be a disaster. I'm sorry, but we'll have to replace Suzanne.'

Gulping down my guilt an idea occurred to me: Sybille.

There were benefits to working at the balloon factory. Apart from the sheer excitement, the place was full of dashing young men. Many were sailors, some training as aeronauts, others up in the rafters, hanging ropes and grappling irons. And lunch was provided, a bonus at a time of rapidly rising prices. We all felt the populace was behind us, watching us, pinning their hopes on us: a way out of the mess the politicians had landed us in. Cakes and biscuits arrived daily from well-wishers.

Guilt engulfed me to the extent I felt like giving up, telling the authorities why I was here. To hell with Moritz and the Prussians.

That night when I arrived home a slip of paper was wedged in the door.

Monique Chérie,

Sorry about the other night, I can hardly think of anything else.

Please come for supper tonight, I have something special. Can't wait to see you – 7.30 sharp.

Your loving friend,
J x

I allowed myself time to wash and dress in fresh clothes. Joelie's letter might have been wheedling but I needed a night out despite my exhaustion.

Lily welcomed me: 'I'll inform Madame Lambert of your arrival.'

Mooching round the salon I ventured onto the terrace to be greeted by the sight of two chickens pecking at seeds from a trough.

'Hannah and Hetty,' said a voice. Joelie looked magnificent, except for the lace headdress she persisted in wearing. 'Crèvecoeurs thrive in confinement. These beauties lay an egg every other day.'

Threading her arms around me: 'I am so sorry about last week, Monique. Will you ever forgive me?'

'Probably not.'

'Tell me what you're up to, *chérie*?' she said, looking ill at ease.

I told her about the balloon factory.

'One of my clients is an aeronaut,' she said with a wink.

We settled down to supper. Her 'surprise' was lamb cutlets, two each. 'Purloined from one of my hotels,' she explained.

We discussed the siege: when it would end, food prices going through the roof, the wounded everywhere.

I handed her an envelope. 'Please get this to Sybille. I need to see her on Sunday.'

The following day was Saturday, a Geoffroy-Saint-Hilaire bin day, but I had nothing to report. Although Monsieur Godard did let drop that *Le Washington* was due to fly on the eleventh or twelfth of October.

I arrived at Gare d'Orléans early. 'Twelve more seamstresses have been hired to work on *Le Godefroy Cavaignac* and *Le Christophe Colomb*,' Madame Godard informed me.

'When will they fly?' I said guiltily.

'After *Le Washington*.'

The day was spent sewing the pieces together. Suzanne was close to tears – aware we lagged behind the other pairings. After lunch I asked Madame Worth if she wouldn't mind working with Suzanne. An angry look in reply.

The work was intense, full concentration required as though the aeronauts' lives really did depend on us. At day's end we had completed eleven sections.

Next day was Sunday, a half day, the afternoon off. Francine announced that one of the *marins* had asked her out for the evening.

'Be careful, dear, all men are beasts,' said Madame Worth.

Claudette suggested the rest of us meet somewhere. I declined in the hope of seeing Sybille.

Sybille arrived at rue Mouffetard in the early afternoon. She appeared her usual bouncy self, but I could tell she was putting it on. Sometimes I caught her looking forlorn. I poured her a glass of wine and cut slices from Moritz's *saucisson*. She explained she had heard nothing from Joelie and that her baker friend had refused to pay her more.

'All men are beasts,' I said, aware I had repeated Madame Worth's mantra.

She brightened when I told her there might be a job at the balloon factory.

We walked in Jardin du Luxembourg. Soldiers everywhere. Grim looks on the faces of people going about their business. The occasional crump of distant cannon. 'Ours,' said Sybille, clutching my hand.

The evening was spent at the place on rue d'Assas as opposed to Saint-Germain, which we felt was too dangerous.

Two soldiers insisted on joining us and ordered wine. Sybille flaunted herself. 'When will you brave soldiers rid us of those *salopards d'allemands*?'

'With Trochu in charge we stand a chance, mademoiselle,' said one. 'We will counter-attack once we have strengthened our defences.'

'The wall that surrounds Paris?' I said.

'And the forts, mademoiselle.'

The evening passed pleasantly enough, although Sybille had become raucous and was holding 'Alfred's' hand. The other soldier, Rudi, tried to lure me away: *There's a little place I know, chérie. You remind me of my sister, chérie.* All stuff and nonsense.

I fobbed him off in kind. *I am promised to another*, and so on.

I had a word with Sybille before we left. 'What you do in your private life is your business, but if you want that job be at my place at seven tomorrow morning. Don't be late and don't forget your papers.'

FORTY-TWO

IVE PAST SEVEN on Monday morning, Sybille was at my door looking tired and uncomfortable. Her eyes were puffy and red. And she reeked. I told her in no uncertain terms to avail herself of my bathroom, and plenty of soap.

A while later she emerged – more her jaunty self, especially when I handed her a dish of coffee and a wedge of brioche.

She stared at me. 'Why the wig, Monique?'

'My hair gets in the way. Anyway, I always wanted to be blonde.'

By the time we entered the brick annex she was positively chirpy. I expounded Sybille's virtues to the duty sergeant: her work with me in the uniform factory, her skills as a seamstress. After showing him her papers he took her aside to ask the usual questions. She was flirting with him, of course. I could see it. Bounding over, she wrapped her arms around me. 'I'm in,' she squealed.

I introduced her to Madame Godard. 'We worked together making uniforms. Would it be possible to put her in my team?'

Seeing her about to open her mouth I nudged Sybille with my foot.

Madame Godard looked down her nose as if to say: *Who is this salope?* Instead: 'She can sew, can she?'

'Nearly as well as Cécile.'

'Very well. By the way we've let Suzanne go. How many sections have you completed?'

'Eleven, madam.'

'Eleven, hmm. They have to be sewn by Wednesday night.'

I introduced Sybille to the others. By lunch we had completed six more sections. Two other teams were in place, each working on their own balloon. *Marins* were everywhere: some threading nets made of hemp from which the gondolas were suspended, others filling bags with sand enabling the balloon to gain height when thrown over the side.

By Monday evening we had completed six more sections. 'Not enough,' said Madame Godard. 'Not that I'm blaming you, Madame du Plessis, your team is working well. We are employing more seamstresses to speed up the process.'

The following day our team had been expanded to ten seamstresses. By lunchtime on Wednesday all forty sections had been sewn. 'Now for the hard part, sewing the sections together to form the balloon,' Madame Godard informed us.

After lunch, we hauled two of the twenty-metre sections onto the table, spreading them, flattening them with irons while checking for blemishes in the material, darning them if found.

We were about to start sewing when Madame Godard ordered us to assemble. 'A security check. Form a line,' she told us.

Two policemen appeared as we lined up in front of the table. Having questioned Claudette first they proceeded to work their way down the line. Fortunately, I was at the far end and had time to compose myself. I chanced a look at Marie – Oreste Monnier was standing in front of her. Feeling faint I grabbed onto Sybille. 'Are you all right?' she said.

'Oh, nothing,' I managed to say.

Oreste worked his way towards me. His thin Monnier nose was mean and pinched. His hair had receded; his sideburns were streaked grey. Eight years had passed since he had interrogated me in the Conciergerie on Île de la Cité.

My wig masquerade was about to be tested. Would he notice it and tear it from my head? Did le Merle prey on his mind? The constant draining of funds, hanging on by his fingertips and the skewed notion of loyalty to family and his *conard* twin.

I wondered what to do with my eyes – to look at him directly or avert them, play the shy puss?

'Your papers, madam' – his arm outstretched.

I made a business of searching for my *laissez-passer* and looked at my feet when I handed it to him.

'Madame Monique du Plessis,' he said. I could no longer avoid his stare, so I deadened my eyes and concentrated on keeping the muscles in my face still, neutral, devoid of persona.

'Du Plessis' – rubbing his chin. 'Your family anything to do with the Richelieus?'

I nodded politely.

'Are you a du Plessis or did you marry into the family?'

'Married, monsieur,' I said, aware I had changed my voice, masking my Bourgogne accent.

'So why are you working here, the wife of an aristocrat?'

'He died earlier this year.' I made a play of wiping away a tear and closed my eyes.

'Forgive me, madam, but if you were married to Baron du Plessis, wouldn't that afford you the title of baroness?'

'Shh, monsieur. Please keep your voice down,' I whispered. 'I work here because I need the money. If my colleagues knew I was a baroness it would cause embarrassment for them and for me.'

'I don't believe you. Show me your papers.'

I excused myself and found my reticule. After extracting my marriage certificate, I thanked God I had resisted the impulse to include 'Christine' in my name.

He inspected it. 'Local family, were you? How did you meet the Baron?'

'In Paris, monsieur.'

'When?'

'Early in 1863. We rode together in the Bois de Boulogne.'

'Eighteen… sixty… three,' he said as though deep in thought.

Madame Godard arrived and stood behind him. I implored her with my eyes.

'Can I be of assistance, sergeant?' she said.

He turned round.

I looked at Madame Godard while shaking my head and gritting my teeth.

'No, no. I was just checking Madame du Plessis' papers,' said Oreste.

'Well, hurry up, if you please. We have balloons to sew, sergeant.'

On the point of leaving he turned to me. 'Strange, but I feel we have met before.'

'No… I don't believe I've had the pleasure, Sergeant.'

He stomped away. Madame Godard said, 'What was that all about, Monique?'

'Oh, I don't know. Just doing his job, I suppose.'

The rest of the day my mind was fraught with anxiety: had Oreste recognised me? His last comment worried me. My identity could come to him in a moment of lucidity. Would he put two and two together: 1863? I had escaped the Conciergerie on 14 December 1862. Would he associate *early in 1863* with my escape? Why would he? There was a war on – his time fully occupied.

No, I had got away with it for the time being. Had I been sensible I would have quit my job, upped sticks from rue Mouffetard and melted into the city. Impossible, given Moritz's thugs were watching me day and night. One other factor – I loved my job, the enormity of it, the camaraderie.

Eighth of October 1870 – Lucien's eighth birthday. He occupied my thoughts all day. What I would have given to see him.

At last we had stitched the sections together – *Le Washington* was now entire. Then it was over to the *marins*, who varnished the percaline inside and out. Once done, a wooden ring was fixed to the top of the balloon to which halyards were attached. Ropes were manoeuvred over the rafters, the balloon hauled to its full height. Madame Worth sewed a 'long sock' to the opening at the bottom, to which a large metal fan was attached. Two of the beefier *marins* turned a handle and the balloon slowly inflated. Madame Godard said this was to dry the varnish and to check for holes in the material.

Thankfully, there were none. '*Le Washington* will fly next Wednesday after daybreak,' Madame Godard announced proudly.

Next morning, Sunday, 9 October. Day ten as far as the bins were concerned. After breakfast I wrote out the code – 23b81 – eight thirty in the morning of the twelfth.

Guilt swamped me as I walked to Gare d'Orléans. Redbeard was in tow. So far I had done nothing wrong – not yet betrayed my country. I weighed up the pros and cons for the umpteenth time. Defy Moritz and he exposes me to the police – to Oreste. In this time of war, a fair trial would be out of the question. I would be executed out of hand. I would never see Lucien again. My plans would evaporate – le Merle would slip away from me. As a traitor, on the other hand, I would be endangering the life of the aeronaut, Bertaux, his passengers, and the post that would be lost – letters to the outside world from the government in Paris and from people reaching out to their families. To say nothing of the pigeons that wouldn't fly back to Paris with vital information attached to their wings and legs.

As I approached the bin on the corner of rues Lacépède and Geoffroy-Saint-Hilaire, I felt the paper in my pocket. No, I couldn't do it. I just couldn't. Before entering the station, I ripped the note to shreds.

That night a knock on my door. Fear seared through me as I put on my dressing gown. I opened the door a crack: Moritz.

'No messages in ten days, Kiki,' he said.

'You said I wouldn't see you again.'

'Don't play games with me. I know for a fact a balloon is close to being completed.'

'True, but I don't know exactly when it will fly.'

He forced his way in, sat down and lit a cheroot. 'We know about Lucien,' he said.

'Lucien?'

'Your son, Kiki.'

I could feel the roots in my hair prickle. 'How?'

'Your friend Markham knows Oreste, of course. Oreste told him of your escape from the Conciergerie eight years ago. Want me to continue?'

'You might as well.'

'He told Markham you were arrested outside a house on rue de l'Ouest. More?'

I nodded.

'I had my men track down the owner, Mathilde Wynburne, who told me you had given birth to a child and later abandoned it—'

'Abandoned it? She stole him from me and betrayed me to the police.'

'Don't expect any sympathy from me, *chérie*.'

'From you, no.'

'You see, I know where the Wynburnes live.'

'Rue du 29 Juillet.'

Moritz shook his head.

'Where? Tell me.'

'Don't be naive, Kiki. Incidentally Mathilde didn't have nice things to say about you. She told me about your botched attempt to abduct Lucien. A self-serving little slut, she said. But that's by the by.'

'You bastard.'

Exhaling smoke: 'I'll make it easy for you… Failure to give me what I want and you'll never see Lucien again.'

'Killing a child, Moritz. You disgust me.'

'Oh, and I want the information by Tuesday morning.'

Standing, he got in close, blew smoke at me, and was about to speak when I crunched my heel down on his foot. Then I was on top of him, flailing at him with my nails. I felt demonic, and wrapped my legs about his waist and squeezed. Grabbing a shoe, I smashed it in his face. But he was strong and soon on top of me and forcing his tongue down my throat. A mistake on his part, as I bit down hard. I remember him yelping, and then searing pain in my head and all going black.

Next thing I knew the sun was streaming through the window. I stirred and found myself on the kitchen floor. My head felt as though a needle was being pulled through one of my temples. I wobbled to my feet. Strange, but my first concern was being late for work. A note on the kitchen table.

K,

I enjoyed our little romp. I let myself out.
Remember what I said: Tuesday a.m.

M

I arrived at the station just before lunch. I had no bruises except the one on the back of my head. I found Madame Godard and apologised to her.

'Be late again, Madame du Plessis, and I'll personally throw you out on the street. Do you understand?'

I mumbled an apology and found Sybille tucking into *boudin noir* and potatoes. 'What happened to you?' she said.

'Man troubles, I'm afraid.'

'Are you all right, dear?'

'Not really.'

'Tough one, eh, they're all *conards*, you know.' She stood and put an arm round me. 'Sit down. I'll fetch you something to eat.'

Later, Madame Godard approached me. 'Sorry, Monique, I was a little brusque with you. I can see you are distressed. We live in hard times, my dear. Let me just tell you how much Monsieur Godard and I appreciate your efforts.'

My stomach turned to butter; I wanted to tell her everything there and then. But I couldn't – my brain not connecting with my tongue.

FORTY-THREE

WEDNESDAY, 12 OCTOBER. The day I would become a traitor, a Buffon bin day. I dropped the note in without breaking step, my arm hanging down and letting it fall. I thought about it: if *Le Washington* sailed at eight thirty there was nothing Moritz could do. He'd be too late. I convinced myself I had not yet betrayed *la France*.

A surprise when I arrived at the station: the semi-inflated *Le Washington* was outside. A metal tank was connected via a pipe to the sock at the bottom of the balloon. 'They're filling it with coal gas,' someone said.

Inside the factory Madame Godard told us we could watch the balloon take off.

Outside all kinds of activity: dangling halyards, a sack of post to one side, sandbags, an oompah band playing, pigeons in a green cage, flags flying.

Le Washington slowly inflated, its red and white vertical stripes clean and true. My chest swelled. I had helped create this flying machine.

Monsieur Bertaux and his two passengers were dressed as though it was the middle of winter and they were downing eau de vie. 'Ooh, that's the pigeon fancier Van Roosebecke,' someone said.

Soon the balloon was inflated. Sailors were straining on ropes to prevent it floating away. The men climbed on board. On a signal the ropes were released and *Le Washington* lifted into the air amid cheers and whoops from the crowd. The balloon rose more swiftly than I would have imagined possible. Any pride I would have felt was quashed by my treachery. I later heard *Le Washington* was subjected to heavy fire as it left the enclosure of Paris, without any injury to its passengers – thank God.

My team had expanded to sixteen seamstresses. Madame Godard told us that *Le Jean-Bart* would fly on the sixteenth, that our task must be completed by Friday, the fourteenth. I guiltily stored the information away.

The station was boiling with activity – all the teams had increased in size. Four balloons were under construction, including *Le Jules Favre No 1*. Madame Godard told us it would also fly on the sixteenth. 'We wouldn't want *them* sewing their envelope before yours,' she said to me in a loud voice.

'You heard, mesdames,' I said to the team.

I had a word with Madame Worth as to suitable pairings. Soon we were sewing the pieces together to form the sections. Madame Worth had singled out Sybille as one of our best seamstresses. Sybille kept the jokes coming, mainly at the expense of the *marins*.

I kept my ears open and learnt that *Le Godefroy Cavaignac* would sail on the morning of 14 October, *Le Christophe Colomb* in the early afternoon.

Thursday, 13 October. I wrote out the codes, took a guess at the times – 43b71 and 43q11. It was a Geoffroy-Saint-Hilaire bin day.

I hated myself, but I'd hate myself more were anything to happen to Lucien, so I dropped the note in the bin. Now I really was a traitor. God forgive my immortal soul.

October flew by. I had virtually given up breakfast and dinner, relying instead on food provided at the factory. Rumours abounded

– people eating cats and dogs. Léon Gambetta's escape to Tours by balloon in early October to raise armies in the rest of France gave us hope – only to be dashed by news of our defeat at Châtillon. Then the final blow: Marshal Bazaine's surrender of the army at Metz, our only hope of escaping the mess gone.

I continued my traitorous pursuits, supplied information on five more flights in October. More rumours including the fate of *Le Montgolfier*, which apparently landed in Alsace and 'fell into Prussian hands'. I was, of course, consumed by guilt.

Not a peep from Moritz. I could only assume he was satisfied with what I was giving him. My thoughts were focused on Lucien. The idea of rescuing him was daunting. For a start I didn't know where he lived and I didn't have the time or the support. And where would I house him in the unlikely event I managed to pull off his escape?

I also worried about le Merle, the money I owed Banque Villiard. But I had a plan and drafted a letter.

Société Vins du Cluvé
Paris

30 October 1870

Dear Monsieur Lagarde,

You have not heard from me for some time as I'm trapped in Paris.

As you know I have managed to sell eight of my paintings (before the war) for a total of thirty-three thousand francs, which you have sent to Banque Villiard in Beaune. This amount has repaid most of the debt I owe the bank in the acquisition of the mortgage for the wine estate in Meursault.

As we both know, this debt has to be discharged by 8 January next year.

As things stand, I will not be able to sell the remaining

paintings. Would it therefore be in order for you to discharge the debt, collateral for which would be the paintings secured in your vault?

On 11 August I sent a letter to my avocat in Beaune, M François de Gaalon, to which I have received no reply.

Please telegraph him your reply to me so he can make arrangements.

Attached is a list of the paintings and the values attributed to them (before the war) sufficient to easily cover the debt in normal times.

I am sending this letter by balloon post and pray it reaches you, and that you will advance the funds.

Je vous prie d'agréer, Monsieur, mon considération distinguée, Monique du Plessis

I wrote out two copies of the letter.

Being Sunday, I felt in need of air and decided to walk in Jardin du Luxembourg. Again the strange background noise emanating from Saint-Germain – a low, continuous roar. A gang of youths, swigging from bottles and chanting, 'À bas Trochu!' 'Vive la Commune!' One of them beat out the *rappel* on a drum.

Their intensity frightened me.

Next day, Monday, I asked Madame Godard if I could send a letter on *Le Fulton*, the latest balloon completed by my team.

'Of course, Monique, but it will have to pass the censors.'

'Censors?'

'In case it falls into enemy hands.'

I was not at all keen on anyone knowing my business – that I was a woman of means. 'All right,' I said reluctantly.

'Speak to the guards in the annex.'

After lunch, one of the guards informed me the letter had passed the censor and that *Le Fulton* would fly on Wednesday morning. 'It will require a stamp, twenty centimes,' he added.

Later in the day, rumours were flying: the Reds had stormed the Hôtel de Ville where members of the Trochu government were being held captive.

Sybille asked me if she could stay the night.

Tuesday, 1 November, a Lacépède bin day. I was aware I could be the cause of my own letter not getting through – *Le Fulton* falling into Prussian hands. I had written down the code – 23b80 – the night before in my room away from Sybille's prying eyes.

Redbeard was on duty and I made sure I was on the inside of the pavement as we walked to the station. I dropped the note in the bin without breaking step. Sybille appeared not to have noticed.

We had become firm friends and had the occasional night out together. A couple of times she slept on my floor in rue Mouffetard as she had the night before. As I continued my way to the station a plan formed in my head. I remembered what Moritz had said: wear a red beret if I needed something.

Most of the faces at the station looked worried. Relief, however, when we learnt that General Trochu was still in control and that most of the Red ringleaders had been rounded up.

Lunch was thin soup and stale bread. 'We're like rats in a trap,' said Madame Worth. 'I can't stand it anymore. Look how thin I am, Monique.'

One wag overheard her. 'If there are rats in a trap, I'd kill 'em and roast 'em over a fire.'

With *Le Galilée* due to fly on 4 November I made sure one of my duplicate letters to Monsieur Lagarde was on board.

Three teams continued to work in Gare d'Orléans. Our next balloon was *Le Daguerre*, so named, I was told, after a man who had invented a photographic process. Somewhat nervously I asked Madame Godard if I could have a day off. She looked down her nose. 'If you must, Monique.'

I had decided to visit Dent, Urwick & Co, the *négociant* I had appointed to sell Corbeau Ridge. After concealing myself in a shop to avoid Redbeard, I walked down rue Lacépède towards rue Jussieu and their warehouse opposite Halle aux Vins. Paris had a mournful feel: leaves gathered in clumps on the ground, people asleep in doorways and down alleyways. I averted my eyes to avoid unwanted attention – someone intent on money and food. A gang of youths was walking towards me so I crossed to the other side of the road.

As luck had it, Stanley Dent was in. His clerk led me through the warehouse. The odours reminded me of why I wanted to be in the wine business – part fruit, part rot and the unmistakable tang of tannin pervaded the air. And wood – I breathed in the oaky fragrance. A splotch of red sap on one of the barrels, tiny black flies circulating, settling on the goo. I couldn't help but daub a finger in it, wrinkling my nose at the smell.

Despite the time of year Stanley Dent dabbed his brow while waving me to a chair. 'Good morning, Baroness,' he said in English. 'A glass, my dear?'

Shaking my head: 'A little early, Stanley.'

He poured himself a splash of red.

'Stanley, I haven't properly apologised… for letting you down. Corbeau Ridge. I'm sorry.'

'Think nothing of it, my dear. I heard the Baron passed away. My condolences' – bowing his head.

'Thank you, Stanley. Unfortunately, I'm not involved with Corbeau Ridge anymore.'

'More's the pity, Baroness.'

'I am, however, working on a project in la Bourgogne.'

'Burgundy?'

'Meursault. Our little secret.'

'Meursault is my favourite tipple. Alas, not a drop coming my way in these troublesome times.'

'Stanley, forgive me, but I'm not here to discuss wine.'

'Oh?'

'… Do you know Sir Reginald Markham?'

His face clouded and he dabbed his brow again. 'That mountebank.'

'Do you know where I might find him?'

'If you mean do I know where he lives, the answer is no. We tend not to socialise.'

'Oh?'

He sipped his wine. 'About three years ago Sir Reginald came into a title, the Earl of… um—'

'Bradford. He inherited coal mines, I believe.'

'That's right, somewhere in Yorkshire. He sold his wine business. No longer bothered, I suppose, what with his coal.'

'So why would he visit Paris?'

'I wasn't aware that he did. Perhaps he can't bear to be away, the attractions here, if you know what I mean.'

'Stanley, you wouldn't happen to have the name of the person he sold to, by any chance?'

'I do, and I have the address.'

Jotting on a slip of paper he handed it to me. 'If you propose dealing with Markham, be very careful, my dear. He who sups with the Devil…'

With Stanley Dent's words in my head, I walked onto rue Jussieu and waited for his clerk to wave down a cab.

My next stop was rue du 29 Juillet, but I needn't have wasted my time. No one emerged from number 6 in the two hours I loitered there. I decided to burn off my frustration and walked back to rue Mouffetard.

The streets were grim, rubbish everywhere and horse droppings. A couple of boys rifling through a dustbin on the corner of rue des Écoles. I was tempted to dip into my reticule, hand them centimes, but thought better of it.

Instead of going home I tried place Scipion. But the stalls had packed up for the day.

For the first time it really struck me how awful Paris was. And the feeling it wouldn't get better. Try as I might in my old Kiki way, I was unable to rally myself. I checked my pantry – no eggs, no bread, no meat, some old potatoes, a couple of wrinkled apples, milk and the stub end of Moritz's *saucisson*. I thought of the boys at the dustbin, that I was fortunate. I had a job I enjoyed, a roof over my head, money and ration cards to buy meat. Finding the time to queue was another matter. I sliced the remains of the *saucisson* and poured myself a glass of water. As it was my only day off in a long time, I sought the refuge of my bed.

Saturday, 5 November. I awoke early, a plan fresh in my head. I had just over five hundred francs – a reasonable sum, although the price of eggs was now seven francs a dozen, a chicken eighteen, to say nothing of the queuing. It could only get worse. Were it not for my 'Markham money', I would have been worried. But I reckoned I had enough for what I had in mind.

This time I would not use Joelie – one of her *I-know-just-the-right-man* contacts.

Breakfast was an apple and a small glass of milk. I could feel my ribs. My figure was losing its shape, my skin its lustre. Working in the factory made it hard to shop. I resolved to visit place Scipion and spend some of my reserves.

I joined a queue of complaining women. Eventually it was my turn to be served. A dozen eggs, a chunk of cheese, some milk and sixteen francs later I joined the file for the butcher. After five minutes I had barely moved. In danger of running late for work, I gave up.

On entering the station my spirits soared. Sybille, God bless her, had saved me some cake donated the day before.

Three balloons were in production: the *La Gironde*, *Le Niepce* and *Le Daguerre*. The standard of lunches had further declined –

soup and a lump of cheese that particular day.

I invited Sybille to supper. Outside was dark and cold. The weather had turned; dampness pervaded. We clung to each other. People wandered the streets as though lost. The cafés were full, though – wine one commodity not in short supply. Inside my apartment I lit the petroleum lamp by the front door as well as the oven. Sybille nursed the flames while I washed and changed.

We dined on omelette – four eggs with plenty of cheese. I put the plates on the table while Sybille poured the wine.

She raised her glass. 'Forgive me asking, Monique, but how can you afford all this?'

I decided to trust her and told my story: my marriage to an older man, fleeing to Paris, my various jobs in the city, my marriage to Armand. I neglected to tell the parts about being wanted by police, my time as a prostitute, my escape from the Conciergerie, that I was in fact a baroness. 'Armand left me some money. Enough to support myself modestly, as you can see.'

'Do you have any children?'

'A boy, but not with Armand – from my time in Bourgogne.'

She sipped her wine, her eyes sparkling. 'With your first husband?'

'Truth is, I don't know. About the time I ran away I had a dalliance with a navy cadet.'

'How exciting.'

'Not really, not when one's struggling to survive in Paris.'

'I suppose you're right. What happened to him?'

'I tried to find him in Brest – the Naval Academy there. But I was too late. His ship had already sailed for Mexico.'

'The war there?'

'It's quite possible that he's dead.'

'Oh, I am sure he isn't. What happened to your child, Monique?'

I poured more wine and described my attempted rescue of Lucien.

'The Tuileries? I used to walk my child there, the child I was responsible for.'

A tingle down my spine. 'When?'

'In the early to mid-sixties, working as a nanny for a family in rue de Castiglione.'

'That's only two streets down from rue du 29 Juillet.'

'I had friends, other nannies, who lived in the 29 Juillet.'

In that instant I viewed Sybille in a different light: a person who would have almost certainly laid eyes on my Lucien. 'Lucien was born in 1862,' I said. 'He would have been a three-year-old in the mid-sixties.'

'There were always a lot of children in the Jardin.'

'Lucien had a dog. Pogo. A terrier. White with black markings.'

Sybille pursed her lips. 'There were also a lot of dogs. What number on 29 Juillet?'

'Number 6.'

'I'll make enquiries.'

'Please. I want to know if the Wynburnes still live there. They might well have moved. It's very important to me.'

She nodded.

'What about you, Sybille? How do *you* survive?'

'On three francs a day… just.'

'And your baker friend?'

'Oh, I still see him. I wouldn't get by without his little treats.'

'Has Joelie been in touch?'

'No. Not yet anyway.'

A wave of compassion washed over me. Strange. Sybille was a fighter, took it on the chin with no complaints and was always there to make a joke, raise the general morale, including mine. 'You could always move in here,' I found myself saying. 'I have plenty of bedding and we could put a mattress in the corner. You'll have some privacy. Anyway, I could do with the company.'

'Would I have to pay rent?'

'You insult me.'

'Please don't think me ungrateful, Monique, but let me sleep on it.'

'In your own time. And talking of sleep you might as well stay the night. It's horrid outside.'

Next morning Sybille accepted my offer; she would move in on Sunday afternoon.

On the way to work I told her I was looking for an 'investigator' type.

'Try Alfred, the sergeant in the annex. He's ex-police.'

'Oh, him. How do you know about Alfred?'

'Don't be silly, Monique. He likes to flirt with me.'

On Sunday I learnt that *La Gironde* was due to fly on Tuesday, 8 November in the morning. At just before one o'clock I met Alfred – Sybille waiting patiently – and explained to him what I was looking for.

Scratching his chin: 'I might have someone, an investigator, you say. I'll do some digging, ma'am.'

I thanked Alfred and we took our leave, Sybille blowing him a mischievous kiss. We crossed the river, walked along quai Henri IV holding on to our berets as a chill wind gusted down the cut of the Seine. Turning right onto rue Saint-Paul we eventually arrived at Sybille's *pension* on rue des Minimes. I kicked my heels, waiting outside for her to gather her things. But not long, before she emerged carrying two hessian sacks. 'My worldly possessions,' she declared.

We discussed food – our ration cards: hers was fully stamped, mine wasn't. She *knew a place*. She reminded me of Joelie, sometimes, a lot less calculating, though.

Her butcher was on boulevard Beaumarchais, close to place de la Bastille. He had some horse meat, three hundred grams or three days' worth of stamps in my ration book and costing me seven francs fifty. At first I had baulked at the idea: images of Lapin and

Leveret baked in a pie. Sybille told me not to be a 'prune'. 'We'll smother it in spices.'

People and soldiers were gathered in place de la Bastille – the National Guard, Sybille explained. We decided to skirt the area and scurried down rue du Petit-Musc onto Île Saint-Louis, crossing the river over Pont de Constantine to La Rive Gauche.

FORTY-FOUR

I FELT NOTHING but contempt for myself when I dropped the message in one of the bins on the way to work. The lives of those on *La Gironde*, *Le Daguerre* and *Le Niepce* were in danger from what I had done, to say nothing of the messages on board. I was sure Sybille hadn't noticed a thing. I stole a look behind me – Blackbeard was on duty.

During lunch Alfred handed me a scrap of paper. 'Known Hippo for years, ma'am,' he said. 'He's reliable, an ex-*sergent-de-ville*.'

I read the note.

Hippolyte Faure
Pierre of Café Troubadour on rue de Charonne knows
where to find him. Mention my name.

I showed it to Sybille. 'Rue de Charonne, near place de la Bastille, where we were yesterday,' she said.

It occurred to me that 'Hippo' might know Oreste Monnier. I asked myself if there was any reason why Hippo would connect me with him.

'Why do you need someone like Hippolyte Faure?' said Sybille.

'It's like this. A certain gentleman whose name you don't need to know raped me in a well-known hotel.'

'Bastard. What will you do if and when you find this man?'

'Umm, I'm not sure. Cut off his penis?'

'Good idea. Types like that should be repaid in kind.'

There was nothing I could say – the look on my face would have given me away.

'Oh, so you have something else in mind?'

I sighed. 'There's more to it than that.'

Work on *Le Daguerre* was near completion, the sense of urgency no longer there. I asked Madame Godard if I could leave early… five o'clock. Luckily, she was in a good mood.

I told Sybille I would be home at seven o'clock.

Crossing the Seine via Pont d'Austerlitz, I walked to place de la Bastille and asked for directions. Soon I was outside Café Troubadour on rue de Charonne. The Bastille quarter was rough compared with Saint-Germain, the people greyer and glummer, the streets strewn with litter, the stench of poverty. I recoiled when a rat flopped out of the top of an overflowing bin. An old soldier in a filthy uniform played an accordion. I dropped centimes into his kepi.

The Troubadour was nearly full. No women. Mainly tradesmen, some in the early stages of inebriation and making a noise, others nose down in their drinks. Nothing for it but to brazen it out, so I stepped up to the bar and waited to be served. I was in my working clothes, my hair tucked up inside the short blonde wig. Even so, one man pawed at me, demanding my attention. I batted him away and told him in a loud voice that I was looking for Pierre.

'I am Pierre,' said the man behind the bar.

Pierre was not what I'd expected – young and clean-shaven. 'I am looking for Hippolyte Faure,' I said.

'Who's asking?'

'Monique,' I said, handing him Alfred's note.

He looked me up and down then walked through an archway

at the back… soon to reappear. 'Go on up. Second floor,' he said.

I felt my way up a narrow staircase to the light at the top. A door was ajar. The stairs creaked. 'Come in,' said a voice.

Medium height and clean-shaven, he was an older version of Pierre. 'Hippolyte Faure,' he said. 'Friends call me Hippo.'

'Alfred told me where to find you.'

'That scoundrel.'

The room was large, windows on three sides. To my left a stove, a basin with crockery in the rack above. A curtained-off area was to my right – where Hippo likely slept. He sat behind a desk with two neatly stacked piles of paper on top. He indicated a chair. 'How is Alfred?' he said.

'Well enough. He keeps us under control at the factory.'

'The balloons?'

'I'm a seamstress there.'

'How can I be of service, ma'am?' – steepling his fingers.

'Tell me about yourself, Monsieur Faure. If you don't mind, that is.'

'Not much to tell… I was a *sergent-de-ville* in the Onzième, retired in '68 and bought this place. Pierre's my son.'

My mind was working: Oreste was based on the Left Bank, some way from the Onzième. Despite my disquiet I handed him the note.

Sir Reginald Markham, the Earl of Bradford
Aged about 50. Nearly 2 metres in height. Pale skin with
black hair, tinged grey. Dark sideburns. Black eyes.

M Gagnon, concierge of Hôtel Brighton

Philippart et fils, négociants
3 quai de la Tournelle

'An Englishman, eh?' said Hippo.

'Ruthless. Very dangerous and very rich.'

'What do you need to know, ma'am?'

'His address, monsieur. Monsieur Gagnon at the Brighton might know.'

'And Philippart fils?'

'Markham used to be a *négociant*. Sold his business to the Philipparts three years ago.'

'Ruthless, you say?'

'And extremely sure of himself and as strong as a lion.'

'Madam, may I ask—?'

'No. Just his address, if you please.'

'Madam, forgive me, but you're wearing a wig?'

I glared at Hippo. Time for me to take off my beret.

'That's why,' I said, snatching the wig away. I stood and ruffled my hair. 'Do you think I'd walk around the Onzième looking like this, monsieur? In *these* times.'

'Madam, if you meant to create an impression you certainly succeeded. May I enquire of your name?'

'My name is of no relevance to you. And I don't want you discussing me with Alfred. Is that understood?'

'Perfectly, ma'am.'

'Can I rely on your help? If so, please state your terms.'

'Eight francs a day, two days payable in advance.'

I nodded. 'Your terms are acceptable, monsieur, but subject to a maximum of four days.'

'Should be time enough.'

'When can you start?'

'Tomorrow.'

'Tomorrow's Wednesday,' I said, handing sixteen francs. 'Sunday's a half day at the factory. I'll return here in the afternoon.'

A while later I entered my apartment. The candles and lamps were lit; a pot simmered on the stove. A pungent smell pervaded the air. Sybille handed me a glass of wine. 'Did you find what you were looking for, dear?'

'I don't want to talk about it.'

Sybille was not only good fun, but she knew how to cook *pot-au-feu*, despite the fact it was horse meat. She had been at it for a couple of days, marinating the meat in God knows what.

She ladled some into bowls. 'Enough to last three days,' she said. 'It will improve with age and we'll slice whatever we can find into it.'

I spooned some into my mouth. 'Mmm, tastes good,' I said. 'A bit like beef.'

I may have been crafty and out for myself, but my decision to have Sybille as a housemate was a masterstroke.

Saturday, 12 November. The launch of *Le Daguerre*. The aeronaut was Sylvain Jubert, one of the many *marins* in the factory. Ernest Nobécourt loaded six cages of pigeons on board. Monsieur Pierron, the other passenger, climbed into the gondola with a dog tucked under his arm. The oompah band was there, together with dignitaries and other hangers-on. Cheering as the *marins* let go of the ropes – *Le Daguerre* lifting away. Sybille sniffled into a handkerchief; something to do with the gallant Jubert, I suspect.

More excitement when *Le Niepce* was launched.

I later learned that the occupants of *Le Niepce* witnessed *Le Daguerre* being shot out of the air and falling into Prussian hands. I felt sick inside. It was not as though I could have confessed to the Godards – too late for that now. Something I should have done a long time ago.

Next day after lunch I walked to Café Troubadour. It was Sunday and busy: noise and smoke in profusion. Laughter. Thankfully Pierre spotted me.

Upstairs, Hippo indicated a chair. 'The information you required, ma'am' – handing me a slip of paper.

15 place Dauphine

I placed the note in my reticule.

'I'd get rid of that if I were you.'

I ripped it to shreds. 'Was he easy to find, monsieur?'

Hippo spread his hands. 'A friend of a friend knows Monsieur Philippart.'

'Do I owe—?'

He shook his head. 'The search occupied very little of my time.'

I was of half a mind to ask him to find the Wynburnes but thought better of it.

On leaving the Troubadour I walked down rue de Charonne, crossed place de la Bastille onto rue Saint-Antoine and rue de Rivoli. Lengthening my stride I passed the Hôtel de Ville and kept my head down. Beggars were everywhere; a woman was touting her body to passers-by. Litter and manure were piled on the pavements. I covered my nose from time to time.

Paris had gone to the dogs. When would it ever end?

A child tugged my coat, his huge brown eyes imploring me. He wore no shoes; his legs and feet were streaked with grime. He couldn't have been much older than Lucien. I have no idea what possessed me and, on impulse, I grabbed his hand and told him to come with me. Turning left at Pont Neuf we walked across the river onto Île de la Cité. Place Dauphine was to our left. The boy complained and dragged on my arm. I felt like dropping him there and then. But my stubborn streak came to the fore, so I tightened my grip. Soon we were standing outside number 15.

This was where the Devil resided. Close to the fleshpots, the hotels: Le Meurice and the Brighton on rue de Rivoli, where he could abuse women as he pleased, with no one the wiser, and those 'in the know' turning a blind eye, abetting him, even – Monsieur Gagnon, for example, the concierge at the Brighton.

A cab drew up. A man alighted, paid his fare. I manhandled the boy into the back of the carriage and followed him in. 'Rue Mouffetard,' I instructed the driver. I removed my wig, let my hair down over my shoulders, all the while smiling at the boy.

He looked at me but remained silent.

Once home Sybille took control. Thank God. No sooner had she told me to boil water, she was ordering me to buy clothes. 'There are plenty of second-hand shops, giving the stuff away. Go now. Now!' she screamed.

When I returned, the boy was wrapped in a towel and eating from a bowl of leftover stew. Sybille clucked over him. 'Little mite,' she repeated. 'Poor little mite.'

That was how I met Tomas – Tommy, as we called him. The longer he was with us the less chance I had of sending him away. I did not want to send him away; and he reminded me of Lucien – his brown eyes – and he must have been about the same age. Anyway, I would not have dared to raise the subject with Sybille. And it was November and raining outside.

With Tommy fast asleep in a corner, Sybille asked me what we were going to do with *the poor little mite*.

'We keep him here. I don't propose to feed him up, put some francs in his pocket and send him back out onto the streets.'

'I should think not.'

I kneaded my chin. 'We could find him work at the factory.'

'Umm, a reasonable idea, but not yet. He's in need of rest and food.'

'You're right, Sybille.'

Sybille's turn to rub her chin. 'There's another alternative… we use him as a servant. He can queue for food and keep the oven alight, the wicks primed, wash our clothes, clean the floors.'

A light went on in my head: the paintings under my bed.

442

Tommy was bound to be inquisitive, and I hadn't forgotten the lesson I had learnt at Hôtel de Londres – my stolen francs.

'No, Sybille. Sorry.'

'Why?'

'I have my reasons. Anyway, how do you know we can trust him?'

The following morning with misgiving looks from Sybille, we took Tommy to the factory. Sybille used her wiles, and Alfred let him inside. At first Madame Godard was not keen. Nevertheless, she gave him a job as a sweeper.

Tommy slept in a corner on the floor of my apartment. He never said very much but told Sybille he was from Belleville, that his father was dead.

One day a few weeks later he disappeared.

Activity at the factory was reduced – the weather and the shortening daylight hours. Despite gas rationing, heating and lighting were installed. The smell of gas pervaded the place. The supply of cakes and treats had dwindled to virtually nothing. Lunch as well.

We were working on Le Jacquard and considered ourselves lucky to have a job. I had not seen Moritz in over a month, although the two 'Beards' continued to lie in wait. How they did it, God alone knows, especially in the cold and dark.

Rumours of smallpox outbreaks in Belleville and La Villette. Eggs were fifteen francs a dozen. We earned three francs a day. Other stories: people eating their pets – unsurprising with meat rationed to thirty grams a day. Rice was still available, as were tea, sugar and coffee. Coal and coke were in short supply. Most of the trees in the city had been felled for use as firewood.

The hopes of Paris were pinned on Trochu's plan for a breakout across the Marne – his 'Great Sortie' – set for the end of November. The name of General Ducrot was on everyone's lips. The city gates were closed. A sense of urgency, excitement even, despite the gloomy weather. The strain manifested itself in the factory, people praying to themselves, others in a trance. At first the news was good – Ducrot's divisions had crossed the Marne – but when the wounded started streaming back in, we learned the awful truth. The sound of artillery could be heard inside Gare d'Orléans. By 4 December it was over: the Prussians and their allies had beaten us again.

The teams were hard at work: no noise, just concentration on the job in hand. We were professionals, knowing exactly what to do and when to do it. *Le Denis Papin* was our latest creation and due to fly on 7 December.

Early December. While trying to cope with the lack of food and fuel, we Parisians learnt of the death of Alexandre Dumas. Some said he died of a broken heart. The news certainly broke my heart. He was a hero, larger than life, his stories fantastical and entertaining. Strange, but his death made me think of Madame Thierry. I moped for a while, my head full of the Musketeers and of times gone by.

Mid-December. The Seine had frozen over. Despite the blankets piled on my bed I was a shivering, starving wreck. One night there was a knock on my door: Sybille asking if she could share my bed.

'I'm not like that,' I replied.

'Don't be daft,' she said. Soon she was asleep and snoring. At least the bed was warmer.

Christmas Day 1870. We had the day off. Joelie had invited us to lunch. To my surprise a soldier was staying in one of her rooms. Gaston had been wounded in the Great Sortie, his right leg in a cast. Somehow, Joelie had procured a couple of rabbits. Gaston occupied one side of the table, his leg propped on a chair. Copious amounts of wine and brandy were consumed and, of course, Sybille flirted with Gaston.

Joelie was in her cups. I had never seen her that far gone. She glared at Sybille from time to time. I do believe she was jealous. Her voice was slurred. She had a go at me – accused me of abandoning her. As the evening progressed, she became an embarrassment and so I stood to leave. Grabbing my arms she forced me back onto one of the ottomans. 'You know something, Kiki? It was me, Joeline, who took your money from the de Londres, not that mouse Séverine.'

I couldn't believe what I was hearing, rendered me speechless. I just sat there.

'Why do you think I befriended you? Charity? Rescuing you from the Conciergerie entailed huge personal risk. Caught and I would have gone to prison… And the use of my apartments – you've been coming and going for years. You forget how I helped you in your futile attempt at rescuing your son.'

I managed to find my voice. 'You've ruined my life, Joeline. That money would have seen me through my pregnancy. Instead, I had to beggar myself to the Wynburnes and lost my child. Why? Why did you do it?'

Sipping her cognac: 'How do you think I got started—?'

'—in your disgusting business. You've used me through and through. You sold me to Armand, for God's sake. How can you live with yourself?'

Sybille came over, sensing trouble, perhaps.

'A minute, Sybille, please,' I said.

'Yeah, get lost,' said Joelie.

'You sure?'

'I said get lost.'

Sybille hesitated, then slunk away.

'I—'

'Worse still, you put me in the hands of Reginald Markham.'

'Reg—?'

'The Earl of Bradford. You didn't even get his name right. You're losing your touch, Joelie. Your reputation will collapse. Your "girls" will abandon you. You're not long for the gutter, *chérie* – a fifty-centime-a-trick slut begging for it.'

Joelie stood, tottered, cognac spilling onto the carpet. She pointed to the door. 'Get out! Get out!' she screamed.

I will never forget her face, her coarsened features.

Walking home I was shaking with rage. Sybille put her arm round me. Then we heard what would become a familiar sound: the crump of distant guns.

After a while Sybille said, 'What was that all about?'

'A long story, dear.'

FORTY-FIVE

EARLY JANUARY 1871. The Prussians were bombarding Paris; their guns felt close. There were awful stories – a girl, for example, cut in half by a shell while walking in the Luxembourg. There was no let-up in the production of balloons in the week before the New Year. My team had excelled itself, completing the *Le Bayard* in record time. Then there was a lull in production.

Sunday, 8 January 1871. The day my debt was due to be repaid to Banque Villiard. I prayed that one of my letters had reached Monsieur Lagarde and that he'd had the wit to forward the funds to Beaune. I was down to 210 francs. I thanked God the rental moratorium was still in force.

Sybille and I were spending twelve francs a day, six francs over our wages. I had five weeks' worth of cash left. I didn't mind subsidising Sybille; how I would have coped without her, I don't know.

That night a knock on the door while we were eating our supper. Moritz, I thought. In fact it was Tommy, who promptly collapsed to the floor. He was drenched and his hair was matted. After dragging him to the bathroom we stripped off what remained of his clothes. He was all skin and bone, and covered in bruises. A look from

Sybille told me I was on hot-water duty. After some 'poor little mites', Sybille had him tucked up on a mattress. 'It's touch and go,' she said.

The following morning we left him in the apartment. I worried about my paintings – he was an urchin, after all. *Le Vaucanson* was due to fly later in the week. Launches to us had become routine.

Monday, 16 January. Freezing cold and barely light when we entered the station. A sailor bundled past us pushing a wheelbarrow full of glass and rubble. 'We've been hit,' he said. A group was gathered on one of the platforms. We hurried over and offered our help. Monsieur Godard was shouting out orders. Sybille pointed to a gap in the roof, twisted metal and glass strewn below.

Someone handed me a brush, Sybille as well. We began sweeping. Others gathered and gaped. Madame Godard arrived and told us to pay attention. Wiping her brow: 'We have been hit by a Prussian shell. A decision will be made later in the day.'

'What decision?' a voice cried out.

'Whether to continue to fabricate balloons here, of course.' She rubbed her chin. 'I'll need a dozen volunteers to help clear the mess. The rest of you can go home.'

'Will we be paid?' the voice again.

'Yes, for today, that is.'

A collective sigh of relief.

I turned to Sybille. 'I'm worried about Tommy. I'm going home.'

'I'll stay,' she replied. 'Nothing better for me to do.'

I arrived home, feeling rather pleased I had the day off with pay. Tommy was up and about. He grunted when I opened the door – he was monosyllabic at the best of times. He looked better than I'd seen him in days. I told him we were going out for food.

We queued for milk and cheese. At forty francs, a dozen eggs were out of the question. A *livre* of cheese was thirty, although rice was only two francs and milk three francs a litre, though I was sure it had been watered down. Tommy's eyes darted everywhere and soon he was gone. An hour later, as I was being served, he returned, opening a bag to reveal five large potatoes. His grin was infectious despite the missing teeth.

Back home I boiled two of the potatoes and grated cheese. We ate in silence, occasionally grinning. Afterwards, I read *Les Misérables* to him. He shook his head when I handed him the book. He was illiterate – hardly a surprise.

Sybille returned home early and gave me the news – the balloon factory at Gare d'Orléans had ceased operations. 'They worry about the flammable gas and the proximity of the Prussian guns. They're transferring operations to Gare de l'Est.'

'Gare de l'Est… that's on the other side of Paris.'

She spread her arms. 'The Godards have cut the workforce down to twenty of us. You, Madame Worth and I are among the lucky ones, as is Francine – a policy of first in, last out. By the way we had a visitor after you left, that policeman, the one who inspected us when we were working on *Le Washington*. I overheard him asking Madame Godard if you still worked there.'

I fought to compose myself.

'You've gone white,' said Sybille. 'You all right?'

'Yes. Fine. What was her reply?'

She arched an eyebrow. 'She said that you had the day off.'

I retreated to my room and tried to work out what to do.

Next day I rose at six, half an hour earlier than usual. It was pitch-black outside. On the way back from the bathroom I nudged Sybille awake.

To my surprise Blackbeard was at his post. I wore my red beret for the first time in three months. Sybille and I walked down rue Mouffetard. Five minutes later I chanced a look; Blackbeard was fifty metres behind us. The walk to Gare de l'Est was grim, especially along boulevard de Sébastopol. Drunkards were everywhere. Broken glass, vomit, rubbish, beggars with their hands out and women on corners – it *was* still dark. Sybille and I huddled together; without her I would never have risked it. Again I cursed myself for not having retained money from the sale of my paintings. At least it was not so cold.

We started work on *Le Général Cambronne* – named after a soldier who swore at an English officer when asked to surrender at the Battle of Waterloo.

On the walk home, I told Sybille I was expecting someone to knock on the door that night. 'Don't answer it,' I said. 'I will slip a note under—'

'A note—?'

'I don't want questions, just your cooperation. Understood. And I need Tommy to do something for me.'

'Tommy? You be careful with Tommy. He's only just recovered and—'

'—he is sleeping on my floor and eating my food.'

'Oh, he owes you something, does he?'

I stopped, grabbed Sybille by the shoulders and glared at her. 'You have to trust me, Sybille. The move from Gare d'Orléans has thrown me. Trust me, *please.*'

We arrived home to a warm apartment. Tommy, bless him, had kept the oven going. Over supper I told him I expected a knock on the door. 'I want you to do something for me, Tommy.'

Despite Sybille's poisonous looks I ploughed on. 'When I give the word you're to go down to the square and hide yourself. A man will enter the building and leave soon afterwards. I want you to follow him. Is that understood?'

I received a crooked smile.

After dinner I went to my room and wrote a note.

Factory moved to Gare de l'Est. Instructions required.

Placing it in an envelope I re-entered the living room. 'Leave now,' I said to Tommy.

No sooner had the door closed than Sybille was on me like a wolf. 'I don't know what you're up to, Monique, but if harm comes to that boy… well.'

We shot each other looks. I heaved a sigh of relief when she went to bed.

I attempted to read my book, gave up and snoozed, woke and snoozed again… the feeling of guilt and worry. Tommy, I tried to convince myself, was tough, a creature of the streets.

Then it happened, the *rat-tat-a-tat-tat, tat-tat* of Moritz's signal.

I stood and slipped the envelope under the door then looked out of the window overlooking the square. I needn't have bothered – the night was as black as Hades.

The next hour was torture – no more dozing or reading. I put on the kettle, removed it from the heat when it boiled, repeating the process.

A knock on the door. Tommy with his lopsided grin. I put my arms round him, Sybille stirred – or rather, her maternal instincts stirred – and she was out of bed and hugging him too.

I handed him a mug of tea. 'Well?'

'Rue Auber, number 22, near the new opera house.'

'What did he look like?'

'Tall with a red beard, ma'am.'

'Well done, Tommy' – pressing a one-franc coin into his hand.

The rest of the week was one of mind over matter – my task to survive each and every day. Mid-week, the army attempted a breakout, only to be beaten again at Buzenval. The National Guard streamed back into Paris, carrying their wounded. The boulevard de Sébastopol was more depressing and dangerous than ever. Then another blow: news of the army's defeat at Le Mans with huge casualties sustained. The atmosphere in the factory was palpable – a matter of keeping our heads down and sewing. There was talk of surrender. I wished they would just get on with it. I felt anger... men were destroying the world, ruining our lives playing soldiers.

Sunday couldn't come soon enough. We'd been given the whole day off with pay. Sybille and I decided to give each other space – leaving me with Tommy. Food weighed on my mind and so we walked to place Scipion. Once again, he proved his worth, producing half a *saucisson* from God knows where. Back home I sat him down and tried to teach him spelling.

Mid-afternoon we walked in the Luxembourg. Tommy gave me a cockeyed smile before racing off to find something to steal, no doubt. A tap on my shoulder: Moritz looking oily and well fed – the cat that got the cream.

'Who's that urchin?' he said.

'A gamin. I've taken him under my wing.'

'Oh, I see, a sort of Lucien substitute,' he said through his shark-toothed smile.

I thought of asking him for news of Lucien but couldn't see the point.

'So you've moved to the Gare de l'Est?'

'At least you can read.'

He sneered. 'While I'm here you might as well tell me what you're working on.'

'*Le Général Cambronne.* And no, I don't know when it will fly.'

He stared at me, his eyes intent. 'For what it's worth, Kiki, you've done an outstanding job.'

'Don't.'

'I'll let you into a secret... a ceasefire. Next week, perhaps.'

'So what?'

'Balloons will cease to play a part. I'll have to find something else for you to do.'

'Haven't you profited enough from me, monsieur?'

'You're still alive, my dear, and therefore still useful. Meanwhile, continue to work on your balloon.'

'I need money, Moritz. Food prices. In your world it doesn't matter. You're obviously well fed.'

'And you have a household, the urchin and that woman who lives with you. You're not a…?'

'And if I was, would it matter?'

'Possibly… we could dangle you in front of a, how do I say, woman of a certain persuasion.'

'Well, I'm not.'

Tipping his hat: 'I'll be in touch, Kiki.'

'I said I needed money' – holding out my hand.

A greasy leer as he dug into a pocket, producing his wallet and handing me fifty francs.

I took it. 'Is that all?'

Sighing, he gave me another fifty.

Tommy ran up just as Moritz had left. Feeling flush, I handed him a one-franc coin. As he bounded away, I heard that undercurrent of sound again. And something else: a crackling noise as though fireworks were exploding.

A ceasefire would change my life – not having to brave boulevard de Sébastopol anymore. And Moritz, what would he have in store? Would I be able to travel? Sell my paintings? I felt a lot better with Moritz's one hundred francs in my reticule.

Much the same the following week, although the damage at the boulevard de Sébastopol end of the Hôtel de Ville meant we had to take the long route into work via place de la Bastille and boulevard de Magenta. It took us over an hour. God, I was fed up at the time.

Ceasefire rumours were on everyone's lips. On Saturday, the day of *Le Général Cambronne*'s flight, the news came through – the armistice had been agreed. But not before *Le Général* had taken off, so at the time we didn't know. We also didn't know that *Le Général* was to be the last balloon to float out of Paris.

Had the authorities known, the launch would have been one of great fanfare and ceremony. Instead, it was perfunctory – no bunting, no oompah band, just a few officials and us, the workers. There were no passengers or pigeons on board, just sacks of post and the aeronaut.

Sybille elbowed me in the ribs. 'Don't look up,' she hissed.

I sneaked a look. Oreste Monnier was staring in my direction. I pretended not to have seen him. I could hear the blood pump behind my eyes. I wanted to run but forced myself to act out the part of admiring the launch. I had to face facts: Oreste had recognised me. It was over. I had to disappear, but where? Saturday was payday and so I asked Sybille to collect my packet.

When she started asking questions, I shushed her: 'I'll see you at rue Mouffetard. Return there immediately. Immediately, do you hear? I'm in trouble.'

On the way out of the station I bumped into Madame Godard and told her to hand my wages to Sybille. 'Are you all right, Monique?' she said.

'A family problem. I must go. Excuse me.'

She mumbled something but I was gone. I tried to work out where I was and turned down rue de Paradis onto rue la Fayette. Half-running, I soon arrived at François Petit's gallery on rue Saint-Georges. It was boarded up. What to do with the paintings? Joelie would have been the most obvious, but since our Christmas Day eruption I had avoided her. Monsieur Bonifay was a possibility, but it was likely the police had questioned him. Anyway, I hadn't seen him in a long time. The Hôtel de Londres? No, they hadn't seen me for years either and the staff would have changed. Crossing the Seine via Pont Royal I cast a wistful look up and down the river. *La Fleur de l'Yonne* was nowhere to be seen.

I racked my brains. Oreste and his police could well be on the way to rue Mouffetard – a matter of extracting my address from Sybille.

As I crossed rue de Lille a wagon carrying wine gave me an idea: Stanley Dent. He was English, kindly and reliable, and no one would know of our connection. I prayed Dent, Urwick & Co was open for business. When I arrived home Tommy was there. 'Go downstairs and find me a cab now!' I told him.

Having pulled the paintings from under my bed I lugged them down to the street. Tommy had snared a fiacre and helped me on board.

He looked at me with his big eyes. I forced myself to shake my head.

When I arrived at the warehouse the large wooden doors were shut. Dent, Urwick was closed. Tears pricked my eyes and I clenched my fists. There was nothing for it but to go to a hotel. But, as I was about to reboard the fiacre, the wicket gate opened and a man stepped out, a janitor type.

'Excuse me,' I said. 'Is Dent, Urwick opening today?'

'Course not, what with the troubles, ma'am.'

'I have to see Monsieur Dent as a matter of urgency. You wouldn't happen to know where he lives?'

Scratching his stubble he gave me a look; his eyes had a certain gleam. Money. So picking out a ten-franc note from my purse I dangled it in front of his nose.

Licking his lips: 'Five rue de Médicis, ma'am.'

I gave the cabby the address. Rue de Médicis ran along the side of Jardin du Luxembourg, a short walk from where I lived. I rapped on the door; a maid opened up. 'Is Mr Dent home, mademoiselle?' I enquired in English, my heart in my mouth.

She smiled. 'May I ask who is calling?'

'The Baroness du Plessis.'

Stanley Dent helped me carry the paintings inside his house. 'Always a pleasure seeing you, Baroness,' he said.

Fifteen minutes later I left without my paintings. Stanley Dent's parting words: 'I will guard them with my life, my dear.'

My thoughts crowded in on me as I walked to rue Mouffetard. I would pack and leave immediately. I prayed Sybille was there.

She was, but so were Oreste Monnier and two policemen. Tommy was absent, thank God.

Sybille looked aghast when Oreste ordered one of his men to restrain me. 'Why are you doing this?' she cried.

Oreste read out the charges, officiousness personified. 'Christine Monnier, you are wanted for questioning in connection with the murder of Augustave Monnier on the ninth of January 1862 and escaping police custody on the fourteenth of December in the same year.'

Sybille, bless her, started wrestling with the policeman. 'Let her go, you *conard*,' she shouted.

Oreste nodded, and the other policeman grabbed her, pinning her arms behind her back. 'Any more of that, mademoiselle,' said Oreste, 'and I'll arrest you as well.'

'Oreste,' I said more calmly than I felt, 'I will come without any fuss, but I need to make arrangements with Sybille. And I need to pack a bag.'

As he ummed and ahed it took all my willpower not to attack him. 'You have ten minutes,' he said at length.

With a nod from Oreste the policeman released his grip.

Sybille followed me into my room and I shut the door.

'The door will remain open,' said Oreste.

Sybille started peppering me with questions. 'Who's Christine…?'

'Shut up and listen,' I said, dipping into my reticule. 'This is all I have… just over two hundred francs. Take it.'

'No… I can't.'

'*Take it!* Now listen… they'll probably lock me up in the Conciergerie. I need you to find me a lawyer.' Shaking her: 'Do you understand?'

Writing down the name and address of my landlord: 'When the moratorium ends, he'll be after his rent... forty francs a month. I haven't paid him since October.'

She tried to hand me my pay packet.

'Keep it.'

'But—'

'When they let me out, I'll need a place to return to. For what it's worth, I did not kill my first husband, who just happens to be the twin brother of that *gros con* there.'

'Is it true... did you really escape?'

'I did.'

Shaking her head: 'There was always something about you, Monique.'

I put my arms around her. 'Look after yourself and Tommy. And don't forget the lawyer.'

FORTY-SIX

AFTER EIGHT YEARS I was back in the Conciergerie, in a
single cell. It smelt of urine, was narrow and dank. Pale
light strained through a slit of a window with a bar across.
An oil lamp flickered from a niche in the wall. I had managed to
pack two sheets and a thick blanket – fortunate, given the state
of the bedding. After arranging the bunk, I lay down. To take my
mind off my predicament, I opened *Les Misérables*.

A while later food was served – thin soup with grains of rice, a
chunk of bread, a small jug of *gros rouge*. Then I must have fallen
asleep.

I woke. Stretched and sat up. Light strained through the window. I
had no idea how long I'd been asleep, but it must have been morning.
A tin pot under the bunk and, squatting, I 'performed the necessary'
– just in time, before the door opened. Breakfast was a mess of
porridge and water from a jug. Later, I was led down a windowless
passage to a tiled room, where I washed and slopped out the pot.

Back in my cell I sat on my bunk and tried to think my
predicament through. I must have fallen asleep and awoke to the
clanking of the door – Oreste accompanied by a guard.

'I trust you spent a comfortable night,' he said. After clicking
his fingers, the guard brought him a chair.

'Eight years ago, you escaped from here, *from me*. What happened to you in the meantime?'

'Do we…?'

'We do.'

I sighed. 'I lived in the countryside married to a *gentleman*, who didn't rape me twice a week. He died last year.'

Opening his notebook: 'The Baron Armand du Plessis.'

I shrugged.

'You showed me your papers at the balloon factory, remember?'

'So?'

'Were you happy with your husband?'

'What's it to you?'

'And you moved to Paris?'

'Just in time for the war to break out.'

'Around July… hmm, what did you do before you worked in the balloon factory?'

'I sewed uniforms.'

'Where?'

'Fourteen rue de Vaugirard… Is this really necessary, Oreste?'

He stared at me. 'I'm trying to understand how you could afford to pay for an apartment in rue Mouffetard.'

'As I said my husband died…'

'Well?'

'Well, what do you think?'

'He left you some money?'

'Well done, Oreste.'

'What were you doing at the balloon factory?'

'Isn't that obvious?'

'Answer the question.'

'*Sewing balloons*, of course.'

'Then how do you explain this?' he said, holding a square of paper in front of my face.

I smiled while choking down my panic, scratched my head

while reading it: 73b11. I played for time. 'What does it mean?' I said thoughtfully.

'You know what it means.'

I made a face. 'Umm, it ends with seventy-one, does it have something to do with this year?'

Handing me a pencil and paper: 'It's code, write it down.'

I obliged: 73b11.

He studied my writing, lines wrinkling his forehead. Luckily, I had taken the precaution of writing out the codes with my left hand. My face was a mask. I worked it out: *Le Gutenberg* sailed early in the morning of 17 December.

'You see, when I saw you in early October, I couldn't work out who you were. It bothered me. Your disguise worked. Then one night it came to me, my dear sister-in-law Kiki.'

I feigned disinterest. Inspected my nails.

'I had you followed. We worked out that two men were aiding you – thugs, bearded, one red, the other black.'

'And yet this is not my writing, monsieur.' I was tempted to ask him what happened to the 'Beards', but how stupid would that have been?

'You are, were part of a spy ring. Spying for the Prussians against France, your country.'

'I am aware of my country, Oreste.'

'Enough. Your escape on the fourteenth—'

'—of December 1862,' I said through a yawn.

'Quite. I want the name of the person, persons who helped you.'

'No names, Oreste.'

'A nun, was she? Ingenious, I have to admit, escaping the Conciergerie disguised as a nun.'

I shrugged again.

'We have ways of extracting information, Kiki.'

'Do your worst, monsieur.'

For three days they left me alone. Perhaps Oreste had better things to do – keeping the Reds under control. I worked it out: *Le Général Cambronne* sailed on 28 January, so that day was 1 February.

On my way to ablutions, someone passed me in the passage. 'They've signed the Armistice,' he whispered.

In the afternoon I had visitors – Sybille and a gentleman whom she introduced as Henri Torrès, the lawyer. 'He's the best,' she said.

I offered my hand. 'Christine Monnier, monsieur.' No point in telling him I was a baroness or giving him my married name – a title would adversely affect me in those 'Red' times. What's more, Oreste had never questioned my name. Why would he?

Sybille gasped, 'Christine Monnier? That's what the policeman called you. So you're not Monique du Plessis?'

I shot her a hard look.

Henri Torrès was a small, gnomish man, with a full beard and spectacles. Taking off his coat he looked at Sybille. 'Would you mind, mademoiselle?'

Standing to leave Sybille handed me a bag. 'See you later, *Christine.*'

The lawyer opened his valise. 'I will ask you some questions, madam.'

'Before you start, I need to be apprised of your charges.'

'Fifty francs as an engagement fee and five francs per hour.'

I winced. 'Please proceed.'

'I have spoken to Sergeant Monnier. Three charges are levelled against you: the murder of Monsieur Augustave Monnier on the ninth of January 1862, your escape from police custody on the fourteenth of December the same year, and lastly, divulging information apropos the production of balloons to agents of the enemy.'

'I am guilty of the second charge, monsieur.'

Making notes: 'The first charge – I need some background, your marriage to Monsieur Monnier.'

I related my past to him in detail: my family, the piece of land, my wedding, the arrangement, the 'device', my relationship with Junius Girard, Madame Gaillard, Benoît, his son Guillaume, the dog fight, Florian, my escape and Madame Thierry. I omitted the brand – he didn't need to know. I also failed to tell him about Lucien.

'Tell me about Madame Thierry?'

'Why? I've just told you. She was my schoolteacher in Beaune and helped me to escape. I don't want her dragged into this – her name ever mentioned. Is that understood?'

He nodded. 'The witness statements – Madame Gaillard's and Benoît Ligerot's.'

'Nothing but lies, monsieur. They both hated me.'

'Go on.'

'My husband and Marie Gaillard were lovers.'

'While you were married?'

'No, before.'

'What happened?'

'They were unable to conceive, so I was given to understand. I was used. My brothers wanted the land. My husband wanted an heir. Simple. Trouble is, they failed to take account of my feelings.'

'And Monsieur Ligerot?'

'A family retainer, the winemaker, been there for years, part of the *ancien régime*, so to speak. He resented me, I—'

He raised a hand. 'I understand, madam… And Florian, the stable boy who helped you?'

'He disappeared. I can assure you he knows the truth… what happened that night. He may have gone to Marseilles, India possibly.'

'And Junius Girard?'

'He joined the navy, became a marine. He sailed for Mexico in 1862. There was speculation that he had been killed there.'

'How do you know that he sailed for Mexico?'

'I went to Brest, the Naval Academy there.'

'Seems strange you would go all the way to Brest to find him.'

'Strange…? Apart from Florian and those liars, he was the only other person who knew the truth of that night.'

His eyes narrowed. 'Your husband… did you have children together?'

I hadn't expected this. I didn't want Oreste knowing about Lucien: finding him, using him as a pawn against me. 'No, monsieur,' I replied.

His eyes flickered over mine. 'Hmm… the spying allegations?'

My pulse quickened. Apart from the half-lie on the question of children I felt confident because I had told him the truth. I composed my features.

'A simple question, madam, did you leave the note Sergeant Monnier showed you? The one you allegedly placed in the rubbish bin on rue Lacépède?'

I played for time. 'You're my lawyer. You act for me. I'm paying you—'

'Ah, whatever you tell me will go no further. It would, however, be helpful if I was in possession of the facts.'

Sucking in my breath: 'I did, monsieur.'

'Why?'

'I can't fully explain but they had something over me, something very important to me.'

'So important that you cannot tell me.'

'I'd rather not.'

'Important enough to betray *la France*?'

I stood. 'I've told you the truth. I feel ashamed. I hate myself. But I had to do it. They—'

'They?'

I told him of Moritz and the 'Beards', omitting Moritz's address.

'All right, what you have told me is mostly the truth. For what it's worth, I believe you did not order the dogs to attack your husband.

Why would you? The dogs were his, not yours. Why would they obey *you*? Unfortunately, we have the witness statements, but in a court of law I believe we can argue in your favour on the basis of reasonable doubt.'

'Are you sure?'

'I am confident, madam. The treason charge, on the other hand, is more serious, given the extraordinary times we live in. Spy mania is rampant. Traitors are shot out of hand. In times like these, justice tends to take a back seat.'

'Oh dear.'

'You were wise to employ my services, madam. Otherwise, they would have rushed through an excuse of a trial and…' he said, making a clicking sound while drawing a finger across his throat.

'What will happen now?'

'I will study the witness statements. Try to have the murder charge waived. The spying charge is another matter. You will be questioned… keep denying the accusations. We'll play for time.'

'Why?'

'As I said, we live in extraordinary times. Regimes come and go. Take Louis-Napoleon, for example.'

After more assurances Monsieur Torrès left me. Strange, but I felt a glimmer of optimism.

I opened Sybille's bag. Three hard-boiled eggs, half a *saucisson*, a bottle of milk, a flagon of wine and a bar of soap. *And* a folded piece of paper.

A governess friend of mine told me the Wynburnes moved to number 94 rue Blanche in Montmartre in the summer of 1866.
Courage!

I leapt off the bunk and poured myself a mug of wine. The Wynburnes must have moved as the result of my attempted repossession of Lucien. Sloshing back the drink I felt a sense of morbid delight at having caused the Wynburnes so much inconvenience and worry.

Lucien. I searched for his face in my memory: his eyes, nose, mouth and ears, his hair. The way he'd twisted away when the maid had approached. I could see him in my mind's eye. And 'Pogo', the only word he had ever said to me. I clung to it, held on to it.

The days passed. I was close to finishing *Les Misérables*. Oreste interrogated me several times, always the same – had I written the coded note and what did it mean (although I was sure he had worked it out)? And who had put me up to spying, and why?

I refused to answer his questions – referring him to Monsieur Torrès. The last time we met I gently led him to the subject of le Merle. 'By the way, who is running the estate, Oreste?'

'Why do you want to know, Kiki?'

'A passing interest. After all, I *was* married to the owner. I always look for it on menus, in wine shops, but it's never there.'

'Things have been hard. Marie runs the place with the help of local labour.'

'Oh, so you still retain an interest?'

Shuffling his feet: 'Of course I do. As you know, my brother had no heirs.'

I decided not to mention that I should have been 'the heir'. Instead: 'Augustave couldn't afford to pay his taxes.'

'How come you know that?'

'Monsieur Guiod, the Mayor of Beaune, told me.'

'Did he now?'

'He also knew of Augustave's passion for dogfighting.'

Oreste looked as though he was about to divulge something. Instead, he averted his eyes.

I tried to keep him going. '*Phylloxera*. What's the latest news, the current thinking?'

He shook his head. 'It's rampant in the south, as far as the northern Rhône, I'm led to believe.'

'So just a matter of time.'

'Why all these questions, Kiki?'

'Just interested, that's all.' Changing the subject: 'The National Guard seems to have become a lot more assertive. The Reds. They'll take over, you know.'

'Nonsense.'

'They are everywhere.'

'Those *conards*, I detest them and everything they stand for. General Vinoy will bring them to account.'

'Vinoy will go the same way as General Trochu.'

'Vinoy has just taken over.'

'He doesn't stand a chance.'

'You're opinionated for a—'

'—woman, yes.' I shot him a look. 'When will I go to trial, Oreste?'

'In due course,' he said, standing up and taking his leave.

Sybille had been bringing me food and news. One thing I noticed was the improvement in the food. She explained that since the Armistice food had been flowing into the city. The British had been very generous, apparently. She was allowed to visit me once a week.

Tuesday, 21 February. Sybille handed me a bag of food. 'I've become an Amazon du Seine,' she announced.

'A what?'

'We will fight alongside the National Guard.'

'So, you are a Red?'

'A patriot, Christine. The government has let us down. It is time we true Parisians took control of our own destiny.'

'You're a fool.'

'No. Adolphe Thiers and his government are not even in the city. They're in Bordeaux running France from the provinces, for God's sake. There have been demonstrations. Talk of one this week.'

'Bordeaux? Demonstrations? What does it all mean?'

'That Paris will govern itself. Us. Not Monsieur Thiers and his cronies.'

'This will lead to no good, civil war even.'

'Christine, you don't understand the feelings out there. People hate the new regime, especially the police. The Reds have this place under constant surveillance. I am taking a risk in coming here. The Reds will think I'm reporting to the police as an informer.'

'Really?' *Informer* – Sybille's words had sparked a worm of an idea in me.

'Yes. People like Raoul Rigault and—'

'Rigault… I saw him years ago. Joelie and I were on a night out, a café in Saint-Germain. He half-scared me to death.'

'He *really* hates the police. Loathes them. Mention his name to Sergeant Monnier and you'll get a reaction… an explosion more like.'

My worm was now a snake.

We continued to talk. I mentioned Lucien.

'There is nothing I can really tell you,' said Sybille. 'The Wynburnes live in rue Blanche and that's it.'

'And Tommy?'

'Poor little mite. He's put on weight, though. Runs errands for me.'

'For the Amazons.'

'Yes.'

'Sybille, one thing… no one's ever called me Christine. I'm Kiki to my friends and family.'

'Kiki?'

'Yes.'

FORTY-SEVEN

A FEW DAYS later Henri Torrès visited me. 'They won't drop the murder charge, Christine,' he said without preamble.

'That doesn't surprise me.'

'Sergeant Monnier takes his brother's murder personally.'

'Brother? They were twins, you know.'

'Twins… interesting. Hmm, for what it's worth, we can exploit the situation… his private crusade… his vendetta. He shouldn't be handling a case in which his family is involved.'

'Very unprofessional.'

'According to the witness statements, you instructed the dogs to attack your husband.'

'Lies.'

'They both used the same words, almost exactly.'

'Of course.'

'As I said last time, I'm not too concerned with the murder charge.'

'Henri, Sybille told me something interesting the last time she visited me.'

'Go on.'

'That this place and the Préfecture are being watched by the Reds and the National Guard. Last time you talked of spy mania. She mentioned Raoul Rigault.'

'That maniac.'

'Sergeant Monnier blew his top when I mentioned Rigault to him.'

Henri Torrès cocked his head. I think he knew where I was trying to lead him.

'Forgive me, Henri, but what are your politics?'

'I'm a monarchist, but not for Napoleon. I would favour a Bourbon restoration.'

'Despite all their corruption and cronyism?'

'I would rather have a constitutional monarchy along British lines. But that will never happen. France is France.'

'So you do not agree with Blanqui and Flourens, or Rigault for that matter?'

'I detest the so-called Reds. Give them power and we will have a repeat of the First Republic, the 1790s all over again. A bloodbath with no one in charge, the various factions pitted against each other. Rule by the mob.'

'You're not a republican, then?'

'I think I have made myself clear, madam.'

'What will happen?'

'To Paris… there's a chance of civil war. The citizens of Belleville and the poorer *arrondissements* have had enough; they are fed up with the old ways – poverty and the fact we lost the war. The National Guard are on their side despite the one and a half francs a day the government pays them. With the Thiers government in Bordeaux, I believe the Reds will form their own "government". They already have a name for it… the Commune.'

'The Commune? Yes, I've heard it on the streets. "*Vive la Commune*".'

'If they do, there will be civil war… restricted to Paris. By the way, what are *your* politics?'

'Anything but the Commune.'

He shifted in his seat. 'Why the questions? What do you have in mind, Christine?'

'Kiki.'

'Kiki.'

'I wanted to know whose side you're on – the same side as Sergeant Monnier, it turns out. So this is how I want you to proceed…'

When I had finished, he stared into my eyes and nodded, which I took as a sign of respect.

A few hours later Henri Torrès and Oreste Monnier entered my cell.

Oreste pulled a face while glancing at Henri. 'He tells me you are prepared to give me two things in return for your liberty.'

'I am, provided the terms of my acquittal are legally binding. In writing.' I looked at Henri.

'I have spoken to the Avocat Général of Île-de-France who has agreed.'

'Who will keep the document?'

'There will be one original, no copies, to be held by me, madam.'

'That's good, Henri, but I want another signed copy for my safekeeping.'

Oreste turned to me. 'Monsieur Torrès tells me you have the address of the so-called Moritz who, how do I say, coerced you into doing something you would otherwise not have done.'

I looked at Henri. 'Proceed, Madame Monnier,' he said.

'Number 22 rue Auber.'

Oreste made a note. 'What does he look like?'

'Overfed, beautifully dressed, sleek and he sports a waxed moustache. Oh, and he has a small, neat scar high up on his right cheek.'

'You realise the address of a spy ring is of no particular value given the war has ended.'

'Really? Heard of the Commune, have you? "*Vive la Commune*".'

Wrinkling his lips: 'Of real interest is what you're prepared to do for France, Kiki.'

'When will I be released?'

'You'll stay here for the time being… for your own good and in preparation for the mission we have in mind for you. We start tomorrow,' he said, standing to leave.

With Oreste gone I turned to Henri: 'The document for my safekeeping. I want it sent to my lawyer in Beaune. As a backup, you understand, were anything to happen to you or to me.'

'Very wise,' he said. 'His name and address, if you please.'

I gave him François de Gaalon's details. Then: 'I don't quite know how you pulled that off, Henri.'

'I persuaded him that a conviction for murder was highly unlikely, given it happened over nine years ago, that the witness statements were flimsy, to say nothing of his personal involvement.'

'Bravo.'

'I appealed to his vanity – that him running a spy deep in the Commune would look good with the Thiers government and therefore the furtherance of his career.'

'I didn't think of it like that.'

'Kiki, you have to realise what's happening. There were huge demonstrations in place de la Bastille today. The police fear the Commune will take over and they'll all be shot. Civil war is a certainty and Sergeant Monnier knows it. "What's the point in finding her guilty and shooting her?" I told him. "Use her talents against the Communards". '

'Talents. You flatter me, Henri.'

'Far from it… I've seen how your mind works. That coded note – you wrote it out with your left hand.'

I smiled and pulled the appropriate face.

Next morning Oreste entered my cell and handed me some clothes. 'From now on you have to think and act like a Blanquist… a Red. Your life depends on acting out the role with conviction. We have two weeks to prepare. Your looks are important. You're scrawny, not the Kiki I remember from le Merle. You need to fatten up and make yourself strong, ready for the fight.' Handing me a sheet of paper: 'Memorise these names.'

I scanned the twenty or so names. Raoul Rigault's headed the list. 'Rigault again?'

'As I said, he hates the police. He has people watching this place for police spies – who goes in and out.'

'Police spies?'

'Agents who have infiltrated the Red clubs, the National Guard.'

'Something I will have to do.'

'Yes, and highly dangerous. Rigault and his like can sniff out a spy just by looking at him.'

'Or her.'

'Quite.'

'When can I go home?'

Ignoring my question: 'Your friend Sybille, tell me about her?'

This was a test – a question I had not anticipated. It hadn't occurred to me, but Sybille and I were now on opposing sides. 'We met in the uniform factory and became friends. After it closed down, I secured a job at the balloon factory. Once I was in, she was in. I introduced her to the Godards.'

'She lives with you.'

'We pooled our resources during the siege, kept each other going.'

'What is she doing now?'

'She has joined the Amazons du Seine.'

'Has she now?'

'Harm her, Oreste, and I'll withdraw my cooperation and to hell with the consequences.'

'Oh, so noble, Kiki.'

'When can I go home?'

'I need to think about it.'

Before leaving he reminded me to put on the clothes and to memorise the names.

He had given me a blue dress, a red coarse-woollen top with long sleeves and a hat – a white sort of mob cap. I stripped down to my underwear and put them on. I didn't have a mirror but now I was Kiki of the Commune. I must have looked ridiculous.

Oreste had said *fatten up*, and the quality of what I ate markedly improved. The siege over, the flow of food into Paris was almost back to normal. My weight improved and I began my exercise regime of sit- and press-ups.

One question gnawed at me: why was I still there, a prisoner in the Conciergerie?

Next day, the day before Sybille's weekly visit, Oreste entered my cell. 'Your friend Sybille,' he said without preamble.

'What about her?'

'We have to give her the impression you are still a prisoner awaiting trial. You will need to change back into your old clothes.'

'I could join the Amazons.'

Rubbing his chin: 'No… I want you in the heart of the enemy camp. As an Amazon, you'll be the same as a soldier in the National Guard, on duty obeying orders. You could end up anywhere – in one of the forts, on the ramparts. Not of much use to me there. And how would we communicate?'

There – I had my answer. I was to remain in the Conciergerie.

Sybille arrived in the morning with food, a change of clothes and fresh bedding. She was a saint. Guilt riddled me – now that I had to lie to her. She asked me if I had made any progress.

'Henri is stringing things out, insisting the witnesses to my husband's death travel to Paris to testify.'

One thing Sybille didn't know – could never know – was that I had been accused of spying. As far as she was concerned, I was about to be tried for the murder of my former husband and my escape from the Conciergerie – in her eyes, a heroic act and worthy of admiration.

We discussed her cash position, the rent moratorium and food prices. And Tommy.

'What's happening on the outside?' I asked her.

'*Mon dieu*, I don't know where to start. Thiers and Bismarck signed the Treaty on Sunday. Alsace and Lorraine are no longer part of France and the *conard* Germans entered Paris yesterday. Demonstrations take place almost daily.'

'Hell, how do I get out of this place?'

She laughed. 'Use your feminine wiles.'

'Forget it.'

'Some of the looser ladies have already snared themselves a German.'

'They'll regret it.'

'Ah, I almost forgot. The National Guard has appropriated the cannons, the ones in place de Wagram. Towed them to the heights above Montmartre.'

Montmartre. The very name made me think of Lucien.

I asked about her Amazons. She enthused: the training, their uniforms, her co-Amazons – Nathalie Lemel and Elisabeth Dmitrieff, Madame So-and-So – their march-past with the National Guard on Sunday. I made a mental note of the names.

'Sybille, coming here is dangerous. You told me the Reds had this place under surveillance. The police loathe the National Guard and vice versa. Taking the cannons will only heighten the paranoia, and you being an Amazon…'

'You don't want me to come here anymore?'

'It's *dangerous*, Sybille.'

She sulked and I fobbed her off. 'I'll be out of here in no time. I promise you.'

We embraced. When the door clanged shut, I hung my head in shame.

I had the feeling Oreste didn't know what to do with me, how to deploy me. He tried to keep me busy – his latest crusade was codes and the use of the telegraph. He was clearly impressed I knew the Morse code.

One morning he gave me a piece of paper with the alphabet written in two lines of thirteen letters each.

A B C D E F G H I J K L M
Z Y X W V U T S R Q P O N

'Learn the matching letters off by heart. For example, C equals X and X equals C.' Handing me a pencil and paper: 'Write down a sentence: "The frog ate the toad".'

I wrote: G S V U.

'No spaces,' he said.

I wrote again: G S V U I L T Z G V G S V G L Z W.

'Correct.'

'There's a weakness… easily decipherable – the letters GSV repeated.'

'Ah, I was coming to that. No "thes" or "ands"… "Frog ate toad".'

I wrote again: U I L T Z G V G L Z W and studied the code.

'It's still decipherable, the positioning of the vowels.'

'Where did you learn all this, Kiki?'

'It's common sense. A suggestion: every day we alter the code. Day one the top line starts with an A. Day two it starts with a B, the A replacing the Z on the bottom line and so forth.'

'Complicated. You can't write it down for want of discovery.'

'I'll remember it. The letters will rotate anticlockwise.'

He looked at me, a look I had seen before – one of grudging respect.

'How do I courier the messages to you?'

'Don't you think I've thought of that?' he snapped.

'Tell me.'

'No point, not until I set you amongst the Communards.'

I gave him the evil eye.

'All right, through one of the embassies.'

'Which one?'

'Forget it.'

'And the courier?'

'I'm working on it.'

'Huh.'

Almost as soon as he had left the cell, an idea occurred to me: Tommy.

Two weeks had passed since Sybille's last visit. *Les Misérables*, long since finished, lay on the floor. Oreste visited every day to test me. 'Day eight – "PIGEON",' he would say, for example, and I would have to answer immediately. 'Day ten – "FOX",' and so forth.

I was tempted to ask him if the police had cracked Moritz's code but thought better of it.

One day he handed me an envelope.

rue Mouffetard

12 March 1871

Dear Kiki,

Sorry to bring this up but I've almost run out of money – two weeks left. As you know, my pay is one and a half francs a day.

The moratorium was revoked at the beginning of the month and so I've had to pay five months' rent.

We could move out. No problem. The little mite is well and missing you, as am I.

Love,
Sybille

Oreste took the note and read it.

'Who's "the little mite"?'

'Tommy... a gamin. We rescued him during the siege.' I hesitated: 'He would make an excellent courier, knows Paris like the back of his hand. Nimble-fingered too. He could pick your watch in the blink of an eye.'

'Sounds like a good idea.'

'To keep him I need to pay the rent.'

'You expect the state to pay?'

'I am in here against my will, to spy *for* the state.'

'I'll look into it. By the way, we apprehended your friend Moritz.'

'Good. What's his real name?'

Shaking his head: 'No, I can't divulge that. I *can* tell you he is Belgian. A mercenary who'll work for anyone who pays.'

'What will happen to him?'

'He'll be tried and shot.'

I pulled a face. 'What's happening on the outside, Oreste?'

'I don't have time to discuss such matters. I must go.'

I was tempted to tell him about Reginald Markham's link to Moritz but resisted. Although the idea of 'Reggie' being shot was appealing, I would deal with him in my own time.

I refined the code. On day fourteen, a different twenty-six-letter grid would be employed and so forth every thirteen days. Other refinements included the names of the so-called Reds, which we abbreviated – Rigault, for example, was code-named 'Pig'. I had a name for the code: the Alphabet Wheel.

I had the first twenty-six grids in my head and used tricks to remember the matching letters.

FORTY-EIGHT

THURSDAY, 16 MARCH 1871. Oreste blundered into my cell out of breath and dabbing his narrow Monnier forehead with a handkerchief. 'It's happening,' he gasped.

'What's *happening*, Oreste?'

'The Commune is taking over. Thiers is about to announce the evacuation of key government personnel to Versailles.'

'When?'

'Within the next forty-eight hours.'

'Including you?'

Pulling a face: 'Yes.'

I felt weak – the eels slipping and sliding. 'Where does that leave me?'

'You'll remain here. You are to be "rescued" by the Communards. They will find you down here, a prisoner of the hated old regime. Change into your Red clothes right away.'

I was too *bouleversée* to argue and changed into my blue-skirt ensemble.

Oreste gathered my discarded clothes. 'These will have to be burnt.'

My turn to pull a face.

'Your file upstairs is in the name of Christine Monnier. The first entry is 1862. I have doctored it. Entries referring to the spying charge have been removed. As far as anyone is concerned, you're here accused of the murder of Augustave and your escape from the Conciergerie.'

I thought of what he had said. 'What if they follow through with the charge of murder? Put me on trial?'

'Unlikely. Quite the opposite, in fact. You may look "suitable" in their eyes, someone of their ilk. A good cover, so to speak.'

'I have to think this through.'

'We don't have time.'

'One thing, there is no point in destroying my clothes. I am neither a Communard nor a supporter of Thiers. I am a woman charged with murder – pure and simple. These Red clothes may make them suspicious.'

Oreste rubbed his chin. 'You are right' – handing back my clothes.

He looked away as I changed. 'With you in Versailles, how will I courier the intelligence to you?' I said.

'Through the British Embassy on rue du Faubourg Saint-Honoré, using Tommy as your courier.'

'And the embassy, how will they know who to forward the messages to?'

Rolling his eyes: 'Staff there will open the note, recognise it as code and pass it to the appropriate attaché. All has been arranged.'

'It could be a message from anyone. I have a suggestion.' Taking a pencil, I made a sketch of a blackbird.

He smiled. 'Huh, ingenious. Le Merle. Good idea. By the way, we believe Raoul Rigault will become chief of police. He's your target.'

'Rigault. You sure?'

'He will be at the centre of power, a leading Communard. I want you to get close to him, ingratiate yourself. Do whatever it takes.'

He turned to leave. 'Oreste,' I said, 'haven't you forgotten something?'

He shook his head.

Rolling my eyes: 'Day one. The code. We need to fix the date.'

Slapping his forehead: 'How could I?'

'Today's the sixteenth. Day one should be Monday, the twentieth of March.'

Nodding he left, locking the door behind him. The *conard* hadn't even wished me luck.

My target was Rigault. Once again, I was going to have play the whore.

The next person I saw was the guard who brought in my supper: cold meats and vegetables, leftovers dumped on a plate – the *demi* of *gros rouge* my only consolation. Then nothing. No food. No human contact.

Night and day merged into one. I had no concept of time. I tried counting to sixty to gauge the sense of a minute, repeating the process sixty times. I was bored and slept intermittently. Played games in my head, the code in fantastical combinations. Pangs of hunger – strange how they ebbed and flowed.

The square of light had disappeared up the wall. I turned over to block out the cell, drew my nails across the sheet, the scratch loud in my head as if I were picking at the strings of some strange instrument. I must have fallen asleep.

I awoke. The light was now high on the opposite wall – morning outside. I rose and checked the grate at the bottom of the door. No food… what did I expect?

Nothing I could do but lie down and consider my predicament again. No sound but the *whump-whump* of my heart. The gloom held the reek of decay. I exhaled. The walls. I wondered whose breath had mouldered the stone, an aristocrat or two in the time of the guillotine?

What day was it? They had slammed the door shut yesterday, or had it been the day before?

Waves of anger, starvation, prayer, anger again. Fear. Would Oreste's plan work? Could I trust him? I reached for the tin, took a sip – no more than a day's water left.

I saw Lucien in my mind's eye. The park. Framed the only word he had ever said to me: P-O-G-O, my lips moving, my tongue fat in my throat.

I couldn't sleep. My life came back to me as if it was yesterday. The boy in the church…

After what I imagined was three days, I did something I had never done before – I shouted and screamed for attention.

No one came. I must have fallen asleep again.

At first, I thought my imagination was playing tricks, the sound of muffled voices. Then: 'Which one?' someone said. 'Try it,' someone else. I staggered to my feet and shouted, '*I am here and alive. Help.*' Soon the door was opened and I must have collapsed to the floor.

Next thing I knew was a voice saying, 'She's awake,' and something being stuck in my mouth and someone feeling my wrist.

My first word was *water*, followed by *food*. Soon I was sitting up in bed, a woman with a red sash round her waist feeding me bread and soup. I recognised the type: Sybillesque and Red and generous, and prone to say things like *poor little mite*. Her name was Agnès, a nurse from Belleville.

She told me what had happened: the Commune had been established and was governing Paris; Thiers and his gang had fled to Versailles; Generals Thomas and Lecomte had been shot dead in Montmartre trying to retrieve the cannons of behalf of the Versaillais army. For the first time I heard the word *barricade*. The Communards were preparing to defend their new-found power. Agnès told me the date: 'The twentieth of March, Christine.'

Day one.

The next day I was sufficiently recovered, so they transferred me back to my cell. Later I was taken to an interview room where a young man was seated. His tousled hair, pince-nez and beak of a nose reminded me of a student. His eyes were blue and intent, the irises flecked with yellow – similar to Augustave's, only colder.

'I have read your file, Madame Monnier,' he said without preamble. 'You are accused of murdering your husband and escaping the Conciergerie eight years ago. Tell me what happened before and after your escape?'

I gave him my story. No oohs or ahs from this cool fish. He appeared to feign interest, even when I told him of my work in the balloon factory under the direction of Eugène Godard, the aeronaut.

A man strode into the room, slamming the door behind him. He was imposing; his beard was thick and full; his tortoiseshell glasses were strung with a cord looped over his right ear. You could feel the energy literally pulsate out of him. I recognised him... the rabble-rouser I saw with Joelie in Saint-Germain. Instinctively, I took the initiative. 'Ah, Monsieur Rigault, I saw you speak in Café de la Renaissance many years ago.'

'Who are you?'

'Christine Monnier.'

'Prove it.'

'My name or the fact I saw you?'

'The latter.'

'You said something about having a man shot. That's it. "One day I'm going to have you shot".'

He laughed – a great harrumph of a laugh. 'I remember it well. But you might have read it in the newspapers.'

'I was there, monsieur.'

Raoul Rigault was one of those people you couldn't imagine ever having been a child; he was old-young, if that makes sense.

He stared at me as though he was looking into my very soul. I remembered what Oreste had said of him: his ability to sniff out a spy just by looking at him (or her!).

He turned to the young man. 'Is she who she professes to be, Coco?'

Coco related what he had learnt: where I lived and where I had worked. When it came to my escape from the Conciergerie, his interest was piqued. 'How on earth did you manage *that*?' he said.

'I was disguised as a nun.'

'Which order?'

'Carmelite.'

'Who helped you?'

'Joeline Lambert, a friend.'

'Joeline Lambert… where have I heard that name…?' He hummed and hawed, then appeared to have remembered. 'Yes, that's it. She's a *sous-maîtresse*, a madam. An exploiter of women… Were you exploited, madam?'

I felt myself blush. 'For a short while, monsieur, until I met my husband.'

'One of Madame Lambert's clients?'

'As a matter of fact, he was.'

'Excuse me,' said Coco, 'but you are accused of murdering your husband.'

Rolling my eyes: 'I was referring to my *second* husband, monsieur.'

'His name, please?' said Rigault.

'Armand du Plessis.'

'So, you were Christine du Plessis.'

'No. Monique.'

'Why Monique?'

'Monique was my "professional" name.'

Shooting me a sly look: 'Do you have any other names?'

'Several, but I can tell you I was born Christine Vellay on the twenty-fourth of July 1846.'

'Huh, I was born in the same year.'

I curled my lip as if to say, *So what?*

'What did your husband do?'

'Which one?'

'The one you murdered.'

'I did not murder him, monsieur.'

'Answer the question.'

'Not until you rephrase it.'

He sighed and looked fit to throttle me. Then: 'All right, the one you are accused of murdering.'

'He was a *viticulteur.*'

'Where?'

'Meursault, monsieur.'

'Ah, I love Meursault,' said Rigault. 'Which *domaine?*'

'Le Merle.'

Screwing up his eyes: 'I don't think I've had the pleasure.'

I pouted, put on an act.

'A little test, if you wouldn't mind…'

I continued to pout.

'Name the vineyards running north from Nuits-Saint-Georges in the direction of Dijon?'

I shot him a look, one of theatrical distain. 'Vosne-Romanée is the first, then Vougeot, Chambolle-Musigny, Morey-Saint-Denis, then Gev—'

'All right, that's enough, you know your wines, whatever your name is.'

'My name is actually Kiki.'

Rigault held his head in his hands. 'Aargh!'

'An abbreviation of Christine, Kikine, a childhood nickname.'

'What did your second husband do, madam?'

'He lived in the Loire, near Tours.'

'Lived?'

'He died just before the war.'

Pulling a face: 'Du Plessis, you say. I recognise the name. Was he an aristo?'

'The Baron du Plessis.'

Rigault's turn to curl his lip. 'Which means you are a baroness.'

'Not something I am keen to advertise in these republican times, monsieur.'

'Ah, so *what* are your politics, *Baroness?*'

'I don't have strong feelings one way or the other. All governments seem the same to me – full of idealism to start with, only to become corrupt. Though I do have some sympathy for the poor of Paris. They *always* lose.'

Another harrumph. 'Huh, you are certainly opinionated.'

'Just observant, monsieur.'

He turned to Coco. 'I want *Kikine* here investigated, the balloon factory, her lease, her birth and marriage records. We need someone to identify her.'

'Monsieur Godard knows me as Monique du Plessis, the name on my lease.'

Squeezing his nose: 'Kiki, I'm dining tonight with friends. I would be delighted if you could join us?'

I slowed myself down. '…I need to go home, monsieur.'

Coco looked at the file. 'To your Amazon friend, Sybille Duval.'

I nodded. 'And Tommy.'

'Who's Tommy?'

'A gamin I rescued from the streets some months ago. I've sort of adopted him.'

'You won't be going anywhere until you've been vetted.'

'That's right, I'm afraid,' said Rigault. 'Coco, find Kiki somewhere comfortable to sleep.'

Agnès led me up two flights of stone steps to a good-sized, musty-smelling room with packing cases in a corner. I opened the only window. Cold air rushed in. Leaning out, I inhaled it in great lungfuls.

Agnès brought in a pitcher of water, a basin, a small towel, a knob of soap and then took her leave. I plumped myself down on the bed and said a prayer for Sybille and Henri Torrès. I was still a prisoner at Raoul Rigault's convenience. What did he have in mind for me? I noticed the way he had looked at me. How to handle him? So far, I had been bold and appeared unafraid. I felt pleased with myself – I had obeyed one of my core rules: never lie when you can be found out. I hadn't lied and had landed myself in the middle of the web, like a fly, just where Oreste wanted me. But flies were eaten when careless.

I stood at the window, breathed in the air again. Saint-Germain was below me, the green expanse of the Luxembourg in the distance.

The bell of Notre-Dame struck eight times as Agnès led me downstairs to a courtyard where a policeman held the door open to a fiacre. She handed the driver some francs. It crossed my mind that I could jump out and run away, lose myself in the city. After a short ride we stopped outside Café Anglais on boulevard des Italiens – close to Durand-Ruel's gallery on rue Laffitte.

The restaurant was packed, laughter and cigar smoke filled the air as the maître d' guided me through the salon to a private room. Inside was equally raucous, one table with eight people seated including two women. Rigault stood, blew out a cloud of smoke. 'I present Madame Kiki,' he shouted.

'You make me sound like a woman of ill repute, Monsieur Rigault.'

'Whoa, oh no, Madame Monnier.'

I cast a glance at the diners. To my horror, Babette was there. Her hand was below the table doing something with one of the men. She glazed me with a look but appeared not to have recognised me.

I took it in – the bottles and the piles of food, the cigars, the flushed faces. My earlier bluster came to mind, the one about government and corruption. It was here in front of my very eyes, and yet the Commune was only a few days old.

'Sit down,' said Rigault, handing me a glass of wine. 'Kiki here knows a thing or two about the grape. Close your eyes, Kiki. Enlighten us with your expertise.'

'I don't play games with wine, monsieur.'

'Go on, woman.'

I made a play – sipped the wine, rolling it round my mouth, inhaling the bouquet. 'It's not a Bordeaux. It smells like a Bourgogne. Perhaps it's a Volnay' – inhaling again. 'No… on the other hand it could be a Pommard.' (I knew it was a Pommard – I should – it was made only four kilometres from where I was born.) I teased them, said at length, 'Yes, it's a Pommard.'

Monsieur Rigault showed me the bottle… it was a Pommard, Domaine de Montille. 'Well done, Kiki,' he said.

A man lurched to his feet. 'Kiki, I'm Théo, Théo Ferré. I work with Raoul.' He was small with a full beard; his eyes were black; he too wore a pince-nez. He was one of the names on Oreste's list. A chill ran down my spine. 'Where are you from?' he said.

'From the dungeons of the Conciergerie—'

'She murdered her husband,' said Rigault.

'Oh, how exciting,' said the other woman, the one next to Rigault. She was young and blonde and extravagant with her make-up, the rouge overdone. And later revealed to me as Madame Martin, an actress.

'Don't be absurd, *chérie*,' said Rigault.

The man next to me was dressed as a National Guard officer and placed a plate in front of me. 'Help yourself,' he said.

Thanking him, I spooned confit of duck, mashed potatoes and carrots onto my plate. I hadn't seen food like this since my days at Château Bèze.

Théo wobbled to his feet again. 'To the new chief of police' – holding his glass aloft.

Monsieur Rigault scowled and drained his glass – refilled by Madame Martin.

'Tell us about Renoir,' said Théo.

'Don't be a bloody bore.'

'Go on,' said the officer.

Rigault sighed. 'Very well… As you all know I was on the run from the police.'

Laughter.

'I escaped by train from Gare de Lyon.'

'No.'

'Living feral in the woods of Fontainebleau. I was desperate.'

'Never.'

'I hadn't eaten for three days, was cut and bruised, and then I came upon a clearing—'

'—where a young maiden was undressing herself.'

More laughter.

'Shut up, Théo.'

Théo pulled a face.

'—where Renoir was at his easel. At first, he did not understand my predicament. Then he draped a smock over me, and stuck a palette and a brush in my hands. Now I am a *Realist*. He hid me in his cottage for a couple of weeks. Fed me. Then I made my way back to Paris. *Voilà.*'

'Did he teach you how to paint?' I asked.

'Alas not, Madame Kiki.'

'A wasted opportunity.'

Madame Martin whispered in his ear and he was off on a different tack.

The evening proceeded in a similar vein – his friends toadying him. He was very much the dominant male. When he thought he had been bettered or gainsaid, he stood and shouted, especially at Théo. He appeared to know everyone and everything. My National Guard neighbour made the mistake of mentioning religion. Rigault went puce. 'That lot, don't get me started… a sanctimonious load of spongers, whose only stock-in-trade is fear. I feel compelled to have the whole lot shot.'

I was relieved that Madame Martin had his attention and not mine. Sometimes, though, I caught her looking at me in my dowdy shift. Perhaps she was trying to work out if I represented a threat.

A bottle of cognac was placed on the table, reminding me of the de Bonnetains, my 'training'. I remember thinking I was the only one sober when the revelries eventually spiralled to a close.

I shared a cab with Rigault and Madame Martin who dropped me off at the Conciergerie. I climbed the long flights of stairs to my room and crawled into bed.

The following morning Agnès escorted me 'next door' to the Préfecture de Police. She left me in a room with a view of the Seine. Soon Coco da Costa entered with a gentleman – none other than Eugène Godard. 'Do you know this woman, Monsieur Godard?' said Coco.

'Of course I do.' He bowed. 'Good morning, Monique.'

I smiled. 'Good morning, Monsieur Godard. I trust Madame Godard is well?'

Coco said, 'Tell me about Madame du Plessis, monsieur.'

'She was one of our best seamstresses. She joined us at the outset and led one of our teams.'

'Teams?'

'Yes, there could be up to twenty women in one, depending on how busy we were.'

'Is she trustworthy?'

Monsieur Godard rolled his eyes. 'I would trust her with my life, monsieur.'

I squirmed, smiling sweetly.

Coco thanked the aeronaut and showed him to the door. He turned to me. 'You are free to go, Madame Kiki.'

'What about the charges against me… murder… escape?'

'We have other rabbits to skin. The courts are full to bursting.'

'Monsieur, thank you… I would love to walk outside in the spring air but I can't afford to do so… not a centime to my name. I owe rent, unable to work during my incarceration, I might add.'

'So what?'

'I could be of use to you.'

Folding his arms: 'Explain.'

'I am fluent in German and proficient in English.'

'Not much use in the situation in which we find ourselves.'

'I know how to use the telegraph, Morse code.'

He curled a tuft of hair round a finger. 'Report here at nine tomorrow morning. I'll talk to Citizen Rigault.'

I was in the open air for the first time in two months. The sun warmed my face. A soft breeze wafted down the Seine as I leant over the side of Pont Saint-Michel and watched the river flow below. What had transpired was akin to a dream – the charges against me had been dropped. Did things like that really happen? Perhaps in extraordinary times they did.

Walking up boulevard Saint-Michel, it struck me that Paris was a happier place. It *was* spring. There was an excitement to the place, the feeling of us Parisians being in this together: Paris against the world. And there was plenty of food. Passing a patisserie, I was tempted to indulge in a pastry, but of course I was bereft of francs.

With the 'hidden' key I let myself into my apartment. I could hardly contain myself yet felt let down that no one was there to share my joy. I checked the larder – almost empty save a tranche of cheese, a jug of milk and a small tin of coffee. I sighed with relief – the oven was alight.

Apart from stripping off Sybille's sheets and making my own bed I spent the day in idleness, basking in my liberty while being free of guilt. Early evening Sybille walked in. Shrieking, she threw her arms round me. Tears everywhere, we blubbed like babies. She was wearing her Amazon uniform and poured wine as I began to lie to her about my release.

She had been promoted to corporal, proudly pointing to her stripes. She let me know she reported to barracks at Caserne Lobau early every morning.

My nasty little spy mind stored the information away. 'How is Tommy?' I asked.

'He still lives here, although some nights he's away. He always seems to have money, though.'

'Ah, on the subject of money…'

'As you know I had to pay five months' rent at the beginning of March, which I did on condition I settled the next three months in arrears.'

'Well done, Sybille. So, we owe 120 francs at the end of May. How are we going to pay?'

'We still have about eighty francs. Oh yes, I didn't tell you, but a policeman dropped round and gave me fifty francs.'

I smiled. I didn't want her to know where it had come from and changed the subject. 'Do you still see, um, you know, your baker friend?'

'No, but I am seeing someone, a National Guard called Eric. He's rather more generous. No "cakes" required.'

I laughed. We drank and talked in the expectation of Tommy coming home. By midnight, I bid Sybille goodnight and climbed into my own bed.

FORTY-NINE

THE FOLLOWING MORNING I made an effort, dressing in one of my more seemly outfits – mauve with flared sleeves – applying some blusher and eyeliner to my gaunt face. The weather was pleasant as I walked down to Saint-Germain. Then a feeling: a presence behind me. I turned round. Moritz. I nearly jumped out of my skin.

'Thought you had got rid of me,' he said, tipping his hat.

'Sergeant Monnier told me you were to be tried and shot.'

Moritz was the same as ever: smooth and pleased with himself, and beautifully attired. 'Ah, but I persuaded him otherwise,' he said.

'A pity.'

'I told him I thought you might be unreliable, him in Versailles and you here.'

'You told him about Lucien?'

'And lose my stock-in-trade? I did, however, persuade him that I had something on you. That while he was tucked away in Versailles, he needed someone to keep an eye on you… in case you strayed.'

'He pays you to do this?'

Bowing: 'A modest retainer, madam.'

'You're like a turd on the bottom of my shoe. You make me sick.'

He smiled. 'I know where you live and on whom you are spying.'

'I'm not spying on anyone as yet.'

'No?'

'I was just on my way to the Préfecture de Police.'

'Really?'

'To try to secure a job.'

'Excellent.'

'By the way, what happened to your two bearded friends?'

'Oh, that would be telling, madam.'

Coco led me upstairs to the room overlooking the Seine. Rigault was pacing up and down, smoking a cigar. 'Ah, Madame Kiki,' he said, waving me to a seat. 'Coco tells me you want something to do. Elaborate, if you please.'

'I haven't a cent—'

'Your personal circumstances are of no interest to me.'

'I can use the telegraph, the Morse code.'

'Go on.'

'I'm fluent in German and proficient in English.'

'Are you a stenographer?'

'Shorthand? I had a job as an accountant for three months and learned the rudiments. It shouldn't take me long to get used to it. I'm a fast learner. I'm also quite well read.'

'Well read, eh? Have you tried *The Communist Manifesto* by—'

'—Karl Marx and Friedrich Engels. No, not yet. Though I've just finished *Les Misérables* by—'

'—Victor Hugo, a friend of mine.'

'I was saddened when Dumas *père* died.'

'He was a romantic but a good republican. A *bon vivant* and highly entertaining. I met him a couple of times. Coco?'

'Hmm, Madame appears capable.'

'Be more explicit?'

'We could use someone with accountancy experience.' Without warning, Coco stuck his nose in my face. 'Twelve and a half per cent of five hundred?'

Curling my lip: 'Sixty-two point five, monsieur.'

'Two per cent of 624?'

'Twelve point four eight.'

'What's—?'

'Enough, Coco, the woman knows her arithmetic.' Tugging his beard: 'Hmm, we do need someone to appropriate funds from the central committee.'

'And perform clerical tasks. An assistant for you.'

'A dogsbody. Employ her,' said Rigault, sweeping out of the room.

Closing the door, Coco impressed on me how fortunate I was, that I would receive four francs a day, six days a week. 'Although you will work on Sundays, when required.'

In those days, the Préfecture was a two-storey building on quai des Orfèvres. Chief of Police Rigault occupied a large office on the upper floor overlooking the Seine – Coco da Costa a cubicle adjacent to him. I was assigned a desk next to Coco's – empty except for a pen, a box of steel nibs and a pot of ink. With nothing to do, I introduced myself to one of the *sergents-de-ville* occupying the floor. His assignment, he explained, was to vet the prisoners of the previous regime, releasing those deemed as loyal to the Commune.

'What did you do before this?' I asked him.

'I was a sergeant in the National Guard. Le Villette. And you?'

'I was a prisoner accused of murder.'

'Of whom may as ask?'

'My husband, nine years ago.'

'Well, you're in good company here.'

I returned to my desk in time for Coco to hand me an armful of files. 'We need a record of the prisoners we release – name, date of birth and address, and next of kin. And of those we retain. The sergeants will provide you with the information you require.'

'How many prisoners are there?'

'For you to find out, Kiki.'

I picked up the top file, marked 'EXPENSES'.

'And you are to keep an eye on expenses. The Central Committee control our funds and will require an account of our expenditure.'

'Understood, monsieur.'

'One last thing,' he said, feeling a pocket. 'Your *laissez-passer*… for entering the Préfecture and navigating your way round the city.'

I inspected the pass – signed by Citoyen Rigault over a black stamp with the date, 22 March 1871, and the words 'Préfecture de Police'.

The next ten days I was inundated. The Mazas, La Roquette and Sainte-Pélagie were full of wrongdoers against the *ancien régime*. Agitators and Reds of various hues: Blanquists, like Rigault, Proudhonists, who were anarchists, and Jacobins, who wanted to abolish almost everybody and everything. Some were members of the International Society, disciples of Marx and Engels. Others were just thugs, exploited by the Reds. All were against the monarchy and its substrate. The majority emanated from Belleville and La Villette. Rigault wanted as many of them freed as soon as was practically possible. The job of the sergeants was to separate the wheat from the chaff. My job was to tabulate the results.

I felt compelled to give something to Oreste – feed the beast, so to speak. At home, I worked out that the next day was day thirteen of my Alphabet Wheel. Accordingly, I wrote down the 'Wheel' for 1 April.

M N O P Q R S T U V W X Y
L K J I H G F E D C B A Z

On another piece of paper I converted the message – 'FOUR HUNDRED REDS RELEASED' – into code.

S J D G Q D K U G T U G T U F G T M T X F T U

I dropped the Wheel in the oven and watched it flare. Folding the coded message in two I drew my identification symbol thereon.

I hid the message between the pages of a book. Tommy was home so, before retiring to bed, I told him to wake me before he left in the morning.

Tommy's gap-toothed smile greeted me when he shook me awake. After dressing I gave him instructions in my room so as not to disturb Sybille. Taking him by the shoulders I fixed him with my eyes. 'You are to tell no one about this, *no one*, including Sybille. It's our secret, just you and me, Tommy. Understood?'

He nodded enthusiastically.

I cursed myself. 'The four hundred', were they of any value to the Thiers government? Was I taking an unnecessary risk? Playing with Tommy's life? Parlaying his life for Lucien's?

The Préfecture was chaos. Rigault strode past my desk in a wake of alcohol, smoke and body odour. I could hear him in his room ranting and raging at Coco.

I felt embarrassed at the fools they were making of themselves and sought refuge with the sergeant in the booth next to my desk. Knocking on his door I let myself in. He wasn't there. My eyes were drawn to the gun on his desk. Picking it up I weighed it in my hand. It was heavy but I managed to open the breech – a circular chamber with six bullets inside.

An impulse overwhelmed me. My hairs prickling when I concealed it in my clothing. Before I knew what I was doing I was out of the door and headed for the latrines on the ground floor. On the stairs I met the sergeant. 'They are arguing,' I said. When he tried to engage me in conversation, I pulled a face: *I really do need to go.*

Standing on tiptoes inside the cubicle, I stretched and placed the gun inside the cistern. A thought, and taking it out I removed the bullets. Putting it back I made sure it did not interfere with the flushing mechanism.

At my desk I worked on my 'lists' and kept my head down. After a while the sergeant stood in front of me. 'My revolver is missing,' he said. 'You wouldn't by chance have seen anyone enter my office?'

'I've been stuck here, Marcel, apart from when I met you on the stairs. Are you sure you haven't mislaid it? Let me have a look for you.'

'No, it's quite all right. By the way, the Communards plan to break out on the third.'

Marcel had unwittingly given me some real intelligence. That night I coded a message.

REDBREAKOUTTHIRD

Sunday was my day off. Having given Tommy his instructions I lay in my bed worrying. At noon he returned, his lopsided smile telling me that all was well. Sybille was out. And wrapping my arms round *the little mite* I enthused, telling him we were going to the Luxembourg. I had money in my purse and intended to spend it. Once there I gave Tommy a couple of francs and he raced away. Then I heard it – the rumble of artillery. *Crump. Crump.* A collective moment of hesitation before people started running pell-mell in different directions. Tommy bowled up with ice cream all over his face – he couldn't have cared less. Determined not to have our day spoilt we made our way to rue d'Assas, where we shared sandwiches and a drink. I wondered if my message had reached the Versaillais.

Monday. Pandemonium reigned in the Préfecture. Mid-morning, Rigault beckoned me to a room where a priest was seated. 'Please take notes, Madame Monnier,' he said.

I felt sorry for the cleric, a Jesuit – meek and mild as he sat there in his cassock – more so when Rigault glared at him.

'What is your profession?' demanded Rigault.

'Servant of God.'

'Where does your master live?'

'Everywhere.'

Rigault turned to me: 'Take this down... "describing himself servant of one called God, a vagrant".'

That was the day I learnt that Rigault planned to apprehend the Most Reverend Georges Darboy, Archbishop of Paris, no less.

Was this news worthy of the risk I would have to take? To say nothing of Tommy. It occurred to me there might be 'publicity value'. But who was I to judge? No, I decided it wasn't worth it.

Next day there was terrible news for the Communards. Gustave Flourens had been executed during the sortie the day before. It crossed my mind that I might have been responsible.

Rigault was in a rage, shouting orders and raving about his hero Auguste Blanqui, then arguing over Archbishop Darboy, the efficacy of arresting him. An argument he must have won when Darboy was arrested later in the day and imprisoned in the Mazas. I knew – I did the paperwork.

Added to the confusion, Citoyens Rigault and Ferré required that all correspondence be dated according to the Revolutionary calendar. That particular day was 4 April 1871 or 14 Germinal in the year 79. My diary had two dates for the same day.

At midday, when Rigault was away at a Commune meeting, I visited place Dauphine located next to the Préfecture on Île de la Cité. Number 15 was boarded up. I assumed that Reginald Markham was back in England, away from the madness of Paris.

The Préfecture had its hands full: issuing passports, providing lodgings to disadvantaged families, establishing neighbourhood police stations, recruiting and organising agents to root out Versaillais spies. The prisons were full again – with enemies of the Commune.

Rigault was a man possessed, his energy boundless, as were his appetites. His dinners in the Préfecture itself are fabled. Often, I witnessed staff cleaning up from the night before. I became adept at making myself 'grey' – dressing down, no make-up and no eye contact – wanting no part in his Bacchanalia, avoiding him socially.

The Central Committee was forever objecting to his expenditure. My job was to mollify them – provide them with written excuses, feeble though they were.

I do believe they were frightened of him. He did as he pleased – the dictator of his domain. On 13 April he arrested Gustave Chaudey, an old friend of his, for opening fire on demonstrators at the Hôtel de Ville, killing Théodore Sapia, another friend.

After he arrested *l'Abbé* Simon, a gang of market ladies from Les Halles turned up at the Préfecture demanding the *abbé*'s release. To my surprise he let the priest go – the only time I saw Rigault back down.

He was drunk on power, but somehow knew it would end, so he might as well binge and whore himself while it lasted. I would swear he had aged ten years in two months.

The rate of his arbitrary arrests was so high that he and Théo Ferré were forced to resign – Rigault soon to reappear, however, as *Procureur* of the newly formed Revolutionary Tribunal. He had almost total power. The new chief of police was an ally, so Rigault remained in the Préfecture.

Ideologically I was on the side of the Versailles government. For a while, though, I felt compassion for the Communards. Although, when I think back on it, they were anarchists bent on destruction. Those at the top were corrupt, especially Procureur Rigault.

Barricades had been erected since the start of the Commune. By mid-April their construction had become frenetic. The one at place de la Concorde connecting rue Saint-Florentin with Jardin des Tuileries was reported as vast. One Sunday we walked there. It was immense and wide – two metres high and nearly as thick, and made of sandbags and barrels – in front a huge ditch five metres deep. According to one of Sybille's Amazon friends it had cost eighty thousand francs to build. Tommy larked around on the top before a guard shooed him away.

I had provided no intelligence in five days. The last thing I wanted was Moritz at my door. Then I was handed a list: the barricades that needed policing. I counted the sites – fifty-six in all – an intelligence goldmine. I worked out what day it was on my Alphabet Wheel.

The bombardment was incessant, far worse than the Prussian offensive. At the beginning of May, the Commune appointed Louis-Nathaniel Rossel to oversee the defence of Paris: the coordination of the National Guard and the erection of additional barricades.

One morning it came to my attention that a major barricade had been constructed across the top of rue Blanche on place Blanche in Montmartre. A splinter of fear down my spine as it dawned on me that I could have more than just the Wynburnes to contend with. I was tempted to approach Rigault, explain my dilemma to him in the hope he would send in a squad of police to rescue Lucien. But for some reason I held back. The process being out of my control, I suppose.

Early May and Rigault was more irrational than ever. Breakfasts in the Conciergerie with his cronies; Théo Ferré was always there,

Coco as well. I made myself scarce, although on 10 May he roped me in, this time at Les Trois Frères Provençaux in the Palais-Royal.

Veuve Clicquot and Nuits-Saint-Georges were served with Chateaubriand aux Truffes. The room was full of cigar smoke and ribaldry – Rigault presiding at the head of the table. An end-of-the-world feeling – no one seemed to give a damn. I was stuck between Pilotell and Ferré, whose hand wandered to my thigh, which I flopped away in exchange for a black-eyed stare.

The self-styled Pilotell was one to avoid. A caricaturist by trade and vain to the rooftops he carried out 'errands' for Rigault – making people 'disappear', I would imagine.

Rigault ordered me to settle the bill – 75.25 francs, including 13.50 for 'Cigars-Cazadorès'. I informed the quivering maître d' that the Committee of Public Safety would 'pick it up'. Much wringing of his hands, but what could he do? Later the bill found its way to my desk – my task to fob off the Central Committee.

The news was always bad. Rossel resigned as the head of the Communard army. Fort Vanves was abandoned. Out of spite, Adolphe Thiers' house was destroyed, Coco gleefully bringing back a tile from the roof.

FIFTY

MAY 16 1871. The day they pulled down the column in place Vendôme, the one with Napoleon Bonaparte at its top.

People in the Préfecture tried to witness the event and went there in the early afternoon, but the cables snapped. 'A farce,' as someone described it.

I arrived there at just after five o'clock in time to see it fall in a huge zigzag through the air, the ground shaking on impact – pigeons skittering away, a gasp of collective breath. Then further absurdity, the emperor detaching himself from the plinth and appearing to leap from his immortal shackle, his laurel-wreathed head rolling into the gutter.

The general shock was palpable – stunned silence – then people started to drift away. Walking down rue de Castiglione I spotted Pilotell when he turned his head to speak to his companion, a tall man in a top hat. The man turned to reply. I felt myself quake... Reginald Markham. *What could these two have in common?* I asked myself.

I followed them onto rue de Rivoli. They strolled, chatting amiably, it seemed. I pulled my hat down over my forehead.

Soon they stopped, their heads bobbing in conversation. Markham offered Pilotell a cigar. Then Pilotell continued down the street. Markham had disappeared. Soon I was at the spot where they had been talking – outside Hôtel Brighton, strangely enough.

Next evening, a huge explosion rattled the windows of the Préfecture – the munitions factory on avenue Rapp had been blown up. Immediate accusations of sabotage: of Versaillais spies at work. Rigault was beside himself.

Coco told us to go home. The cubicle was empty and, after bolting the door, I picked the revolver from its hiding place. From what little I understood of guns I knew the firing mechanism had to be dry. Outside I found a quiet place on the other side of the river. Wiping the gun on my shift I then slotted the bullets into the chamber – calmly, deliberately.

A pall of smoke hung over the west of the city as I walked down rue de Rivoli. Bizarre, but I felt no fear. I found myself justifying what I had to do – the morality.

The location was no stranger to me. Apart from the night there with Markham, the Hôtel Brighton was next to the Welcome café where I used to lie in wait for Lucien. I was dressed in my work clothes except for the mob cap. The employees' entrance was via a door on rue du 29 Juillet. Acting the part of a chambermaid I soon found my way to the female changing room. Making sure no one was about I tried the lockers – all were locked. I breathed in deep to steady my nerves. A maid walked in. We acknowledged each other – my face averted. 'I'm new here,' I said.

'Oh, yes?' she replied, undoing her pinafore.

'Someone should be here to meet me.'

'Since the Communards took control things have gone to shit,' she said, tossing her clothes into a laundry basket.

She was of a similar build to me, so I took my time. After more chit-chat we bid each other 'goodnight'. Once she was gone, I made for the basket. Soon I was dressed in the hotel's livery.

Stashing my work clothes, I found my way to the backstairs. I prayed Markham had taken his usual room on the fourth floor. I felt the gun in my reticule for reassurance. A prayer as I knocked on the door. The sounds of someone on the other side, a bolt sliding back…

She was thin and pretty, wore a negligee, a cigarette dangling down from a languid hand. I knew her from somewhere. Then it came to me: Madame Martin, Rigault's actress friend at Café Anglais.

'Madam, I've come to turn down the sheets' – avoiding her eyes.

She appeared not to have recognised me. 'A bit early, aren't you? Oh well, come in.'

'Sorry, ma'am, my first day…'

A bit early, aren't you? Madame Martin, it would seem, had stayed for more than one night. For a moment I thought I had come to the wrong room.

In the bedroom, however, there were signs of Markham everywhere: a cigar butt in a flute of champagne, a very large pair of shoes at the end of the bed, a pyjama top with RM embroidered thereon.

As I straightened the sheets, I thought it through: Pilotell, Markham, Madame Martin, Rigault and Moritz were all connected.

Madame Martin was a complication. What to do with her?

In the salon I took out the gun and waved it at her.

Her eyes flared and she stood up. 'Don't. Please,' she said.

'Do exactly as I say. The bellpull, I want you to cut the cord.'

'With what?'

'A knife, scissors. Use your imagination.'

Appearing to hesitate she opened a drawer and took out a knife. Climbing on a chair she cut the cord and stepped back down, placing the knife on a table.

'Hand me the cord then turn around,' I said.

'Reggie will kill you.'

I coaxed her to the bathroom and tied her to a towel rail. A flannel was to hand, which I stuffed in her mouth. Tearing a pillowcase into strips I secured the flannel by tying one of the strips round the back of her head. She tried to spit it out, to no avail.

In the salon an open bottle of champagne. Pouring myself a flute I drank it down in a mouthful.

Not long before there was a knock on the door. 'It's me,' said a male voice in English.

'Coming,' I said, imitating Madame Martin's tones as best I could.

I opened the door. The gun was in my hand.

Markham stood there, a cigar in his mouth, a bottle of champagne in one hand. Dragging on the cigar: 'Ah, Kiki, I was wondering when you would turn up.' Indicating the gun: 'Put that silly thing away.'

I pointed it at his head. 'Sit. Place both your hands on the table. Take them off and I won't hesitate.'

'Where is Madame Martin?'

'In the bathroom, indisposed, you might say.'

'You are dressed as a chambermaid. Fitting, given your class.'

'Hands on the table, Reggie.'

He put the cigar in an ashtray, his hands on the table.

'Tell me, Reggie, why is Madame Martin here?'

'Raoul tired of her so I took her off his hands.'

'So, you know Procureur Rigault?'

'You catch on quickly, Kiki.'

'And Théo and Pilotell and Coco?'

'All personal friends of mine.'

'Makes sense, given their stock-in-trade.'

'Pray enlighten me?'

'Oh, indiscriminate murder, rape, general debauchery, that sort of thing.'

'Mind if I open the champagne? I'm a tad parched.'

'Hands on the table, Reggie.'

He sighed wistfully.

'And of course you will be acquainted with Moritz.'

'Moritz… never heard of him.'

'A dapper fellow, overfed and very pleased with himself, a scar on his right cheek. A Belgian.'

'Oh, him. Calls himself Moritz, does he?'

'Does he have a name?'

'And betray a personal friend? You'd think the lesser of me, Kiki.'

'After you raped me, Moritz blackmailed me into spying on the balloon factory. Why?'

'Why? We wanted to shorten the war with Fritz, of course.'

'We?'

'Her Majesty's government.'

'In London?'

'I can't imagine where you would find another "Her Majesty" with Eugénie now gone.'

'You are a British agent?'

He grinned and clapped his hands.

'Hands on the table, Reggie. Next time I will shoot.'

He pulled a face. 'Napoleon was a buffoon, not a patch on his uncle, but dangerous nonetheless. We knew that once France lost the war she would be overrun by extremists, that chaos would reign, albeit temporarily. In a few days the Commune will be finished, with Thiers in control.'

'Why Thiers?'

'Why do you think?'

'Tell me.'

'Britain requires a strong France to counteract the growing strength of Bismarck and his German Empire. The balance of power in Europe is to be maintained at all costs.'

'Britain always takes the weaker side.'

'As we did against the first Napoleon.'

'And what will become of "your personal friends"? Rigault… the others.'

'Oh, them, they are buffoons as well, ruffians, communists worse still. They will die fighting or be executed afterwards.'

'Are you in touch with Oreste?'

'Your charming brother-in-law – matter of fact, I am. I came up with the idea of using you to spy on the Préfecture. He didn't need much persuasion.'

'I thought—'

'God, you're naive, Kiki.'

'Well?'

He sighed. 'Oreste had the sense to know the Commune would be defeated. We convinced him that, once it was over, an ever-so-grateful Thiers would appoint him as chief of police of Paris.'

'But what about the Commune?'

'As I said, we knew the extremists would take control. But we still have to rid ourselves of them.'

'And that's when I became useful again?'

'I convinced him that, rather than having you tried and executed, he could use you against the Commune, against Rigault specifically. The plan had the backing of my government. I saved your pretty little neck, Christine.'

'That's why the messages were couriered through the British Embassy.'

'Well done, Kiki. Clap, clap.'

'He was prepared to drop the murder charge against me, the so-called murderer of his precious twin.'

'He was persuaded by my government's point of view. I had to drag him across the line – your information invaluable to Thiers. As I said, he will become Thiers' chief of police.'

Anxiety spiralled through me – the prospect of Oreste paying off the mortgage. 'So why were you friends with Augustave?'

'Do I really have to explain?'

'Try.'

'I was a *négociant* – a perfect cover for what I do. I enjoyed it. I *enjoy* France, what it has to offer, especially Paris, if you know what I mean. Augustave was a useful idiot, a diversion. The dogs. The fights amused me, and then you murdered him.'

'I did not.'

Rolling his eyes: 'I *know* that.'

'Did you arrange with Joeline Lambert to meet me here in this room?'

'No, I wanted a woman for the night. I had no idea it would be you. I have never had the pleasure of Madame Lambert's acquaintance.'

'So, when you found out who I was, you used me.'

'Afraid so, Kiki, that little monogram on your cunt.'

'Why did you rape me?'

'I enjoyed it and I wanted to bring you to heel.'

'I'm not a dog, Reggie.'

He raised his eyebrows.

I could feel my resolve draining out of me. Everything he said made sense: the Prussians, France, Europe and the balance of power, the wretched Communards, Adolphe Thiers. He had used everyone against themselves in the interests of Britannia, of 'Her Majesty'. *And* he had used me. The thing is, though, he abused me… his one mistake.

He must have sensed my preoccupation and suddenly leapt out of his chair. I pulled the trigger, the gun recoiling in my hand, the chandelier above him instantly splintering, shards of glass pinging and clinking.

Then he was on me, the gun spinning away. Picking me up, he threw me against the table which shattered under my weight. I was not sure how, but the knife Madame Martin had used was within reach and so I grabbed it with my right hand. Then he was on me again and sticking his tongue down my throat. I let him have his way and responded in kind. And when he was unbuttoning his trousers, I thrust the knife as hard as I could in his side.

'You fucking bitch!' he screamed, wrapping his giant hands around my neck. I stabbed and stabbed again with every ounce of my strength. He continued to squeeze and I kept stabbing. He had the strength of the devil but eventually his grip loosened and he rolled off me onto his back. Then *I* was on top of *him*. He was groaning and rasped, 'You don't know what you have done.' I stabbed him one last time, through his Adam's apple. The entry point bloomed like a rose; his shirt drenched in blood. His legs twitched and then he was still.

I slewed off him and lay there panting, my heart thumping against my ribs. I sucked in the air in great gulps. I was covered in blood, its sweet metallic smell. My throat gorged; I spewed uncontrollably on the carpet. I felt cold, started shaking, the sweat sticky damp on my back. Whimpering, I staggered to my feet, tears streaming down my face. Blood was everywhere *and* glass – the carpets and chairs were ruined. Markham's champagne – I twisted off the cork and drank from the bottle. Retched again. I tried to avoid Markham's stare, his vacant eyes.

My brain began to function – what to do? My clothes were covered in blood, as were my face, my hands, my arms and my hair. I searched the room for water.

A sound in the bathroom – Madame Martin; I had completely forgotten her.

A jug of water stood on a side table in the bedroom. Undressing down to my underwear I pulled a sheet off the bed and washed myself as best I could. Leaning over a bowl I poured the remains of the water over my head, drying my hair on another sheet.

Opening a wardrobe, I sifted through Madame Martin's clothes. Her costumes were unsuitable, but I settled for a high-collared dress and put it on. It would do. Her brushes and combs lay on a vanity unit. Brushing my hair I stared at the mirror. I looked awful and applied some of Madame Martin's powder and a dab of rouge, rubbing it in with my fingers. Lastly, I took off my shoes, cleaning them as best I could, wiping off the blood and drying them on a sheet.

I decided to leave Madame Martin in the bathroom – no need for her to see my face, identify me. Back in the salon, I retrieved my reticule and the gun, wrapping it in a serviette. An idea… and, opening one of the windows, I smeared the sill with the bloodied sheet, leaving the window slightly ajar. I delicately opened Markham's frock coat, searched the pockets, extracting his wallet – 210 francs inside. I scattered the remaining contents and dropped it on his body, as I imagined a thief would have done.

With a final glance at Markham, I opened the door and retraced my steps to the changing room where I dressed in my work clothes. Outside, I was back in the real Paris, the one of worried people scurrying down its streets – of barricades. The thump of cannon was close, reminding me of something Markham had said: *the Commune will be finished*.

On Pont Royal I dropped Madame Martin's dress, the maid's uniform, the knife and the gun in the Seine. Walking home I tried to work out my situation: would the Préfecture associate me with the murder of Reginald Markham? Madame Martin was a worry, though I was almost certain she hadn't recognised me. And what of the chambermaid? The police would know that Markham's assassin was a woman once Madame Martin was questioned.

I would carry on as though nothing had happened.

FIFTY-ONE

THE FOLLOWING DAY a massive cannonade, which seemed to never end. Heeding reports of Versaillais troops in the Bois de Boulogne we barricaded the Préfecture. Sending messages to rue du Faubourg Saint-Honoré was nigh on impossible.

Just after lunch, a flustered-looking Pilotell entered Rigault's office, swiftly followed by Théo who slammed the door behind him. After a while they emerged sombre-faced. Soon it was round the office: an English associate of theirs had been found dead in a hotel, murdered by all accounts. Then Madame Martin hurried past my desk and barged her way in – screaming from the other side of the door as I made myself scarce in the latrines.

On Sunday the Versaillais army was in Paris. All day the ringing of the tocsin bell from churches urging the Communards to arms for one final effort. The world had gone mad.

No sign of Sybille in the apartment, though I saw Tommy who was clearly enjoying himself, bringing back souvenirs – cartridge casings and lumps of masonry, one piece in the shape of a fleur-de-lys. I handed him what I thought would be my last message to Oreste.

I ventured outside in the afternoon to the sound of cannons. The air was full of smoke. Shreds of burnt paper fell like snow, littering the ground. I made my way down rue Royer-Collard towards the Luxembourg where I was confronted by three barricades. Communards of all descriptions manned them. Most were decked in red – belt, tie, scarf and pantaloons – and going about their business, some ripping up *pavés* to add to the piles. One lieutenant, palm out, ordered me to turn round. After inspecting my *laissez-passer*, he was more civil but insistent. 'We're expecting trouble, ma'am. For your own good, I cannot let you pass.'

It dawned on me that Markham was right: the Communards didn't have a chance – nor did I. I conjured up the map in my head, the route that would take me to rue Blanche and Lucien. A near-impossible task – a woman making her way through a battlefield to the Red stronghold of Montmartre.

Monday, 22 May. Panic. The feeling we were about to be overrun, that the Préfecture would soon be under siege. An order crossed my desk: all bridges spanning the Seine were to be blown up – one more madcap idea from Messrs Rigault and Ferré. They appeared bent on destroying the city's heritage in some vainglorious, self-centred crusade. I could hardly believe it at the time. I was of a mind to say something but could see no point. They imagined they could do anything – have anyone shot. After lunch I received the order: Archbishop Darboy was to be moved from the Mazas to La Roquette. I whispered a prayer – the unthinkable was now probable.

More bad news: the Trocadero quarter had been taken by the Versaillais, followed by the order to cover the Palais de Justice in oil with a view to setting it alight. Something awful happened, and they were set on revenge.

By late afternoon I had made up my mind to leave the Préfecture. With the few items I possessed, I made my way downstairs. As I walked across the courtyard a fiacre pulled up. Pilotell stepped out followed by a *sergent-de-ville* with a prisoner in tow – a small fellow, his face covered in blood. The 'boy' was wriggling, twisting and turning. The sergeant swore. Wanting nothing to do with Pilotell I swerved to my left – too late as the boy stood stock-still. 'Madame Kiki,' he said through bloodied lips. '*Aidez moi*. It's me. Help.' At first the words did not register; then my heart sank – the boy was Tommy.

'Sergeant, arrest that woman!' screamed Pilotell as he grabbed hold of Tommy.

'Leave him be!' I retorted as the sergeant clamped my arms behind my back.

Pilotell smirked. 'I have always had my suspicions, Madame Kiki.'

I was hauled up to Rigault's office. Ferré was there, Coco too.

Rigault snatched a piece of paper from Pilotell. 'What does this mean?'

Despite my fear it was time to make my presence felt so, taking off my beret and wig, I undid my hair so that it fell around my shoulders. Standing to my full height: 'It is code, monsieur, what did you think it was?'

Rigault went puce. 'Code?'

'Informing the Versaillais of barricades to be erected at Croix-Rouge, rue Madame and rue de Babylone.'

'How did this urchin come to possess it?'

'I gave it to him.'

'Why?'

'So it could be passed to the Versaillais.' I nearly added, *Stupid*, but held back.

'You're a spy—'

'—since the day you released me from the Conciergerie.'

'I warned you,' said Pilotell.

Rigault ignored him. 'To whom do you pass the messages?'

'Before I tell you, I want an understanding.'

'Fat chance.'

'I want Tommy released. He's an innocent, an errand boy.'

'You're in no position to make demands.'

'Well?'

'I'll think about it.'

'That's not good enough.'

'All right, I'll let the little bastard go. He'll get himself killed anyway.'

'Answer the question,' said Pilotell.

I acted it up, tossed my hair. 'To a Monsieur Moritz of 22 rue Auber,' I lied.

'Moritz? Who is this Moritz, for God's sake? Explain or I'll have you taken away and shot,' said Rigault.

'Moritz reports to Sergeant Oreste Monnier of the Versaillais police.'

A sly look from Pilotell. 'We received a message an hour ago – that an urchin was being used to courier messages to the British Embassy.'

'Why would Sergeant Monnier, the recipient of her intelligence, betray her?' said Coco.

Ferré rubbed his chin. 'With the Versaillais in the city he had no further need of her services.'

'That can't be right' – Coco again.

I said, 'The answer is simple, messieurs: Le Blaireau believes I murdered his twin brother, Augustave, nine years ago.'

'Ah, the murdered husband,' said Coco. 'The reason you were in the Conciergerie.'

Ferré said, 'Apart from the alleged murder of his twin, what else did your brother-in-law have over you?'

'Nothing.'

'With him in Versailles, why didn't you ignore him?'

'Moritz… he has some power over me.'

'Yes?'

'Moritz has access to my child—'

'Your child?'

'Taken from me nine years ago.'

'You don't look old enough' – Ferré with a leer.

'Are you saying that your brother-in-law knew nothing of the child?' said Coco.

'That is correct.'

'Why the motif, the bird?' said Pilotell.

'To distinguish my message from others.'

'Others?'

'I don't know. So, my messages got through to him, all right!'

'A blackbird?'

'A *merle*, yes.'

'Why?'

I wasn't going to let him know about le Merle and shook my hair. 'We needed something recognisable between us – something to do with my hair, perhaps.'

'Back to Moritz, whoever he is,' Coco said. 'I don't understand how he came into the picture in the first place. Was it something to do with the child?'

'No.'

'Well?'

'An English agent put him on to me.'

'His name?' said Rigault.

'Reggie.' Ha, that stopped them in their tracks. They all looked at one another wide-eyed, then at me.

'You know that Reggie is dead?' said Coco after a while.

'I do, monsieur,' I said somewhat triumphantly.

For a moment no one spoke. Stunned silence. The shaking of heads. I remember looking across to the windows, the sun sparkling on the Seine, and wondering if this was my last sight of something beautiful.

At length Rigault said, 'Much though I admire what you've done, I'm afraid I am compelled to have you shot.' Addressing the *sergent-de-ville*: 'Marcel, escort Madame Kiki to La Roquette. A single cell. Don't take your eyes off her till she's under lock and key.'

'Why not take her downstairs and shoot her now?' said Coco.

'Why waste a cell on the bitch?' Ferré said.

'Shut up, Théo. Get her out of my sight, sergeant.'

In normal times, Île de la Cité to La Roquette takes half an hour by cab. An hour later we were stuck in traffic – carts and people everywhere and the barricade on rue de la Roquette blocking our path. We could go no further and walked the rest of the way.

Ever since La Bastille's destruction in the Revolution, La Roquette had usurped its distinction of being the main prison of Paris, its primary place of execution – the reason Archbishop Darboy had been transferred there – a frightening, monstrous place with its six-sided building and turrets. Marcel handed me over to the prison authorities. The inside was menacing, the smell of stone and bodies, the rotting straw. But I was used to imprisonment. I held fast to my courage as I underwent the iniquities of incarceration.

Monsieur Pinet, the warder, escorted me to a single cell, leering at me through gapped teeth before locking the door. The cell was filthy and reeked. The pallet was stained. But it was May, the weather warm and dry.

I sat and closed my eyes, recalled the scene in Rigault's office – Théo Ferré's comment: *Why waste a cell on the bitch?* Had Rigault something else in mind? I couldn't believe this was where it would end. My life. Destined to die as a twenty-four-year-old, the mother of a son I barely knew, never to see Alie or sweet Arlette again. Or Sybille. Or Joelie for that matter. It didn't seem possible, yet there I was in La Roquette awaiting my fate.

I stood and paced the cell and patted my pockets – something inside one of them: my *laissez-passer*. I dozed fitfully, kneading the cross at my throat the occasions I prayed. The scene in the stables seemed a lifetime ago. I thought of Madame Thierry – what I would give to see her one last time.

I tried to conjure up the image of Junius – his face was round and he had brown eyes, like Lucien's. His smile, the shape of his mouth, his chin, eluded me. What had happened to him? Did I care? I imagined him clinging to the wreck of his ship, somewhere in the Gulf of Mexico. Was he dead, as per the rumours?

I thought through my interrogation again – Pinotell's sly look when I mentioned Oreste's name. *We received a message an hour ago*, he had said. Only Oreste and Moritz knew what I was up to. Moritz had no motive in betraying me. Oreste knew that Rigault and his collaborators would deal with me once they knew I was spying on them.

Half asleep, I awoke to the sound of the cell door scraping open. Raoul Adolphe Georges Rigault stood there holding a bottle of champagne and two glasses. His face was red and sweaty. And when he removed his jacket, the familiar stench of his body odour. I attempted a smile.

'I am here to celebrate your perfidy, Kiki,' he said, filling the glasses.

'You have come to gloat, monsieur.'

'Not to gloat. But, how shall I put it… to revenge myself upon you. Yes.'

I felt my skin crawl.

'So, you killed Reggie?'

'He deserved it.'

'Why?'

'He raped me then used me to spy against my country.'

'Ahh. I will have to be careful.'

'Oh?'

'I would be obliged if you took off your clothes, Kiki. You see, I don't have much time' – slurping his champagne, foam clinging to the fuzz of his beard below his lip.

'What do I get out of this, monsieur?'

'A glass of champagne. *Une petite mort.*'

'An orgasm, Raoul? I hardly think so.'

Handing me the bottle: 'Consider this as your last "meal", Kiki, with me the main course.'

Curling my lip: 'You smell, monsieur… always have. I'd rather fuck a pig.'

'We can do this your way or mine.'

It occurred to me to comply – gain an advantage. After all, I had done this before – inured myself to the process, locked down my senses… Augustave, the loathsome de Goffre, Joelie's clients. *And* Reginald Markham, nothing on God's earth could be worse than that. So I stood and did what I have done many a time: teased off my shift and stepped out of my pretties.

'That's better,' he said, licking his lips before tearing himself out of his clothes.

After glugging down champagne, I lay on my back and hitched up my legs. He was on me like a hog, no foreplay and grunting. His skin was slick with sweat and God did he stink. It was over in seconds, and rolling off me he apologised.

I don't know what possessed me but, while he was dressing, I went for the bottle and slashed at his head. I managed to land a blow before he ripped it out of my hand. 'Good try,' he said, panting. 'Terrible waste.'

Soon he was dressed and ready to leave.

'What's to happen to me?' I asked him.

'You'll be taken out and shot tomorrow morning, four o'clock – the first shift. You won't feel a thing. Adieu, Kiki.'

The door clanged behind him, the key squealing in its roundel. Then silence.

I was in a terrible mess and did my best to clean myself – difficult, there being no water. I felt the tears well and let myself go.

FIFTY-TWO

I AWOKE WHEN Monsieur Pinet and a guard entered my cell. 'It's your time, madam,' said Pinet.

'Am I entitled to a priest?'

'None are available.'

'The archbishop?'

His mouth flopped open. 'How do you know?'

Soon I was in the inner courtyard, my hands tied behind my back. A hint of light, but gloomy, the massive walls obscuring the dawn. I was led to a wooden post at the bottom of one of the turrets. It was stained, the wall behind splattered with blood. I shivered and muttered a prayer. A soldier approached. Strange. The way he moved – a familiarity, a recall, of something in my past – the tilt of his head. His uniform was one I didn't recognise. He stared at me. His eyes – I could just make them out. His beard was ragged and streaked. 'Think of your mother,' he murmured, dipping his head to my ear… that movement again.

'Florian,' I whispered.

'What…? H-how could you know my name, madam?'

I bowed my head. 'There's a cross around my neck.'

I could feel his hands as he tried to find the chain.

'There,' he said, looping it over my head.

'Look at it, Florian.'

He patted a pocket and then struck a match – a flare in the gloom – his features gaunt and shadowy as he examined the cross, his fingers running over it, turning it. A sharp intake of breath: 'Kiki.'

'Florian.'

Silence… as though he was trying to make up his mind. He looked around, seemed to come to a decision. 'Shush, Kiki,' he said, inclining his head in the direction of three soldiers in the same strange uniform. One was inspecting the breach of his *Chassepot*; another was smoking a pipe; another, very large, was leaning against a wall.

Monsieur Pinet walked into the courtyard.

'*Merde!* Wait here,' Florian said before loping towards his men. He was angular, lean yet powerful. After a brief huddle he strode back to me. 'Follow my instructions to the letter, Kiki.'

One of his cadres joined us. 'Walk between us, look straight ahead,' he ordered as they marched me towards the arch from where I'd emerged. Soon we were in a long, vaulted room full of soldiers asleep. At the end of one of the bunks a chair with a uniform draped thereon. 'Put these on and tuck up your hair,' he said.

I did not know it at the time, but I was dressed in the uniform of the Foreign Legion. Florian carefully placed the foraging cap on my head and made adjustments. 'There,' he said. 'Follow me and Carlos.'

The three of us walked down a passage to a large wooden door. The stench was awful, acrid yet sweet. I had to prevent myself from throwing up.

After a while, Florian dragged out a woman's body, hefting it onto his shoulders. 'This one will do,' he said nonchalantly.

In the courtyard, he dropped the body by the stake. Handing me a *Chassepot* he instructed his men: 'Aim for the head, boys.'

We aimed at the figure and Florian shouted, 'Fire!' Closing my eyes I squeezed the trigger, the butt thumping into my shoulder.

The volley echoed off the walls. 'Congratulations, Kiki,' he said, 'you have just shot yourself. Follow me.'

'What happened to Monsieur Pinet?' I said.

'You'd rather not know.'

'Ah.'

'Tell me why you are here,' he said as we walked down a passageway.

'I was to be shot as a spy for the Versaillais. Oreste Monnier was my controller. He blackmailed me.'

'Oreste Monnier?'

'He had something over me. He knew where my child was,' I lied.

'Your child?'

'A boy – eight years old – held captive.'

'Where?'

'Rue Blanche, Montmartre.'

'Montmartre... a long way away under the circumstances.'

'That's where I'm going if I get out of this hole.'

We continued down the passage, Florian's head lowered as though deep in thought. 'Can I persuade you otherwise?' he said once we had returned to the sleeping quarters.

'Not a chance.'

Scratching his beard: 'All right. Stash your clothes in a backpack while I talk to my men.'

He handed me an empty pack. Remembering my *laissez-passer*, I concealed it in my uniform.

Florian's men returned. 'Horst and Jean-Baptiste,' he said, introducing them. 'You've already met Carlos.'

The men grunted. The giant touched his cap.

Two minutes of intense activity as the legionnaires armed themselves with pistols, bayonets, pouches, sabres and knives. Florian handed me a holster containing a revolver, which I buckled round my waist. Then he gave me a *Chassepot*, bayonet fixed. 'I hope you won't have to use this,' he said, 'but you look the part, private.'

'Private?'

'Private Duval.'

No one blocked our path or asked questions. We were the 'first shift' and on our way out of La Roquette for something to eat. Soon we were on rue de la Roquette. Ahead was our first barricade. 'Time for me to change,' I said.

Two minutes later I was dressed in my day clothes again. The barricade was strung across the road at its junction with boulevard d'Austerlitz. I swaggered up to the sergeant in charge. 'A fine day for it, Sergeant,' I said.

'Says who?'

'Citoyenne du Plessis, special assistant to Procureur Rigault' – showing him my *laissez-passer*. 'These soldiers are my escort.'

He saluted me. 'Please proceed, Madame Citoyenne.'

The same happened at place de la Bastille and rue de Rivoli. The weather was sublime: blue skies, a gentle breeze. I was enjoying myself: my authority, the magic of my *laissez-passer*, my four legionnaires – menacing and armed.

'You know where you are going?' said Florian.

Rolling my eyes: 'I've rehearsed the route in my head many times, *dear*.'

He grinned, his teeth white and even against the tan of his face. He looked as though he had been in parts foreign and hot. I could see him in some long-lost outpost in the deserts of North Africa. He had retained his Bourgogne accent, though – a comfort to me at the time.

We turned right at Châtelet and encountered another barricade. The *laissez-passer* continued to weave its spell. The faces manning the barricades were grim and exhausted. A squad of Amazons on the other side of the road as we headed for Les Halles. I prayed for Sybille.

A cannonade, the first of the day, in the west and not far away, its rumbling, shuddering crump reverberating off the surrounding buildings.

A wolfish grin from Florian.

Another barricade. 'The station at Montparnasse has been taken,' the sergeant in charge informed me. 'The Versaillais are heading for Montmartre, ma'am.'

'You certain?' said Florian.

'They took Parc Monceau yesterday and are attacking Batignolles from the north. General Ladmirault. We'll see them off, don't you worry, sir.'

Florian shook his head as we moved away. 'He's in cloud cuckoo land. They'll be massacred, professionals against this *rabble*. Ladmirault is one of the best.'

We trooped through Les Halles. At Saint-Eustache we turned north along rue Montmartre. The very name filled me with fear. The nearer we were to Montmartre the noisier it became, with cannonades every minute or so. Men roaring and screaming in the distance – muskets discharging, the sound echoing off the walls. And smoke, a grimy haze, the smell of cordite. I couldn't help but wrinkle my nose.

As we crossed rue Réaumur, Florian grabbed my arm. 'The men, Kiki. We need breakfast.'

I nodded. Who was I to argue? We turned left onto place de la Bourse. A café on a corner was open, something I found extraordinary. Florian ordered wine, brioche and *saucisson*.

The four of them laughed and joked. They talked of North Africa, their exploits there. The banter was constant – taking potshots at each other given any opportunity.

Breakfast arrived. Jean-Baptiste poured himself a glass of wine, sniffed it. Turning to the waiter: 'Two more bottles of this piss, if you please, *garçon. Now.*' He splashed my glass. I sipped. 'Not exactly Château Lafite,' I said.

'Oh no, not another *conard* wine expert,' said Carlos.

'I'm afraid so,' said Horst. 'Fucking Florian thinks he knows the grape. Bah.'

'He should,' I said. 'He was born and raised in Meursault.'

'As were you, I suppose, mademoiselle?'

'We are childhood friends.'

'Childhood sweethearts, more like. Ooh la la,' said Carlos.

Florian turned a shade of pink under his beard.

Jean-Baptiste cut the *saucisson* into large chunks and proceeded to swallow one whole.

'Where are your manners, you Breton pig? A lady's present,' Horst said.

'Mind your manners, Fritz,' Jean-Baptiste retorted.

'*Du bist Deutscher*,' I said to Horst.

'He's from the gutters of Hamburg,' said Carlos.

'A rat from the sewers,' said Jean-Baptiste.

Raucous laughter. Carlos holding his sides.

The waiter placed two bottles on the table together with a large bowl of cherries.

'We didn't order these,' said Jean-Baptiste, stuffing a handful in his mouth.

'The time of cherries,' said Florian.

'You always like this?' I said.

'Yes, especially after an execution.'

'Yeah, I'm looking forward to some proper killing,' said Horst.

'Stick it up some Frenchies, eh?' said Carlos.

'And where are you from, Carlos, if I might enquire?'

'Seville, mademoiselle' – bowing his head.

'He thinks he's a conquistador,' said Horst, hawking out a stone.

'A conquistador of *merde*,' said Jean-Baptiste through a mouthful of fruit.

'Of ladies' hearts, more like,' said Florian.

'You remind me of the musketeers. Florian, d'Artagnan, of course.'

'You flatter us.' Carlos bowed again.

Horst sat up straight and looked at Florian. 'What's our mission, captain?'

'To rescue a child – an eight-year-old boy.'

'Where?'

'Montmartre.'

'Shouldn't be too difficult' – Jean-Baptiste dunking a square of brioche in his wine.

'Could be tricky, seeing as today's action will be *in* Montmartre.'

'This child, is he related to you, ma'am?' said Carlos.

'He's my son, Carlos.'

They all looked at Florian. 'Not guilty,' he said, holding up his hands.

A gamin approached our table, his hand out, his eyes pleading. Florian dipped in his pocket and flipped him a coin. 'This will be difficult,' he said. 'The Versaillais are well trained. Ladmirault's no slouch. Not like the *conard* Communards.'

A shell burst close to the Bourse, the noise deafening. My companions turned not a hair. They talked some more of Algeria – the scrapes they were in. Standard conversation, repeated ad nauseam, no doubt – shared experiences unique only to them and good for morale.

It was time to go. They all tossed francs onto the table and stared at me. I opened my palms. 'I've not a sou to my name,' I said.

Horst rolled his eyes. 'Typical' – chucking in more coins.

Smiles all round as we stood and adjusted our kit.

Soon we were walking down rue Réaumur. The men held their *Chassepots* at the ready, their eyes darting from side to side. Near the end of the road we turned right down a passageway to emerge on boulevard des Capucines, close to the new opera house. At the entrance to rue de la Chaussée-d'Antin, we were confronted with a barricade where I presented my *laissez-passer*. The corporal was reluctant to let us through – wanting us to stay and fight on *his* barricade. I explained that we were under orders from Procureur Rigault to deliver a message to our fellow Communards in place Pigalle. He pulled a face then waved us through.

The noise was intense as we ran half-crouched towards la Trinité. My life was catching up with me: poor food and desk-bound, to say nothing of the spells in prison and Rigault's attentions the night before. The *Chassepot* made my arms ache, and I swapped hands every hundred metres or so. Apart from my role in the firing squad I had no idea how to use it. Had it not been for Florian I would have ditched the thing.

Halfway up d'Antin, another barricade. Cheering, guns firing, the air full of smoke. A gang of women ahead of us was harnessed to a *mitrailleuse*. About twenty National Guards were in position, some taking shots from the top and through slots in the barricade. Screams as one toppled backwards. A woman pulled him to the side.

Carlos shouted, 'Sniper high and right.' Looking up I saw a soldier on the roof, a *Chassepot* clamped to his shoulder. Horst took aim and fired, the soldier instantly slumping forwards, his weapon cartwheeling down.

Then an explosion, debris flying everywhere. 'They've blown a hole,' shouted Florian. 'Stay to the side.' Grabbing my spare hand, he pulled me to the left. 'Stay behind me,' he said. 'And keep your head down.' The *mitrailleuse* was now in the breach, the women unharnessing themselves. One of the guards toppled off the top of the barricade, his head pumping blood. All five of us were within touching distance. Despite the carnage I felt unassailable, such was my phalanx of legionnaires.

A roar from the other side of the barricade; the *mitrailleuse* jolted backwards; bodies littered the breach. Two of the women stepped forward, thrusting down with their bayonets. Versaillais soldiers on top of the barricade, one slashing down with his sabre and screaming.

'This will do us no good,' said Florian. 'We have to retreat. Now!'

He pulled me into an alley. A bullet bit into a section of wall above my head. Strange, but I felt no fear. We tried to conceal ourselves as best we could – Horst flattening himself against a doorway.

The din of people killing one another echoed off the walls. More roaring, some cheering, and then guardsmen and some of the women were running down d'Antin. A soldier ventured into our alley and started shouting. Two of his comrades arrived. Horst raised his *Chassepot* and shot one through the head. Jean-Baptiste and Carlos waded in and, seconds later, all three Versaillais were splayed on the ground. One moved. Carlos stood over him, dispatching him with the stock of his firearm.

'Change into their uniforms,' said Florian. 'One by one while the others keep guard.'

Jean-Baptiste said, 'They won't fit me, captain. You change, I'll guard.'

Soon Carlos and Horst were wearing the red trousers of the Versaillais. Carlos started to stuff his legionnaire's uniform in his backpack. 'Leave it,' ordered Florian.

Florian levered off his boots and was lowering his trousers when two Versaillais entered the alley. Jean-Baptiste fired his weapon. One of the guards screamed, clutching his neck, while Horst fired his pistol at the other who fell in a heap – dead before he hit the ground.

'Perfect,' said Florian. 'The one on the left is small. Take his uniform, Kiki.'

Soon I was dressed as a Versaillais. Only the massive Jean-Baptiste remained in the uniform of the foreign legionnaires. Florian said to him, 'Dump the bodies out of sight.'

This done, Florian gathered us around. 'We are now soldiers of the army of France – Versaillais – Jean-Baptiste is our prisoner. Check your uniforms for papers.'

'Huh.' Jean-Baptiste shrugged. 'You whore-mothers couldn't hold me if your pathetic lives depended on it.'

I searched my pockets and produced a ration card. 'I am Pierre Dubois.'

'Pity about the beard,' said Florian.

All was relatively quiet on rue de la Chaussée-d'Antin and we edged onto the street and turned left towards the shattered barricade. Bodies lay everywhere. At least five of the women appeared to be dead. I could hardly bear to look. One groaned. I went over to her. 'Leave her!' barked Florian.

We clambered through the breach. Versaillais were streaming the other way. A lieutenant stopped us, telling us to turn around. 'Paris is that way,' he said, pointing.

Florian stood tall. 'The name of your commanding officer, lieutenant?'

'Captain Leroy.'

'I report directly to General de Ladmirault. I'm on my way to him on important business' – inclining his head at Jean-Baptiste.

The man snapped to attention. 'Yes, sir.'

Soon we were past Sainte-Trinité and on rue Blanche itself. Number 94 was at the place Blanche end of the street. We climbed through a smashed barricade, the dead and dying all around us.

'Ninety-four?' said Florian.

'Ninety-four, on the right.'

I was in a fever of anxiety as we stalked up rue Blanche. Were the Wynburnes in? Had they fled to the countryside? Their house was one in from the corner of rue de Douai. Fear corkscrewed through me as we drew near – the corner house was blasted away on the ground floor. Jean-Baptiste charged the front door to number ninety-four, but it didn't give way. Florian stepped through the breach, me behind him. Stepping over debris we arrived at the party wall – also breached. I tried to calm myself as I followed Florian into the Wynburnes' fortress, my mouth dry, my breath hot. We climbed a blown-out staircase, stepping on the sides of the treads. Florian tried the door off the landing but it was locked. Revolver at the ready, he blasted it. A scream from the other side as he kicked his way in.

Mathilde and John Walter Wynburne were sitting at a table in their Sunday best. Mathilde was huge in her blue crinoline dress, her face puffed and red; a bead of sweat ran down her cheek. John wore a dove-grey frock coat. He was thin and emaciated, as though some vile succubus had drained him down to a mere husk. They didn't appear to recognise me.

'Where is he, Mathilde?' I said, my voice even.

She turned her vacuous eyes on me – staring through me, not at me.

I removed my foraging cap, my hair tumbling down.

'You,' she said after a while.

'Where is he, Mathilde?'

Lifting a finger, she pointed at the ceiling.

'Shall I?' said Florian.

I shook my head and mounted the stairs, my heart thundering in my chest. There were three doors off a landing. After trying one, I entered another. The wallpaper was blue, the curtains drawn. A boy seated at a desk, wearing glasses, his nose in a book.

'Lucien,' I whispered.

'Who is it?' His voice was thin.

'Your mother.'

He looked up. 'You are not my mother. She's downstairs.'

He was a Girard, not a doubt in my mind. His face was round – like Junius's. And he had a gap between his front teeth. He removed his glasses. I stared into his eyes; they were brown and glowed with intelligence. My eyes. I wiped away a tear.

'Where is Pogo, Lukie?'

'Pogo is dead.'

'Oh dear.'

He shrugged.

'What are you studying?' I said, sniffling.

'Carl Gauss's *Princeps Mathematicorum*, madam.'

'I love arithmetic too. You should meet my friend Madame Thierry. She knows a thing or two.' I stepped towards him and took his hand. 'We have to go, Lukie. My friends downstairs are waiting for us. Can I help pack your bags? We'll take Carl Gauss with us.'

'Has the fighting stopped?'

'It has, my darling.'

'You say you are my mother?'

'I know everything about you – your birthday, the eighth of October 1862. You have a birthmark just above your belly button.'

A look of comprehension, a shift in his eyes. He shook his head as though he was trying to understand the enormity of what I had told him.

A mirror hung on a wall. I bent down. 'Look into my eyes, Lucien.'

He stared at me intensely.

'Now, look in the mirror.'

He stood and stared at his reflection. He turned to me: 'They're the same.'

'As is your nose… turns up slightly up at the end.'

He felt his nose. Then a look; I was taken by surprise – pure Junius for an instant in time, the way his mouth hung open, the gap in his teeth, his countenance. 'If you are my mother… Are you saying that you were married to my father?'

'If you mean the man downstairs then no, John Wynburne is not your natural father.'

'Then, who is my father?'

'A man called Junius, from my hometown in Meursault. I loved him very much.' I failed to add: *at the time*. Guilt suffused me.

'What happened, madam?'

'It's a long story – you were taken from me when you were a month old.'

'Why?'

'As I said, a long story.'

'Oh. What is your name, may I ask?'

'Christine, Christine Vellay. My friends call me Kiki.'

Reaching out his hand: 'I'll come with you.'

A while later we walked down to the first floor. Florian was standing there, tall and straight, calm and quiet as though he had not a care in the world. He smiled at me, his head inclined as though he was trying to plumb my very soul. Mathilde sat stunned and silent. John Walter held his head in his hands. 'I should never have listened to you,' he kept repeating.

Mathilde looked at me. 'Are you really taking him away?'

'He is my son, Mathilde.'

'We had better be going,' said Florian.

The three of us descended the stairs. Stepping through the rubble, we emerged onto rue Blanche. Jean-Baptiste, Horst and Carlos stood there nonchalantly. Carlos winked at Lucien and took his bags.

It was strangely quiet. The sun shone; the sky was blue. A gust of warm wind ruffled my hair. Sparrows tweeted, dusting themselves in a potted plant nearby. Lucien gazed up at me and held out his hand. We started to walk back to the heart – the heart of the city.

To Paris.

ACKNOWLEDGEMENTS

I started writing *The Time of Cherries* in the spring of 2019.

First, I must apologise to family and friends… bored brainless with Kiki and her peregrinations.

I must thank Valerie Dolat and her team at Archives Municipals de Beaune for maps, shop names, building works and wages in Beaune in the 1850s and 1860s.

Thank you to Jericho Writers for convincing me to cut my rather crude manuscript from 175,000 words to a more manageable 140,000 plus.

I wish to express my gratitude to my friend Philip Nourse for providing me with sage advice and his proofreading and photographic skills.

Many thanks also to Carol Cole who stepped into the breach at the right time, providing me with a final proofread and comments.

Thank you to The Book Guild for publishing the novel.

Finally, I am very grateful to my long-suffering wife, Sarah, for providing me with space and time to complete the undertaking.

I rummaged through many books for information, including:

The Franco-Prussian War by Michael Howard.

The Fall of Paris by Alistair Horne.

Elihu Washburne: The Diary and Letters of America's Minister to France During the Siege and Commune of Paris by Michael Hill.

Paris in Peril by Henry Vizetelly – his description of balloon manufacture at Gare d'Orléans was invaluable.

The Communards of Paris, 1871 edited by Stewart Edwards.

The Rise and Fall of the Paris Commune in 1871 by W. Pembroke Fetridge.

Massacre by John Merriman

Phylloxera by Christy Campbell

Baedeker's Paris – for information on hotels and restaurants.

And many thanks to Paul-Louis & Flavie Durand-Ruel for their guide to the price of artworks in 1870.

And to all those people I have omitted to mention, my apologies and thanks.